Hair slicked b[...] n her face, she emerged from the [...] rising from the sea and headed straight toward him. He'd forgotten how she walked . . . the gentle sway of her hips seduced with every step. The air between them fired with a familiar charge, the sharp, full-bodied awareness that he'd felt from the first moment he'd seen her across the crowded hall of Stirling Castle all those years ago.

His entire body went rigid. The sark she wore was completely transparent, clinging to breasts fuller than he remembered, but just as tantalizing. The cool air against her wet skin only made things worse. Her nipples beaded into two tight buds like berries waiting to be plucked.

He swallowed, trying to clear the taste from his mouth. Ten damned years and he could still taste her on his tongue, still remember the sweet press of her breast against his teeth as he'd sucked her deep into his mouth. His nostrils flared; he could still smell the fragrant honeysuckle of her skin.

Not even his steely control could prevent the sudden rush of blood surging through his veins. He swore under his breath, the lack of control infuriating him. But the vile oath didn't begin to summarize his anger at the realization that no matter how he felt about her, he was only a man, and for all his vaunted control, a hot-blooded one at that.

And Jeannie had a body that would tempt a eunuch.

Also by Monica McCarty

Highland Warrior
Highland Outlaw

Highlander Untamed
Highlander Unchained
Highlander Unmasked

HIGHLAND

A Novel

SCOUNDREL

MONICA McCARTY

BALLANTINE BOOKS • NEW YORK

Highland Scoundrel is a work of fiction. Names, characters, places, and incidents are the products of the author's imagination or are used fictitiously. Any resemblance to actual events, locales, or persons, living or dead, is entirely coincidental.

A Ballantine Books Mass Market Original

Published in the United States by Ballantine Books, an imprint of The Random House Publishing Group, a division of Random House, Inc., New York.

BALLANTINE and colophon are registered trademarks of Random House, Inc.

ISBN 978-0-345-50340-4

Cover illustration: Aleta Rafton

Printed in the United States of America

www.ballantinebooks.com

OPM 9 8 7 6 5 4 3 2 1

To Maxine, my own little red-haired lass.
May your road to love
come a lot easier than
any of the characters I write about . . .
and not for *at least* another fifteen years.

Acknowledgments

Writing a back-to-back trilogy is tough, but the hard work doesn't end when I hit the send button. There is an enormous amount of work that goes into turning a raw manuscript into a novel. Thanks to Kate for her wisdom, flexibility, and speed in keeping the whole process going by juggling reading and revisions for one book, synopses for the next, and copy edits and galleys for the previous. Thanks to Kelli for keeping everything on schedule. A special thanks to the copy editors and to the Ballantine production team. The cover gods have shined not once, but twice on both trilogies—thank you for your brilliance in capturing my strapping lads!

To Jami and Nyree for the whole gamut: plotting, problem-solving, revising, cheerleading and the occasional psychiatry session. Boy am I glad I went to that San Francisco RWA meeting in early 2003.

To my fellow "Team Onica" traveler Veronica: I think another trip to Scotland is in order, we deserve a rematch on that pub quiz (this time without all the "football" and British TV questions). To our cohort and guide Iain Watson: thank you for a fantastic journey around Argyll. Your knowledge of the history and locales was truly amazing—not to mention all those romantic lines of prose you suggested. I still haven't found the right place for "give this bird a swift one," but I'm sure it will come to me.

To all the usual suspects, including my agents Andrea,

Annelise, and Kelly; Emily and the web design team at Wax Creative; and the brainstorming gang: Anne, Candice, Barbara, Carol, and especially Penny and Tracy, who helped with the initial concept of this book at lunch a very *long* time ago.

And finally, most of all, to my children and husband, who with each book only seem to grow more understanding (either that or I'm growing more deaf).

Chapter 1

Near Aboyne Castle, Aberdeenshire, Autumn 1608

Jeannie went to the loch on a whim, which was notable in itself. Rarely did she give in to an impulse or flight of fancy. If the apple had been Eve's downfall then "that little voice" in the back of her head barraging her with "good ideas" had been Jeannie's. Over the years she'd learned to ignore it, leaving little of the impetuous girl who'd come so perilously close to ruin. Whenever Jeannie felt the urge to do something, she forced herself to stop and think, and invariably ended up reconsidering.

But not this time. The pull of an unusually hot day so close to Samhain, and the knowledge of how refreshing it would feel to swim in the cool waters of the loch before the sun gave way to the gray of winter proved too tempting. As was the thought of escape. Just for a little while. To carve out a moment of peace and solitude where the troubles of the recent months could not find her.

It was only a swim. For an hour, no more. She would bring a guardsman. And her pistol. Something she kept close to her side of late.

She couldn't stay locked away forever, a prisoner in her own home. The short outing to the loch was just what she needed. She was almost out the door when a voice behind her halted her in her tracks. "Going somewhere, Daughter?"

The sharp voice of her mother-in-law, teeming with censure, set her teeth on edge. If mourning the death of her husband wasn't enough, Jeannie had been forced to contend with the oppressive presence of his mother, the formidable Marchioness of Huntly, for the past few months as well.

She clamped her lips together, biting back the ready retort that it was none of her blasted business. Taking a deep breath she turned around and even managed a smile—albeit one that stuck to her teeth. "It's so lovely outside today I thought I'd go for a quick swim in the loch. I'm taking a guardsman with me," she offered, anticipating the objection.

She didn't know why she was explaining herself. Nothing Jeannie did ever met with the Marchioness's approval. Jeannie had never been worthy of her son when he was alive, and now that he was dead could never hope to be. Why Jeannie still bothered trying to please her, she didn't know. But she did. To do otherwise was to admit one more failure to her husband and *that* she could not contemplate.

The Marchioness returned a smile that was every bit as forced as her own. Her mother-in-law might have been an attractive woman at one time, but over the years the sourness of her temperament turned outward, taking a toll on her countenance. Sharp lines of disapproval were mapped across her face, and the corners of her mouth turned down in a perpetual frown. Tall and frail—from the constant fasting she did to prove her discipline as well as her devotion—she looked like a strip of salted herring left to dry in the sun.

Jeannie had always hated herring.

"Are you sure that is wise?" It was criticism masked as a question—a particular skill of the Marchioness's.

The woman seemed to take distinct pleasure in questioning—and by implication, criticizing—everything Jeannie did. It was ridiculous. Jeannie was nearly eight and twenty, but standing before the older woman she felt like a recalcitrant bairn. The Marchioness shook her head and tisked in a poor attempt at motherly fondness. "You know what happened last time you went off by yourself."

Jeannie clenched her fists at her side, resenting the implication that the recent abduction attempt was in any way her fault. Though they'd been beset by cattle reiving since Francis's death—a widow being perceived as an easy target—bride abduction hardly followed. How could Jeannie have foreseen that her regular morning ride would be seen as an opportunity to claim her wealth and lands by such a barbaric practice? "I have my pistol and, as I said before, Tavish will be with me. Another score of guardsmen are well within shouting distance. The loch is barely beyond the castle gate."

"A woman alone is always a temptation. You need more protection than a simple guardsman can provide."

Jeannie knew where this was heading and she would not allow the Marchioness to browbeat her into remarriage to a man of her choosing. Jeannie hadn't had a choice in her first marriage—it was either that or disgrace—but she had no intention of marrying again. "I'll be fine."

"Of course, you know best, dear," her mother-in-law said chirpily, but Jeannie wasn't fooled. "Francis did always say that once you put your mind to something it was like trying to stop a charging boar."

But Francis had said it with love and affection, not with condemnation. For a moment Jeannie wavered. Then she realized how ridiculous this was. She'd worked hard to atone for her past mistakes, and she'd be damned if she would be made to pay for them forever. "It's only a swim." She almost added "for God's sake," but knew the satisfaction of the blasphemy would be dulled by the week of reparation that would follow to her intensely devout mother-in-law.

"Of course," the Marchioness said, quite put upon. "I was only thinking of your welfare."

Jeannie repressed a groan. Guilt was another particular skill of hers. "I appreciate your concern, but there is nothing to worry about. I'll be fine."

And before she could change her mind, Jeannie stepped through the door and out into the sunshine. She trotted down the stairs and crossed the yard to where Tavish waited. As they made they made their way across the forested glen to the loch, Jeannie tried to put her mother-in-law out of her mind. The Marchioness might have put a damper on the spontaneity of her outing, but Jeannie had every intention of enjoying herself.

A short while later she had her wish. From the first moment she'd jumped from the rock perched a few feet above the loch into the shock of icy water she'd felt reinvigorated. Freed from the grief and guilt she'd been mired in since her husband's death. Now, with the warm afternoon sun beating down upon her face, floating aimlessly atop the pool of blue-green, she felt relaxed. The gentle sway of the undulating water lulled her into a state of peace that she'd not felt in a long time.

She paddled around on her back a little longer, though the hour she'd initially allotted had come and gone. A soft wind swept over her, the wet skin of her exposed chest prickling with gooseflesh. Suddenly, the warmth on her face vanished, replaced by a dark shadow. Opening her eyes, she gazed up into the sky to see the clear blue stretch of sky marred by a thick roll of clouds.

A sign, it seemed, that her moment of peace was gone.

She rolled over and plunged through the water one more time, diving deep and swimming the twenty or so feet to the edge of the loch before bursting through the glassy surface in an explosion of water and light.

Trudging through the hip-deep water up to the shore with the goopy silt of the loch floor squishing between her toes, the hint of a smile curved the corners of her mouth. She felt lighter. Happier. Almost refreshed. For the first time since Francis had died, Jeannie felt as if she could breathe. The horrible smothering tightness in her chest finally had loosened its virulent grip.

She'd been right to come. For once an impulse had not led her astray.

Emerging from the water, she wrapped her arms around her chest in a futile attempt to ward off the blast of frigid air. Teeth-chattering, she gazed down and blushed. Every inch of her body was very clearly revealed in the sodden ivory linen plastered to her damp skin. She glanced around, hoping that Tavish had kept his promise to watch over her from afar. If not, he was certainly getting an eyeful. In her current state, as her old nursemaid used to say, very little was left to the imagination. But it was remarkably still . . . and quiet. Almost unnaturally so.

A whisper of disquiet swept across the back of her neck.

No. She pushed it aside. The Marchioness's doom and gloom would not spoil this day.

She ran the last few steps to her belongings and snatched a drying cloth from the top of the pile to wrap around herself. Going right to work, she rubbed the swath of linen over her face and limbs, removing as much of the water as she could from her skin before using the cloth to squeeze some of the excess from her hair. But the long, thick waves would take hours to dry even sitting before a fire.

Cursing her strange apprehension, which she fully attributed to her mother-in-law's interference, she glanced around one more time to make sure she was alone, then yanked her wet sark over her head, letting it drop at her feet, before reaching for a fresh one.

Bent over, naked as the day she was born, Jeannie heard a sound behind her. A sound that turned her blood to ice and made every hair at the back of her neck stand up in fear.

The guardsman never saw it coming.

Engrossed in ogling the woman swimming in the loch, he crumpled at Duncan's feet like a poppet of rags. Out cold, blood trickled from the gash at his temple.

Duncan could almost feel sorry for him. It wasn't the first time this woman had been the cause of a man's fall from grace.

Not that it was any excuse for such an egregious failure in his duty. If he were one of Duncan's men, there would be severe consequences beyond a knock on the pate for the lapse. His men were revered for their discipline and control, as much as they were feared for their dominance on the battlefield.

Bending over the prone man, Duncan quickly divested the fallen warrior of his weapons, and then returned his own dirk to the gold scabbard at his waist. The blow from the heavy, jewel-encrusted hilt wouldn't do any lasting damage, but the pain in the man's head when he woke would give him something to think about. But that wouldn't be any time soon, buying Duncan time enough to complete his unpleasant task.

This was a meeting better had alone—and without interruption.

He heard a splash coming from the loch, but resisted the urge to look at what had so enthralled the guardsman. He knew. Instead, the man feared from Ireland to across the Continent as the Black Highlander—dubbed not just for the color of his hair but for his deadly skill at warfare—motioned for his men positioned at the edge of the tree line to keep an eye on the guardsman in case he stirred, and circled around the loch to the place where she'd left her belongings.

If leaving the castle with a worthless guardsman to frolic in the loch was any indication, Jeannie hadn't changed one whit. He'd half expected her to be meeting a lover for a tryst, and had waited before approaching her just to make sure. But she was alone—this time at least.

He moved through the trees as soundlessly as the wraith some might think him. He'd been gone a long time.

Too long.

Only now that he was back did he allow himself to acknowledge it.

Ten years he'd bided his time, forging a new life from the ashes of his old to replace the one denied him by birth and treachery, waiting for the right moment to return. Ten years he'd waged war, honing his skills and laying scourge across countless battlefields.

Ten years in exile for a crime he didn't commit.

For so long he'd forced everything that reminded him of the Highlands from his mind, but every step that he'd taken across the heathery hills, grassy glens, rocky crags, and forested hillsides of the Deeside since he'd landed in Aberdeen two days ago had been a brutal reminder of how much he'd lost.

This place was in his blood. It was part of him, and he'd be damned if he'd be forced from here again.

Whatever it took, he would clear his name.

Duncan flexed his jaw, steeling himself for what lay ahead. His controlled expression betrayed none of the fierce turmoil surging through him as he neared the reckoning ten years in the making.

Anger that had taken years to harness returned with

surprising force. But emotion would never control him again and he quickly tamped it down. For many years now, Jeannie Grant—nay, he reminded himself bitterly, Jeannie Gordon—had been nothing to him but a harsh reminder of his own failings. He'd put her out of his mind in the way that a man wants to forget his first lesson in humility. Rarely did he allow himself to think about her, except as a reminder of a mistake he would never make again.

But now he had no choice. As much as he would like to keep her buried in the past where she belonged, he needed her.

The splashing grew louder. He slowed his step as he wound through the maze of trees and brush, taking care to stay well-hidden as he drew closer. Even in the heavy thicket of trees, his height and breadth of shoulder should make hiding impossible, but over the years he'd become adept at blending into his surroundings.

He stopped near the rock where she'd left her clothes, keeping hidden behind a wide fir tree.

Every muscle in his body tensed as he scanned the dark mossy-green waters of the loch . . .

He stilled. *There.* The pale oval of her upturned face caught in the sunlight, illuminating the perfectly aligned features for only an instant before she disappeared under the water.

It was her. Jean Gordon, née Grant. The woman he'd once been foolish enough to love.

He felt a hard jerk in his chest as the memories flooded him: the disbelief, the hurt, the hatred, and finally, the hard-wrought indifference.

His name wasn't all that she'd destroyed. She'd taken his trust, and with it, the idealism of a lad of one and twenty. Her betrayal had been a harsh lesson. Never again would he allow his heart to rule him.

But that was a lifetime ago. The lass wielded no power over him now; she was merely a means to an end.

His gaze intensified on the stretch of water where she'd disappeared. A frown betrayed his unease. He knew she was a strong swimmer, but she'd been under a long time. He took a step toward the loch, but was forced to step quickly back when she suddenly exploded out of the water like a sea nymph in a spray of effervescent light. She'd surfaced near the shore, perhaps only twenty feet separated them now, enabling him to see her clearly.

Too damned clearly.

Hair slicked back, and water dripping from her face, she emerged from the loch like Venus rising from the sea and headed straight toward him. He'd forgotten how she walked . . . the gentle sway of her hips seduced with every step. The air between them fired with a familiar charge, the sharp, full-bodied awareness that he'd felt from the first moment he'd seen her across the crowded hall of Stirling Castle all those years ago.

His entire body went rigid. The sark she wore was completely transparent, clinging to breasts fuller than he remembered, but just as tantalizing. The cool air against her wet skin only made things worse. Her nipples beaded into two tight buds like berries waiting to be plucked.

He swallowed, trying to clear the taste from his mouth. Ten damned years and he could still taste her on his tongue, still remember the sweet press of her breast against his teeth as he'd sucked her deep into his mouth. His nostrils flared. He could still smell the fragrant honeysuckle of her skin.

Not even his steely control could prevent the sudden rush of blood surging through his veins. He swore under his breath, the lack of control infuriating him. But the vile oath didn't begin to summarize his anger at the realization that no matter how he felt about her, he was only a man, and for all his vaunted control, a hot-blooded one at that.

And Jeannie had a body that would tempt a eunuch.

But his earlier allusion to Venus—the goddess born in sea foam from the castrated genitals of Uranus—was a well-placed, brutal reminder of what this woman could do.

Even as an innocent girl, she'd possessed an undeniable sensuality. A primitive allure that was deeper than the mere physical beauty of dark flame-red hair, bold green eyes, ivory skin as smooth as cream, and soft pink lips. It was something in the tilt of her eyes, in the curve of her lush mouth, and in the ripe sensuality of her body that spoke to a man of one thing: swivving. And not just any swivving, but gritty, mind-blowing, come-until-you-pass-out kind of swivving.

With her youthful curves ripened into the full blush of womanhood the effect was even more pronounced.

Worse, he knew from experience it wasn't all for show. She was every bit as wanton as she looked.

Jeannie was one massive cockstand—sex and carnality personified.

He knew seeing her again after all these years would be unpleasant, but he was unprepared for the fury of emotions unleashed inside him by the undeniable pull of the very thing that had been his downfall: desire.

He didn't know what he'd expected to feel: anger . . . hatred . . . sadness . . . indifference? Anything but lust.

Years ago he'd wanted her, been foolish enough to think he could have her, and been firmly put in his place.

But he wasn't a lovesick lad anymore, seduced by words of love and a body more deadly than any weapon he'd ever faced in war. He was a man hardened by the harsh blow of disappointment.

The sharp edge of lust dulled.

And then she removed her sark.

His stomach clenched and his breath came out in a hiss. Every muscle in his body went taut with the strain of curbing his reaction. Heat and heaviness tugged at his groin. His body wanted to thicken, but he fought it back. He had only one use for her now and it wasn't to satisfy his baser urges.

Lust and emotion would never defeat him again.

To prove it he forced himself to study her—coldly, dispassionately, as a man might admire a good piece of horseflesh. His gaze slid down the curve of her spine, over the soft flare of her round bottom, and down the firm muscles of her long, shapely legs, taking in every inch of creamy bare skin.

Aye, she was beautiful. And more desirable than any woman he'd ever known. Once he would have given his life for hers. Hell, he had. Just not in the way that he'd ever anticipated.

His eyes lingered and then shifted away, satisfied. Whatever was between them once had died long ago. Her considerable charms were no threat to him now.

Focused on the task at hand, Duncan realized that he could turn her nakedness to his advantage. He had her on the defensive and he knew that with Jeannie that was a good place to start.

Eyes hard, steeling himself for the unpleasantness of what was to come, he stepped around the tree.

Jeannie didn't think. She heard the crack of a twig behind her, the sound of a footstep, and reacted.

Instead of grabbing the sark, her fingers closed around the cold brass handle of her puffer pistol. She murmured a silent prayer of thanks for the foresight she'd had to leave it primed.

She swung around, leveling the gun in the direction of the noise. All she could see was the gigantic shadow of a man so tall and heavily muscled he made her heart jolt in a moment of sheer panic.

She'd learned only too recently the extent of her vulnerability at the hands of the Mackintosh scourge who'd tried to abduct her. She was strong, but even the strongest woman was no match physically for a fierce Highland warrior—and this one certainly qualified.

He started to say something, but she didn't give him a chance. She wouldn't be taken again. Squeezing the trigger, she heard the wheel lock click, smelled the burning, and then a few seconds afterward, the kick of the blast sent her stumbling back.

The brigand let out a vile curse and slid to his knees, cradling his stomach. Her recent instruction paid off, her aim true.

He had his head down, but vaguely it occurred to her that his clothing was far too fine to be that of a brigand.

"A knife in the back wasn't enough?" he groaned. "You've decided to finish the job?"

Every muscle, every fiber, every nerve ending curled on end—an instinctive reaction of self-protection. The rich, deep sound of his voice resonated, probing the farthest reaches of her memory. In the dark forgotten place she'd locked away forever.

The blood drained from her face, from her body. Her heart constricted with a dull throb.

It couldn't be . . .

Her eyes shot to his face, taking in the hard square jaw rough with dark stubble, the wavy jet-black hair, the firm nose and wide mouth. Handsome. But hard—too hard. It couldn't be him. Then she looked at the eyes beneath the steel of his knapscall. Crystal clear, as blue as the summer sky, they bored into her with an intense familiarity that could not be denied.

Her chest tightened to the point of burning. She couldn't breathe.

The shock was such that she could have been seeing a ghost. But this was no ghost. The prodigal son had returned. Duncan Dubh Campbell had finally come home.

For one ludicrous moment her heart leapt and she stepped forward. "You came back!" she cried before she could call the words back, all the hope of the innocent young girl who didn't want to believe that she'd been deserted by the man she loved in her voice. At one time, she would have given anything to see his face again.

At one time. She jerked back.

That was before he'd broken her heart. Before he'd taken her innocence, promised to marry her, and left her without a word. Before she'd sat by the window for days on end, staring at the horizon, praying with every fiber of her being for him to come back to her—for him to believe in her . . . in them. Before she'd wept and wept until every last bit of love for him had been purged from her soul.

Her heart twisted as the memories came flooding back. Not one word for ten years. Only the first had hurt. The other nine had been spent alternating between hatred and self-recrimination.

Duncan Campbell was the last man she ever wanted to see again.

Many times she'd dreamed of putting a lead ball in his stomach, she'd just never thought it would actually happen. Her first instinct was to rush and help him, but she forced herself not to move. Once she thought she'd known him better than anyone else in the world, but this man was a stranger to her.

Her mouth fell in a tight line, refusing to think about the blood rushing between his fingers as he tried to staunch the bleeding that flowed into a crimson pool at his side. *He wouldn't die . . . would he?* She shook off the fear and found her voice. "What do you want?"

Despite the pallor of his skin, his gaze burned as his

eyes slid over her, lingering on her breasts and between her legs.

All of a sudden she realized why. Dear lord, she was naked.

Her cheeks burned more with anger than with embarrassment as she quickly yanked a dry sark over her head. Eager to shield herself from his eyes, she left the kirtle in the pile and grabbed the plaid she'd brought to lie on, wrapping it around her in a makeshift *arisaidh*.

"Still fond of swimming, I see," he said.

She flinched, not missing the heavy sarcasm in his voice at the pointed reminder of a night she longed to forget. Anger burst inside her. After all he'd done to her, how dare he taunt her with memories of her naïve foolishness. Her fingers tightened around the pistol she still held in her hand. Were it re-loaded, she just might shoot him again. Her gaze met his just as intently and she smiled coldly. "And you're still a bastard."

She caught the glint in his blue-eyed gaze and knew her barb had struck. If Duncan Dubh—aptly named, though it should be for his black heart and not his coloring—had a weak point in the steely armor that surrounded him, it was the nature of his birth.

He covered his reaction so quickly, if she didn't know what to look for she might have missed it. But they knew well how to hurt one other, that skill had been honed to perfection years ago.

The smile that curved his mouth was about as warm as the icy mountaintops of the Cairngorms that surrounded them in the dark of winter. "Some things never change," he said matter-of-factly.

But he had.

She stared into the face that was at once heartbreakingly familiar and completely different. The youth had become a man. If anything, the passage of time had only served to make him more attractive—something she would have thought impossible. The black hair and blue eyes had always been a striking combination, but with age his boyish features had become more sharply defined and chiseled. He wore his hair shorter now—the soft waves that had fallen to his jaw had been cropped to just past his ears. The deeply tanned skin had been weathered by the elements and nicked by war, yet it only served to make him more brutally masculine—imposing, almost dangerous.

Despite his undeniable appeal, nothing stirred inside her. Looking at him she didn't feel anything. He'd killed what was between them long ago.

"We don't have much time," he said. "The shot will have been heard." He shook his head. "I can't believe you shot me."

He was trying not to show how much pain he was in and his mouth was quirked, revealing the dimple in his left cheek. She sucked in her breath, stunned by the aching familiarity. By the reminder. Her heart pounded in a hard panic as the force of everything she had to lose by his return came crashing down on her. "Why are you here, Duncan?"

"I came back to prove my innocence." He looked at her. "I need your help."

He held his face impassive, but she knew how much those words had cost him.

"Why would I help you? I thought I betrayed you?" She couldn't keep the twinge of bitterness from her voice.

Nothing flickered on his expression. "And I thought you claimed otherwise?" he challenged.

He sagged backward, falling from his knees to the ground, but she made no move toward him. Any compassion she might have felt for shooting him paled beside the danger his return could bring. He'd nearly destroyed her once before, he would never have the opportunity to do so again.

And now it wasn't just her life at stake.

Her eyes narrowed. "Now you wish to listen to me?" She laughed harshly. "You are ten years too late for that. You should never have come back, Duncan. The only thing waiting for you is a noose. And I'll be happy to help them put it around your neck myself."

Chapter 2

❖❖❖

Ten Years Earlier
Stirling Castle, Stirlingshire, late summer 1598

Maybe this wouldn't be so bad after all.

Jeannie Grant stood between her father and aunt in the middle of the great hall of Stirling Castle, feeling the tension gradually ease from her neck and shoulders. A short while later she even found herself smiling—*really* smiling—at one of the courtiers she'd been introduced to and realized that she was actually having fun.

Had she worried for nothing?

When her father, the Chief of Grant of Freuchie, had insisted she accompany him to answer King James's summons, she'd resisted, anticipating the worst. Veiled looks. Sly remarks. Whispers like the ones that had followed her when she was a girl.

But her mother's fall from grace had happened eight years ago and many, many scandals ago. With the inevitableness of dawn, new misfortune had risen to take its place. Indeed, they'd arrived earlier to find the castle buzzing about one of the queen's ladies in waiting who'd been sent from the court in disgrace.

Jeannie didn't know the circumstances, but she could never take pleasure in another's pain. She'd spent almost half her life living under the shadow of her mother's scandal. Janet Grant had run off with a "BloodyEnglishman" (her father didn't separate the two) when Jeannie was just nine years old.

She'd learned all too well how scandal and gossip engulfed everyone they touched in misery—even the innocent. Especially the innocent.

With her father and aunt locked in conversation with an old acquaintance, Jeannie took advantage of the free moment to catch her breath. She looked around the glittering hall, the massive room crammed to the wooden rafters with colorfully clad courtiers—a veritable feast of silk and satin for the eye. Her mouth twisted. So much for the "small gathering" her father had promised.

She gazed toward the crowd at the far end of the room, still waiting for her first look at King James and Queen Anne. But thus far she'd been unable to catch a wide enough opening between the silk wall of hooped skirts and puffy slops worn by the courtiers surrounding Scotland's royal couple.

Above the din of voices she could just make out the gentle strum of the lute and the haunting melody of her favorite song—despite being written by an Englishman—"Greensleeves." The familiar words floated through her head:

Alas, my love, you do me wrong,
To cast me off discourteously.
For I have loved you well and long,
Delighting in your company . . .

She fluttered her fan a few times in front of her flushed cheeks, stirring the stagnant, warm air. Four enormous chandeliers hung from the ceiling, laden with masses of candles, casting a magical glow across the room. But as beautiful as all those candles were, they also made the room hot. Still, the heat and noise only added to the feeling of excitement surging through the hall.

"And this must be your daughter," a man said.

Automatically, Jeannie turned to greet the new-comer; her gaze meeting the twinkling gray eyes of a distinguished-looking gentleman of middling years, per-haps a few years older than her father's eight and forty. He was short, not much taller than her handful of inches over five feet, and built like a barrel. His white hair had thinned and receded up top, but he more than made up for the loss on his face. His impressive mustache was long and thick, curling up into two perfect points on the ends. He reminded her of a sea lion, albeit without the gruffness. The jovial smile on his face belied any thought of that.

"Aye," her father said. "My eldest daughter, Jean." Her father turned to her. "Daughter, I'd like you to meet an old friend, the Laird of Menzies."

Menzies. Castle Menzies was in Perthshire, near where her mother had grown up.

"Not so old that I can't admire a beautiful lass," the laird said with a chuckle, taking her gloved hand and of-fering a gallant bow. He shook his head and said softly, "I'd recognize that hair anywhere."

Instinctively, Jeannie stiffened, bracing herself for what was coming next. A comment about her hair was invariably followed by a knowing shake of the head and the inevitable, "just like her mother." As if red was some kind of mark for a spirited and adventuresome—if occa-sionally ill-conceived—temperament.

The Laird of Menzies's remark had not just affected her; her father tensed as well.

But to her surprise, rather than a subtle barb, the old laird said, "Your mother could light up a room with her beauty and her smile. Such energy, such light. She was a breath of fresh air, your mother." He smiled with a wist-ful shake of his head. "I was sad to hear that she was gone." He met Jeannie's gaze and the crinkle around his eyes deepened. "I've never seen her like since, but I see you have some of that energy about you as well."

Jeannie could detect no animus in his voice to suggest a different meaning. When she looked into his eyes all she could see was kindness.

She blushed and mumbled a quick thank you. It had been so long since someone said anything nice about her mother that she was at a loss as to what to say. So often reminded of the bad, she forgot the good.

The memories of her mother were faint, coming to her only in flashes. The tinkle of her laugh. The scent of rosewater and the French wine of Champagne that she loved. The thick auburn hair so like Jeannie's own blazing red in the candlelight. The beautiful ball gowns that would have made England's Queen Elizabeth curse with envy.

Janet Grant had loved the young King James's court at Holyrood Palace and disliked returning to the inhospitable "wilds" of the Highlands—so she avoided it. She'd been like a beautiful butterfly flitting in and out of Jeannie's life.

Flitting, that was a good word for it. Her mother never followed a path, only where her fancy led. She fancied herself in love with Grant, the Laird of Freuchie, so she'd married him. Four children later, with the husband she'd loved no longer dancing attendance on her, she fancied herself in love with the BloodyEnglishman— for he had no other name in their household—so she'd run off with him.

For Jeannie, the pain of her leaving never lessened. It didn't help that her mother had quickly regretted it. The damage had been done. Donald Grant refused to take her back. The love he bore his wife could not stand in the face of the blow she'd dealt to his pride. Despite their Norman forbearers, her father was every bit a proud Highland chief and forgiveness was not in his vernacular.

Her beautiful, impetuous mother had died less than a year later in a carriage accident—the result of a madcap drunken wager—leaving Jeannie, the eldest, to pick up the pieces and burdened by a legacy of the danger of impulsivity.

"Jean is nothing like her mother," her father said sharply.

Realizing his misstep, the Laird of Menzies stammered an apology and moved away.

Jeannie had heard the note of defensiveness in her father's voice and tried not to let it upset her. Her father might have insisted that she stop hiding in the countryside and join him at court, but it didn't mean he wasn't worried about the prospect of setting her free in the environment her mother had loved so much. The presence of her dour aunt as chaperone attested to that.

She did not doubt that her father loved her, but sometimes she would catch him watching her and she would see something in his gaze. It was almost as if he was holding his breath, waiting for her to make a mistake.

Worse, she knew that his fear was not completely unfounded. When an idea struck her, she felt it so strongly it was hard to dislodge. It always seemed right at the time. Like when she'd hidden that horrid Billy Gordon's clothes when he was swimming in the lake so he was forced to walk home naked or when she was six and decided to walk to Inverness because there was a shop that sold confections she liked or the time she'd served her father's best claret to her poppets and the hounds had passed out drunk.

But she didn't do things like that anymore.

She wanted to ease the worried look on her father's face, to assure him that he spoke true, that she was nothing like her mother. That nothing would ever induce her to be so rash.

But doing so would only cause him more pain, so Jeannie kept her promises to herself and changed the subject.

The wait was at an end. The Laird of Grant had arrived.

Duncan Campbell eyed the crowd that had spilled out into the courtyard, effectively blocking the entrance to the great hall. But it did not deter him. Though he'd rather muck the castle stables than suffer through another evening of court entertainment—which too often meant the drama taking place off the stage and not on it—he had a job to do.

He forged his way through the throng as purposefully as a *birlinn* cutting across the waves. More than one young woman saw him coming and stumbled "accidentally" into his path, murmuring apologies while casting him an inviting glance. That a few looked at him with something more than a dalliance in mind was a new experience for him. News traveled swiftly at court, and word of his being named captain of his father's guard and keeper of Castleswene had not escaped notice. Apparently for some, his new position was enough to blur the stain of his birth.

But no manner of enticement, no matter how bold, would steer him from his course. He'd spent the past few days cooling his heels, waiting for Grant to arrive and now that he was finally here Duncan was anxious to proceed. His father, the powerful Campbell of Auchinbreck, had sent him to court to persuade the Chief of Grant to join forces with the king and the Campbells in the impending battle with the Earl of Huntly. His father was giving him a chance to further prove himself, and Duncan had no intention of squandering the opportunity. So he disentangled himself with a polite smile, before purposefully continuing on his way.

Upon entering the hall, a wave of heat and the sickly sweet stench of sweat masked with too much perfume hit him hard. He grimaced. What he wouldn't give for a fresh breath of heathery Highland air.

He scanned the room, searching for Grant. As on the battlefield, his prodigious height proved useful and his gaze traveled unobstructed over the sea of swarming courtiers.

His younger brother Colin dragged up beside him, having had a bit more difficulty in navigating through the crowd. "Damn it, Duncan, slow down. Gad brother, you must be blind. Lady Margaret's lovely breasts were wedged so firmly against your arm, she was practically serving them up on a platter."

Duncan's gaze slid down to his brother's. At eight and ten few things interested Colin more than a pair of lovely breasts. Hell, at one and twenty Duncan wasn't altogether disinterested himself. He arched a brow. "I saw them."

"And you didn't stop and offer an encouraging word?" Colin asked incredulously. "That field may be well plowed, but 'tis a bountiful harvest all the same. She's a lusty lass. A real screamer, I hear. Thomas said he had to put his hand over her mouth to prevent her from waking the whole castle."

Duncan frowned. Whether she was free with her favors or not, he didn't like to hear his brother speak with such coarseness about a lass. "I've no time to dally with the lasses, Colin. I've other matters to attend."

"How much time do you need?" Colin paused as the young woman in question approached, her eyes sweeping over the brothers with interest. His gaze followed her round backside as she sauntered past, hips swaying enticingly. Only when she'd moved out of sight did

Colin's gaze return to him. "The lass is panting after ye. Grant has only just arrived. Surely your talk can wait an hour?"

"The sooner I speak with him, the sooner I can persuade him to see reason." And the sooner he could return to Castleswene and prepare his men for battle.

"You've a mind for only one thing," Colin said with a shake of his head.

His brother's look of utter disgust tugged a wry grin from Duncan. And when he saw Colin's eyes following another comely lass, he laughed and said, "As do you, little brother."

Colin grinned, not bothering to deny it.

If Duncan was ruthless in his determination to make a name for himself, it was because he had not the luxury of anything else. Duncan didn't envy Colin the freedom afforded by his position, he accepted his place with the same pragmatism he would anything else he couldn't change.

For a bastard he was more fortunate than most. When his mother had abandoned him, his father had brought him into his household and raised him alongside his half brothers and sister, treating him no differently. If anything, his father often found it difficult to hide his favoritism toward his bastard son. But it was Colin, younger by three years, who was the Laird of Auchinbreck's heir and *tanaiste*. Not even his father's love could change that.

But Duncan hadn't let the circumstances of his birth impede him. He'd worked hard for what he'd achieved and in some ways he suspected it was all the more satisfying. He'd been made captain and become the right-hand man of his cousin the Earl of Argyll *in spite* of his birth, not because of it.

It was a good start, but only the beginning of what Duncan intended to achieve.

Returning to the task at hand, Duncan renewed his search for Grant.

Suddenly, he stilled.

It was the laugh that drew him. Soft and sweet, filled with a natural exuberance that seemed utterly out of place among the throng of jaded courtiers.

His gaze shot to the source and he froze. He made a sharp sound—his breath catching hard in his throat. His body charged, filled with an awareness unlike anything he'd ever experienced before.

He stared transfixed with only one word springing to mind: *magnificent*.

The lass was a beauty, there was no denying that, with thick dark waves of titian hair, big green eyes, flawless ivory skin, and small, delicate features.

But the hall was filled with beautiful women. It was something more. Something that seemed to reach inside him and tug with all the subtlety of a whirlpool. Something hot and primal.

An image flashed before his eyes of her naked in his arms, her cheeks flushed, her lips parted, her eyes soft with pleasure. The image was so sharp, so real, his body reacted. Blood surged through him, pooling in his groin. The hard result was as instantaneous as it was unwelcome.

What the hell was the matter with him? He was acting like an untried lad.

"What's wrong?" Colin asked.

"Nothing," Duncan said, knocked from the temporary stupor. His brother was watching him curiously. "The lass," he said, with a nod in her direction. "Who is she?"

Colin gave him a strange look. "Can't you guess?"

"What do you mean?"

"She's standing next to the man you've been not very patiently waiting to arrive for the past week."

Stunned that he could have missed something so important, Duncan looked back in her direction just in time to see her exchange a fond glance with the older man hovering protectively at her side. The very man he'd been searching for, the Laird of Grant. It was clear the two were close.

"Must be his daughter," Colin added. "You know what happened to his wife."

Grant's daughter? Hell. Duncan felt a surprisingly sharp stab of disappointment, knowing without needing to be told. Notwithstanding his recent promotion among the ranks of his father's guardsmen, the daughter of a powerful Highland chief was well beyond the reach of a bastard son.

His jaw flexed in a hard line. It was no use getting angry over things he couldn't change. He'd found Grant, and daughter or no, he had a job to do.

He'd only taken a few steps toward them, however, when he was waylaid by his cousin, Archibald Campbell, the powerful Earl of Argyll.

"There you are, Duncan. I've been looking for you. Come with me, there is someone who wishes to speak with you."

Duncan frowned. "But Grant has arrived."

"Grant can wait," his cousin replied, and then smiled. "The king cannot." Seeing Colin beside him, Archie said almost as an afterthought, "You can come along, too."

Duncan followed his cousin to a small antechamber off the hall. He should be thrilled with the opportunity—moments ago he would have been. Instead he felt an unmistakable twinge of disappointment.

Disappointment that had nothing to do with Grant and everything to do with his daughter.

*   *   *

There it was again, Jeannie thought. That odd sensation of being watched. She'd felt it earlier, but when she'd looked around and found nothing unusual, she wondered if she'd imagined it.

Only half-listening to the woman beside her, Elizabeth Ramsey—who had delighted in telling Jeannie every detail of the latest scandal to hit the court within two minutes of meeting her—Jeannie tried once again to find the source of that eerie sensation.

She stilled, noticing him right away—though he wasn't looking in her direction. It was impossible not to. Tall and broad shouldered, his lean muscular frame honed tight as a bowstring, he stood out among the Lowland courtiers and smattering of Highlanders like her father who'd answered the king's summons.

Her body hummed with a strange energy.

At first, due to his height and muscled build, she wondered if he was perhaps a guardsman—the champion warrior of some great lord. But the quality of his fine clothing belied that possibility, as did the air of consequence and authority in his proud stance. She was still wondering when he turned around.

She gasped. The minstrels stopped. The chaotic whirl around her stilled. Every nerve ending, every fiber of her being came alive with a charged jolt. Awareness radiated through her from head to toe and she felt an odd squeeze in her chest.

She'd heard the bards sing of love that could strike like a lightning bolt and thought it a romantic exaggeration. Now she wondered.

His eyes met hers and held.

A second shock followed closely on the heels of the first. His eyes were otherworldly—a clear cobalt blue that belonged to the heavens. The contrast with the dark ebony hair that fell in soft waves to his jaw was enough to stop her heart from remembering to beat.

Handsome seemed utterly insufficient to describe him. His brow cocked speculatively and she blushed, realizing she was staring. But she couldn't look away.

Apparently the lack of maidenly modesty amused him and the faint hint of a smile appeared on a countenance that appeared otherwise unaccustomed to the movement, revealing the deep crater of a dimple in his left cheek. On such a serious countenance it was a charming incongruity, and her heart tumbled a little farther.

His gaze shifted back to the man at his side who'd said something to him, breaking the connection.

"Who's that man over there?" she asked Elizabeth. Before the other woman could answer, Jeannie shifted her gaze, recognizing the man beside him. "Standing next to the Earl of Argyll."

Elizabeth followed the direction of her gaze and let out a dreamy sigh. "His cousin, Duncan Campbell. Isn't he gorgeous?"

"Argyll's cousin?" Jeannie replied, apparently not hiding her interest as well as she should have.

Elizabeth Ramsay's eyes sparkled with mischief. "Don't get any ideas. Well not any permanent ones at least." She giggled. "I wouldn't mind a wee ride on that stallion myself." Jeannie's eyes widened at such ribald talk, but Elizabeth didn't notice. She was still gazing hungrily at the man she'd called Duncan. "He's Campbell of Auchinbreck's *natural* son."

Jeannie experienced a flicker of disappointment. Despite Elizabeth's crudeness, she was right. A bastard son—even one of a powerful man like Campbell of Auchinbreck—was not a proper suitor for the daughter of Grant of Freuchie.

Discovering that he was a bastard should have discouraged her, but there was something about him. Something that rose above the circumstances of his birth. The stamp of authority and the unmistakable aura of a man who knew his own worth.

"There she is," the woman whispered, unable to hide her glee.

"Who?" Jeannie asked distractedly, still focused on Duncan Campbell.

"The one I told you about," Elizabeth said with a much put-upon roll of her eyes. "Lady Catherine Murray. Lady Anne's sister." Lady Anne was the lady-in-waiting sent from the castle in disgrace. "I can't believe she didn't leave with her sister."

Jeannie's brows gathered above her nose. "Why, the girl did nothing wrong."

Elizabeth looked at her as if she couldn't believe she could be so obtuse. "But her sister did, and she's tainted by association. Bad blood, you know."

Jeannie's mouth fell into a hard line and Elizabeth blushed, realizing her mistake.

"Of course I didn't mean . . ."

Me. Jeannie might not be the gossip of the moment, but it was clear that her mother's transgressions had not been forgotten. Nor had Jeannie forgotten what it felt like to be the brunt of forked tongues.

Excusing herself, Jeannie squared her shoulders, lifted her chin, and walked over to the girl who was doing her best to pretend she didn't know that everyone was whispering about her.

Though his cousin was talking to him, Duncan was vaguely aware of a heightened buzz whirling around the room, the whispered voices rustling like leaves caught up in a gust of wind. And Grant's daughter appeared to be right in the eye of the storm.

After he'd caught her staring at him with such refreshingly innocent candor, he'd wanted to approach her—despite the fact that she no longer stood with her father.

But then something had clearly upset her and she'd very determinedly marched over to another young woman.

The strange thing was that no one else had joined them.

"Have you heard anything I've just said?" Argyll said, the annoyance in his voice managing to get Duncan's attention.

"What's going on over there," he said, motioning to the two girls.

Argyll lifted a brow. "I thought you didn't like gossip."

Duncan gave his cousin a hard stare; he knew very well he despised it.

Archie shook his head, realizing Duncan wouldn't bite. He shrugged. "Just the latest court scandal. Apparently, one of the queen's ladies-in-waiting went to bed with her candle too close to the bed hangings. The fire was put out quickly, but caused a commotion. When the servants rushed in to put it out, the lady was stark naked." The young earl paused for dramatic effect. "Unfortunately for her, the man in her bed was not her husband."

"What does that have to do with them?"

"The dark-haired one is her sister, Lady Catherine Murray." Archie was watching him carefully—too carefully. "The other is Grant's daughter. But I suspect you know that."

Duncan shot him a quelling glance. His eyes narrowed. So the sister was being shunned and Grant's daughter had decided to stand up for her. Good for her.

"Odd company," Archie noted. "You'd think Grant's daughter would want to avoid a connection."

"What do you mean?"

"Do you not remember Grant's wife? She caused quite the uproar when she ran off with the Englishman."

Duncan's eyes hardened. He bit back the rush of anger. He understood too well. "Introduce me," he said.

His cousin's gaze leveled on him. "Why?"

Duncan turned to him. "Because you are going to ask Lady Catherine to dance."

Archie didn't bother hiding his amusement. "And why would I want to do anything so noble?"

One corner of Duncan's mouth curled up. "Because that's just the kind of man you are." He paused. "You just need me to remind you."

It was horrible. No one was talking to them. Jeannie could see the toll it was taking on the other girl's fragile demeanor. She knew from experience that pride was the only thing keeping Lady Catherine from dissolving into a pool of tears.

All the memories of those years following her mother's scandal rushed back to her in a hot, painful wave. The shame. The embarrassment. The lonliness.

But then she looked up and he was there—Duncan Campbell—with his cousin, one of the most powerful men in Scotland.

She barely heard Argyll's voice carrying out the necessary introductions. She couldn't turn her eyes from the man standing before her, nor did she hide the wave of gratitude that flooded out toward him.

This was his doing. She knew it.

Dear Lord, he was even more impressive up close. His coloring—the blue eyes set against black hair—was a breathtaking combination. The clean lines of his handsome face were cut in sharp angles and hard planes. He was younger than she first thought—the air of command and authority was misleading—perhaps only a few years older than herself.

And he was tall, much taller than she realized. She stood six inches over five feet and he was nearly a foot taller, towering over her in a way that was not threatening, but oddly calming. And his shoulders . . . a strange shiver shuddered through her. Broad and muscular, the black fabric of his doublet stretched over the hard shield of his chest.

He had the build and presence of a warrior—a man who would protect and defend to his last breath.

He took Lady Catherine's hand and bowed over it, then did the same to hers.

Her breath caught in a startled gasp at the first touch. Heat poured through her and it felt as if every nerve ending in her body had come alive. She didn't want the moment of connection to end. Their eyes met and she knew he'd sensed her reaction. Perhaps felt it, too. He held her hand an instant too long. For a moment she wondered if he meant to let it go, then reluctantly he released her.

Her heart was beating too fast. Her skin felt flushed and sensitive. Her breath was coming in short gasps. Everything inside her seemed to be tossing about wildly like a boat in a storm.

What was wrong with her?

The two men took turns asking a few polite questions, but even the sound of his voice affected her. The dark, rich timber and the sultry halting lilt of the Gael sank deep into her bones.

He exchanged a look with his cousin, right before Argyll asked, "I hear them starting a reel. I'd be honored if you would dance with me, Lady Catherine."

The look of relief that swept over the girl's face made Jeannie's heart squeeze with happiness. In standing up with her, Argyll—second only in power to the king in this room—had made a powerful statement of support.

Lady Catherine accepted eagerly and Jeannie gazed up at the man left standing before her. "Thank you," she whispered. He nodded his head in acknowledgment, not pretending ignorance. "You can't imagine what this must mean to her."

One corner of his mouth curled up. "I think perhaps I can."

Their eyes held and something passed between them. Something strong and significant. She had the strangest sense that he understood exactly what she meant.

"And what of you, my lady, do you wish to dance?"

Right now, if it meant she could be with him longer, she would follow him anywhere. A wide smile broke across her face. "I would love to."

He took her hand and led her to the dance floor.

Jeannie hoped he would never let it go. The future suddenly seemed exciting and full of promise.

Chapter 3

After two weeks of surreptitious courting, Jeannie was even more certain that Duncan was the man for her.

She better be with what she was risking.

Her heart fluttered as fast as the wings of a humming-bird. Anticipation and danger were a potent combination. Her senses were on full alert, honed to every inch of her surroundings. In the torchlight, the long, narrow hallways seemed a forbidding labyrinth of cold stone and dark shadows.

Adjusting the hood of her cloak, she was careful to keep her face concealed as she crept silently down the winding passageways of the palace, slowly making her way to the adjoining great hall.

The sound of voices coming toward her put her heart in her throat. Quickly she ducked into an alcove, heart pounding in her ears as she waited for the men to pass. From the clatter of metal that followed in their wake she assumed they were guards. Only when the footsteps had faded did she dare to breathe.

That was close. It gave her a moment's pause. Maybe she should turn back? Discovery would be disastrous. She'd be hard-pressed to find a plausible excuse for her current circumstances. A late night trip to the guarde-robe? A midnight snack? A spot of fresh air? She winced, hearing the snickers already. There was only one reason for a young lady to be traipsing around the castle by herself in the middle of the night and everyone would know *exactly* what she was up to.

A secret assignation was about the last thing Jeannie ever imagined that she would be doing. If her brother and sisters could see her now they wouldn't believe it.

She sighed, shaking her head. How the righteous had fallen. She'd always tried to set a good example for her younger siblings, which made her current situation all the more astonishing.

This is different, Jeannie told herself. She'd never been in love before . . . well not like this at least. The boy from the village who'd used her for target practice with water-filled pig's bladders when she was ten and the stable lad who'd cornered her for a slobbery kiss four years later didn't count.

Duncan was different.

Any initial qualms she might have had about his birth had been quickly erased. The past two weeks of stolen conversations and observing him had solidified what she'd felt that first night: Bastard or no, Duncan Campbell was a man to admire.

He was a natural-born leader with all the presence and authority of a chieftain. He seemed destined for greatness, something his family had obviously recognized. Not only had his father made him captain of his guardsmen and keeper of Castleswene, he was much closer to his cousin than she'd realized. Duncan was said to be Argyll's right-hand man.

And he'd chosen her, singling her out amongst the other women eager for his attention. He danced infrequently, but when he did it was with her or the wife of one of his companions. He seemed to be looking for reasons to seek her out—even recently joining the morning hunt. It was even more exciting because she sensed that courting women was the last thing on his mind—clearly he was at court on important business. But courting her he was.

Her father would undoubtedly be disappointed; he'd hinted at future plans for her, but he loved her, and Jeannie was confident she could bring him around.

Eventually.

But she couldn't wait for eventually.

She felt a prickle of conscience, which she quickly brushed aside. It was only a bit of harmless fun that was all.

Then why were her hands damp, her skin flush and sensitive, and her heart fluttering wildly with excitement?

"Meet me," he'd said earlier, his deep, lilting voice seeping into her pores and warming her skin.

That voice . . . a girl could get lost in the dark promises hidden in its silky depths. It really wasn't fair. How was she supposed to resist?

From any other man she would have quickly dismissed the suggestion. But with Duncan, what you saw was what you got. If he intended to seduce her he would tell her—not lure her with the promise of a midnight swim. He exuded nobility and integrity. She trusted him.

"I couldn't," she protested weakly, but they both knew how badly she yearned to say yes. She chewed her lip for a moment, what he was suggesting was outrageous, impossible . . . wasn't it? "If anyone discovered us—"

"No one will discover us, I'll see to that. You won't regret it." His eyes darkening with a promise that sent shivers sweeping over her body. *Everywhere.* The shivers seemed to be getting stronger and more demanding with each day. "It's going to be hot tonight—uncomfortably so. Just think of how refreshing the water will feel. You said you loved to swim? Well, I promise you there's nothing like a refreshing dip under the light of a full moon." He paused and looked into her eyes. "We can be alone." He reached out to sweep a stray lock of hair from her face, and she sucked in her breath. The rough pad of his thumb brushed the curve of her cheek. The sensation of his touch was as overwhelming as it was dangerous.

She looked furtively around, worried that someone might have noticed the intimate gesture. But the crowd gathered in the hall was too caught up in the dancing and fine claret to notice the burgeoning love between the young daughter of Grant of Freuchie and Campbell of Auchinbreck's bastard son. She suspected Duncan's brother Colin had guessed, but he'd left a week ago.

And then he leveled the death knell. "I must leave soon. Perhaps as early as tomorrow."

Her heart twisted. Just the thought of him leaving made her panic. When would she see him again? Was he asking her to meet him so they could discuss their future?

He hadn't let her answer, withdrawing before she could say no. But the look in his eyes . . . it was as if he knew the temptation he offered would be too sweet to resist.

Still, she'd had every intention of not going. The lessons of her mother were well learned. But once the seed was planted it could not be dislodged. In her heart she wanted to meet him and her head soon grew weary trying to convince herself otherwise. For years she'd heeded caution, but not this time.

I'm not my mother.

The chance to be alone with him after two weeks of stolen moments under the watchful eye of her father and aunt was simply too tempting to ignore. Having cared to avoid drawing suspicion, the subtle flirting provided by the occasional dance wasn't enough. She wanted to feel his arms around her, to look up into those piercing blue eyes, and hear the words that had been hanging between them from the first. To feel his lips on hers for the first time.

There was an urgency—a restlessness—wrestling inside her that she couldn't fully comprehend. But she feared that if she didn't take a chance, Duncan Campbell would be lost to her forever.

So here she was, throwing caution to the wind, traipsing through the palace in her nightclothes, ducking through doorways, waiting in alcoves for guards to pass, following the call of her heart.

She heaved a sigh of relief when she left the great hall and stepped outside into the *barmkin*. Moonlight spilled across the courtyard, bathing the outer close in a sultry, celestial light. It was brighter outside than in, which also presented a problem: where to hide.

The great hall at Stirling Castle was the largest ever built in Scotland and its massive walls should have provided ample shadows, had they not been washed white with lime. It might make the building a beacon of royal supremacy from miles around, but it also made a poor backdrop against which to hide from the numerous guardsmen milling about.

"By the North Gate," he'd said. She wished he'd been more specific. But then again, she hadn't really thought to be here.

Taking a deep breath, she darted across the courtyard to the edge of the kitchen buildings—and waited.

Where was he?

She bit her lip. Perhaps this was a bad idea?

All of the sudden, she felt an arm snake around her waist, and she was yanked against a chest that was as hard as a stone wall. She would have cried out, but he covered her mouth with his hand and whispered in her ear, "Shhh, it's me."

Once her heart started beating again, she became very aware of the press of his body against hers. She'd never been this close to a man. It felt strange . . . and exciting. His body was hard and unyielding, yet she felt safe and protected. Heat and the faint scent of a woodsy soap teased her nose. She had to resist the urge to inhale deeply, he smelled incredible.

But he'd nearly scared her half to death.

She turned on him, with every intention of giving him a piece of her mind for startling her like that, but he gestured for her to be quiet with a finger to his lips. The amusement dancing in his eyes, however, told her that he was very much aware of her intentions.

The hint of roguish mischief charmed her like nothing else. It was so different from the way he normally was. Over the past two weeks she'd watched him—closer than was proper, no doubt. Duncan's serious, no-nonsense reputation was well earned. What he'd been denied by birth, he made up for with ambition and industry. But with her he was different. When he smiled, it felt as if he was giving her a special gift—a secret gift—meant only for her.

As if it were the most natural thing to do, he took her hand and led her through the tunnel of the North Gate into the Nether Bailey below, avoiding the Guard House. The warmth and strength in the connection was both comforting and intimate. She'd become far too used to it.

He'd exchanged his court attire for a *leine* and *breacan feile*. It was the first time she'd seen him in the traditional Highland garb and she was surprised how much it suited him, though she suspected that even dressed in rags he would look like a king. The inherent nobility in his bearing and proud visage could not be denied. But the simple shirt and belted plaid emphasized his raw masculinity, giving her a glimpse of the fierce warrior he was reputed to be.

When they reached the postern gate in the curtain

wall, he whispered for her to keep her head down and tucked her under the crook of his arm. When he made a ribald jest to the guard at the gate about going on a "wee ride" with his "lady friend" she knew why. Heat blasted her cheeks.

"It's Argyll's cousin, let him pass," the guard said. "Where's your companion tonight, Campbell?"

Duncan laughed and mumbled something about his new countess.

When they were clear of the gate and he released her, she turned to him accusingly, "You let him think I was one of your doxies!" Her eyes narrowed. "Just how often do you do this, Duncan Campbell?"

" 'Tis the first," he said with an apologetic twist of his mouth. "My cousin and I often partake of the ale in the village, that's all." She was still trying to decide whether to believe him. "I'm sorry to embarrass you, but I thought it would prevent questions. It did." There was an awkward silence as they navigated the path down the rock upon which Stirling Castle sat. Finally he said, "You came," as if he didn't quite believe it.

She gave him a sidelong glance from under her lashes, unable to read his expression. The implacability that she found so frustrating was no doubt what made him such a prized negotiator by his cousin—he gave nothing away. He would make a fortune gaming, she thought wryly. "Did you think I would not?"

Duncan Campbell gazed down at the lass all but hidden by the hooded cloak beside him, not quite believing that she was real. In truth, he'd wondered that every minute he spent with her over the past two weeks.

Jeannie Grant had enchanted him. It wasn't just the fiery hair, emerald eyes, and ivory skin so smooth and luminous as to invoke allusions to goddesses and other heavenly creatures—even to a man utterly unfamiliar with such romantic notions. Nor was it the tall, lithe figure and soft round swell of what appeared to be a very generous bosom beneath the stiff fabric of her stomacher. (Although, as any man of one and twenty, he did occasionally find his gaze dropping.)

It was her vibrancy, the spirit that seemed to bubble inside her, despite her obvious efforts to contain it behind a staid and decorous manner. He, better than anyone, understood the reasons why she fought so hard to repress her natural exuberance. Living under a black stain was something they had in common—he for his birth and she for her mother's scandal. Abandonment, he supposed, was also something with which he was familiar.

Yet despite what she'd been through, it had not put a damper on her spirit. And for the serious Duncan that vitality was an elixir. Like a moth to the flame, he was drawn to her in a way that he'd never been drawn to a woman before.

He knew she wasn't for him, but he couldn't keep away.

Of certain, no lass had ever made him lose focus like this—a war with Huntly was looming for God's sake and here he was sneaking around for a midnight swim just to have the opportunity to be alone with her.

Before meeting Jeannie, Duncan's sole focus had been making a name for himself and earning the future that would have otherwise been his were it not for one thing: legitimacy.

But he'd never been forced to confront the inherent limitations of his birth. Marriage had seemed something in the future. Another means to advance himself. Never would he have dreamed of reaching so high. But from the first moment he'd seen Jeannie Grant he'd wanted her, wanted her in a way that he'd never wanted anything—or anyone—before. Knowing that his birth might prevent him from having her was a bitter draught to swallow and for the first time he felt something akin to bitterness.

Making it all the more surprising when Jeannie made it clear his birth didn't matter to her. She returned his attentions so wholeheartedly he'd actually allowed himself to believe that a future between them might be possible.

To that end, when he returned to Castleswene, he intended to broach the subject of an alliance with his father. But he hadn't been able to resist seeing her alone before he did.

Had he thought she'd come? She shouldn't have. But no matter how hard she tried to suppress her spontaneity and thirst for adventure, he knew her well enough to know that she would be hard-pressed to resist. "I wasn't sure," he hedged.

They'd reached the bottom of the rocky hill upon which Stirling Castle was perched. She tossed back her hood and turned to him, hands on her hips and emerald eyes flashing. "I think you are an arrogant rogue and knew very well I'd come."

He tossed his head back and laughed. Did she have any idea how adorable she was? Her innocence and utter lack of pretense were as rare as they were enchanting.

A rogue. No one had ever accused him of that before. Serious, focused, determined, ambitious, ruthless, aye. But Jeannie brought out a side of him that he hadn't known existed. The playfulness in her that was so foreign to him was contagious. Two weeks in her company and he felt more carefree than he had in his entire life.

He caught her wrist and spun her toward him. They weren't touching but his body fired with awareness simply from having her near. Reaching down, he tilted her chin to look deep into her eyes. The incredible baby softness of her skin under his fingertips was almost unreal. "I'll not apologize for wanting you alone, lass."

Her eyes scanned his face, lingering on his mouth. He stilled, his entire body consumed by the sudden flare of desire and the urge to kiss her. He heard her sharp intake of breath and knew she felt it, too—the hard pull that seemed to draw them together.

His eyes dropped to her mouth, her lips parted invitingly below his. God, they looked so soft and sweet. Her subtle floral perfume had wrapped itself around him, drawing him tighter. Just one taste . . .

He swore silently and dropped her wrist. He hadn't brought her out here to seduce her.

But he knew he was playing with fire. He couldn't look at her without getting hard. He'd seemingly lost control of his body, succumbing to the ailment that plagued men of his age—his mind obsessed by thoughts of one thing.

She dropped her gaze, but he could see the heat on her cheeks as if she didn't quite understand why he'd pulled away. Hell, he was trying to protect her. Sometimes he had to remind himself how damned young—and innocent—she was.

"Come," he said gently, indicating the path through the trees to the north. "The loch is only a short walk from here." It was dark, but the moon provided more than enough light to navigate through the sparse birch trees.

Not quite trusting himself to touch her with heat still surging through his body, he resisted the urge to take her hand again and they walked side by side for a few minutes in companionable silence. That was one of the things he found so special about her—they were just as comfortable talking as not. "How did you get away from your eagle-eyed warden?"

She glanced over at him, a sheepish look on her face.

"My aunt has a certain fondness for a glass of claret before she goes to sleep."

He grinned. "And let me guess, you made sure she had an extra?"

Jeannie bit her lip, an innocent, girlish habit that drew his attention to her lush sensuous mouth, to the pink fullness of her lips, arousing a decidedly non-innocent response in him. A mouth like that could drive a man wild with erotic images. Those pink full lips stretched tight around . . . hell, he adjusted the source of discomfort and focused his attention back on her.

"Actually, I had an entire flagon sent up," she admitted. "I didn't want to take any chances."

He chuckled, appreciating the foresight and ingenuity. "Done this before, have you?"

She turned to him, aghast. "Of course not—"

She stopped, seeing his expression and realizing he was teasing. Their eyes met and she burst into laughter. The soft tinkling sound made something in his chest expand and he thought he would be a happy man if he could listen to her laughter for the rest of his life.

He knew it with a certainty that should surprise him. Duncan didn't make gut decisions; he made rational ones. But not this time.

He'd never believed in fate, but there was no other way to describe what he felt about Jeannie Grant. The strength of those feelings made him uneasy. Romantic love was the province of troubadours, not of warriors. He'd thought himself immune to the weakness of emotions. Not that he wasn't capable. He loved his family, but it wasn't the same. The intensity, the ferocity of what he felt for Jeannie he feared as Achilles must have his tendon.

It was moving too fast, but for once in his life he couldn't seem to stop himself. When it came to Jeannie, his prized rationality and control had deserted him.

He only hoped she felt the same. He thought she did—that this connection was not merely one-sided—but she was so young. And her propensity to follow her heart, wherever it may lead, did not necessarily augur well for steadfastness and depth of feeling.

A few more minutes of walking brought them to the edge of a small pool. No more than a half mile from the castle, they might have entered another world. Surrounded by trees on one side and a jagged staircase of rock that disappeared into the hillside on the other, it was a lush oasis that seemed more suited to a remote part of the Highlands. The full moon was poised low in the sky, hanging right over the center of the loch. It couldn't have been in a more picturesque position had he hung it there himself.

"It's lovely," she said softly beside him. "However did you find it?"

He shrugged. "It's a popular spot." When he saw her expression, he amended, "During the day."

"Perhaps this isn't a good idea."

He cocked a brow. "You aren't going to turn around now, are you?"

She chewed on her lip, her tiny white teeth pressing into the soft pillow of pink. "I don't know . . ."

God, she had no idea what she did to him. Heat built inside him, pooling in his groin. He forced his gaze away from her mouth. Time to cool off. He quickly divested himself of his clothing and weapons. Rather than the two-handed *claidheamh da laimh* and longbow he preferred on the battlefield, at court he carried a pistol, a short sword—mere ornament for Lowland courtiers—and a dirk. After unbuckling his thick leather belt, he removed his plaid and tossed it beside the rest of his belongings. In deference to the innocence of his companion, he kept on the linen shirt that fell almost to his knees.

Flashing a jaunty grin at her flushed face, he said, "Suit yourself," before running to the edge of the loch and diving in.

The cold water washed over him in an invigorating shock, cooling some of the lust from his blood. He surfaced some distance away from where she was standing, but he could see her indecision clear enough in the furtive glances she kept casting from the ground at her feet to the water.

He treaded for a few minutes, watching her struggle and trying not to laugh. "It feels amazing in here," he taunted. "You don't know what you're missing."

She put her hands on her hips and glared at him. "You are not a very nice man, Duncan Campbell."

He grinned. "I never claimed otherwise."

He heard her mutter something unflattering before her hands began to work the ties of her cloak, letting it slip to the ground in a pool of black. He stilled, all joking suddenly cast aside, as he was utterly transfixed by the spectacle on the shore. Watching her undress like this was the most erotic thing he'd ever beheld. Pure torture, but he could not look away.

Though from this distance the plain ivory linen nightraile was modest, his body fired at the realization that all that separated her from nakedness was a thin swathe of fabric. Fabric that when wet would become virtually transparent. The relief he'd felt only moments ago from the cold water suddenly vanished. He went as hard as a damned spike, grateful for the dark water that hid the force of his reaction from her view.

She kicked off her slippers and pulled the combs out of her hair. The long locks tumbled down her back in a thick, shimmering wave of fiery auburn. He wanted to bury his face in its softness, feel it fall on his naked chest like a silky shroud as she rode him. He nearly groaned at the vivid images.

All her hesitation gone, she ran toward the water, following his path and diving in.

He saw the splash and the ripple of water as she swam under the water toward him. His heart pounded something fierce as he waited for her to surface. His entire body throbbed with desire. How the hell was he going to keep his hands off her?

She broke through the water a few feet away, hair slicked back, droplets of water sparkling on her skin in the opalescent moonlight like faerie dust, a smile of pure pleasure spread across her radiant face. Did she have any idea how beautiful she was?

His chest tightened. If there'd been any doubt before, there wasn't any now: He loved her. Loved her with an intensity that took his breath away. He'd never thought himself capable of feeling like this.

"You were right, you fiend. It feels wonderful."

The laughter in her voice made him smile. "Ah, then I'll refrain from saying I told you so."

"You just did," she quipped playfully, before putting her hands together and pushing enough water to thoroughly douse him. After shaking his head to clear the water from his face, he fixed his gaze on her with predatory intent. "So that's how it's going to be, is it? Hasn't anyone every told you never start a war you can't win?"

He lunged for her. She squealed with laughter and kicked backward to evade his grasp.

Her eyes sparkled mischievously as she tisked her head in mock disappointment. "A braw Highland warrior like you? I expected better. You'll have to do much better than that if you are going to catch me."

And with that she disappeared under the water.

He grinned and gave chase. Practically raised in the water, Duncan was the fastest swimmer in his clan. Last year he'd come in second to Rory MacLeod at the swimming competition at the Highland Gathering. Next year he intended to be first.

He didn't expect it to be much of a chase, but Jeannie surprised him. What she lacked in strength, she made up in agility and speed.

She was quick, he'd give her that. A wolfish smile curled his lips. But not quick enough.

He held back, lulling her into a false sense of security for a few minutes, before catching up with her in a few powerful strokes. With one hand he reached out and latched his fingers around a slim ankle, pulling her back until he circled her waist. The ivory linen of her night-raile puffed out like a sail, revealing long, shapely legs. She tried to wriggle free, but he held her firm, her efforts only succeeding in stirring his body to painful awareness. He pulled her around to face him when they burst through the surface, both of them gasping big gulps of air from their underwater struggle.

Her eyes shone with laughter as she tried to push away. "Let me go."

"I don't think so," he said, snuggling her more firmly against him. God she felt amazing. Chest to chest, hip to hip, legs entwined—he could feel every glorious inch of her. From the soft pillow of her lush breasts, to the hard point of her nipples and bones of her hips, to the sweet juncture at her thighs, to the strong, lean muscles of her legs. They could have been naked, there was nothing between them but water and wet fabric.

Playing with fire . . .

All of a sudden she seemed to become aware of their position—of their very intimate position. And there could be no doubt of his very prominent state of arousal. Her eyes widened and he heard the erotic little catch of breath in a small gasp. But she didn't move. The innocent curiosity in her gaze only fanned the flames of his desire—and his agony.

"You cheated," she said, her voice husky.

He was intensely conscious of the heavy rise and fall of her chest against his. Of her soft breasts crushed to his chest. Of the hard point of her nipples branding him. He forced his attention back to their conversation. Cheated . . . he arched a brow. "How so?"

"You grabbed my ankle."

He shrugged. "There are no rules in warfare. A good warrior takes advantage of any opportunity."

She bit back a smile. "And what of honor?"

He smiled wickedly. "Overrated."

"Wretch." She giggled and tried to push away again. This time he let her go. He didn't know how much longer he could hold her like that and not kiss her.

She swam to the edge of the loch and levered herself up to sit on a long flat rock that served as a ledge over the water. Planting his hands on the edge of the rock, he pulled himself up beside her. He caught her staring at his flexed arms, but she quickly turned away, embarrassment staining her cheeks. He fought a grin. Apparently, the prominent muscles in his arms developed from the constant sword training served another function other than dispatching enemies.

She'd brought her knees to her chest, hiding her nakedness from his view, but he wouldn't have trusted himself to look at her anyway. They sat in contented silence, the exertion of their swim seeping from their bodies as they watched the reflection of the silvery moon bob on the rippling black water.

"You'll be leaving soon?" she asked.

He nodded. "Aye, the situation with Huntly has deteriorated. I need to return to Castleswene to report back to my father." He wasn't sure how much she knew of their reasons for being at court.

King James was furious with the recalcitrant Earl of Huntly and intended to rein the Great Lord in. Not only had Huntly refused to either renounce his Catholic faith or leave the country as required by last year's decree, but he'd also been accused of conspiring with the king of Spain to restore the papist religion to Scotland. Huntly's continued defiance was an embarrassment to King James who was trying to assert himself as heir—a Protestant heir—to the aging English queen.

"There will be war?"

Apparently she knew enough. "It seems unavoidable—unless Huntly agrees to the king's demands to renounce his faith."

"Which he won't do."

"Probably not," he admitted.

"And you will fight?" She couldn't keep the trepidation out of her voice.

"Aye." She looked like she wanted to say something, but he cut her off. "It's what I do, Jeannie." There was something inside him that drove him and he couldn't give it up—not even for her.

She gave him a long look but didn't respond. Instead, she asked, "And what is my father's part in all of this?"

He shrugged. "That's up to him. But the king hopes he will be persuaded to see the virtue of our side."

Jeannie considered him thoughtfully. "In other words, King James is hoping to take advantage of the current feuding between my father and Huntly."

It was an astute observation. Her father had been furious with Huntly's role in the murder of the Earl of Moray—enough to break his vassal duty and feud with his lord. The king hoped to drive the wedge even further between the two. "Aye," Duncan admitted.

She wrinkled her nose. "I suppose it's possible, but the feud with Huntly has waned. The fighting was severe and I doubt my father would like to see it renewed. I would think it more likely that he would stay neutral—it's not his battle. The Grants repudiated the Catholic religion years ago." She untucked her feet from under her and dropped them back down into the loch, kicking carelessly on the surface of the water. Even her tiny arched feet were adorable.

Duncan gave her a measured look, for all her naïveté she was more aware of the political situation than he'd realized. She'd echoed her father's response to Duncan's appeal almost verbatim. "Your father says much the same, but he might be forced to chose a side whether he wants to or not." And sooner than he realized. The king had given a royal commission to Argyll—his lieutenant—to march against Huntly before the month was out. "You are close with your father?"

She gave him a wry smile. "Probably more than is typical for a daughter. We're all close—my father, brother, sisters, and I. Circumstances . . ." her voice dropped off. She sighed deeply. "Well, suffice it to say, there is strength in numbers. A unified front is an easier position from which to defend."

He knew she referred to her mother's scandalous past. They'd never spoken of it directly. Such conversations were not easy on the dance floor.

She spoke matter-of-factly, yet somehow Duncan sensed that it was only a façade. "It must have been very difficult for you. You are the eldest, are you not?"

She nodded. "Yes."

"How old were you when she left?"

"Nine."

Only a bairn. Duncan felt a sharp spur of rage directed at the woman who could thoughtlessly abandon her children like that. "And you stepped into your mother's shoes."

Jeannie shrugged. "As much as I could, but I was young." It was clear she didn't want to talk about it. "It was a long time ago, I hardly ever think about it anymore."

He doubted that was true. He suspected she thought about it every day. "You never really get over a parent leaving you."

The unintentional revelation took him aback. He never talked about the circumstances of his birth. But with Jeannie . . . it was different. He found himself wanting to share things with her. He sensed she would understand.

Her gaze sharpened. "Speaking from experience?"

It was his turn for the wry grin. "Perhaps."

She was quiet for a moment almost as if out of respect for his memories. "You are close to your father as well?"

He nodded. "Aye. I'm fortunate."

"From what I hear, I think it is your father who is fortunate. You've made quite a name for yourself already. He must be proud."

The praise warmed him, probably more than it should. "Inquiring after me, have you?"

Her cheeks flushed adorably. "Of course not!" Seeing that he was teasing, she smiled and mumbled under her breath, "Arrogant jackanapes." She tossed a loose piece of stone into the water. "If you are leaving, does that mean your mission has been a success?"

He lifted a brow.

"I assume it is you who was given the task of convincing my father."

This time the insight surprised him. She had a sharp mind, more so than he'd realized. "I'm cautiously optimistic."

"In other words 'no,' but you haven't given up."

He laughed and shook his head. "You would make a horrible politician with such a blunt assessment."

She returned his grin. "I fear you are right. My father is always telling me that I think with my mouth and that

I don't necessarily need to say aloud whatever pops in my head."

He grinned. "It's enchanting. But you are right about your father. He is not convinced, but I might have a new proposition for him. Perhaps a way to sweeten the bargain."

Jeannie turned her face to his and his breath caught in his throat. The moon bathed her delicate features in an ethereal light. She was so young. Unspoiled. With her damp hair strewn around her shoulders, she could be a sea nymph or a mermaid.

He ached to touch her. To mold his hand against the soft curve of her cheek. To lower his face to hers and feel her lips move under his. He wanted her more than he'd ever wanted anything in his life.

"What kind of bargain?" she asked.

He looked into her eyes. "Perhaps an alliance by marriage?"

Her gaze scanned his face anxiously as if looking for a crack. "What are you suggesting?"

The excitement in her voice gave him courage.

He wanted to tell her what was in his heart. That from the first moment he'd seen her he knew that she was his. That he'd never felt like this before. That she'd brought laughter and levity to a life that had been consumed by duty and ambition. But words were the province of the poet and the bard; Duncan was a man of action. He would show her how he felt, show her for the rest of his life if she would have him.

He took her hand. It felt so tiny and soft in his. It was too soon, but he found himself asking, "Marry me."

His heart, his breath, everything stopped as he waited for an answer, a sign . . .

The balance of his life seemed poised on an edge, waiting to tumble or soar at her decision.

Chapter 4

Marry me. Who would have thought two simple words could bring such happiness? Joy burst inside Jeannie in a cacophony of effervescent bliss. Slowly, her mouth curved into a wide smile and tears filled her eyes.

Gazing up into the darkly handsome face, she nodded. "Yes. Yes, I'll marry you."

The look he gave her would be etched in her memory for all time. For one unguarded moment, he opened his heart, showing her the full force of his love.

Duncan Campbell was not a man to sing her ballads of love, or compose odes to her beauty, but the depth of his feelings was perfect in its simple purity. This strong young warrior loved her, and in him, Jeannie had found a solid future—he would never let her down.

He returned her smile, his teeth flashing white in the semidarkness. Gazing into the unworldly blue of his eyes, she had never felt happier.

And then, because nothing could seem more natural, he lowered his head and touched his mouth to hers.

She sucked in her breath. The soft silk of his lips, the subtle taste of him, the warmth of his breath a shock of sensation. But by time she'd started to process what was happening, he was already lifting his head.

She blinked her eyes, dazed, feeling the swift disappointment of a bairn who'd been offered a sweet confection, given one taste, and had it quickly snatched away.

Reading her thoughts, he chuckled softly and cupped

her face in his hand, sweeping his thumb over her bottom lip. "I've wanted to do that since the first moment I saw you."

A thrill raced through her. "Do it again," she blurted, before discretion could intervene.

His face darkened; heat simmered in his eyes. He lowered his mouth and kissed her again, this time harder, firmer, coaxing her lips with his.

Her senses awakened like the petals of a flower in the sun. Instantly, she became aware of everything about him: his rich, spicy taste, the heat that seemed to radiate from his powerful male form, the rough scratch of his jaw on hers.

The chaste kiss felt like a brand, so wholly did it consume her.

She'd never experienced anything like this before. The connection was more powerful than she could have ever imagined. Nothing had ever felt so right.

Passion unfurled inside her, spreading over her in a warm flush of excitement and eager anticipation.

He started to pull away, but she made a sound of protest and leaned into him. One kiss wasn't enough; she wanted more.

He groaned and the kiss intensified. His mouth was both tender and demanding as his lips moved over hers. She sank against him, her body dissolving in a pool of liquid heat. She brought her hands up to rest on the solid frame of his shoulders to steady herself. God, he was strong. She recalled her fascination with the power of his body when he'd emerged from the water. With the wet shirt molding his chest and arms, she could see every ridge, every bulge, every chiseled block of steely muscle in his arms.

Now she could feel him and the thrill was even more powerful. The lean muscles flexed under her hands—as if he was straining. Holding back. Fighting for control.

She sensed the danger, but she was too caught up in the whirlwind of sensation drowning her senses to worry about it.

Following his lead, she kissed him back, sinking into his mouth, into his chest, into him. She couldn't get close enough.

He made a pained sound deep in his chest and circled his arm around her waist, nestling her more firmly against him. Her skin seemed to sizzle at the contact. Her breasts pressed against his chest, the taut bead of her nipples straining even closer. She could feel the pounding of his heart. It was a heady sensation, knowing that she could affect him so.

His hand caressed her jaw, gently urging her mouth open. A thrill shuddered through her when his tongue slipped between her lips and into her mouth, filling her with heat and spice.

His hand threaded through her damp hair, cradling the back of her head as he brought her mouth more fully against his with a deep, guttural groan.

God it was incredible. His taste. The closeness. The erotic feel of his tongue sliding against hers.

He demanded a response—and she gave it. Meeting his thrusts with her own, twining and circling, desire coiling hot inside her with every stroke. Her entire body felt alive, sensitive and flush with excitement. A strange tickle of awareness gathered between her legs.

This was where she was meant to be. In his arms, snuggling against his warm, protective chest, kissing him . . . touching him.

She felt as if she'd been caught in a powerful current, carrying her into a sea of unknown delights. She couldn't think about anything other than how amazing he made her feel. Her body throbbed with heat, every nerve ending on edge, anticipating, poised for something she didn't understand, but knew with every fiber of her being that she wanted.

He'd only meant to kiss her. Just one kiss to seal their bond. But Duncan hadn't expected the fierce kick of desire and passion that flared between them like a raging inferno.

The eagerness of her response nearly unmanned him. She had no idea what those little sounds of pleasure and the insistent wriggles of her body did to him. He struggled to find the reins of control as he found himself quickly descending in a dark tunnel of desire more powerful than anything he'd ever experienced.

Never had a kiss aroused him to such a state. Hell, never had making love aroused him to such a state.

He couldn't get enough of her. The honey sweetness of her mouth, the delicate floral scent that lingered on her hair and skin, the lush softness of her body pressed against his. He wanted to eat her up. To taste every exquisite inch of her.

Sinking his fingers through her damp, silky hair, he brought her mouth more fully against his, devouring. His tongue thrust against hers, mimicking the primal rhythm of what he wanted to do to her. Of what was quickly becoming the only possible outcome.

They were moving quickly to the point of no return. If he didn't stop soon, he wouldn't be able to.

Playing with fire . . .

He would have wrenched away, but her hands slid over his shoulders, bringing him closer to her, exploring the muscles of his arms and back. Instinctively he flexed under her fingertips and her murmur of appreciation set off a flare of masculine pride he didn't know he had. The knowledge that she was just as aroused by him as he was her roused primitive instinct in his body. The urge to possess—to make her his—surged hot and hard inside him.

Continuing her innocent exploration, her fingers trailed down the front of his shirt, between his ribs, over the ridge of muscles at his stomach, stopping perilously close to the sensitive head of his manhood. He hissed, grabbing her wrist and pulling her hand away before she could go any farther.

He was hard as a damned rock, his cock throbbing painfully—insistently—against his stomach. One sweet pump of her hand and he would go off like a keg of gunpowder.

He kissed her harder—deeper—just thinking about her tiny soft fingers wrapped around him. Lust pounded through him; his pulse racing out of control.

Needing her under him, he carefully leaned her back, cradling her in his arms to prevent her from lying on the cold rock. His mouth slid over her jaw, below her ear, down the long smooth column of her throat. The wild pounding of her heart urged him on like the frantic beat of a drum.

Touch her. Take her. Make her yours. The voice of temptation drowned out everything else.

He cupped her breast with his hands, groaning as the round lush flesh poured through his fingers. With only a wet nightraile between them, there was little to impede his exploration. Her breasts were every bit as incredible as he'd anticipated. High and firm yet soft and round. And generous—mouthwateringly generous—the nipples as tight and hard as two pink pearls. She moaned, arching her back instinctively into his palm.

Her responsiveness, her unfettered passion, just might be the death of him. What she lacked in experience was more than compensated by instinct and enthusiasm, her movements pure and unconscious. With Jeannie in his bed, he would never need—never want—another.

My wife. God, he couldn't believe his good fortune.

His mouth found the hollow at her throat as his fingers closed around her breast. Scooping the soft flesh in his hand, he weighed its ripe fullness, squeezing gently and sliding the pad of his thumb over her very tight, very small—and, he suspected, very pink—nipple.

She gasped, her body stilled, waiting . . . nay, begging for his touch.

If he wasn't just as eager as she was, he might be amused. But with Jeannie he felt none of the detached confidence that had characterized his previous sexual encounters. He was just as caught up in the sensory frenzy as she was.

But he was still in control.

He smoothed his thumb over her again and the shudder of surrender that wracked her body nearly undid him. He swelled even harder and had to grit his teeth against the urge to bring her hips to his, position himself between the sweet cleft of her legs, and sink into the warm, wet heat of oblivion.

He rolled her nipple between his finger and thumb, pinching it lightly as his mouth and tongue devoured the baby soft skin of her neck. She was so damned sweet, practically melting in his mouth. Her scent, her taste, enveloped him. It was Jeannie. Only Jeannie. She was all that mattered. All that he could think about.

The tie at the neck of her nightraile had come loose, and he kissed a path to the deep cleft between her breasts, burying his face and inhaling her warm feminine scent.

Her breath hitched in innocent anticipation. He slid his tongue beneath the fabric along the round curve of her breast, slowly licking up to the very tip.

She stilled, the soft rasp of her breath the only sound to break the silence of the night. He almost wished she would stop him. The thread of his control was quickly dissolving into nothing. But she'd given over to him completely, any maidenly shock overpowered by curiosity and an innate sensuality. He would stop, but first he would give her pleasure.

He flicked his tongue over the puckered skin of one delectable nipple before drawing it between his teeth with one tender suck.

The force of her moan hit him deep in his groin.

He sucked harder, swirling his tongue around the rigid peak until she arched, pressing herself deeper into his eager mouth.

Her hips moved insistently against his erection. A throbbing ache crashed over him. Restraint making every inch of his body clench.

He knew what she wanted. His hand slid under the hem of her nightraile, lifting it high upon her thigh.

Her skin was like velvet under his rough fingertips as he slid his hand between her legs. He was going too fast, but he'd outpaced his experience. It wasn't the physical act—he knew well enough what to do—but nothing had prepared him for this kind of urgency, the indescribable need to join not only bodies, but souls.

Like Jeannie, he was acting on instinct, and right now all he could think about was giving her more pleasure than she'd ever imagined.

His finger swept over her.

His cock jerked, the soft heat, the creamy dampness under his fingertip forced him over the edge. She was so wet.

He'd just reached the limits of his restraint.

She gasped at his intimate touch, her entire body arched, suspended in a moment of shock and anticipation.

He didn't give her any time to think, but sucked her nipple deep into his mouth and slid his finger inside her. Heat and dampness surrounded him.

She cried out when he entered her, unable to hide her pleasure.

God, she was wet and tight and so damned responsive. Did she have any idea how beautiful and irresistible she was with her flushed cheeks, sweetly parted lips swollen from his kiss, and her luminous gaze soft with desire.

He wanted her more than anything he'd ever wanted before, enough so that for the first time in his life he didn't trust himself to stop.

Jeannie knew she should be shocked. And she was, but just not enough to stop him. Not when it felt so incredible.

She had knowledge of what happened between a man and a woman—living in a castle with little privacy provided a basic lesson in the fundamentals—but never had she imagined that a man's touch could rouse such intense sensation, such incomparable pleasure. The grunts and groans she'd heard so often in the middle of the night suddenly made perfect sense.

Nor could she have imagined the connection—the intimacy—forged by a kiss and a caress. She felt bound to him. A part of him. Possessed and possessing at the same time.

When he held her in his arms, kissed her, touched her, she felt as if nothing could ever come between them. She felt safe . . . secure . . . loved. He belonged to her and she to him.

She knew what was happening, knew where this was headed. But she didn't care. The lessons of a lifetime of preserving her virtue suddenly felt silly. He would be her husband. Every instinct, every fiber of her being told her that this was right—that nothing that brought such pleasure could be wrong. Any qualms disappeared in the heated excitement of the moment.

His mouth on her breast, sucking her nipple had sent off wave after wave of white hot pleasure, but it was nothing to the sensations aroused by his hand between her legs.

The strange tickle of pleasure she'd felt before had concentrated to a strong, needy pulse.

The strangeness, the shock, quickly faded as heat pooled around his finger. She felt soft and wet and desperate for his touch. Her thighs parted, opening a little wider. Trusting him to give her pleasure.

Her body felt possessed by a higher power. It was as if he'd taken her to a magical place where all that mattered was letting go and giving way to the incredible feelings building in her body. Except that it wasn't her body to control anymore, but his.

God, what was he doing to her? It was incredible. The heel of his hand rested on her mound as his finger circled inside her, caressing, plunging in and out until her hips started to lift to meet his wicked stroke.

Something warm and tingly was building inside her. She writhed, arching against his mouth, her thighs closing around his hand, craving the friction.

Her hands clutched his shoulders, his back, craving his weight and his heat. Her body possessed by a power that she could not control.

"Oh, God," she cried out.

He lifted his mouth from her breast and met her half-lidded gaze. "Don't fight it, love. Let it come."

She shook her head. She knew this wasn't all of it. She wanted him to share her pleasure. She needed him. All of him. The thick column of his erection burned against her thigh. "I want you," she moaned. "Please."

Jeannie felt the change, sensing the moment he lost control. Sensed when the passion took on a force of its own. He radiated sexual energy, his body hard and determined.

Duncan knew what she wanted.

Her soft plea was too much. Every muscle in his body stretched taut, pulled to the very limit of restraint. Blood surged through his veins. His head pounded, his erection throbbed. He felt like he was about to explode.

There was a time he could have stopped, but that time had passed.

Somehow his cock replaced his finger and he was pushing inside her. His jaw was drawn into a hard line, the vein in his neck pulsing with the effort to find a thread of restraint to hold on to.

She was too tight and he was too big, but she was achingly wet and eager for him. He scooped his hand under one leg, bringing it to his hip, opening her wider for him.

He held her gaze as he pushed inch by paralyzing inch inside her. It was the single most powerful moment of his life. He didn't know himself capable of this kind of emotion. This wasn't just about lust, but about the joining of two people into one. God, he loved her. So much that it almost scared him.

Her body gripped him like a hot fist. Sweat poured off his brow as he fought the urge to sink inside her in one powerful thrust. It would hurt, but he wanted to make it as pleasurable for her as possible.

Slow . . .

He should never have looked down. The sight of her soft pink flesh stretched around him made every muscle in his body clench. He couldn't breathe, couldn't think, as white hot lust surged through him. The last thread of control snapped.

His eyes met hers. "I'm sorry," he said through clenched teeth. "God, I love you so much," he bit off before plunging through her maidenhead in one deep stroke.

Jeannie thought her heart would explode. "I love

you—" *Too,* she started, but her words were lost when he thrust inside her and the sharp piercing pain made her cry out.

Her eyes met his—more in surprise than accusation. The sudden interjection of pain brought a swift curtailment of pleasure and with it a sudden flicker of panic. Dread washed over her. *What am I doing?*

He was inside her; she was no longer a maid. That much was obvious. There was no mistaking the fullness of him inside her. He was a big man—a very big man—and she could feel every thick inch of him.

What they'd just done could not be undone.

His gaze burned into hers. His jaw was clenched tight and all the muscles in his neck and shoulders flexed. He was pulled as taut as a bowstring, holding himself completely still. He didn't seem to be breathing. From the look of him, she wasn't the only one in pain.

"I'm sorry," he said tightly. "There is some pain the first time. I didn't want to hurt you, but I couldn't . . ." his voice dropped off.

He's embarrassed, she realized. He was so confident and controlled, sometimes she forgot that he wasn't much older than she. Though undoubtedly he'd had more experience, it warmed her to know that in some ways he was just as carried away as she was.

"I'm fine," she said automatically, realizing that she was. The pain had lessened considerably, replaced by the sudden awareness of the wicked intimacy of their position. Her leg was wrapped around his waist and she could feel the weight of him between her legs. A shiver of desire rekindled inside her. He was inside her, filling her.

He bent down to kiss her gently on the lips. "Are you sure?"

She nodded, lacing her hands behind his neck. Looking into his incredible blue eyes, she had to fight the wave of emotion thickening her throat. "I love you."

A wide grin spread across his mouth. "And I love you."

How fortunate they were to have found one another so young. Her heart squeezed, thinking of the lifetime they had to look forward to.

He kissed her again, this time more demanding, his tongue sliding in and out with long carnal strokes.

All of a sudden, she understood. She felt herself warm and then soften around him as her body awakened to the pleasure he could bring. Her fingers dug into his shoulders insistently as the kiss spiraled out of control. It wasn't enough.

He felt so hot and big inside her, and anticipating the pleasure he would bring, her hips nudged against him.

He growled in her mouth, murmuring an oath before he started to move. It was as if her small movement had set him free.

It was incredible. The sensation of him pumping in and out of her in long rhythmic strokes flooded her with heat. The jarring force of each thrust shuddered through her in wave after wave of tingling sensation. His big, muscular body posed hard above her.

She felt the heavy feeling building inside her again. Felt the tight coiling in her womb.

Her pulse raced and her breath quickened.

He sank deeper and deeper. Harder and harder. Faster and faster.

Her mind went black. All she could think about was him. He was giving her something, something that hovered just out of her reach.

God, right there.

She arched her back and cried out as the pressure crystallized, then broke apart. Her womb tightened as wave after wave of contractions spasmed through her.

He joined her, leaning his head back and let out a sound of pure masculine satisfaction. His big body stiffened and then shook as the power of his release tore through him—and into her, flooding her with warmth.

When the wave of pleasure had ebbed, he held himself still over her for a moment, looking into her eyes. "I've never felt anything like that before."

The warmth in her heart spread to her cheeks. "Really?"

He shook his head, his dark hair slumping across his brow in a way that made him appear roguish and heart-stoppingly young. He rolled to the side, but still kept her tucked under his shoulder and snuggled against the hard curve of his body. The warmth between her legs suddenly felt chill and empty in his absence.

They were silent for a moment, staring up at the canopy of stars. Jeannie was finding it difficult to figure out exactly what had just happened. One moment they were kissing and the next they were making love. The feelings he aroused in her had been too powerful to ignore. Nor could she feign regret for what had happened. Duncan Campbell had made her a woman. He'd awakened a new side of her that she hadn't known existed and given her a glimpse of heaven in the process.

Who would have imagined that the joining of a man and woman could be like that? With her rudimentary knowledge of the marital act she'd thought the concept somewhat . . . strange. Never could she imagine how her body would crave his like that.

She might not have planned to give him her virginity tonight, and admitted it might have been more prudent to wait at least until they were formally betrothed, but she was not sorry that it had happened. He loved her and she loved him. They were meant to be together, she knew that more now than ever.

Her elation, however, was somewhat tempered by his continued silence. He was quiet. Too quiet.

Jeannie ventured a glance at him from under her lashes, the implacable expression once more affixed to his face. He seemed lost in thought. Like her, he was probably contemplating the significance of what had just occurred. But unlike her he did not seem as happy about it. His next words confirmed her suspicions. "I'm sorry, Jeannie. When I asked you to meet me tonight, I never meant for this to happen."

"You have nothing to apologize for. I know you didn't bring me out here for this, but I'm not sorry that it did."

He gave her a skeptical look. "You're not?"

She shook her head. "We are to be married, aren't we? I'd wager it isn't uncommon for betrothed couples to anticipate their wedding night."

The hint of a smile cracked his stoic demeanor. "Probably not." The smile fell, the look he gave her was filled with consternation. "But you must realize that a betrothal is not a foregone conclusion." Something flickered in his gaze—it looked almost like pain. "Your father might have a few objections."

Because of his birth. Jeannie studied his face in the darkness. Except for the tightness around his mouth, his expression was still—too still. The lack of reaction spoke much. Though Duncan never let on that his being a bastard bothered him, for the first time Jeannie realized that it did.

It struck her that she really knew very little about him. She dispersed the sudden pall that had been cast over the moment with a vow to change that as soon as possible—she wanted to know everything about him.

"I will just have to persuade him then that you are the only man for me." When Duncan didn't appear relieved, she added, "Don't worry, my father loves me, he will want to see me happy."

"I hope you are right. My father's support will help. I will speak with him immediately upon my return. With any luck we can be wed as soon as the banns are read." He gazed up at the moon. "I better get you back to the castle before you are missed."

He stood and helped her to her feet. She wobbled a little, her legs as unsteady as a newborn colt. Once she'd recovered her balance, she put her toes to the edge of the rock and turned back to look at him over her shoulder. "Race you back," she challenged.

"You're on," he said.

Together they dove into the blackness and raced toward the other side of the loch where they'd left their clothes.

This time Jeannie won.

She spent the better part of the walk back to the castle threatening him with bodily harm if he ever let her win again—her newfound knowledge of his body and just what parts to threaten already coming in handy.

Chapter 5

Despite Jeannie's assurances, Duncan still could not convince himself that in making love to her he hadn't somehow failed them both.

He took full responsibility for what had happened. He was the one with experience.

But nothing like that had ever happened to him. Never had he so completely lost control. He'd felt lust before, but it wasn't simple lust that he'd felt with Jeannie. It had been much more complicated—bigger. He hadn't just wanted to take her body, he'd wanted *her*.

But love was no excuse.

Taking her innocence was a black mark against him—one that would only be lifted when they married.

He'd played with fire and burned them both. He'd made a mistake; he just hoped to hell it wasn't an irreparable one.

She'd better be right about her father.

At least Duncan could count on his father's support. That knowledge was the only thing keeping his rising apprehension in check.

After a very public and thus unsatisfactory departure from Jeannie where he was unable to say half the things he wanted to, Duncan pushed hard across the Highlands to Knapdale and Castleswene. In his eagerness to secure his father's assistance in speaking to Jeannie's father, the journey by land and sea that would normally take upward of three days took less than two.

He found his father in the laird's solar, the small antechamber off the Great Hall.

He appeared to be in deep discussion with a few of his *luchd-taighe* guardsmen, but as soon as Duncan entered he ushered them away.

The Chief of Campbell of Auchinbreck rose from the bench behind the great table, clasping Duncan's forearm. At the same time, Duncan clasped his with a firm shake in what amounted to a half handshake, half embrace.

Blue eyes met blue. Though Duncan had equaled his father's height of a hand over six feet, his father had at least two stone on him in solid, battle-wrought muscle. At just past forty, his hair was mostly light brown with just a few stray strands of gray at his temple.

His father's implacable countenance betrayed none of his thoughts, but Duncan had caught the sudden spark in his gaze when he'd entered the room. His father couldn't completely mask his pleasure in seeing him.

Once the perfunctory greetings were exchanged, his father settled back in his chair, and Duncan remained standing, facing him from across the enormous carved oak table. Over ten feet in length and three feet wide, it dominated the small room.

The hard, battle-scarred face, so like his own, studied him thoughtfully. "Grant was not convinced?"

Duncan stiffened. Did his father have another man at court? Colin had left nearly a week ago—so the report couldn't have come from his brother. Had his father not trusted Duncan to complete his task? The blow to his pride packed a surprising wallop. "You've already had a report?"

"Nay," his father said. The hint of recrimination in his voice suggested he'd guessed the direction of Duncan's thoughts. "I know you too well. I could see the moment you walked into the room that you were on edge."

His father was right, though it wasn't for the reason he suspected. Duncan was confident that Grant would join the king's forces—something had caused a change of heart in him the day of Duncan's departure—but that confidence didn't extend to Duncan's bid for his daughter's hand.

"Grant was initially reluctant, but I think he can be persuaded. The king has made it clear that he expects to have his support."

"So it's either anger his king or anger his lord."

"Aye, and James is not as easily ignored now that he appears the most likely choice to be named Elizabeth's heir. The king will soon have the power of England's navy behind him—Grant would be taking a risk to defy him." Duncan furrowed his brow. "Though until a few days ago I thought he might do just that."

The observation seemed to please his father. "Ah, he must have received my missive."

"Missive?" Duncan questioned casually, tamping down the urge to bristle again.

"Colin had a suggestion when he returned from Stirling Castle; I thought it a sound one. Perhaps it helped." Colin? Duncan was taken aback. What did his brother have to do with this? His father's hard gaze scrutinized his face. "But this is good news. What is it that has you amiss?"

Duncan clasped his hands behind his back, forcing himself to stand still though the urge to move was strong. He couldn't recall ever being this apprehensive about anything. He almost didn't know where to start. "I, too, have a proposition that I hope will solidify Grant's alliance with our side." Duncan waited.

"Go on."

He took a deep breath. "I have asked Jean Grant, the

laird's eldest daughter, to be my wife, and she has agreed." The shock on his father's face could not be more profound. Before he could respond, Duncan added, "I anticipate there might be some objection and would ask for your help in persuading her father to see the benefit of the alliance."

His father shook his head. "It's impossible."

The words were so unexpected it took Duncan a moment to realize what he'd said. He stiffened. "I don't understand. The lass is agreeable."

For the first time in Duncan's recollection his father appeared to be at a loss. His normally implacable expression was all too readable. He looked dumbfounded, aggrieved. "Whether the lass is agreeable makes no difference, other arrangements have been made."

"What other arrangements?"

"The missive I mentioned. It was to propose an alliance between your brother and the lass."

The blood slid from Duncan's face. "Colin?"

His father nodded. "He was quite taken with her."

"How could he be? They barely exchanged three words."

"Three words or a hundred, the offer has been made and cannot be rescinded."

Duncan couldn't believe this was happening. "But if Grant hasn't agreed—"

"It doesn't matter." A pained expression appeared on his father's face. He met his gaze unflinchingly. "Surely, you see why it would be impossible now."

His chest burned. Duncan could see. Too well. Having the heir exchanged for a bastard would be perceived as an insult.

A sliver of what could only be termed resentment, something he'd never experienced before, wormed its way inside him.

He clenched and reclenched his fists at his side. He

didn't care. He wouldn't give her up—not Jeannie. The thought of his own brother married to the woman he loved . . .

"You'll have to find another lass," his father said, more gently than Duncan had ever heard him speak.

Duncan shook his head stubbornly. "There is no other lass." His voice was hollow and ragged. He needed to make his father understand. "I love her."

The flicker of compassion in his father's face was cold comfort. "I'm sorry."

This was the last thing Duncan had expected. He'd always been able to count on his father's support. Always. "You can't do this."

"It's already done."

The cool finality of his tone set off a flare of anger inside Duncan. "You don't understand . . ."

All of a sudden his father did. Fury quickly drowned out whatever sympathy his father had just felt. He jumped to his feet, reached across the table, and grabbed Duncan by the edge of his leather doublet—his eyes as hard as ice. "What the hell have you done?"

Duncan wrenched away. He wasn't a lad anymore, ready to take whatever punishment his father dolled out. He wasn't proud of what he'd done, but neither would he be taken to task for it. "Nothing more than what is natural between two people who love each other and intend to marry," he said evenly, not shrinking from the anger in his father's cold gaze.

"What the hell could you have been thinking?" The look his father directed at him was one Duncan had never seen before—of disappointment and disgust. "Obviously you were thinking with what hangs between your legs and not your head."

"It wasn't like that." But he knew it was.

His father slammed his hand down on the table with such force the room shook. "Call it what you will, but it doesn't change the fact that what you have done could well jeopardize everything we've been working for. I trusted you with an important mission and this is how you repay that trust?" Duncan's face went white. "Do you think Grant will join us if he discovers you have seduced his daughter? The king is counting on his support and if this war against Huntly fails because of this you can be damned sure who he will blame. You've dishonored yourself and this family." His gaze chilled. "You've reached too high, boy."

Duncan flinched, feeling as if he'd just been stabbed in the back by the person he'd trusted the most in this world. *Bastard. Mongrel. Whoreson. Scoundrel.* He thought of all the disparaging comments people had made over the years about his birth, but how it had never mattered because his father hadn't felt that way.

He was wrong.

His eyes pricked with heat. Furious, Duncan fought off the emotion. He was a man, and it was clear he had only himself to rely upon. He told himself it shouldn't matter. His bastard blood would not dictate his future, but it didn't dull the pain of having his father so brutally shove the shame of his birth down his throat.

Duncan straightened his back and squared his shoulders, summoning every ounce of his stubborn Highlander pride. He'd never let his father know how much he'd hurt him. "You do not need to remind me of the circumstances of my birth. I am well aware of my bastardy. It didn't matter to the woman I hoped to marry, I never expected it to matter to the man who made me so."

He saw the flicker in his father's gaze and knew his barb had struck. Beneath his anger, Duncan felt a wave of sadness. Never again would he look on his father as his ally—his champion. Perhaps he'd been a fool to do so in the first place.

That which had been left unsaid his whole life had

now been said, and it would never be the same between them again. He wasn't the equal of his brothers and sister. He was an outsider and always would be.

With a pained glance, Duncan turned on his heel and left.

Freuchie Castle, Moray, Two Weeks Later

Jeannie could barely contain her excitement as she moved about the Great Hall attending to the comfort of their unexpected "guests."

Her heart fluttered like the wings of a butterfly. Duncan was here.

After two long weeks, she would finally see him again.

She smiled at Colin Campbell and thanked him for the compliment, her father was quite proud of the castle *cuirm*. Though there was a superficial resemblance between Duncan and his younger brother, Colin did not yet have the air of authority possessed by Duncan. At eight and ten only a few years separated them, but Colin seemed a mere lad in comparison.

She answered his questions about their brewing method as best she could and tried to prevent herself from constantly looking past his shoulder toward the door, waiting for Duncan to exit the laird's solar with her father, his father, and the young Earl of Argyll.

The throng of Campbell warriors had arrived with little warning, seeking not just a night of Highland Hospitality, but also, she realized, to conscript her father and Clan Grant into joining them.

War with Huntly, it seemed, had become unavoidable. Though she knew it was unwarranted, she couldn't prevent the prickle of fear at the thought of Duncan marching off to battle. The thought of losing him . . .

She forced herself to push away the ill omen, knowing it was bad luck to think of death.

But the realization that this was how it would be for the foreseeable future as the wife of a warrior was sobering.

She'd been surprised that Duncan had not waited to see her, but had immediately retired to the solar with her father and his guardsmen. She'd hoped for a wee bit of reassurance before the subject of their marriage was broached to her father, but he hadn't even looked at her.

She knew her father would not be easily persuaded, but had full faith in Duncan. He would fight for her, of that she was sure. Surely her father will see him for the man he was?

Still, she couldn't help being nervous. Not for the first time, she wiped her palms in the folds of her skirts. Her father was so distracted lately, out of sorts, with mysterious riders coming and going at all times of night. Perhaps it wasn't the best time . . .

Heat flooded her cheeks, realizing that Colin was staring at her. He must have asked her a question. "I'm sorry?"

"I was just asking whether you enjoyed the hunt?"

Jeannie nodded. "Very much. Though I'm fearfully out of practice with a bow."

"I would be happy to help you reclaim your former glory."

Jeannie laughed. "I'm afraid I was never that accomplished. Are you a bowman as well?"

He arched a brow. "As well?"

The gesture was so reminiscent of something Duncan would do that it took her aback for a moment. "I . . . I've heard that your brother is an accomplished archer," she stumbled, the heat in her cheeks no doubt giving far too much away.

He gave her a strange look, before his mouth curved in a wry smile. "There is little that my brother does not do well."

He said it matter-of-factly, but Jeannie detected a sudden hardening in his gaze and wondered whether there was something behind the observation. It must be difficult having a brother as accomplished as Duncan—he was quite a lot to live up to. "You have more than one brother, I believe," she said, turning the conversation from Duncan. It was too hard for her to feign disinterest.

Colin nodded. "Jamie is a squire for our cousin Argyll at Inveraray. I also have a younger sister, Elizabeth. She's at Inveraray as well with the countess while we are away." He was looking at her so intently that Jeannie self-consciously swiped her face with the back of her hand, worried that a crumb of the cake she'd pilfered from the kitchen had lingered on her face. "I hope that I will be able to take you hunting soon. I should like to get to know you better."

Jeannie smiled. "I should like that . . ."

But her words fell off because at that moment Duncan entered the room.

Instinctively her eyes shot to his, seeking that connection she'd grown so accustomed to.

But the gaze that met hers was nothing like she was used to. It was hard and black and filled with an emotion she'd never seen in him before—rage.

The last two weeks had been the most difficult of Duncan's life as he struggled with what to do. His duty demanded he step aside—at least until the battle with Huntly was won. But every instinct warred against it. Jeannie was his, and he wanted her. He'd never begrudged his brother his position as heir and *tanaiste,* but he did so now.

To walk into the hall and see Jeannie and Colin together set off every ugly emotion he possessed, and some he didn't know he had—anger, resentment, and even jealousy.

He'd be damned if he'd stand aside. Not this time. Not with Jeannie. He would bide his time, but whatever it took, she would be his wife.

He felt his father's presence at his side. "Have care, lad, you wear your emotions for all to see," he warned under his breath. "We have what we came for, do not do anything to give Grant cause to reconsider."

Grant had agreed not only to march with them toward Strathbogie Castle to battle with Huntly, but also to consider the betrothal with Colin. It had taken every ounce of Duncan's self-control to sit there and hold his tongue while a marriage between his brother and the woman he loved was being bantered back and forth.

But to see them together . . . his forbearance apparently had its limits. A hot dirk seemed firmly wedged between his ribs. Just for a moment, the easy smile Jeannie bestowed upon his brother made Duncan wonder if she would be as opposed to the match as he wanted her to be.

His brother was the heir, and he was a bastard. A favored one, to be sure, but for how long if he defied his father? Marriage to Jeannie could well jeopardize his position with his father and cousin—everything he'd fought so hard to achieve could be gone.

Duncan didn't respond to his father, but forced his gaze from Jeannie and tried to get a rein on the angry emotions surging through him. He'd do best to avoid her until he could see her alone—which, by the look of it, might not be for some time.

The Great Hall of Freuchie Castle, the stronghold of Clan Grant, had been set out for a spectacular feast. The large, cavernous room with its high-beamed ceilings and colorful tapestries adorning the plastered walls seemed ablaze in candlelight and silver.

Above the fireplace on a thick wood mantle sat the fabled Skull of the Comyn—the macabre trophy taken after an ill-fated romance between a Comyn and a Grant a few hundred years ago. Legend had it that if the skull was ever lost, so too would the Grants lose their lands in Strathspey.

Turning back to the feast, he noted the great platters of roasted game and hearty root vegetables set out upon the festively decorated tables laden with flagons of claret and the castle *cuirm*.

Considering the late notice of their arrival, it was an impressive display. And he knew who was responsible. He should be pleased to discover that the woman he intended to marry would make a fine chatelaine, but instead it only served to make him angrier, driving home everything he might deprive her of.

He wasn't the only one to appreciate her efforts. The battle-hardened Grant chief fairly beamed with pride as he gazed approvingly at his beautiful young daughter. Jeannie caught her father's gaze and smiled, her cheeks pink with pleasure from the unspoken praise.

The simple exchange unsettled him. The easy affection from the normally gruff warrior was a harsh reminder. Duncan knew how close they were. Would Jeannie really be able to defy her father and run away with him if necessary?

The Campbells took their seats at the high table. Duncan was seated on the end, Colin, he couldn't help but notice, had been seated next to Jeannie.

Duncan filled his tankard to the rim with ale and spent the better part of the next two hours keeping it that way. But not even the dulling haze of drink could take the edge off the foulness of his temper.

Once he glanced up to find Jeannie staring at him.

Their eyes met and held for an instant before he quickly turned away, but he'd caught the look of confused hurt in her gaze.

She didn't understand why he was so angry, why he was avoiding her. But any twinge of guilt he might have felt was smothered by the tinkling sound of her laugh, floating down the long length of the table minutes later.

Anger simmered dangerously inside him. He didn't need to look to know who the recipient of that laughter was. Instead, he clenched his jaw and reached for his tankard.

He won't even look at me.

Jeannie fought the panic rising in her chest, but as the evening wore on she couldn't ignore the truth—something was wrong. Horribly wrong.

Duncan hadn't broached the subject of an alliance with her father, of that she was sure. Her father was in too good of spirits.

Had Duncan reconsidered? Did he no longer wish to marry her?

No. She couldn't believe that of him. It had to be something else.

I should go to him. Perhaps he didn't realize . . .

She took a few steps toward him and stopped. Heat crawled up her cheeks when she realized what she was doing—chasing him down, running after him. Making a fool out of herself.

She hadn't been able to prevent her gaze from drifting down the table to him for most of the meal, hoping for some sign, some meager show of reassurance.

Look at me. Please, look at me.

But she was to be disappointed.

The only time their eyes met, he looked away so sharply, Jeannie felt as if he'd struck her, so powerful was the blow.

It was as if he didn't know her. As if he'd never held her in his arms and joined his body with hers. As if he'd never said he loved her.

She'd heard the stories of other girls at court who'd been foolish enough to succumb to a handsome face, silken tongue, and promise of marriage. Girls who'd been disgraced. But what she and Duncan had was different . . . wasn't it?

She felt ill, fighting back the queasiness rising to the back of her throat.

This couldn't be happening.

Despite the blade slowly forging its way into her heart, she did her best to entertain her guests. She'd been surprised to find Colin seated beside her—rather than the Earl of Argyll as befitted his rank—but Duncan's brother proved to be an amusing dinner companion, undoubtedly much more so than his grim cousin would have been. But he was no substitute for the man she wanted beside her.

After the meal, when the tables were cleared for the dancing to begin, she waited anxiously, half-hoping that Duncan would seek her out. Instead, it was Colin who asked her to dance. With one last glance toward Duncan, who seemed to be partaking of copious amounts of the castle *cuirm,* she followed Colin to the dance floor.

"Is everything all right?" he asked.

Jeannie looked up at Colin and managed a wobbly smile. "Yes, thank you. I'm sorry if I seem a bit distracted. I'm afraid the day has been quite hectic."

Colin waved off her apology. "You've done a magnificent job. Your father is a fortunate man to have you." He gave her a sly smile. "Though I expect he won't for much longer."

Jeannie glanced at him in surprise, wondering if he knew something about Duncan. But his gaze was perfectly guileless. She exhaled slowly, realizing it had merely been a general observation. Thankfully, she was saved from having to reply by the demands of the reel.

She loved to dance, but not even the enlivening steps and joyful sounds of the pipes could lift her flagging spirits. The last notes had just been played when out of the corner of her eye, she saw Duncan leave the hall. Muttering a quick excuse to Colin, she wound her way through the dense crowd of raucous clansmen and followed him outside—pride forgotten with the urge to talk to him.

The midday meal had extended well into the evening hours and the sun was just beginning its descent when she exited the hall.

After scrambling down the wooden forestairs, she stood at the bottom, looking back and forth, wondering where he could have gone to. The yard was deathly quiet. With the feasting inside, only a handful of guardsmen kept watch at the gate.

Freuchie Castle was a "Z"-shaped tower house with a large *barmkin* surrounded by a tall *barmkin* wall. A few wooden outbuildings lined the south side of the wall, including the stables and barracks. Deciding that the latter was the more likely, she headed across the yard.

The large door opened with a shaky squeak and she stepped inside.

It was dark, and it took her eyes a moment to adjust. But she'd found him. Duncan was sitting on his pallet with his back against the wall, a flagon at his side. Her heart beat fraught with concern. She'd never seen him drink so heavily—he seemed on a mission to get drunk.

His eyes met hers. They stared at one another for a long pause. He tossed back the contents of his cup and slowly stood. "You shouldn't be here."

"Neither should you," she said, refusing to be hurt by his rudeness. "Did you not care for the feast?"

Piercing blue eyes bored into her with a dangerous intensity. The anger that she'd sensed earlier had only grown worse. The calm control that she'd always admired in him had fled, to be replaced by a dangerous volatility. "Not as much as you did," he said.

Jeannie sucked in her breath, stunned by the unexpected lash of vitriol in his voice. She heard the sharp accusation but could not guess its source. "What is that supposed to mean?"

His hard jaw was pulled tight, the corners of his mouth white. "Nothing," he said stiffly. "Return to your guests, my lady."

My lady? She took a tentative step toward him. Where was the man she knew at court? The one she'd given her heart—she gulped, her *body*—to? "Duncan, what's wrong? Why are you treating me like this?" A hot ball lodged in her throat and tears gathered behind her eyes. "Tell me. Did I do something wrong?"

He stared down at her and their eyes met. The anger that had raged so furiously inside him just as quickly died. His expression softened. The vise squeezing around her heart loosened. Once more he was the man she'd fallen in love with.

He shook his head. "Nay, love. You've done nothing wrong."

"Then what is it? Did it not go well with your father?"

He made a sharp sound low in his throat. "You might say that."

He was hurting and instinctively she wanted to sooth his pain. She put her hand on his arm. "Tell me."

He stared at her hand for a moment, then lifted his eyes to hers, his voice toneless as he informed her of his father's refusal to help them and of the proposed betrothal with Colin.

She shook her head, stunned. "That's impossible. My

father wouldn't arrange my marriage without telling me." Would he?

"Nothing has been formally agreed. I assume he is waiting to speak with you."

"And when he does, I will tell him it is impossible. That I love another."

He was watching her carefully, too carefully. "Are you sure that is what you want?"

"Of course. How could you even think—"

She stopped. Her eyes narrowed. "Just what did you think, Duncan Campbell?"

He shrugged. He meant it to look a careless gesture, but Jeannie could see the tension in the stiff set of his shoulders. "Colin will be chief."

Was that the reason for this anger? She took a step back and gazed up at him, shaking her head with incredulity. "You're jealous."

He folded his arms across his chest, every inch the proud Highland Warrior. "Don't be daft."

Momentarily distracted by the prominent bulge of muscle, it took her a few seconds to respond. Forcing her gaze from the rock-hard arms, she looked into his eyes. "How could you even think I would consider marrying anyone else?"

"Don't you understand, Jeannie? Without my family's support I will have nothing but my sword for us to live on."

And all that he'd worked for would be lost—a brutal blow for an ambitious man like him. Her heart caught. Did he regret his vow? She took a deep breath, no matter what it cost her she would not force him to marry her. "Do you still wish to marry me?"

He appeared shocked by her question. "Of course."

Jeannie tamped down the spike of relief. "Even if it means risking your position with your father and cousin?"

Duncan straightened as if she'd impinged his honor even by the suggestion. "I know well what is at stake." Piercing blue eyes bit into her and the raw intensity of his voice left her no doubt. "I love you and would walk through the fire pits of hell to have you."

Jeannie smiled through the tears. That was the most beautiful thing anyone had ever said to her. "Can you not afford me the same courtesy of knowing my own heart? I wouldn't want to marry your brother even if he was the king himself. I only want you." Her heart pounded in her chest as she grappled with the importance of what she was about to say.

Never would she have imagined herself in this position. She thought of her mother. Of the destruction she'd left in her wake. But this was different. She would not be leaving a husband and children behind. Her father would be hurt. Her brother and sisters disappointed . . .

She took a deep breath. No matter the cost, she would follow her heart. "I will marry you even if it means we must do so without our families' permission."

His eyes scanned her face, seeming to realize what that must have cost her. She could see the relief wash over him and he pulled her into his arms, hugging her against him as if he would never let her go. She lifted her face to his and he kissed her. A tender, poignant kiss that tugged on every string of her heart. Heat and happiness washed over her.

Lifting his head, he cupped her chin and looked deep into her eyes. "I hope it doesn't come to that. When this war with Huntly is won I will think of some way to persuade my father to help us."

Jeannie nodded, wanting to believe it was possible, but fearing what would happen if it didn't. She couldn't shake the feeling that something horrible was going to happen. "What if something goes wrong? Can't we just leave right now?"

His expression hardened, his gaze challenging. "Would you have me leave my clansmen to fight without me? I am captain until my father tells me otherwise."

She winced, hearing the admonition in his voice. Of course he would never leave his men. He would do his duty not just because he had to, but because it was who he was—a warrior. A leader. She'd recognized it in him from the first; it was one of the things that had drawn him to her. He would not be the man she loved if he did differently, no matter how much she wanted him to be safe.

She laid her head on the wall of his chest, taking comfort in the steady beat of his heart. She would never forget the way he smelled—clean and fresh as a warm sea breeze. "I don't want you to go."

He sighed and stroked his hand over her hair as if he was soothing a child. "I know."

She lifted her head. "It will be dangerous."

"Aye."

"What if you are hurt?"

His mouth curved. "I will recover."

"But what if you . . ."

He stopped her with a look. He was right, she shouldn't even think it.

He cupped her chin in his big hand. "I will come back to you, my love. On that you may depend."

She was. "Just make sure that you do." Her eyes twinkled mischievously. "With all your parts intact. I find that I am most looking forward to being a wife."

He grinned, revealing the roguish dimple on his left cheek. Her heart squeezed. The dark as midnight hair, the cobalt eyes, the strong, masculine features . . . he was so handsome, sometimes she couldn't believe he was really hers.

"Don't worry, lass, whatever it takes we will be man and wife."

Chapter 6

◈

Early the next morning, Duncan rode away from Freuchie Castle, his head considerably clearer than when he'd arrived. He hadn't realized how much the situation with Jeannie had been weighing on him. Now that it was resolved, and he was secure in the knowledge that no matter what befell them, they would find a way to be together, he could focus his full attention on the task at hand—namely the commission given to his cousin Argyll to pursue the rebel Huntly with Fire and Sword.

After weeks of planning, the fighting was finally upon them and Duncan was eager for it to begin. He was always like this before battle: restless, senses heightened, blood surging a little faster through his veins. The strange sensation of having never felt more alive at the moment the possibility of death drew near.

He knew Jeannie had been worried and wished he could help her understand how it was for him—why he needed this. On the battlefield, men weren't judged by their birth, but by their skills. On the battlefield—leading, making decisions, fighting—he was in his element. On the battlefield, he would make a name for himself, one where "bastard" did not signify.

He wiped the dust and sweat that had gathered at his brow beneath the helm of his knapscall, squinting against the blinding sunlight as they drove east. Ahead lay the Hills of Cromdale and beyond that their destination, Drumin Castle. Drumin was strategically located at the juncture of the Rivers Livet and Avon, a good place from which to plan the attack on Strathbogie—Huntly's stronghold—reputed to be one of the finest castles in Scotland. Ironically, Drumin Castle also belonged to Huntly, but was currently under the stewardship of Jeannie's father.

Duncan scanned the wide stretches of rolling heather-covered hills for any sign of a disturbance. Enemy scouts would be watching for them. With so many men, they would not have the advantage of surprise. It was inevitable that Huntly would know they were coming.

Their plan was to muster at Drumin with the other clans who'd answered the king's call to arms, and await King James's orders to attack. King James himself was only a few days march south in Dundee. Argyll was in charge until he arrived, though Duncan suspected his cousin wouldn't willingly relinquish control.

His cousin was chomping at the bit to prove his mettle. Archie was one of the most important magnates in Scotland, but his relationship with the king was at times strained. Both were young men in their prime, recently freed from the leading strings of guardians, eager to establish their authority. At times that pursuit put them at loggerheads. Undoubtedly it hadn't escaped the king's notice that in the Highlands, Argyll was referred to as "King Campbell."

Duncan rode beside his cousin at the head of a force of nearly two thousand Campbells. With the rest of the clans and men who'd answered the king's call, they would be nearly ten thousand strong. In addition to Grant's men, they would be joined by their cousins, Campbells of Lochnell and Cawdor, MacLean of Duart, the MacGregors, the Mackintoshes, and the MacNeils.

A significant force, aye, but few of those were trained soldiers—even fewer had protective armor or a mount.

He glanced around behind him at the long line of foot soldiers, seeing precious little silvery steel glinting in the sun, only the occasional knapscall and habergeon, the sleeveless coat of mail, such as he wore.

"Something bothering you, cousin?"

Duncan turned to find Argyll watching him. He frowned, considering the question. He supposed there was. "I'd hoped to see more men on horseback."

From any other source, Duncan knew the comment would be perceived by his cousin as a criticism, but they'd been fostered together and Duncan never hesitated to speak his mind. It was probably why Argyll relied upon him—he could trust Duncan not to toady to him. Not that his cousin always heeded his advice. Nay, Argyll had a mind of his own, unfortunately with all the arrogance of youth and position.

"What disadvantage we have in horsemen will be more than compensated by our superior numbers. If the rebels manage to rouse a quarter of the men we have I will be surprised."

Duncan refrained from commenting on the relative skill of their men, some of whom were armed only with swords or pikes and had probably only answered the king's summons for the plunder. Huntly's numbers would be much smaller, that was true, but they would be trained and better equipped.

But that would change. When the king and the Frasers, Irvings, Forbeses, and Leslies arrived they would have many more horsemen. "You are probably right," Duncan agreed.

Argyll quirked a brow—the sardonic look emphasizing the sharp angles of his dark, Gallic ancestry. "Probably?"

Duncan grinned. Archie liked to believe he was *always* right. "Aye."

"There's no doubt about it, there will be a rout.

Huntly won't escape punishment this time." Argyll was unable to mask his glee. "Not even James can ignore a conspiracy to take his crown and put it on the head of a papist."

The bitter rivalry between the two earls was well known. It infuriated Argyll to no end that despite Huntly's persistent failure to renounce his religion—and his outright defiance—the king continued to show "Geordie," his boyhood companion, favor. Seeing "Geordie" brought to heel—not to mention laying claim to some of his lands—was something Argyll had looked forward to for a long time.

When Duncan didn't disagree, his cousin eyed him slyly. "Where did you disappear to last night?"

He held his face impassive. "I was tired. I went to bed."

"Hmm . . ." His too-observant-cousin didn't believe him. "It's funny," Archie offered ironically. "Our beautiful young hostess seemed to disappear about the same time as you did."

The muscle in Duncan's jaw jumped. "Is that so?"

The problem with foster brothers was that they knew you too damned well. Duncan shot his cousin a warning glance, one that was ignored.

Realizing he'd struck gold, Argyll smiled like a cat that had just cornered a fat mouse. Like many young men recently wed, he seemed eager for everyone around him to share his fate and had been encouraging Duncan to find a wife. "The suggestion of a betrothal between the gel and Colin surprised me—at Stirling I was sure that you wanted her."

His blasted cousin saw far too much. Duncan gave him a hard look. "Would it have mattered?" he asked, unable to completely bite back the bitterness in his voice.

Argyll considered the question, but not for long. The

answer was painfully obvious. "Nay, I suppose not." His cousin never shirked from telling him the truth—no matter how harsh. In that they were alike. "How badly do you want her?"

Duncan looked at him, but he didn't need to answer, the fierce intensity in his gaze said it all.

"I see," Argyll said in a measured tone. "It's a pity. Colin will never be half the leader you are."

"He's young yet," Duncan defended automatically, as always fiercely loyal to his younger brothers and sister. He'd always been close to his half siblings, even more so in the year since their mother had passed. His father's wife had tried, but had never been able to get past her resentment of Duncan's place in her household. Perhaps it would have been better if his father hadn't shown him so much favor. But fortunately, their mother's coldness had never affected his relationship with her children.

As lads, Colin and Jamie had tailed after their older brother, mimicking everything he did—including dragging around weapons that were too big for them—with eagerness that bordered on idolatry. Growing up, there had been surprisingly little rivalry between the brothers, which Duncan supposed was partially do to the age difference. As Colin grew into manhood, he suspected that would change.

It certainly would once he found out about Jeannie.

Now that his anger had waned, Duncan could see that Colin was not to blame for what had happened. While at Stirling, Duncan had taken care to keep his interest in Jeannie to himself. That his brother had taken one look at her and fallen in love . . . well, he could hardly blame him.

Duncan frowned, realizing he hadn't considered that his brother might have feelings for the lass. He would have to do what he could to ensure that Colin understood that there was never an intention to hurt him.

But he knew Colin. His quick-tempered younger brother would be furious.

"So this problem with the lass," Argyll said. "Is that why you are not riding beside your father?"

Duncan looked over his shoulder, through the dust and throngs of soldiers, catching sight of Colin and his father riding side-by-side near the rear of the clan. Aye, he'd purposefully avoided both of them, exchanging only a few words since the feast yesterday. The chill between him and his father had not waned the last two weeks. He raised a brow. "Do you not enjoy my company, cousin?"

"Better than most, I suppose," Archie said wryly. All jesting, however, fell by the wayside with his next words. "Whatever problems you have with your father, keep it away from the battlefield and do not let it interfere with your duty." His dark eyes gleamed hard, like two pieces of polished onyx. "I won't let anything get in the way of seeing Huntly brought to heel—especially not a disagreement over a lass."

Duncan gave him a hard glare, forgiving his cousin for the slight only because he knew of the treacherous circumstances in which Archie had recently found himself, at the center of an assassination attempt by men he'd trusted. Duncan knew how the betrayal still ate at him—and probably always would. "You should know me better than that."

Argyll didn't answer right away. "There is no one I trust more, but there is no one I trust completely." The look in his eye was one of bitter melancholy. "It is a lesson you should take to heart, cousin. It might save you from making a painful mistake."

Watching Duncan ride away, when every instinct clamored to stop him, was one of the most difficult things Jeannie had ever had to do.

When her mother had left, it had been in the dead of night. Jeannie never had the chance to stop her. To beg her not to leave. To tell her that if she left she would never come back.

If only Jeannie had been older, she might have realized what was going on. She might have been able to stop her.

But she was old enough now. Standing at the window in her tower chamber, watching as the last of the Campbell soldiers and the bold yellow standard of the Earl of Argyll faded from view, she clenched a damp, lace trimmed square of linen in her hand.

It will be all right, she told herself.

Duncan is not my mother. He will return in a few days and we will be married.

Nothing will go wrong. Even her father had agreed to side with Argyll and the king. To go against Huntly, his lord, her father must be certain of a victory.

Tucking the cloth in the sleeve of the embroidered green silk doublet she wore over her French gown, Jeannie sighed and started to turn from the window, stopping when something caught her gaze. A movement in the copse of trees north of the castle. A rider emerged, almost as if he'd been waiting for the last of the Campbells to leave, and rode hard across the moors, up the small rise, and under the iron castle yett.

She wrinkled her nose, thinking it strange, but giving no more though than that. After washing the sadness from her eyes with some water she'd poured into a basin, Jeannie emerged from her chamber refreshed to head downstairs. Her father and his men would be leaving soon to join the others at Drumin Castle and she must see to the preparations.

Father . . .

She forced herself not to think about it. He would come back. He always came back.

　　She crossed the hall, teaming with servants still busy cleaning the mess from the celebration the night before, and stopped outside the door to the laird's solar.

　　It was partially open and she could see a man standing before her father. Tall and broad shouldered, if a bit gangly, he looked vaguely familiar. It took her only a moment to realize he was the rider she'd seen emerge from the trees a short while ago. But the quality of his clothing and the costly mail coat were far too fine to be that of a messenger.

　　She raised her hand to knock, hesitating. The rider had turned slightly and removed his steel bonnet, revealing thick waves of golden blond hair damp with sweat. Jeannie smothered a gasp with her hand.

　　She recognized him. Francis Gordon, the Earl of Huntly's second son. They'd met a few times over the years before the feuding had begun. She'd thought him handsome, in the way that a young girl fancies a lad half-a-dozen years older. Now, compared to Duncan's dark masculine beauty, he seemed almost pretty. But Francis had always been kind to her, making it a point to smile and wink when he caught her staring at him.

　　Her heart pounded. What could he be doing here? Looking around furtively, seeing that no one was paying attention to her, impulsively she slipped into the shadows behind the door.

　　"You took a risk," she heard her father say. "What if someone had seen you?"

　　"I was careful," Francis said, his tone dismissive.

　　"You came alone?"

　　"I thought it best. My men are waiting for me in the forest."

　　"Aye, the fewer people who know the better. I don't want to take a chance of Argyll or the king getting word before it is done."

　　Before what is done? Jeannie feared that she didn't

want to know. Francis Gordon's presence did not augur well.

"So we are agreed," Francis said. "You will wait for our signal. When the first cannon shot is fired, you and your men will retreat."

Huntly had cannon? *Dear God.*

She waited for her father to deny the treachery, but was to be disappointed.

"Aye." Her heart sank. "A War Council will be held at Drumin tonight. Argyll is eager to battle. I'll see what I can do to encourage him and send word when I can about the battle plan." Jeannie sagged against the cold stone wall, not wanting to believe what she was hearing—her father intended to join the Gordons and betray the Campbells.

She listened in a daze as they discussed more details of the battle, including Huntly's intention to move on the much larger force. A move that was sure to enrage Argyll. It wasn't until her name was mentioned that she snapped out of her horrified stupor.

"And the lass is amenable to the arrangement?" Francis urged.

Her father hesitated. "Jean is a good girl, she will do her duty."

Francis's voice sharpened. "You mean you haven't told her yet."

"I thought it better to wait. I didn't want to risk an accidental slip of the tongue."

Jeannie frowned at the implication. She could keep a secret.

"I'll not take an unwilling wife—betrothal or not."

Wife? The blood drained from her face and her heart jolted to an abrupt stop. Her father had betrothed her not to Colin Campbell, but to Huntly's son?

Her father started to offer him assurances, but Jeannie

had heard enough. She slipped out from behind the door and moved into the hall, too stunned to think clearly.

Her mind raced, thousands of possibilities converging in the realization that she couldn't let this happen. Her father's betrayal of the Campbells would forever doom her future with Duncan. Worse, her father's retreat would put the Campbell forces at grave risk. Men would die.

Duncan could die.

She bided her time, knowing what she had to do. When she saw Francis Gordon slip out of the laird's solar, she took a deep breath and walked into the room he'd just departed.

Seated in a large chair opposite the cold fireplace, her father appeared to be in deep thought and didn't notice her right away. She sniffed, smelling the strong peaty scent of *uisge-beatha*. Sure enough, he held a half-filled glass in his hand.

It gave her hope. Perhaps, there was a chance. Perhaps, betraying the king and the Campbells did not sit as easily with him as he wanted Francis Gordon to think.

"Father."

He looked up sharply, startled to see her.

"What is it, Jeannie lass? I'm busy."

She wanted to present a carefully reasoned argument about why he should not go through with it, but her emotions got the better of her. She gazed entreatingly at the man she'd always thought a noble knight. At the familiar dark hair dusted with gray, at the green eyes so like her own, at the well-worn, handsome face, and simply blurted, "What you are planning . . . you can't do this."

His eyes scanned her pale face, then narrowed. "Listening at doors, daughter? Aren't you too old for that? Spies are tossed in the dungeon."

Jeannie ignored his anger, rushed toward him, and fell

to her knees before him, taking his hand in hers. "Oh, father, I'm so scared. What of the king? He will be furious with you."

"Hush, lass. You don't know of what you speak. The king isn't eager to destroy Huntly, no matter what the Kirk would like. It's Argyll at the head of this war and I'll take my chances with Huntly over an untried youth."

"But men will be killed."

"It's war, Jeannie. Killing is to be expected." He waved her away, clearly preoccupied and in no mood to appease his daughter. "Return to your chamber. This has nothing to do with you."

"It has everything to do with me!" she protested. "I will not marry Francis Gordon. I don't love him."

It was the wrong thing to say.

"Love?" her father shouted scornfully, the years of bitterness at her mother's betrayal erupting in an angry storm. "Love has nothing to do with marriage. This alliance will bind our clans together and end the feuding. You will have more wealth than you can imagine. Enough of this sniveling about love. The contracts have been signed and I expect you to do your duty as you've been raised to do."

Jeannie shook her head, never had she heard her father sound so unfeeling. "I can't." She bit her lip, knowing this was the worst possible time in which to reveal her love for Duncan, but she had no choice. Otherwise it could be too late. "I"—her voice broke—"I love another."

Her father snatched his hand away from hers and peered down at her coldly. "Who?"

"The Laird of Auchinbreck's eldest son."

"Colin Campbell?"

She shook her head. It took him a moment to figure out what she meant.

"Duncan Dubh, the bastard?" he asked, incredulous. "You can't be serious."

Jeannie lifted her chin. "The manner of his birth is of no import—"

"It's of every importance," he shouted, standing and lifting her harshly to her feet. His fingers dug into her arms as he shook her. "You're a fool if you think I would ever agree to such an arrangement." His face was livid with rage. "I expected more of you." The disappointment in his voice cut her to the quick. "You are so like your mother."

He said it as if there could be no worse comparison. Yes, her mother had made mistakes—but she wasn't all bad . . . was she?

He was studying her face too intently. "Just what have you done?" he asked, suspicion creeping into his tone.

Jeannie shrank back. "N-nothing," she lied.

He stared at her face as if not sure whether to believe her. "So quick to fall in love are you? But what do you really know about Auchinbreck's bastard?"

"I know all I need to know. Surely you can see what kind of man he is? He will make a name for himself. Already he is greatly esteemed by his father and cousin. I love him and I know if you just give him a chance—"

He slammed his glass on the table with such fury the amber liquid sloshed over the edge of the glass. "I will hear no more of this. The betrothal has been agreed upon. Return to your room and if I find you have been lying to me, I will see you locked in the tower like your Great-Aunt Barbara. It's what I should have done with your mother."

Jeannie's eyes widened. Her great aunt had been locked in the tower when she refused to marry any other than the man she loved. She'd died there and even today "Barbie's Tower" was said to be haunted by her ghost.

She gazed up into the cold, hard eyes of a familiar stranger. The transformation in him couldn't have been more extreme. God, he meant it. What happened to the man who'd taken her on his lap when her mother left, wrapped her in his big, strong arms, and dried her tears?

But she'd never defied him before. She'd always been the dutiful, biddable girl, trying to atone for the mother who'd left him—who'd left them all. He might love her, but it was not without boundaries—and she'd just crossed them.

She shivered to think what he would do if he ever found out about what she'd done with Duncan.

He must have seen the fear in her eyes. His gaze softened, and he took her hand. "I'm sorry, lass, I should not have said that. I know you aren't like your mother. You've always been a good girl. I know I can count on you to do what's right. To do your duty to your clan, can't I?"

She'd hit a nerve, more raw than she'd realized. He would never have spoken to her so otherwise. Her mother's betrayal had cut deeply. What would it do to him if she did the same? "Y-y-yes, father." Her voice shook.

His face brightened and he managed a smile. "There's a good lass. Now we'll forget all this unpleasantness. I won't hear another word about a Campbell in this keep. Francis Gordon is a good man, you'll come to care for him."

But she'd never love him like she did Duncan.

Jeannie fled from the solar, running across the hall and up the stairs, not stopping until she'd reached her tower chamber.

For hours, she stared out the window, shivering despite the warm day and the plaid she'd wrapped around her shoulders. Long after her father and his men had gone, she stood up, knowing what she had to do.

I can't let him die.

Her attempt to make her father see reason had not worked. She prayed she faired better with Duncan.

"I am of the opinion . . ."

Duncan hoped to never hear those words again. They seemed to ricochet back and forth in his head like a musket ball, leaving him with a splitting headache. The raised voices were all starting to run together.

If this was what a council of war was like, Duncan would stick to fighting. He'd rather take his chances against a claymore and hagbut any day over listening to the same argument go round and round for hours.

Gathered in the great hall of Drumin Castle were the elite of King James's Highland forces: chiefs, chieftains, and a few trusted captains like Duncan—each of whom insisted on putting forth their opinion. Like a room full of competing cooks who each added seasoning to the pot, all they'd ended up with was salty gruel.

Duncan had been listening to the arguing for the better part of three hours now, and the other men were finally coming to the realization that he'd made hours ago—Argyll could be as stubborn as an old mule.

His cousin had set his course and would not be swayed. No matter how vehemently the council argued otherwise.

On arriving at Drumin Castle, they'd been surprised to learn that Huntly had moved his forces to Auchindoun—only a few furlongs away. Argyll wanted to strike a quick blow against his nemesis and attack on the morrow, before the king and the other clans from the south arrived with their horses. His cousin believed their advantage of position and numbers would be enough.

His chief advisors argued against it. Duncan's father,

Cawdor, MacLean, and MacNeil, all agreed that it would be precipitous to attack now. Only Grant and Lochnell sided with Argyll.

"We should wait for the king's orders," his father reiterated, ever the steady voice in a sea of discontent. "And for the additional cavalry support."

"By time the king arrives my yellow standard will be flying high atop the tower of Strathbogie," Archie boasted boldly. "We have all the men we need. Our scouts have put their forces at no more than two thousand. We have five times that many."

"But most of Huntly's men are mounted," his father pointed out, much as Duncan had earlier.

"Our numbers will outweigh any advantage of their horses. We have them where we want them." Argyll glared at the chiefs defiantly. "I will not sit back and squander this opportunity."

Duncan knew how important it was to his cousin to prove himself. If they attacked now, Argyll could claim victory for his own. Privately, Duncan was inclined to agree with his cousin. Perhaps the more prudent course would be to wait for the king's men, but if the men held their positions, they would win without them.

"The earl is right," Jeannie's father, the Laird of Freuchie, interjected. "It may take days for the king's men to arrive. With Huntly's men here," he marked a small "x" on the rough map of the area they'd been poring over, "if we move south we can position ourselves here," he pointed to a small hill above Glenlivet. "From there we will have the high ground from which to attack."

All of a sudden, from his seat at the opposite end of the table, Duncan felt his cousin's gaze settle on him. "What do you think, cousin?"

An unnatural quiet descended over the room. Duncan

knew what the men were thinking. What did it matter what the bastard son of Auchinbreck thought?

It was the first time his cousin had made public what many no doubt suspected occurred in private—the earl's reliance on his counsel. A reliance Duncan knew the others resented. Especially their cousin Lochnell, chief of the senior branch of Clan Campbell behind Argyll.

Archie had put Duncan in an awkward position, forcing him to choose between his father and his cousin. If Duncan sided with his father, and Archie followed Duncan's advice where he'd ignored that of more important men, the other men would be furious. If he sided with Archie, as he was inclined to do, he would be seen as pandering to his powerful cousin.

His father had obviously reached the same conclusion. Before Duncan could answer, he deflected the question—and the attention—away from Duncan. "My son is eager to fight by your side whether it's tomorrow or two weeks from now. As are the rest of us, but we do not want to act precipitously."

"I think we should do as the earl says and attack tomorrow," Colin offered out of turn, but no one paid him any mind.

The arguing continued back and forth for almost another hour, but eventually Argyll had his way: They would march tomorrow.

Using a map to delineate their positions, they planned their course. It was decided that the vanguard of four thousand men—mostly on foot—would be divided into three sections. The left flank, including the MacNeils and MacGregors, were to be commanded by Grant. The Campbells, commanded by Duncan's father and Lochnell, would take the center. The right flank would be under the command of MacLean of Duart.

Behind the vanguard Argyll would command the remainder of the army of six thousand men, this time divided in two divisions. "Cawdor will take the left," Argyll said, "and the right . . ."

He looked at Duncan, clearly wanting to give the command to him. Duncan's heart pounded, anticipating the coup. It would be a great honor to be given such a command at his age—no matter what his station.

Again the room fell quiet. The resentment toward Duncan was palpable. Palpable enough for his cousin to sense it.

He saw the flicker of regret in his cousin's eyes before Archie shifted his gaze.

Duncan understood his cousin's predicament, but couldn't mask his disappointment. The day would come when Duncan's right to lead could not be denied, but that day would not be today. He was still too young, too unproven for his cousin to chance giving a bastard such a position of importance above the more senior clansmen.

Colin glanced at Duncan then back to Argyll. Duncan sensed his brother's anxiousness, anxiousness that seemed to be manifesting itself in unusual—even for Colin—brashness. Before Duncan could stop him, Colin volunteered, "I will take the right, cousin."

"You?" Argyll scoffed, not bothering to hide his amusement. "You've barely earned your spurs, boy. Glengarry will take the right."

Colin turned so red in the face, Duncan thought he might burst a blood vessel in his temple.

Damn. Their cousin had about as much tact as a charging boar. Archie didn't have to humiliate Colin like that. Eagerness—even misplaced—should be encouraged.

Duncan half expected their father to intervene, but instead of moving to pacify his son as he often did in these situations where Colin's rash tongue got him in trouble, his father stayed silent, studying Colin with a disturbed look on his face. Something was going on between his father and Colin, but Duncan had been so caught up in his own troubles he hadn't realized so until now.

Colin stewed angrily while the final details of the plan were worked out, and at long last the men stood up to go. Jeannie's father folded the map and started to slip it into his sporran, but Argyll stopped him with a distracted wave of his hand. "No, no. Let my cousin hold the map." Both Colin and Duncan stilled, but it was Duncan who he spoke of. "He will be at my side tomorrow should I have need of it."

His father looked as if he wanted to argue, no doubt assuming as Duncan had done, that he would fight beside his father.

Grant handed it over, giving Duncan a hard look, and for the first time acknowledging Duncan's presence. "If you think that is best, my lord." It was clear he didn't; there was no mistaking the slur in his voice.

Duncan took the map and tucked it into his sporran, meeting the other man's anger and condemnation full force. *Grant knew,* Duncan realized. Any hope that he would be persuaded to the match faded.

Cognizant of his cousin's warning to focus on the task at hand, he stayed silent. But one day he would prove himself worthy of Grant's daughter . . . one day.

Sizing up the situation, his father distracted Grant with a question and drew him away from Duncan. Gradually the men dispersed, leaving the great hall to see to their men before retiring for the night. Duncan would have joined Colin in doing the same, but his cousin held him back, insisting on going over the battle plan in the laird's solar one more time. By the time they rose from the table, it was near midnight.

With so many men having descended on Drumin, the great hall and outside barracks were jammed to the rafters. His father had decided to sleep in tents outside the castle gates with their clansmen. It was quiet as Duncan wound his way through the rows of sleeping men. The night was pleasantly cool, a gentle wind blew from the north.

He was surprised to find a candle flickering and Colin still awake when he pulled aside the canvas flap and ducked inside the small tent.

Colin's face was half cast in the shadows. For a moment, Duncan thought he saw raw hatred gleam in his eyes. "Is something wrong?"

"I was just coming to find you," Colin said cheerfully. Duncan realized he must have been mistaken as to what he thought he'd seen. Colin handed him a folded missive. "This came for you a few minutes ago."

Duncan frowned and turned it over in his hand, seeing his name written in bold, but distinctly feminine, strokes. He stilled. It couldn't be.

"Who is it from?" Colin asked casually. "It looks to be a woman's writing."

"I don't know," Duncan said, but feared he did.

He tore it open and read. Each word fell like dry leaves on flames. His mouth drew in a tight line. He was going to kill her.

Colin sensed something was wrong. "What is it? Is there a problem?"

"Not for long," Duncan said darkly. "There is something I must attend to."

"Now?"

He nodded. "I'm afraid it can't wait."

"But the attack . . ."

"I'll return in a few hours. Get some sleep."

"Should I go with you?"

Duncan shook his head and said grimly, "Nay, this is something I must do alone."

Chapter 7

Jeannie sat on a rickety chair before a small window nervously tapping her foot on the wood floor. The sound, however, was dulled by the thick layer of dirt and dust covering the wide planks. She glanced around the decidedly rustic chamber, trying not to look too closely, but unable to prevent a reflexive grimace. No fireplace, a couple of waxed stubs for candles, a thin bed with a mattress that was probably twice as old as she was, a table with a green pitcher and basin, which at one time might have been copper, dust clouding every surface, and cobweb-strewn beamed ceilings.

Cobwebs meant spiders.

A shiver ran up her arm and down her neck, as if she were feeling them crawl across her skin. She inched forward in her seat away from the wall, sitting a bit more upright on the chair.

What did she expect? She was fortunate to have found any kind of private accommodation this close to Drumin Castle, but nearly every village had an alehouse. The room—or, more accurately, alcove—above this one would have to do.

The guardsmen who'd escorted her on her "emergency" journey to her cousin's would be sleeping in the stables.

She felt a twinge of guilt for the elaborate lies she'd concocted, and a bigger one for the ease with which it had come—it wasn't just the guardsmen, but her brother she'd lied to. She'd thought about confiding in John—the girls were too young—but didn't want to force him to choose between his love for his father and his love for the sister who'd been like a mother to him. So she'd invented a message from their cousin Margaret, the new Lady Lovat, requesting her immediate presence at Castle Fraser. Then, when they'd neared Drumin she'd feigned illness, forcing them to find the nearest accommodation. A little gold had gone a long way in persuading the ale woman to overlook the gentleman who would arrive later, ensure the guardsmen had plenty to drink, and to send her son with a message for Duncan at Drumin.

She wrinkled her nose, looking at the old wool plaid covering the bed. Perhaps the guardsmen had the better end of the bargain; straw might be an improvement. But at least in here she and Duncan would be alone. That is, if he ever showed up.

She peered out the window into the darkness as if willing him to appear. Where was he? She'd sent her note hours ago. What if he didn't come?

Panic pinched her chest. He had to come.

She had to warn him. Though what she was going to say, she didn't know. She could hardly tell him what she'd learned—to do so would not only betray her father, but put his life in jeopardy. She bit her lip. It wasn't only worry about what she was going to say, but she suspected that Duncan wouldn't exactly be pleased to see her. But as Huntly's stronghold of Strathbogie was still some distance, she wasn't in any real danger.

The toe-tapping didn't seem to be easing any of her anxiety so she stood and began to pace, which meant taking only a step or two in each direction in the tiny room.

The sounds of loud, off-key singing, interspersed with laughter filled the night. It was well past midnight, but from the noise below you would never know. The raucous sounds of merrymaking only seemed to increase as the evening wore on, which spoke well for the ale, but not so well for the prospect of sleep.

Not that she expected to be able to rest any time soon. Not until the battle was over.

And perhaps not even then. What if he wouldn't listen to her?

Despair washed over her, but she forced it aside. She would make him understand.

A horseman suddenly burst out of the darkness into the yard below. The shadow of a large man dominated the small circle of light provided by a few torches.

Her pulse took a sudden violent leap, taking her heart right along with it.

It was too dark to make out his features, but his size and fierceness of his movements told her all she need to know: Duncan had arrived.

Taking a deep breath, she sat in her chair and faced the door, waiting with her hands folded calmly in her lap, though the erratic beat of her heart was anything but. For the first time, she wondered if she might have made a mistake in coming. She couldn't escape the knowledge that it was something her mother might have done. But it was too late for second thoughts. Besides, what other choice did she have?

It seemed to take forever before she heard the heavy sound of booted feet climbing up the stairs, coming to a sudden stop just outside the door. Then, finally, the door burst open.

It was a good thing she was sitting, as the force of his anger hit her like a blast from a smith's bellows.

Her lips parted with a gasp and a shiver wound down her spine. *Jesu, he was magnificent.*

Primed for battle, Duncan was an impressive sight. A flush of heated awareness swept over her, her body responding in a distinctly feminine fashion to the blatant display of masculine power. Black leather and steel encased every bulging muscle of his tall, powerfully built body. With his jet black hair and fearsome expression, he looked like a dark knight pulled off the lists of an ancient tournament—fierce, dangerous, and indestructible.

He had to stoop to avoid hitting his head and angle his shoulders to pass through the doorway. Once inside the chamber he'd sucked the cool air right out with his heat.

If the room had seemed small before, now it felt about as big as a mouse hole. A mouse hole crowded with almost six and a half feet of fearsome Highland warrior, his body honed as sharp and deadly as the edge of a claymore. He dominated the chamber, making her at once conscious of his strength—and his fury. Fury that rang every internal alarm bell she had until her entire body seemed to reverberate with the clamor. The tiny hairs at the back of her neck and arms stood on edge, sensing danger. She felt the strange urge to run, but there was nowhere to go. He was everywhere.

His face was a mass of hard lines in the flickering candlelight, the dark shadows emphasizing the square set of his jaw and tight line of his mouth. His eyes narrowed on her with predatory intent, piercing blue appearing almost black. A muscle ticked ominously in his neck—an agonizing tolling of time when it otherwise seemed to stand still. Closing the door, he strode toward her. Even the way he moved was fierce and harshly masculine; he had the long, powerful strides of a lion. She resisted the ridiculous urge to cower, but if she'd ever been inclined to do so, it was now.

He didn't say a word. He didn't need to. Anger radiated from every inch of his powerful, mail-clad form.

She gazed up at him tentatively, looking for a crack in his forbidding demeanor, but finding none. His expression was about as yielding as the steel that plated his chest.

She swallowed, trepidation balling in her throat. No, definitely not pleased to see her.

Duncan had been out of control precisely twice in his one and twenty years, and both times involved the lass seated before him as primly and properly as if they were meeting at court and not in some hellhole alehouse only a few miles from a looming battle.

Tamping down the urge to pull her into his arms and vent his rage for scaring the blazes out of him, instead he pulled out her note from his sporran and tossed it in her lap like a gauntlet. "What the hell—" he stopped, clamping down on the reins of control "What is the meaning of this?"

She picked it up without even looking at it and held it back to him. "I needed to see you."

He ripped the wrinkled parchment from her hand and snapped it open with a flick of his wrist, holding it before her wary, green-eyed gaze. "I can see that," he said, his voice deceptively calm, "right here where it says: 'Come quickly, I must see you. We must act immediately.' " He stuffed the note back into the leather pouch and leaned over her menacingly, his arms on either side of her shoulders, bracing himself against the window sill, his face only inches from hers.

Damn, he could smell her. He inhaled instinctively, drawing in the delicate scent of honeysuckle. And those lips . . . so soft and pink. A mouth like that should be illegal, conjuring images that could murder a man's self-control. For a moment, desire blinded him, threatening distraction, but anger won out. "What it doesn't say," he said in a low voice, "is what possible reason you could have for following me into a damned war zone."

She lifted her tiny upturned nose in the air as haughtily as a queen. Her delicate, regal beauty was laughingly out of place in this hovel. "Stop trying to intimidate me when I'm only here to help you."

At another time he might admire her spirit. He wasn't often challenged when he was in a temper like this. Clenching his fists, he drew a long, ragged breath, searching for patience, but finding it exhausted. "How could putting yourself in danger and jeopardizing not only our future, but also your father's involvement with our side, possibly help me? Do you know what would happen if anyone discovered you were here?"

Her nose wrinkled. "I wasn't thinking of that—"

"Of course you weren't," he said scathingly. "You weren't thinking at all. You just acted, following whatever damned fancy led you to think coming here was a good idea."

She flinched as if he'd struck her. He hated hurting her, but hell if he'd temper his anger and risk her ever doing anything like this again.

"You're wrong," she said woodenly. "I didn't come here on a flight of fancy, I came because I love you and don't want to see you hurt. I'm sorry my presence so displeases you, but I can assure you I'm in no danger—I brought half-a-dozen guardsmen with me."

"No danger?" He could barely contain the fury in his voice. "Do you realize that there are almost fifteen thousand men camped not three miles from here, poised to do battle?" He shuddered to think what she'd told her guardsmen to get them to bring her here.

She drew her brows together over her nose, looking up at him uncertainly. "Strathbogie is still a day's ride—"

"Huntly is no longer at Strathbogie, he's at Auchindoun."

She paled, then chewed on her lip. A surge of heavy heat rushed to his groin and he had to force his gaze away. As always, the intensity of the desire he felt for her was getting in the way, and he didn't like it. The lack of control bothered the hell out of him. He'd never felt like this. Ever. Nor had he expected to. But love had hit him like Thor's thunderbolt. Would there ever come a time when he could think rationally around her?

"Oh," she said softly.

"Oh?" he repeated, his voice booming. "Is that all you have to say for yourself?"

His words had the opposite effect than he'd intended. Her cheeks splotched with angry red. "I do not answer to you, Duncan Campbell."

He grabbed her wrist before she could poke his chest and looked down into her flashing eyes. "You will," he said through clenched teeth. "Once you are my wife, you will damn well answer to me."

She gave him a pitying look, as if he was quite deluded in that respect, and wrenched her hand free. "That's exactly why I'm here."

His eyes narrowed. For the first time he noticed the genuine turmoil in her expression. Whatever had brought her here was significant enough to be causing her grave distress. His anger cooled perhaps a degree or two. Standing, he dragged his fingers through his hair and pushed it back from where it slumped across his face, trying to uncoil the emotions twisting inside him since he'd received her note. He sighed with exaggerated patience. "Why are you here, Jeannie?"

She stood and turned toward the window, her back rod straight and hands fluttering fretfully at her narrow waist. "We need to leave together now. In a few days it will be too late."

Her vague response did nothing to keep his temper in check. He fought the spike of impatience and managed to mask his frustration behind an even tone. "If you haven't noticed, I'm in the middle of fighting a war. I don't have time for puzzles, Jeannie. Explain why you are here, and then you can turn right around and go back home."

She turned to face him, her eyes softly pleading. "There is something . . ." She seemed to catch herself and took another uneven breath. "A feeling of disaster that I cannot shake." She placed her hand on his chest and leaned toward him pleadingly. "If we don't leave now I fear we will never be able to. We will never marry. If there is to be any chance for us, we must go now. Tonight."

His jaw clenched. "And that is why you are here?" He paused. He couldn't believe she would act so precipitously. *But that's exactly who she is.* Blood pounded through his veins, clamoring for release. "A feeling?"

Her eyes scanned his face, shimmering with tears. "Please. I'm asking you to trust me."

"Based on what? A bad feeling? I do trust you, but what you ask is impossible. I will come for you as we planned in a few days—"

"Don't you see," she cried wildly. "By then it will be too late. We must go now!"

Her fear seemed so intense it bordered on irrational. "Is there something else, Jeannie? Some other reason—"

"No," she cut him off, shaking her head adamantly.

Too adamantly. He studied her for a moment. Part of him wondered if she was hiding something . . .

Nay. He recalled how scared she was when he left. This was nothing more than a young girl's fears of war talking. He thought she'd understood how important this was to him, but obviously she hadn't. He was not a man to be led around by leading strings.

He unlaced her hands from around his neck and set her purposefully away from him. "Return home and I'll come for you when the battle is over."

"No, you have to listen to me." Her hand clenched his arm, squeezing. "Something terrible is going to happen.

I don't want you in the middle of it." Her voice had grown increasingly desperate. "Please, if you love me." Tears slid down her cheeks. "I'm asking you to trust me."

Anger hardened inside him. Why was she doing this? Didn't she know how hard it was for him to deny her anything? All he wanted was to make her happy. "I do love you. But what you are asking for is blind obedience not trust. If you have a reason beyond a 'bad feeling,' tell me now."

She looked back at him, eyes wide and pained, and opened her mouth, but said nothing.

"Very well then." The look on her face tore at his chest. He knew he had to get out of here. He strode toward the door. "At first light you will ride for Freuchie and await my arrival." He gave her a long look, not immune to the fear in her eyes. "I will come for you, Jeannie. Of that I promise."

I've failed.

Jeannie stared helplessly at his back, watched as he put his hand on the latch, taking in every heart-wrenching detail of the man who'd claimed her heart from the first moment she'd seen him, as if by doing so she could hold on to him forever. Her eyes scanned the tall, powerful frame, the wide shoulders, narrow waist and long muscular legs, the big callused hands, and the silky black hair that curled at his neck.

He was a fortress of masculine strength—seemingly indestructible.

Seemingly, there was the rub. He might look like a rock, but he was flesh and blood.

Fear, panic, and desperation conspired in one final attempt to make him see what she could not explain: That if he left now, he might never return. "Duncan, wait, you can't go. I . . ."

Dear God, what can I say? How could she make him understand without betraying her father and putting his life—and the lives of her clansmen—in danger?

The politics of who was right and who was wrong in the religious dispute between Huntly and the king meant nothing to her. All that mattered was that two men she loved were on opposite sides—how could she protect them both?

If she told Duncan what she'd learned, she knew him well enough to know that he would consider himself duty bound to inform his cousin of her father's perfidy. He could not stand aside and allow a wrong to go unchecked. Betrayal such as her father intended to a man of integrity like Duncan would not be worthy of understanding or mercy. Duncan would always do what was right and just, no matter the personal cost. She knew that about him.

But if she didn't tell Duncan—or somehow stop him from leaving—her father's treachery would put Duncan in grave physical danger. No matter what she did, Jeannie knew all hope of their family being persuaded to make a match between them was gone. It was the other match that worried her—the one her father had arranged to Francis Gordon and which she'd unwittingly agreed to. She felt a twinge of guilt. Her father had invoked a powerful weapon: duty. She wanted to be a good daughter and defying him would be extremely difficult.

She was caught in an impossible quandary, torn between two conflicting loyalties. Either way she lost.

Somehow she had to convince Duncan to heed her warning, but she had to be careful. He was too astute—he might guess what was happening if she said too much.

He looked back at her over his shoulder, his handsome face set hard against her with cold determination.

It was the way he looked at other people—not her. His ability to shut off his emotions so completely, so easily, unsettled her.

"I need to do this, Jeannie. Don't make it harder than it already is."

Hard? What a prodigious understatement. He had no idea how this was tearing her apart.

She ran toward him and put her hand on his arm, tears of fear and frustration streaming in hot rivulets down her cheeks. She gazed up at him, imploring him with all the love in her heart. "Please, you can't leave like this."

He stood very still and didn't say anything, but the edges of his mouth turned white. He was fighting something. *Me*, she realized. Denying her *was* hard for him. It was a small crack in an otherwise impenetrable façade. Gently, he unlatched her fingers from around his arm and turned away from her.

Her heart twisted with a fresh spike of panic. *He's going to leave. Stop him. Hold on to him.* Not knowing what else to do, she flung herself against him, putting herself between him and the door.

She clung to his mail-clad chest, but he wouldn't look at her. His expression stony and unreadable, only the tick below his jaw betrayed his effort. She couldn't bear that he was holding himself apart like this. "Please, don't be angry with me," she begged, tears choking her voice. "I know you think I'm being silly and was foolish to have come here like this. I can explain." Her chest heaved as she fought to breathe between the sobs. "I'm just so scared."

Perhaps it was the honesty of the emotion that finally penetrated, but suddenly his arms were around her and she felt the comforting security of being held against him. He stroked her hair and murmured soothingly, "I know, my love, I know. But have faith in me."

I do. But I've no faith in treachery.

He gazed down at her and their eyes locked. She couldn't breathe, waiting, hoping. Her mouth quivered as he wiped the tears from her cheeks with his thumb. The tenderness in his eyes gripped her heart. She loved him so much. The thought of life without him was too horrible to contemplate. "Please." She lifted her mouth to his, needing the reaffirmation—needing him.

His fingers tightened around her chin as if he was trying to resist the pull, but the desire and the indelible connection between them was stronger than them both.

He lowered his head and covered her mouth with his, his kiss achingly soft, achingly tender, comforting her with the caress of his warm, silky lips.

Her heart rose up to her throat, the relief to her frayed emotions acute. In the safety of his embrace she knew that everything was going to be all right.

The heat of his body warmed her, gentle and soothing, taking away the chill like the morning sun on a bed of dew.

She tasted him through the salt of her tears, the dark, spicy masculine essence of forbidden fruit. So irresistible it had to be sinful. One taste and she was lost.

But the tender kiss was like a sprinkle of rain on a raging wildfire—too gentle, too sweet to douse the flames of her fear. Only the fierce downpour of passion could tame the desperate maelstrom lashing inside her.

Don't let him go.

She sank against him, seeking the reassurance of his solid strength. Leather and steel bit into her chest, but she didn't care. He was hard and steady, a rock in a stormy sea, and as long as she could hold on to him, nothing could go wrong.

He groaned, sensing her need, threading his fingers through her hair to grip her neck and bring her mouth more firmly against his.

His lips moved over hers, roughly, passionately. The comfort and tenderness of moments before turned hard and possessive. Demanding. All of the emotion that he'd fought to contain exploded in a rush of hot, searing lust. She could taste his hunger, his desire, and her body heated with awareness. Sensation shot through her in hot, shimmering waves. All she could think about was the way that he'd touched her, covering her with his big hands, pushed inside her and thrust until the heavens had parted and she'd glimpsed paradise.

He smelled incredible. She inhaled the wind and the sun, a potent primitive scent that only increased her urgency. It filled her mind with wicked thoughts. She wanted to feel him naked against her. Wanted to slide her mouth and tongue over his chest and taste the salt of his hot skin as he pounded inside her, working them both to a frantic lather.

Her hands clutched his shoulders, gripping hard, trying to bring him even closer. She stretched against the hard length of his body, lifting up on her tiptoes to circle her hands around his neck, seeking . . .

His hand slid down her back to cup her bottom and lift her firmly against him.

Oh, God, yes. Pleasure broke over her in heavy waves. Her body softened. Tingled. The strange fluttering awakened low in her belly, damp and insistent. She circled against him, instinctively seeking friction to ease the anxious pressure.

He growled, a fierce primal sound that called to a place deep inside her. An erotic, carnal place she was only just discovering. She wanted to make him sound like that always. Crazy with need. Crazy for her.

He lifted her leg to circle his waist and pinned her back up against the door. The hard column of his desire pressed insistently between her legs. This time his size did not bring fear, only eagerness. She remembered all too viscerally his fullness inside her, hot and heavy, stretching her, driving her home to oblivion.

She wanted him there now.

And he wanted it, too. Badly. She could feel the hammering of his heart, the taut muscles flexing under her fingertips, the jerkiness of his movements. The air verily crackled with danger. His passion was like a cask of gunpowder in her hands, ready to explode.

His tongue was in her mouth, probing with long, wicked strokes that left no part of her unclaimed. She opened against him, wanting it even deeper. Harder. Wetter. Her entire body ached for him. Need obscured everything else.

No longer bound by innocence, she knew what this man could do to her and she wanted that feeling again. Over and over until they collapsed in a sated heap of naked entwined limbs. Until he never wanted to leave her again.

His mouth dropped to her throat, his hand clutched her breast, squeezing, their bodies undulating toward only one conclusion.

He tugged her stays and bodice down to access her breasts, almost tearing the fabric in his urgency. She cried out when his mouth covered her, when he sucked her deep into her mouth, tugging her throbbing nipple between his teeth as his hips rocked against her.

God, she could feel it. Feel the pleasure building. The heat intensifying, concentrating at her very core.

He fumbled with the ties at his waist. A moment later she heard his sporran and scabbard hit the ground, then felt the air on her bare skin as he lifted her skirts.

She was so wet, so hot, literally shaking with desire, her need all consuming.

He lifted his head from her breast and gazed into her half-lidded eyes. His eyes were hooded, dark with passion, every muscle in his face and neck tight with strain.

"I can't wait," he growled through clenched teeth. "God, what do you do to me?" he groaned, his voice raw and exposed—almost angry.

Positioning himself between her legs, he lifted them around his waist so that her feet were off the floor, and surged inside her with a deep, guttural groan of pure masculine satisfaction.

She gasped from the exquisite force, her back slamming against the door as if to mark his possession. Because that's what it was—possession. She felt his power surge inside her, every inch of his six foot plus muscled frame poised and straining against her. He was so big and hard, filling her completely, the weight of her body taking him even deeper. She let the sensation wash over her, over and over. It was incredible, beautiful in its primitive perfection. She could stay like this forever.

Their eyes met, emotion breaking through the haze of unfettered passion. She felt his love for her as surely as if he'd just reached out and touched her heart. "You are so damned beautiful," he kissed her again, hard and punishing. "You make me lose my mind."

"Good," she whispered, wriggling him even deeper. "I like you this way."

His eyes flared, any control he'd managed snapped. Her legs tightened around his waist as his hands gripped her naked bottom. The feel of his big, callused warrior's hands hard and demanding on her soft flesh sent fresh tingles up her spine. He kissed her again, and his hips started to move, thrusting hard and deep. The force of each stroke shuddered through her, setting off wave after wave of sensation. She gave over to him completely, not knowing that anything could feel like this. Not realizing passion could be so fierce and furious.

Her breath was coming in short gasps, echoing his sharp grunts. Her heart was pounding. Heat engulfed her. She could feel it coming. Faster and faster, he plunged into her, his powerful body surging into her with every thrust.

"I can't," he growled through clenched teeth, his face a mask of tortured restraint. She knew he was waiting . . .

Her body contracted. "Oh, God," she cried out as the spasms ripped through her in wave after hot wave.

But her cries were drowned by his. He held her hips and thrust into her one more time, holding her against him as his body jerked with his own release. A guttural sound of raw ecstasy tore from his chest. Warmth rushed between her legs.

When it was over, Jeannie couldn't move. Utterly spent, utterly boneless, her entire body sagged like a poppet made of rags in his arms.

His breathing was still coming hard when his eyes found hers. "God, I'm sorry."

She looked up at him in surprise. "Whatever for?"

Shame tinged his handsome features. "For taking you like a damned animal. Look at us." Gently he eased himself out of her and lowered her to the ground. Her body chilled, protesting the sudden emptiness and loss of his heat. Her legs were a little shaky but she managed to stand upright—not a small feat with jelly in her bones. Boyish befuddlement clouded his gaze. "I've never been like this before. Something comes over me . . ." his voice dropped off. "You deserve to be worshipped, to be made love to properly. On a damned bed for starters."

He looked so chagrined. She put her hand on his cheek, the rough stubble scratching her palm. "It was wonderful. I love what you do to me." She smiled. "I can't imagine anything more . . ." her cheeks heated, "proper." She tilted her head. "But I suppose there is one way we could rectify the situation."

His gaze sharpened, hot and penetrating. "How's that?"

She glanced past his shoulder to the narrow bed, her fingers starting to work the fastenings of his mail at his shoulders. "You could show me all that I've allegedly been missing."

Heat flared in his gaze. "Do I detect a challenge, my lady?"

She gave an exaggerated shrug, her eyes dancing wickedly. "If you aren't too tired. You were doing all the work, after all."

"I assure you, my love, it wasn't work." He kissed her, nuzzling her mouth with his lips and tongue, then moving onto her ear. "Nor am I tired," he breathed against the damp skin, sending a shiver down her spine. He scooped her up into his arms. "Though I appreciate your concern for my welfare."

She giggled and whacked his chest. "What are you doing? Let me down."

A very naughty grin spread across his gorgeous face. "I think not. I intend to show you exactly how to do this properly."

And he did—twice—though she suspected there was nothing proper about it at all.

Hours later, Jeannie collapsed in an exhausted heap of naked entwined limbs just as she'd wanted. But never could she have imagined the absolute contentment, the intimacy forged in the arms of another. She could stay like this forever, tucked under his arm, her head resting on his shoulder, her cheek pressed to bare skin. This might be her favorite place in the entire world. She inhaled his warm, masculine scent, savoring the moment and knowing she would remember it always.

His soft breathing sounded in her ear, filling her with contentment such as she'd never known before. She smiled, her fingers toying with the smattering of fine hairs that formed a triangle on his chest. He'd earned his sleep.

So had she. He was here, with her, safe.

She sighed, nuzzling deeper into the crook of his arm, and closed her eyes. Everything was going to be all right.

It was her last coherent thought before sleep dragged her under.

It was still dark when Duncan jerked awake.

He swore, furious with himself for falling asleep. He needed to get back to camp before he was missed. Carefully he untwined himself from Jeannie's naked limbs and eased from the bed.

It creaked loudly with the removal of his weight and Jeannie stirred, but did not wake. It was probably for the best. He hated leaving like this, without explanation, but neither did he have time for another scene.

He hadn't meant for this to happen. He'd only meant to comfort her, to calm her fears with a gentle kiss. But he'd tasted her need, felt her urgency in the sweet press of her body against his, and desire had reared up inside him like a wild angry beast demanding to be set free. Would it always be like this between them? Hot and explosive, almost desperate in its urgency?

Even after the first time, his efforts to slow the pace and tease out her pleasure were for naught. Their emotions were too raw, their passion too fiery, their need too violent. He lost his mind when he was with her. A small part of him questioned whether he was equipped to handle something so intense. He'd never thought something like this could happen to him. He'd always felt his destiny lay on the battlefield; love had never seemed part of it. Love only complicated things. He need only look as far as the old tales of Arthur or Tristan to see that.

His gaze lingered on her face, her delicate features almost angelic in repose—were it not for the naughty mouth. Even sleep couldn't hide the decidedly sensual curve of her lips.

His chest tightened, moved beyond words that she was his.

Forcing his gaze away, he squinted into the darkness trying to locate his belongings, which in his eagerness—or frenzy—had been strewn around the room.

Instead he was surprised to see everything folded in a neat pile. He frowned. When had she done that? He shook his head. He must have slept deeper than he'd realized. Given what they'd been doing—and that he'd found release three times in about an hour—it probably wasn't all that surprising. He should count himself fortunate that he woke at all from such a sated slumber.

He dressed quickly and pressed one more kiss on her temple before quietly leaving the room. Less than an hour later, after leaving instructions with the ale woman to rouse the guardsmen at dawn, he pushed back the flaps and entered the dark tent.

He was glad Colin was asleep—he was far too tired for explanations. With only a few hours left until daybreak, he didn't bother to remove his clothes, tossing off only his weapons and sporran beside him before crawling onto his pallet. He was so damned tired.

And morning would come soon enough.

Chapter 8

Duncan's eyes and throat burned from the acrid smoke of gunpowder that hovered like a shroud over the bloody battlefield. Sweat poured from every inch of his body. He was exhausted, dirty, and bleeding from too many places to count. It was a rout all right, just not the way his cousin had planned.

"Fall back!" he yelled to a party of men advancing before him. But it was too late. The cannon ball exploded right in front of them, taking two men with it. Five more explosions followed in quick succession down the line with similar deadly results.

Initially, the sight of limbs torn apart and flying body parts had startled him just as it had the rest of the Campbell forces. It had taken all of Duncan's command to prevent half the troops from deserting at the first blast of the strange, terrifying weapon that attacked with a devastating power never before encountered.

That first cannon shot had proved a harbinger of things to come. By no accident it had been aimed right at his cousin's position, claiming not the intended target, Argyll, but Campbell of Lochnell who rode at his side.

Now, hours later, with the rest of the army deserting all around them, all that was left of the vanguard were his father's men and the right wing under the command of MacLean of Duart.

It wasn't only Huntly's cannon that had decimated them, however, but treachery.

His mouth fell in a grim line. Jeannie's father, the Chief of Grant, had betrayed them, retreating at the first cannonade, taking the entire left position with him, and irretrievably crippling the vanguard from the start.

Had Jeannie known what her father intended? Throughout the long day, the question—or more specifically, the answer he knew—haunted him.

When the smoke from the latest barrage cleared he looked around for the earl. This time his damned cousin would bloody well listen to him: Argyll needed to retreat. It was too dangerous this close to the line, and it had become too difficult to protect him. Their numerical advantage was gone. The men who'd eagerly answered the call, hoping for spoils, had second thoughts at the first sign of difficulty. They had about two hundred fifty mounted men and perhaps a thousand foot soldiers to Huntly's fifteen hundred cavalry, though those who remained with them were mostly trained warriors. But hagbuts and swords, even in the hands of trained soldiers, could not defeat cannon. All that had prevented the center vanguard from collapsing was their superior position upon the hill and the fact that the sun was behind them.

He turned his mount around from where he'd ridden ahead to try to warn the men, and then scanned the line behind him, relieved to see Argyll at his father's side.

His cousin could shoot a musket well enough, but in close combat, skill with a sword was preferable—a man could be skewered before he had a chance to reload. Duncan's father wielded a sword with enough skill for them both.

As had occurred all day, a force of Huntly's men had charged forward after the cannon fire, taking advantage of the gaps in the line created by the explosions. But right away, Duncan could see that this time something was different. There were more men, more horses, and more guns—all aimed directly at his father and Argyll.

He shouted a warning, but it was swallowed up in the clash and clatter of the battle. With a flick of his wrist, he snapped the reins and clapped his heels to urge his horse to a gallop, but the distance to close was too great. His pulse raced. He wasn't going to make it.

Dread rose up inside him.

Through the smoke, through the tangle of moving limbs and mail of fighting soldiers, Duncan saw the barrel of the gun pointed right at Argyll.

Time suspended. It felt like he had one foot dangling over the edge of a cliff, tottering as he fought to pull back. Duncan knew what was going to happen. He could almost see the bullet strike his cousin, and every instinct, every fiber of his being, rushed up to try to prevent it. But time wouldn't stop long enough for him to catch up.

The Gordon soldier pulled the trigger.

He saw the spark. Felt the delay. Heard the blast.

He must have shouted again because his father looked up, caught sight of him barreling toward them, and quickly discerned the reason why. With his sword raised, he threw his body into Archie's with enough force to knock them both from their horses. Stumbling to the ground, his father managed to strike a blow, splaying open the man who'd just fired the gun.

With a fierce battle cry, Duncan arrived at full gallop, cutting down two more. His father's guardsmen rallied behind him, and with a burst of renewed ferocity, fought back the charge.

When it was done, and the Gordons had retreated to prepare for the next volley, Duncan jumped off his horse and plowed through the circle of men who'd surrounded his father and Argyll.

His path was blocked by his cousin. His relief at seeing Archie alive was replaced by anger. Now maybe he would listen. "Damn it, Archie, you need to move back. You could have been killed."

"Duncan, I'm sorry . . ." Archie's expression filled Duncan's veins with ice.

He held his cousin's stare for a long heartbeat and then pushed passed him, knowing what he would see.

No. His chest clamped down so tightly that he couldn't breathe.

His father lay prone on the ground. One of his guardsmen knelt beside him, holding a cloth to staunch the blood gushing from his side. The ball had avoided the plate mail, instead finding a narrow gap of unprotected flesh.

"Father." Duncan fell to his knees.

"I'm fine," his father said, his voice clenched as if even breathing added too much pain.

Duncan's throat tightened. They both knew he lied.

Another cannonball exploded nearby, sending a spray of dirt, rock, and smoke in all directions. He needed to do something before they were all killed. He wanted to go with his father and see him to safety, but as long as men were fighting his duty lay on the battlefield.

"We need to get you back to the castle." He stood and quickly issued instructions to a few nearby men.

"Colin?" his father gasped.

The heir. Something twisted in his chest.

"Safe," Duncan assured him, ignoring the hurt. "I sent him back to get more ammunition. I'll send him to you when he returns."

"Watch . . . over . . . will . . . need . . . you."

Duncan wanted to argue against the implication, refusing to accept that his father was dying, but nodded instead. His father needed all his strength to battle his injury.

Panic suddenly widened his father's gaze. "Must . . . tell . . . you . . . sorry . . ." Another explosion cut off what he'd been trying to say, and the effort proved too much for him as he fell unconscious.

The men hustled his father away and Duncan turned to Argyll, steel in his eyes. "Go with them."

This time the earl didn't argue, but his cousin's face was twisted with hatred. One day Archie would be a great leader, but he did not yet possess the age or maturity to weather a blow of this magnitude to his pride with grace. His face flushed red and his eyes bulged with rage. "It's not fair. Were it not for treachery this would be my moment of triumph." Tears of humiliation streamed down his cousin's cheeks. "This is all Grant's fault. I'll destroy him."

Duncan nodded grimly, but he wasn't thinking about Grant—he had no doubt the Laird of Freuchie would get what he deserved. He was thinking about Grant's daughter. Jeannie's father's betrayal had cut off any possibility of a match sanctioned by their families.

But it might have done more than that. His chest tightened. *She knew.* It was the only explanation for why she'd come for him last night.

And now his father lay dying.

His jaw clenched. He didn't have time to think about the ramifications. Huntly's clansmen from the next charge were just breaking over the rise in front of them.

Out of the corner of his eye, he caught a glint of brass and silver. His father's sword was right where he'd left it, staked like a cross impaled through the chest of the man who'd shot him. The enormous two-handed great sword—almost six feet in length—had been handed down to the Chiefs of Campbells of Auchinbreck since the time of the Bruce. Engraved on the blade was one word: *steadfast*.

Clasping the horn grip with one hand, he slowly

pulled it from the dead Gordon and, brandishing it before him, turned to face his attackers. They were almost upon him.

He fought like a man possessed. Perhaps he was. Bastard or no, his father's blood ran through him, and he could feel the strength of his ancestors behind him as he wielded blow after deadly blow, crushing all who came in his path.

They repelled the attack with ease and were waiting for the next when he noticed one of the MacLean's guardsmen riding hell-bent toward them. The guardsman looked around, obviously searching for a leader. Duncan stepped forward. With his father gone from the field, as captain he was in charge of what was left of his clansmen.

"What is it, Fergus?"

If the MacLean clansman was surprised by Duncan's assertion of command he didn't show it. "It's the Mackintosh. He and his men are surrounded. My laird is doing all he can to hold off the Earl or Erroll." Erroll was Huntly's loyal cohort and fiercest warrior. MacLean had to hold him; if Erroll broke through they were done. Someone else would have to go to Mackintosh's aid.

Duncan didn't hesitate. "Where?"

Fergus pointed to the gap in the ridge on the other side of the burn.

Through the haze Duncan could just make out the skirmishing warriors. Perhaps a dozen men had been separated from the rest of the force and were trapped in a narrow gully between the two hills—completely surrounded by Huntly's forces who were descending on them like vultures.

A quick reconnaissance of the situation proved grim. Any rescuers seemed just as likely to be slaughtered as the men they were trying to reach. Their only chance was to strike hard enough at Huntly's left vanguard, creating enough of a diversion to give the Mackintoshes time to retreat through whatever gap they could create. With a big enough force it wouldn't be as difficult, but Duncan knew he could not afford more than a few men—they were having time enough of it as it was defending their own position. If they lost the hill, they lost the battle.

He made his decision and turned to face his father's men—now his—explaining his plan. He called out the names of five of his fiercest warriors, all of whom he knew to be unmarried and without bairns. His jaw clenched. Like him.

"I'll not force you to go," he said. "There is every chance you'll not return." He looked around the circle of men, seeing no hesitation, but fierce determination on their dirty, scraped-up faces. And he saw something else. Trust. They trusted him—not only to lead them into battle, but to bring them home or follow him to the death. He felt a charge go through him, emboldened, and knew without a doubt that this was his destiny.

Neil, one of the older guardsmen, spat on the ground. "Hell, Captain, 'tis the damned Gordons who'll sup with the devil before the day is done."

Duncan grinned. "Aye, then we'd best not delay—we wouldn't want them to be late for dinner."

With a fierce battle cry Duncan led the valiant charge.

The six Highlanders who rode at breakneck pace, swords held high, into the heart of Huntly's left vanguard should have died that day.

Instead, they became legend.

Jeannie woke with a start. The first golden rays of dawn broke through the dirty pane of glass in the small window and tumbled across the floor. But the sun could not warm the cold emptiness that gripped her heart.

She knew without even looking: Duncan was gone.

She'd failed.

Dread took hold of her and did not lessen its virulent grip the entire journey back to Freuchie Castle. Indeed, it was only made worse when barely an hour into the journey they heard the terrifying sound of loud explosions behind them. Explosions unlike anything she'd ever heard before, but knew to be cannon. Even from a distance she could feel the air reverberate with each deafening boom.

As much as she wanted to know what was happening on the battlefield, she also knew that Duncan was right—it was no place for her. Thus, she hastened back home to do all that she could—wait and pray and hope that he came for her as promised. Her guardsmen did not hesitate at the sudden "change" of plans to return to Freuchie, nor did she need to feign the illness, which was her explanation. Her fear for Duncan saw to that.

It was the longest day of her life. She tossed her needlework to the side and hastened to the tower window once more as she'd done all day—back and forth, unable to sit still. God, she hated waiting. Hated the feeling of utter helplessness. Her life was being played out on a battlefield and all she could do was stand by and wait. What was happening? Who would emerge victorious? Would he still come for her? And the most torturous question of all: Would he live to come at all?

He couldn't be dead. Surely she would know it?

Then, just before nightfall, Jeannie saw the white standard of the Chief of Grant crest the hill from the east. And riding not far behind, her father.

She said a prayer of thanks for his safe return and raced down the tower stairs, through the great hall, and down the forestairs into the *barmkin* below, her heart pounding like a drum. The victorious expressions on her clansmen's faces as they rode under the iron yett answered her first question: The Campbells had lost.

Now, all she could do was wait and hope that if Duncan lived—and she could not bear to contemplate anything else—he did not blame her for her father's treachery.

The triumph over the death-defying rescue of the Mackintoshes was short-lived. Duncan fought alongside the MacLean until the bitter end, but eventually they were overwhelmed and forced to retreat. No matter how bravely or fiercely they battled, Huntly's cavalry and his cannon proved insurmountable. Had the Campbells not lost half their vanguard in the first hours of the battle, they would have had a chance. As it was, they could claim a small victory to have lasted as long as they did. Though he supposed his cousin would not see it as such.

Argyll's flag would fly over Strathbogie Castle this night as he'd promised, but in defeat not in victory. Though it had taken three spears to bring him down, Robert Fraser, Argyll's standard bearer, had fallen to the enemy.

The last whisper of daylight had just faded when Duncan rode through the gates of Drumin Castle, numb and exhausted from the day's events.

They were waiting for him in the laird's solar. The chiefs and chieftains who'd made up the War Council last night appeared changed men—somber, pride in tatters, an air of stunned disbelief permeated the painfully quiet room. These were men not used to losing. And though none would ever give voice to their thoughts, ever present was the knowledge that what many had warned against had come true. But no one could have anticipated Grant's treachery.

Perhaps they should have. Perhaps *he* should have.

Duncan took one look at his cousin and could see that time had not dulled his rage. He was in a dangerous temper. Mouth pulled back in a snarl, eyes narrow and hard, with his sharp, Gallic features he looked like a half-crazed wolf, ready to take a bite out of the first person to look at him the wrong way.

But appeasing his cousin's wounded pride was not what Duncan was thinking about right now. "Our father?" he asked Colin, relieved to see his brother had followed his orders and returned to the castle.

Colin's face was pale and streaked with dirt and blood, his eyes unfocused. He appeared in shock by the events of the day. Duncan couldn't blame him.

"He lives," Colin replied. His relief, however, was tempered by his brother's next words. "But he has not woken since we left the battlefield."

"Where is he? I must go to him."

"In the laird's bed chamber," Argyll said. "But I will have your report first."

Duncan recounted the events after his cousin had left the field, emphasizing the courage and fortitude of the MacLeans and their chief.

"Where is MacLean? Why is he not here to tell of this himself?" Archie demanded.

"He took a pike in the arm and is having it tended."

"Our losses?"

Duncan met his gaze. "At least five hundred men." He didn't need to mention the thousands of untrained rabble who had deserted at the first cannonade.

"And Huntly?"

"Far fewer." Duncan would guess no more than a score—he and his men had been responsible for half of them.

Archie's gaze hardened, his eyes shone black as onyx. "They knew our positions. They knew our battle plan."

A murmuring of agreement went around the table. Campbell of Cawdor spoke up. "Aye, they may as well have had a map, so well did they anticipate our movements. 'Twas probably Grant's doing." He shrugged. "He must have sent a man after our meeting last night."

The mention of Grant seemed to unhinge his cousin. His face flushed crimson. "The filthy, lying viper." He banged his fist on the table. "He will pay for his treachery." He motioned to one of the guardsmen who stood by the door. "You there. Go, find out who was seen leaving the castle last night."

Duncan swore silently, hoping that no one had taken note of his departure. He'd rather not have to explain his meeting with Jeannie. Especially now.

"If that is all, cousin, I should like to go and see my father."

"Go," Argyll said, waving him away. He was almost to the door, when he stopped him. "Wait. Before you go, leave the map."

Duncan opened his sporran, pulled out the parchment and handed it to his cousin. He turned to leave again, when Argyll said, "What's this? A note?"

Damn. In his haste to see his father he must have accidentally handed Archie Jeannie's note.

He held his expression impassive and opened his sporran again, this time looking as he rifled through the contents. He frowned. Where was it?

"Is there a problem?" Argyll asked, the barest hint of uncertainty creeping into this voice.

"I can't seem to find it. I must have lost it during the battle."

If the room was quiet before, it was dead silent now. He didn't need to look around to know that all eyes were fixed on him. He felt a burst of anger, knowing that there were many in this room who would be suspicious of him simply for his blood alone. But Archie would never doubt his loyalty. Duncan's actions on the battlefield spoke for themselves. He would dare any man in this room to say otherwise.

He held his hand out for the return of the missive, but his cousin hesitated. He was tempted to snatch it back, but doing so would only make it look as if he had something to hide.

"Who is it from? It appears to be a woman's hand."

Duncan gritted his teeth and squared his jaw. " 'Tis a private matter."

Only when his cousin unfolded it and started to read, did he recall the wording: *Come quickly . . . we must act immediately.* Wording that might provoke question in even the staunchest of hearts.

His cousin looked up at him with a strange look on his face. "When did this arrive?"

Duncan did not shirk from the truth. "Last night."

"After the council?"

"Aye."

"I warned you to let nothing interfere with your duty to me. Perhaps you should have been focusing on the father rather than the daughter. Convincing Grant to join us was your responsibility."

Duncan heard Colin's sharp intake of breath when he understood the implication of Argyll's words. Damn. He hadn't wanted Colin to find out like this.

Shock registered on his brother's features. "Jean Grant? You were with my betrothed last night?" he asked, accusation ringing in his voice.

"You are not betrothed. It is complicated, I will explain everything, I swear, but later." He looked back to Argyll. "My relationship with Grant's daughter has nothing to do with this." His cousin's criticism, however, was not as easily dismissed. "Perhaps I should have anticipated treachery, but I am not the only one in this room who Grant fooled." His father, Argyll, all of them had believed Grant's anger against Huntly to be real. "If you have something you wish to accuse me of, cousin, do it. Otherwise I shall go to see my father." *Who took a bullet intended for you.* But he left that unsaid.

He waited and when his cousin said nothing, turned and left the room. Archie hadn't accused him of anything, but neither had he defended him. With all that Duncan had been through today, the realization that his cousin could even remotely harbor suspicion toward him stung.

Could Argyll really think him capable of betrayal? Nay, it was only his frustration and anger talking. When his cousin calmed down, he would see the truth. Archie never apologized, but Duncan knew he would find a way to make amends.

For the next two days, Duncan kept a steady vigil at his father's bedside, leaving only to wash the stains of battle from his weary body and make occasional use of the garderobe.

His father lay still and bloodless in the enormous bed, seeming to wither before his eyes. The bleeding had stopped, but he'd yet to regain consciousness. The healer warned that it was likely he never would. But Duncan wouldn't leave his side in the oft chance that he did.

Jamie and Elizabeth had been sent for, but had yet to arrive. Argyll and Colin were frequent visitors, but never stayed long and spoke little. In Duncan's absence, it seemed, Argyll had turned to Colin to attend him as they awaited King James's arrival. The king was enraged, both by Argyll's precipitous attack and by Huntly's treason. Now he was on his way north with thousands of men, intending to bring Huntly to heel.

No mention was made of what had been said—or left unsaid—after the battle. But with MacLean's return, rumors of Duncan's valiant rescue of the Mackintoshes had spread, casting doubt on the suspicion toward him.

Or so he thought. Late in the afternoon of the third

day, Colin burst into the chamber. "You have to leave," he said, gasping for breath.

"Calm down, Colin. What's wrong?"

"They found it."

Duncan frowned. "Found what?"

"The gold."

He laughed. "Well if they found gold, you can be sure it isn't mine."

"How can you make light of this? Don't you see that they think you are guilty? You were angry after the council at not being given a command and with father for refusing your marriage. They think you conspired with Grant."

Duncan wasn't laughing any longer. "Who thinks this? Not Archie?"

Colin shook his head. "Nay, he defended you, but even he could say nothing when they found the bag of gold. Forty gold ducats are hard to explain."

Duncan felt the first prickle of true alarm. 'Twas a small fortune. But it was not his. "There must be some mistake."

"There is no mistake. They searched our tent and found it in the bag you attach to your saddle."

Someone had put it there. Someone who wanted him to look guilty. Grant?

"Anyone could have put it there. Let them bring these spurious charges to my face."

"With the king on his way the chiefs are out for blood. You will be arrested. You must go."

Arrested? "I won't run. I'll stay and prove my innocence."

"Where, from prison?"

His jaw squared. "I'll not leave father."

"He would not want you to stay, not like this."

From the courtyard below, Duncan heard the unmistakable clatter of soldiers.

"Go," Colin said. "I will stay with father until you return. I swear it."

He didn't want to go, but Colin was right. He could do nothing to prove his innocence from prison. And without his father, who would fight for him? Archie would be having a time of it himself, defending himself before the king.

He clasped his brother around the shoulders. "Thanks for the warning, little brother. I've yet to have the chance to explain about Jeannie. I'm sorry if you were hurt, it was not intended."

Colin brushed off the apology. "We were both fooled."

Duncan gazed at him quizzically.

"You haven't heard?" He shook his head. "Jeannie Grant is betrothed to Huntly's son, Francis Gordon."

Duncan froze, every muscle rigid with shock. It wasn't possible.

Was it?

For the first time a shadow of doubt crept into the back of his mind and he allowed himself to consider what he'd been staving off thinking about for days. Why hadn't she told him? And what had happened to the map? He'd had it with him the whole time, removing it only to sleep. He recalled his sporran neatly arranged with his belongings.

And now she was betrothed to Francis Gordon.

It suddenly cast what had happened between them in an entirely new light—a sinister light.

His stomach turned. Had his brain been too addled by emotion to see the truth? Had Jeannie been lying to him? Had she used him? He didn't want to think it possible, but he damned well intended to find out.

Leaving Colin to watch over their father, Duncan slid out of the chamber, down the corridor, past the men coming to arrest him, and into the darkness of the night beyond.

Chapter 9

Jeannie startled awake, wrenched from a deep sleep by a sound. Her heart raced with fright. She didn't breathe, waiting in the darkness for another sound, slowly exhaling when none was forthcoming.

She rolled to the side and settled into the mattress, trying to quickly reclaim the slumber that had just abandoned her, trying not to think . . .

Of Duncan. Too late, she realized, resigning herself to another sleepless night.

In the three days since her father returned she'd learned little of the fate befallen the Campbells. She could not ask her father, and she doubted he would tell her if she did.

Her father was anxious for her marriage to Francis Gordon to secure the alliance and Jeannie knew she would not be able to put him off much longer, especially now that Francis had arrived.

Duncan was alive. He had to be. But why hadn't he come for her? A snippet of a conversation she'd overheard this evening would not leave her. Her father had been speaking with Francis in the solar after the evening meal about the battle, reveling in their success, "thanks to Campbell's map." At first she'd given it no thought, continuing her duties in clearing the hall, until the mention was made of treason and gold.

It couldn't be Duncan that they were talking about, but the prickle of unease would not leave her.

Oh, why didn't he come?

All of a sudden, a man stepped out of the shadows. She gasped, opening her mouth to scream, but he smothered it with his hand.

In the beam of pale moonlight she made out his face. Her body sagged with relief and tears of joy sprang to her eyes.

He removed his hand and she bolted upright. "You're alive!"

He didn't say anything. He was strangely still, keeping to the shadows, maintaining distance between them, rather than enfolding her in his arms as she'd dreamed would happen at this moment.

Indeed, now that her eyes had adjusted, she could see that he had the strangest expression on his face—almost menacing. If she didn't know him she might be frightened by the cold look in his glowing blue eyes, of the cruel flair of his nostrils, of the square set of his jaw. She sensed the tension, the anger radiating from him. "Duncan, what's wrong?"

His eyes scanned her face. "Tell me it's not true. Tell me you aren't betrothed to Francis Gordon?" She paled and he swore. Before she could defend herself he grabbed her arm and dragged her from bed. "How long have you been keeping this from me? Were you engaged that night you sent for me?"

He read her answer and pushed her away, but she clung to him. "Don't you see? That's why I came? I don't want to marry him; I want to run away with you. The betrothal was my father's doing."

"But you agreed."

"I was scared. He was so angry when I told him about you. But I never intended to go through with it. I wanted to tell you, but I couldn't because I feared . . ."

"You feared I would realize that your father intended to double-cross us. You're right. It seems there is much you have kept from me." His eyes bit into her. "Why did you send for me?"

"Don't you see? I feared for your safety."

"Well, as you can see there was nothing to fear, though I'm afraid my father wasn't as fortunate."

Her stomach turned. "Oh, Duncan, I'm sorry. But can't you see there was nothing I could do."

His face was tight and unyielding. "You made your choice."

"That's not fair," she protested. "Surely you can see what a precarious position I was in? If I told you what my father had planned it would be him in danger."

But it was clear he didn't see. To the noble Duncan, honor and integrity would always trump treachery. "Your loyalty to your father is to be commended," he said mockingly. "But tell me Jeannie, just how far does that loyalty extend?"

She didn't like what she saw in his eyes. Her brow furrowed. "What do you mean?"

"You were quite insistent that I not leave. Quite insistent."

She sucked in her breath, not wanting to believe what he was suggesting—that she'd purposefully seduced him. "I was worried about you."

"Is that all?"

"Of course. What other reason could I have?"

His eyes bored into her. "Why did you move my belongings?"

She opened her mouth to deny his charge, then remembered that she had moved his things. Heat pricked her cheeks. "I had to use the garderobe. I almost tripped on them, so I picked them up."

He didn't believe her. "Are you sure it wasn't to look for something? A map perhaps?"

"Of course not—" She stopped, realizing what he'd

said. She swallowed hard. "A map?" Her voice squeaked.

The look he gave her, hard with betrayal, could have cut glass. He took a step back and looked at her incredulously. "God, it was you."

She shook her head, grabbing onto his arm. "No. I took nothing. It's only that I heard my father mention a map."

But her attempt to explain only seemed to damn her more in his eyes. "Enough!" he said, tossing her away from him. "I've heard enough."

"No, you haven't." Anger burst inside her. She stood before him, fists clenched tight at her side. "How dare you come here like this and accuse me of such a heinous crime and not allow me to explain."

"There is nothing to explain. The facts speak loud enough. When I arrived at the alehouse, answering your urgent summons, I carried a map—a map your father clearly wanted. A map by your own admission your father now apparently has." He shook her by the shoulders. "Was it just luck or did he send for you and tell you where to look?" His voice was deceptively calm, but his eyes were wild and dangerous. "Does your betrothed know the depths to which you had to go? Does he know that you've had to whore yourself to a bastard to achieve your ends."

Jeannie gasped, a hot spike of pain stabbing in her heart. Without thinking, she pulled her hand back and slapped him as hard as she could across the cheek.

His face turned with the force of the blow. When he turned back, the look in his eyes froze her to the floor. "Don't ever do that again," he said in a low voice, clasping her arms in a viselike grip.

Her heart raced. She'd never seen him like this. "Let go of me." She tried to wrench free, but he didn't give an inch, holding her firm a few inches away from him as if he didn't know whether to push her away or pull her into his arms.

She could smell the wind on his skin, see the dark stubble that lined his jaw, feel the tautness of his body, and knew how perilously close he was to the edge. She tried to pull him back, tried to make him see reason. "I would never do what you accuse me of. I would never hurt you." She inched toward him and reached up to cup her hand to his stubbled jaw, looking deep into his eyes. "I love you, Duncan. Can't you see that?"

For a moment his gaze softened and she thought her words had penetrated, but just as quickly the steel curtain dropped once again and he jerked his face free of her caress. "It won't work this time, Jeannie. You have fooled me once, but never again. I'll be lucky to escape the net of treason you've cast around me with my life. Was it you who planted the gold or your father? Did I reach too high?" His fingers dug into her arms and his entire body coiled with rage. "God, I should kill you for what you've done."

Jeannie felt something inside her flicker and die. She hadn't done what he accused her of, but maybe in the end it didn't matter. He couldn't love her; he didn't know her at all.

She lifted her chin, to meet his damning stare. "If you truly believe what you are accusing me of, perhaps you should."

For a moment he didn't move, but simply stared at her as if he might believe her, as if he'd heard the truth behind the bravado. But instead of pulling her into his arms, he released her and stepped back. "Good-bye, Jeannie."

He turned his back to her. Panic rose up inside her and held her by the throat. He was really going to leave. "Wait!" She grabbed onto his arm. "You can't go. Not like this. You have to listen to me."

His face barely moved. He stared straight ahead and didn't look at her. "There is nothing more to say."

She felt him pulling away, closing himself off from her. Her worst fear had come true. Tears shimmered in her eyes. "Why are you acting like this?"

"I don't ever want to see you again."

The cool finality in his voice turned panic to hysteria. She lost whatever tenuous hold she'd had on control. All pretense of pride fell to the wayside as she clung to him, her fingers digging into his arms. "No. You can't mean that." He tried to free himself from her hold, but she wouldn't let him go. "Duncan, please . . ." she begged, her words choked with hot tears.

But he was immune to her pleas. Jaw clenched, he forcibly jerked away from her. She collapsed to the floor in a heap, her body racked by uncontrollable sobs. "Don't leave me," she choked.

Without another word, without another look, he slid back into the shadows as stealthily as he'd emerged. A moment later she heard the door open and close.

"No!" But there was no one to hear. He was gone.

Duncan didn't know how desperately he'd wanted to believe her innocence until he'd realized she'd betrayed him. The man who'd walked out of that room was not the same man who'd entered. He was older. Disillusioned. A hard shell. Cold inside.

I should have known. He'd seen her with her father—had he really thought she would leave all that for him?

Perhaps he could try to understand her loyalty to her father, but he couldn't explain the map once in his possession was now by her own admission in her father's. Nor could he explain her betrothal to another man.

He felt a strange burning in his chest, a twisting emotion that could only be described as jealousy. That he knew the man—and were they not on opposite sides might have admired him—made it worse. Francis Gordon was an apt politician, a skilled warrior, wealthy, and if Duncan abided the judgment of the ladies at court, uncommonly fair of face. The perfect match for a daughter of a chief. Unlike him.

He felt like such a fool. Why would she want to marry him when she was betrothed to the son of one of the most powerful men in Scotland? The legitimate son. Duncan had been deluding himself, believing a woman like her could see past the stain of his blood.

Had her father used her to distract him? That was probably the most difficult shame to swallow, that he might have missed the signs of Grant's treachery, failing in his duty to his family, because he was panting after a lass like a lovesick pup.

This was what happened when you thought with your cock. He would never make that mistake again. His destiny lay on the battlefield, not with a woman. He should have recognized that long ago.

Yet part of him refused to believe it had all been a lie. Passion like that could not be feigned. But maybe that's all it was: passion. Maybe she'd moved on when she'd found something better. Hadn't he worried about that very thing? That she would follow her heart when the next impulse struck?

He shook off the memories. Even if she had not been entirely pretending her feelings, she'd made her choice in siding with her treacherous father.

And he'd made his. He would return to his father's side and plead his case to his cousin.

Duncan considered the evidence against him and knew that it was damning. The note. The map. The gold. His anger at his father and at not being given a command. Perhaps one could be explained, but combined they were compelling proof of guilt. He could only hope that when he laid out the facts before the earl,

Archie would find him guilty of being a fool, but not a traitor.

It was near dawn by the time Duncan slipped through the gate of Drumin Castle on foot, leaving his horse—and battle garb—a short distance away. He'd carefully hid his steel knapscall, weaponry, and mail, exchanging them for a simple plaid and bonnet worn down low over his brow so as not to attract notice.

They were looking for him. The three parties of soldiers he'd avoided on the road told him as much, but as the gates were not being watched closely he guessed they did not expect him to return.

He hid in the stables and spent the better part of the day avoiding anyone who might recognize him, waiting for the opportunity to slip inside the castle. Finally, he joined a party of men bringing in peat for the kitchens.

Once inside he'd worked his way back up the stairs from the kitchens to the laird's chamber. Opening the door carefully, he peered inside, relieved to see only Colin and a maidservant. Colin lifted his head when Duncan entered, his eyes red and glassy.

His gaze widened when he realized it was Duncan. "What are you doing here? You shouldn't have come back. Half the King's army is looking for you."

"I had to see father. Has there been any change?"

Colin shook his head mutely.

Duncan knelt beside the bed, taking his father's hand in his. It was as cold as ice.

"Duncan, you can't stay here."

He met his brother's gaze. "I intend to prove my innocence."

Colin gave him a strange look. "You found the proof you were looking for?"

His mouth tightened. "No, but I believe our cousin will listen to what I have to say."

Colin shook his head. "You don't understand. There

is a bounty on your head. You have been tried this very morning and found guilty."

Duncan swore. "Argyll will believe me."

Colin didn't look so sure. Indeed, Duncan suddenly realized that Colin didn't believe him either. "You think I'm guilty."

"No," Colin said reflexively, but without real vehemence.

Duncan held his stare for a long pause. "I see," he said softly, unable to believe how quickly his own family had turned against him. The evidence was strong, aye, but did it erase a lifetime of honor and loyalty? Were his actions on the battlefield supposed to be some elaborate front? It was ridiculous.

"It's not like that," Colin said, trying to make amends. "It's just the lass is beautiful—" He stopped at the sound of footsteps approaching the door. "I'll get rid of them," he said.

Duncan hid behind a tall cupboard near the door until he heard the sound of his brother's voice fading down the corridor.

He knelt beside his father's side again, resting his head against the bed as if willing him to wake and give him guidance.

It was far worse than Duncan had realized. They'd already tried and convicted him. Without proof he would not be able to overturn the judgment against him. With sudden clarity, he realized that he'd been made a convenient scapegoat for the loss of the battle. A bastard was an easy mark. If his cousin and his own damned brother didn't believe him, who would?

He felt drained, as if all the life he'd known had been sucked right out of him. For the first time in his young life, he was at a complete loss. *What can I do?*

He must have spoken the question aloud, because he heard a soft grunt in response. He thought he'd imagined it at first, but when he raised his head his father opened his eyes.

"Father!"

His father moved his head back and forth on the pillow, clearly distressed. Duncan tried to calm him with soothing words, but it didn't work. His father opened his mouth, trying to talk, but only strangled sounds came out.

He was only growing more agitated. His body seemed gripped in a spasm, his eyes wide open. Duncan knew that he needed to get the healer. He stood to run to the door, but his father grabbed his wrist with surprising strength.

Their eyes met and finally he managed to speak, but the words were jumbled and difficult to make out. "Forgive me," his father rasped. "Mother . . . Find . . . MacDonald."

"Father, I can't understand—"

But his words were cut off by a cry, as a violent convulsion wracked his father's frail frame in one last embrace. When it was done, Duncan knew it was over.

His father was gone.

Now it wasn't only the loss of the battle to be laid at his feet for his stupidity, but also his father's life.

He stared with dry, disbelieving eyes for a long time, overwhelmed by what had just happened. By his loss. He never got to tell his father he was sorry. He'd never got to thank him for all he'd tried to do for him.

He heard the door open, but didn't move. For a moment he didn't care if he was taken, but it was only Colin. The ramifications struck him hard. Nay, not only his brother. Colin was now his chief, Campbell of Auchinbreck.

"He's dead," Colin said numbly.

Duncan nodded. "He woke for a moment. Tried to tell me something."

His brother's voice was tight with emotion. "What did he say?"

"I could only make out a few words. It sounded like he wanted me to find my mother." The mother who'd abandoned him at birth. A serving woman—a MacDonald serving woman apparently—who'd cared so little for her child's welfare that she'd never thought to see or even inquire after him for over twenty years. He had just as little interest in her. "I'm not sure he even knew what he was saying."

Colin nodded. They were both silent for a few minutes, paying respect to the father they both loved. "I came to warn you," Colin said. "They've found your horse. They know you're here."

Damn. He hoped they hadn't also found his cache of weapons. He would have to wait until nightfall for the chance to retrieve them.

"It's not safe," Colin said. "You have to go."

Duncan didn't bother arguing. He'd just lost the one man who might have believed in him enough to prevent this gross miscarriage of justice. "Aye," he said. "I'll go."

"The Highlands are not safe for you."

The truth hit him hard. He would have to leave Scotland. The only home he'd ever known. But with his father gone and Jeannie lost to him, there was nothing left for him. He thought of his brothers and Lizzie. They would be better off without him. If he stayed he would only be a source of shame.

He was truly alone.

He made his decision. He hardened his heart against regret, against sadness, against loss. "Ireland," he said. In Ireland there was always room for another hired sword. As a gallowglass mercenary he would have a chance to make his way—on the battlefield.

Colin reached in his sporran and retrieved a handful of coins. "Here, you'll need this."

Duncan took it with a nod. "Take care, Colin. You've been a loyal brother to me. I'll not forget it."

"Safe travels, brother." Something flickered in his brother's gaze—regret? "I'm sorry."

Duncan swallowed the hot ball in his throat. Ignoring the throb in his chest, he bid final farewell to his father and brother.

He left Drumin Castle, left the Highlands, left his home and family, without looking back. His destiny, it seemed, lay elsewhere. But he knew one day he would return. To clear his name and to have a final reckoning with the person who'd destroyed it.

Two days later, he stood at the stern of the boat taking him from Kintyre, his father's sword safely at his side, gazing longingly at the fading coastline. His last thought as it slipped from view was not of the soaring rocky shores, green hills, or crystalline waters, but of emerald eyes and auburn hair—and the woman who'd cost him everything.

Two more weeks had come and gone, and Jeannie knew she could not delay any longer. Her father and Francis had been busy making amends to the king, but soon she knew the subject would once again turn to her marriage.

And Duncan still had not come for her.

Though the humiliating scene when he'd left her was still painfully fresh in her mind, when she'd calmed down, she'd convinced herself that once his anger dulled he would see the truth.

She'd hoped that he would recognize his error on his own, but she was no longer in the position to wait. Swallowing her pride, Jeannie decided to go after him.

With her father occupied in Inverness, she conscripted a couple of guardsmen to take her to Castleswene, the ancient royal stronghold on the west coast of Knapdale.

The Campbells of Auchinbreck were the traditional keepers of the castle, and she knew it was the place Duncan considered home.

A sharp, icy wind from the north bit down on them as they approached the formidable stone castle near dusk. The last pink swirl of sunlight was dipping over the horizon. Austere was perhaps the best word to describe the formidable tower house and curtain wall, reputed to be four centuries old and one of the oldest stone castles in all of Scotland. Perched upon a rocky knoll on the edge of the sea, the towering stone edifice was broken only by a simple arched entry.

Unsure of her reception, Jeannie felt a trickle of trepidation as the small party passed through the gate. If the guardsmen who admitted them were surprised to hear the name of Grant, they did not show it. When she asked the bailiff who greeted her to see Duncan Dubh, however, any pretense at equanimity vanished. Without another word he directed her men to the stables and led her into the keep, leaving her in the great hall to warm herself by the fire to await Duncan.

Immediately upon entering, Jeannie sensed that there was something wrong. A somber air hung over the place, almost as if it had been steeped in a dark cloud. The fires and candles burned low and it was painfully quiet—the few servants she saw moved about silently, heads' bowed, avoiding her gaze.

The wait seemed interminable. Her heart pounded fiercely in anticipation. Duncan had been so angry before, so sure of her betrayal, had he reconsidered? Had he realized yet that she could never hurt him? She gnawed at her lower lip anxiously. Would he hear her out?

She couldn't wait to see him.

Finally she heard the sound of footsteps. Her heart

jumped, then fell when she realized they were too light to belong to a man.

A young girl entered the dimly lit room. Slight and petite, with hair so blonde it almost seemed white, one look at her pale face was all it took to identify her. The eyes gave her away. Elizabeth Campbell was as light as her brother was dark, but they had the same crystal-clear blue eyes of the sky on a sun-filled day.

Duncan's sister was a few years younger than Jeannie—probably no more than six and ten, but her serious expression bespoke someone much older. The black gown she wore didn't help matters; the harsh contrast against her pale skin only served to make her look more severe.

All of a sudden, Jeannie understood the reason for the somber clothing and the horrible pall that seemed to have been cast over this place. They are in mourning. She should have realized. Duncan had told her that his father had been injured. Tears welled in her eyes, her heart going out to him. Poor Duncan! How he must be hurting. That must be why he hadn't come for her.

Elizabeth returned her perusal, then bowed her head in greeting. "Mistress Grant." She held a pause for a long, disquieting beat, tilting her head in a manner befitting a queen. In that regard she was also like her brother. The air of importance seemed to pervade the entire clan. "You are certainly not lacking in courage to show your face around here."

Jeannie's cheeks heated with shame for her father's part in their tragedy. "You must be Elizabeth. Your brother has mentioned you."

The mention of Duncan seemed to strike a strange blow. For a moment Elizabeth's stern expression fell, revealing a painstakingly young girl who was suffering—deeply.

"I'm sorry to appear here like this unannounced. At

this horrible time," Jeannie continued uncomfortably. "I know you must blame me for what my father did—"

"It's not only what your father did." Elizabeth's blue gaze fired with angry sparks. "From what I hear you played quite a significant part in it as well."

Jeannie shook her head. "I swear to you I had nothing to do with it. What your brother accuses me of is not true. I would never betray him." Elizabeth remained unmoved. "Please, I must see Duncan, I would not be here if it wasn't of the utmost importance. I had reason to believe he might be here."

Pain flashed in Elizabeth's eyes. "I'm afraid you are misinformed. My brother is not here."

Panic rose inside her. She had to find him, there wasn't much time. "Please, you must tell me where he is. I need to find him."

Her desperate plea fell on deaf ears. Elizabeth laughed harshly. "So you can finish what you started? Thank you, but I don't care to see my brother swinging from the gallows. Burying my father and mother in one year is horrible enough—I'll not lose a brother as well."

Jeannie paled. "What are you talking about?"

"Thanks to you, Duncan has been convicted of treason." Elizabeth explained how the note Jeannie had written had been turned against him and that gold had been found in his things.

Her eyes widened in shock. He'd mentioned a noose around his neck, but she hadn't thought . . . That was just it: She hadn't thought. "Surely no one could truly believe that Duncan would betray his clan. He is noble to the core. He could never do anything so dishonorable. It isn't in him. He will always do what is right and just, *always*."

Her impassioned defense finally penetrated Elizabeth's anger. Her face crumbled. Tears shimmered in her crystalline blue eyes. "You can't see him. It's too late. He's gone."

For a moment Jeannie's heart stopped, everything inside her constricted so tightly it felt as if she were burning. "Gone?" she echoed disbelievingly, her voice barely above a whisper.

Elizabeth nodded, tears streaming down her pale cheeks. "Two weeks ago. Right after my father's death. I didn't even get a chance to say good-bye," she sobbed, the tears breaking free.

My God. He left me. Shock claimed her breath.

She'd been willing to risk everything for him, and he'd left her without a word. Betrayal knifed inside her. How could he do this to her? *To them.*

"Where?" she asked hollowly.

"Ireland. At least that's what he told Colin."

"I see." Her voice sounded oddly calm, but her body was shaking uncontrollably, like glass about to shatter.

This wasn't the first time someone she loved had left her behind without a thought for the destruction they would leave in their wake. But experience didn't make the anguish any easier to bear.

Suddenly light-headed, she wobbled, her hand instinctively covering her stomach. Lizzie caught her by the elbow. "Are you all right? Here," she said, guiding her a few steps toward a chair. "You better sit down for a minute."

She wasn't all right. She didn't think she'd ever be all right again.

Elizabeth seemed at a loss as to what to do—her instincts for concern tempered by loyalty to her brother. Jeannie wanted to say something, but her throat felt too hot and thick to speak. She stared blindly into the dying embers of the fire, knowing the same sensation inside her heart. There was nothing left but stark, cold emptiness. The flames of love had flickered and died, and in its place leaving only the ashes of what might have been.

"You really cared for him, didn't you?" Elizabeth said, not bothering to hide her surprise.

"I loved him," Jeannie said emotionlessly. Her misfortune was that her love was not returned. Not enough to really matter. And she would pay dearly for her mistake.

"Perhaps you should have thought of that before you betrayed him."

"I didn't—" she stopped, staring into Elizabeth's hard, unyielding eyes so like her brother's. It didn't matter. This girl would not believe her.

"I think you should go before anyone else finds you here."

Jeannie nodded. She had no reason to stay.

A short time later, Jeannie left Castleswene and all illusions of love and happiness behind.

I'm a fool. I learned nothing from my mother's mistakes.

But she would not let him destroy her. Only one thing mattered now: The life of the babe she carried in her belly. The reason she'd been so desperate to find Duncan. She would do whatever it took to protect her child against the scandal her own impetuousness had rained down upon them both.

Chapter 10

❖

Ten Years Later, Present Day

She'd actually shot him.

Duncan would laugh if he could manage anything other than a grimace. The greatest warrior from Ireland to cross the continent brought down by a lass—and a naked one at that. There was irony in it, he supposed, but he was in too much damned pain to appreciate it.

Had he actually thought he could convince her to help him? That she might be willing to atone for the injustice she'd done him all those years ago? He'd held out a small ray of hope.

But this woman who stared at him with hatred in her eyes was not the girl he remembered. She'd changed. All the vivacity and spirit seemed to have been leached right out of her, replaced by calm, cool resolve. Bold green eyes that had once sparkled with excitement now glittered as hard as cold emeralds. A mouth once turned in a perpetual smile and inclined to excited chatter was pursed in a flat line.

What had changed her? Had life been so unkind?

He shouldn't—didn't—care. Hell, perhaps he should even think it fitting revenge for the life she'd stolen from him. But he found he could not muster the enthusiasm for the revenge that had once been his only solace in the long, lonely nights when the unwanted memories struck. Revenge was the province of bitterness, and he'd relinquished that long ago. Now all Duncan wanted was the truth.

If he lived long enough to find it. Not only had Jeannie put a hole in his stomach, she was also apparently eager to put a noose around his neck. Before he wouldn't have thought her capable of such vindictiveness, but he did not doubt the resolve of the woman standing before him. He was glad the pistol she carried only had one shot or he had no doubt he'd find himself riddled with holes.

He heard the sound of footsteps running toward him, his men responding to the gunfire. Summoning what was left of the strength that had not bled out of him, he gritted his teeth, held his hand to his stomach just below the edge of his leather plated cuirass to staunch the bleeding, and fought to a stand.

He staggered. For a moment the pain engulfed him and his mind went black. He tensed, bracing against the firestorm raging inside him, and managed to stave off unconsciousness.

She stood stone still, making no move to help him.

Conall tore through the trees. "Captain, we heard—" He stopped in his tracks, stunned to see Duncan's condition. "What in Hades . . . ?"

Duncan motioned to Jeannie. "Conall. Leif. Meet Lady Gordon." The name curdled in his mouth.

There was a long pause as his men absorbed—none too easily—the significance.

It was Leif who spoke first. "The *lass* shot you?"

"I'm afraid so," Duncan said wryly, finding the patent incredulity in his captain's voice somewhat of a salve to his skewered pride.

Conall whistled and shook his head, crossing thick arms across a chest that would make a bear envious. "The men won't believe this. No one has ever gotten the jump on you."

"Well, she did." Twice, in fact, if you counted her stealing the map while he slept in sated bliss. It was a lesson well learned. He'd never lost control like that again, never allowed himself to succumb to such connubial stupor.

Leif recovered first, removing a square of dirty linen from his sporran and handing it to Duncan. The Norseman had been quick to adopt the practical and convenient leather pouch worn around the waist, in addition to the *breacan feile*, the belted plaid, of the Highlands.

Duncan took the cloth, though it wasn't going to do much good. It was like trying to dam a rushing burn with a scrap of parchment. "There's no time to tarry. We must go before the entire garrison rains down upon us to investigate."

Conall frowned. "But I thought the lass—"

"I was mistaken." Duncan eyed Jeannie, seeing nothing but hardness. "The woman will be of no help to me."

Perhaps he'd been a fool to think she ever would. She'd chosen her side years ago, supporting—nay, aiding—her treacherous father.

For weeks after he'd left Scotland, Duncan had done something he never did: second-guessed himself. He'd racked his head to find another explanation. But either he'd lost the map on the battlefield and it had miraculously ended up in Grant's hands, someone had taken it while he slept the few hours in his tent, or the far more logical explanation that Jeannie had taken it. Her oddly worded note, her determination that he not leave, the rearrangement of his belongings all pointed to her. Still, something ate at him. He couldn't forget how she'd looked that night he'd surprised her in her chamber— the last time he'd seen her. She'd appeared, she'd sounded, she'd seemed . . . *innocent*.

Unable to reconcile the sweet girl he knew with the

manipulative schemer anger had created in his mind, he'd decided to return. Then, right before he was to set sail, word reached him of her marriage to Francis Gordon.

She hadn't even waited a month. Three weeks after he'd left, barely escaping with his life, she'd married. While he'd been agonizing about whether he'd committed a grave injustice against her, she'd been lying in the arms of another man.

The swift marriage confirmed his worst fears. It begat the darkest period of his life, the time when he'd earned his fearsome reputation. Eventually the gut-wrenching betrayal had given way to the faint pinch of discomfort he felt now. But even that tiny remnant of weakness infuriated him.

His men moved to either side of him to hold him by his elbows, but before they had taken a few steps, the sounds of approaching men—by the sounds of it a good many—stopped them. It was too late. The Gordon guardsmen were already there. If he wasn't about to collapse escape would have been possible, but hampered by the ball of lead in his belly . . . Well, Jeannie would have her chance to see that noose around his neck soon enough.

"My lady!" The calls echoed through the trees.

Duncan turned and looked at Jeannie, his gaze locking on hers. He knew better than to put himself at her mercy, but he had no choice. "What's it to be, *Lady Gordon*? Will you help me or turn me in?" Why he bothered to ask he didn't know. He could see the answer in her eyes.

"Here," Jeannie called out, answering the concerned cries of her guardsmen. "I'm here."

At least a score of clansmen broke through the trees, surrounding them, hagbuts and pistols drawn, swords brandished. When they saw the three strangers, they immediately took aim, intending to finish the job she'd started.

At least it would be fast. Ten years of waiting and it all came down to this. He should have known better than to think he would find mercy in the hands of the woman who'd betrayed him. He heard the click—

"Wait!"

All eyes turned to Jeannie. Except for his. His had been glued to her the whole time. Watching. Challenging. Seeing whether she had the stomach to do what she threatened.

"I . . ." she faltered.

She couldn't do it. It shocked him almost as much as it did her. His eyes narrowed. Was there a glimmer of softness left in that cold heart after all or was some other game at play?

Their eyes met for an instant before she looked away, seemingly disgusted with herself. "Lower your weapons. There's been a mistake," she said calmly. "I was caught by surprise. These men mean me no harm."

Jeannie couldn't do it. Her chest twisted, though any emotion for this man had been wrung out of it long ago. *I should. For all the pain and suffering you put me through, I should.*

But as much as she wanted to send him to the devil, at the moment of truth she'd looked into his eyes and the words would not come.

Lord knew why. She owed him nothing. Indeed, he could destroy everything she'd fought so hard to protect. But hers would not be the hand that spelled his doom.

Her spurious decision seemed to have surprised Duncan as much as it did her.

Adam, the captain of her guardsmen, eyed her uncer-

tainly, his gaze flickering to the three imposing warriors.
"Who are they?"

Good question. She thought quickly. "Guardsmen
hired by my brother. Additional protection after the recent events."

She felt Duncan's questioning gaze on her, but ignored
it. Her troubles were no business of his.

Adam straightened. "We have men enough," he said,
obviously taking umbrage at the suggestion that he was
not equipped to see to her protection himself. Ignoring
that Duncan and his men had managed to break through
the perimeter he'd set up easily enough.

"I'm sure my brother meant no disrespect," Jeannie
said, attempting to mollify the disgruntled warrior. "But
you know how upset he was. I will tell him these men
are unnecessary, but until then we need to get him back
to the castle."

Appeased, the captain looked around. "Where's
Tavish?"

"There was a slight misunderstanding," Duncan provided, his voice raspy.

How he managed to stand with a hole in his belly she
didn't know. She bit her lip. Mother Mary, he was pale.

"From where he was positioned, I didn't realize he
was protecting the lass."

There was something in the tone of Duncan's voice
that caught the captain's attention. "I see," Adam said
grimly.

Jeannie looked back and forth between the two men,
realizing she'd missed something. But now that she'd
made her decision, she was anxious to have it done. The
sooner she got him back on his feet, the sooner he would
be on his way. She hoped she wasn't making a huge mistake. "Adam, have your men show our guest to the
tower. We will put him in the empty chamber in the garret."

The significance occurred to her too late. Her chest squeezed. It had been her son's chamber.

Adam lifted his brow in surprise, but did not question her decision to place a guardsman in the tower house. "Aye, my lady."

"I will find the healer."

"I saw her in the garden earlier," one of the younger guardsmen offered.

"Thank you, William."

The handsome warrior beamed at her praise and that she'd called him by his given name. But it was not a sign of particular favor; Jeannie made it a point to know everyone in the castle.

She thought Duncan's eyes narrowed, but she turned her back on him and went in search of the healer. Did he think William was something to her? Let him.

By the time she'd found the healer and they'd started to make their way into the keep, her mother-in-law had had plenty of time to be apprised of the situation. Not surprisingly, Jeannie found her path blocked at the entry.

"I told you no good would come of this flight of fancy of yours," the Marchioness said.

Jeannie gritted her teeth. "So you did. But as you are no doubt aware, a man has been shot and is in need of the healer."

"You shot him." It was a statement, not a question.

"An accident." This time. "I thought he was another ruffian."

And before the Marchioness could issue another one of her I-told-you-sos, Jeannie brushed past her and led the healer up the stairs to the top level of the tower house.

A small landing separated three small chambers. Adam occupied the largest, the one with the view of the surrounding countryside so he could keep apprised of any attack, the nursemaid slept in a mural chamber next to it, and then beside hers was the small chamber that had belonged to her son and was now crammed full with towering, muscle-bound, mail-clad warriors.

She stood at the door as the healer attempted to squeeze around the blond brute. His icy Nordic looks sent a chill running through her. Which was a good thing as it was hot as Hades in here. She didn't know what it was with men—especially warriors—but they seemed to radiate heat.

Duncan lay on the small bed, his feet hanging well over the edge. His face was flush and his eyes, burning with pain or hatred she didn't know, fixed on her.

"Your men will have to leave," she said firmly.

The two henchmen drew themselves up to their full height—barely missing the wood-raftered ceiling—and squared their prodigiously broad chests like two over-protective bears who had every intention of digging in their heels. She met the burly red-haired man's—an Irishman by the sound of him—gaze and smiled sweetly. "I promise not to do him any more harm."

He stilled, then let out a bark of laughter. Something she would wager he did quite a bit of. His rough, ruddy countenance seemed prone to joviality—a foil to Duncan's dour darkness. "Aye, lass, you've a wicked sense of humor." He shook his head. "Hurt him?" He laughed, then turned to Duncan for confirmation.

Duncan nodded. "Go. See to the horses. I'll be fine."

The men moved slowly. The blond one turned to her at the door. "You'll let us know . . ."

"As soon as the healer has looked at him," Jeannie assured him.

He nodded and the two men left. The room seemed infinitely larger—and blessedly cooler.

Mairghread, the healer, was already at work. She examined him for a few minutes before looking up at Jeannie. "I'll need to remove his cotun and sark, my lady."

His men must have helped him remove the leather plated cuirass he wore over his chest. Knowing he was watching her, Jeannie held her expression and tone even. "I'll help you."

She pursed her lips together, steeling herself for the unpleasantness. *It's nothing you haven't seen before,* she told herself. If only he wasn't watching her so intently, those cool, unforgettably blue eyes leveled on her— unflinching and unnerving.

Her hands shook as her fingers worked the leather buckles of one side of his quilted leather cotun studded with bits of metal as Mairghread worked the other. Furious, she forced herself to steady and focused on the task at hand, not on the man, and certainly not on the intimacy of the act to which she was involved. But leaning over him like this, his scent reached out to grab her in its familiar hold. Beyond the warm leather and the faint coppery hint of blood, she caught the sea and the wind—and the elusive masculine spice that had always been uniquely his.

It was really him. All these years and he'd finally returned. A hard wave of longing washed over her, dragging her back.

But she pushed the memories aside. He'd lost the right to affect her.

If it was any consolation—and it was—the removal of his clothing didn't seem to be any more enjoyable for him. He stiffened and clenched his teeth in pain when they tried to move it past his shoulders. A task that was proving impossible. "Cut it off," he said tightly.

Jeannie's brows wrinkled. "Are you sure?" It was a fine garment, expertly worked, and by the look of it costly. Now that she thought about it, everything about him bespoke wealth. From the weaponry his men had removed and set beside him when they laid him down on the bed, to the gold scabbard at his waist, to his clothing. He'd done well for himself—very well. She'd never doubted he would.

" 'Tis no matter," he dismissed without a second thought. "And the sark as well. It will be easier than trying to lift it over my head."

Jeannie reached down and slid the jewel-encrusted dirk from its scabbard, surprised by its weight. She turned it around in her hand, marveling at the workmanship. A weapon like this was fit for a king. Carefully, holding the dirk to his neck, she prepared to score the leather.

"Remember your promise," he said. She eyed him quizzically. "To Conall."

Not to hurt him. Her mouth quirked in spite of herself. "I'll do my best, but the temptation might prove too difficult to overcome."

And then, as if to emphasize her words, she held the edge of the blade to just below his jaw and in one decisive stroke, sliced from the neck to the edge of his shoulder.

To his credit he didn't flinch. Not once. Not even when she slowly slid the blade along the opening at the neck of his shirt. Nor when her fingers accidentally brushed his bare skin.

But she did. The moment her fingertips met smooth, hot skin, she felt the jolt from head to toe. The intense awareness. The full body reaction. The sensation that every nerve ending had come alive. The same thing she'd felt all those years ago.

The weakness infuriated her—her body's reaction seemed the ultimate betrayal. She could, however, control what she did with that reaction. She was no longer an innocent girl with stars in her eyes. So she buried it under years of hurt and disappointment where it belonged.

She could feel his eyes on her, and knew that he'd sensed her reaction, but she kept her focus on the task at hand. She continued wielding her blade through the material and after a few more minutes of struggling and cutting, the cotun and sark lay in shreds at his side.

She stood back to admire her handiwork and choked on the involuntary gasp. The bottom of her stomach dropped to the floor. She'd like to claim that it was from the bloody hole a few inches left of his right hip, but it wasn't the wound that knocked her senseless.

It was the wide span of tanned chest and arms. Forsooth, he was incredible. As imposing a specimen of masculinity as she'd ever seen.

His countenance wasn't the only thing that had changed with maturity. The lean build of youth had given way to thick slabs of finely chiseled, heavily built muscle. It was as if he'd been chipped from stone, each cut precise and honed to perfection, without an ounce of spare flesh on him. From the tight bands layered across his stomach, to the smooth round curves of his arms, he was built for one purpose: battle. And if the numerous scars that lined his chest and arms were any indication, he'd seen his fair share.

Heat spread over her, her limbs suddenly heavy. She couldn't seem to look away.

She wasn't the only one to notice. Mairghread might be approaching three score in years but she wasn't blind, and such a display of masculine strength and power could only be admired.

He was no longer a boy, but a man. A warrior. Jeannie felt a pang in her chest. A stranger. This was not the boy she'd foolishly given her heart to, but a man who'd lived a life that she knew nothing about. The years

stretched between them, separating, snapping any connection they'd once shared.

Her gaze fell.

For the next hour Jeannie worked alongside the
healer, trying to undo the harm caused by her pistol and
overeager trigger finger. When it became clear that they
would need to dig out the ball, Jeannie started to call for
one of his men to hold him down, but he stopped her.

His fingers circled her wrist. She fought a gasp, but
the big, callused hand felt like a brand on her skin. She
was at once cognizant of his strength. He could crush
her bones with one squeeze.

"It won't be necessary," he said.

Jeannie eyed the healer, having some familiarity with
recalcitrant patients of the Highland persuasion. Mairghread rolled her eyes and mumbled something about
stubborn laddies.

"Are you sure?" Jeannie asked, carefully pulling her
wrist free. Her skin tingled, and she had to resist the
urge to rub the warm imprint of his touch away.

"Aye," he replied grimly. "This isn't the first time I've
had a bit of lead in me."

She had to bite her tongue to prevent further questions, though when Mairghread began digging with her
dirk, Jeannie doubted he would have been able to answer. His jaw locked, and every muscle in his neck and
shoulders clenched against the pain that the knife must
be causing. Sweat gathered on his brow, but he held perfectly still and said nothing—not one cry, not one grunt.

But his eyes burned into hers, holding her gaze the entire time. Jeannie's pulse raced, her heart pounded in her
too-tight chest through every agonizing minute, feeling
as if she was seated on the edge of a precipice. When it
was over, she was sure she was more exhausted than he
was.

Mairghread assured her that the ball would not kill

him—and as long as fever did not set in, he would recover well enough. Jeannie shuddered at the thought of fever. Now that the initial shock and anger of seeing him had faded, she didn't want him dead, just gone.

After cleansing the wound with water and giving Jeannie a piece of linen with which to hold against the bleeding, Mairghread left for a few minutes to retrieve some herbs and salves from her storeroom near the kitchens.

Jeannie kept her gaze focused on the wound, but was deeply conscious of being alone with him. Of the uncomfortable silence broken only by the even sound of his breath and the erratic beat of her heart that not even her strong will could tame.

"Why didn't you turn me in?" His voice was flat, emotionless.

She schooled her features in a similar fashion, giving no hint to the turmoil unleashed by his question. By him.

Why indeed when he could do her such harm? She didn't know. Every minute he was here increased the risk of discovery of her secret. And there was her family to consider. Duncan's reemergence would not bode well for either the Gordons or the Grants.

But when the time came to speak against him, it seemed as if every instinct in her body had revolted. Perhaps she wasn't as hard-hearted and vengeful as she'd like to think. But she suspected her reasons went deeper than that. She'd had so many questions after he'd left: Why did he not try to defend himself, why had he been so quick to damn her, why did he leave without saying good-bye? Why did he wait ten years to come back? Questions that needed answering. Maybe then she could finally put the past behind her and have a chance at finding happiness.

She'd failed her husband, never being able to give him

the love he so selflessly gave her; she would not do that to another man.

But she could hardly tell that to Duncan. He was watching her closely—too closely—his gaze hard and unrelenting. Just like the man himself. This stranger who could still make her feel like she was jumping out of her skin with one deep, penetrating gaze. *Fool.*

She gave him a hard look. "I assure you my motives were purely selfish and had nothing to do with any fond memories or sentimentality toward you." He had no reaction, not that she expected him to. If she'd ever harbored a girlish fantasy that he'd longed for her, that one day he would realize how he'd wronged her, it had fizzled that first moment she'd looked into his eyes. He was not here to fall at her feet and beg forgiveness. He was here because he wanted something. She gave him a pointed look. "What do you want from me?"

"Information. Access."

Her skin prickled with alarm. "Nothing would be gained by resurrecting events that are better left in the past."

Anger glinted in his hard blue eyes. That was one thing that hadn't changed. His eyes were still a startling deep blue—a striking contrast to his black hair. She'd always thought him the most handsome man she'd ever seen. That hadn't changed either.

"Easy to say when it's not your name that has been blackened and dragged through the mud for the past ten years. What of justice? Would that not be served?" His gaze narrowed at her accusingly. "What you mean is that it's better for you and your family if the treachery done that day is forgotten."

Heat flared in her cheeks, but she met his gaze defiantly. "Yes, that is exactly what I mean." He was right. Trouble was the last thing her clan needed right now; their situation was precarious enough. With her father-in-law, the Marquis of Huntly, excommunicated and imprisoned in Stirling Castle for once again failing to convince the Kirk that he no longer adhered to the Popish faith, the name of Gordon was not exactly a welcome one at court. Nor did Jeannie want to bring trouble for her brother John, the new Laird of Freuchie, by reminding the Earl of Argyll of her father's treachery at Glenlivet. The king may have forgiven her father his trespasses, but Argyll never had—not even her father's death two years ago had cleansed his sin. Duncan's sudden return would open up all the old hatred. Her eyes locked on Duncan's. "Please, just leave it be."

But her pleas had never had any effect on him. She would never forget the last time she'd seen him. The humiliation was imprinted on her mind. When she'd clung to him like a lovesick fool, begging him to believe her, and he'd coldly—heartlessly—pushed her away and never looked back. He had the same hard, unyielding look in his eyes then as he did now. And she felt the same foolish urge to break through.

"I'm afraid that's impossible," he said, his face a mask of steely determination.

Dread washed over her, knowing that he would not be swayed. He'd set a course and nothing would get in his way—no matter who he hurt along the way. Certainly not her. If she'd ever meant anything to him that day was long past.

She stared at him, searching in vain for an opening, but there was not a weak bone in his body. Even laying in bed wounded, having lost a good amount of blood, he still managed to reign supreme—his authority and raw physical strength undeniable. The promise he'd shown as a youth had been more than fulfilled.

If only it were just physical, but his strength permeated his character as well. And once he was resolved, he was immoveable. Trying to break through to him would be like trying to throw herself through a stone wall.

Only once had she changed his mind, she thought, recalling the night at the alehouse. But then her seduction had been unconscious, not cold and calculated, were she tempted, which she wasn't, to use that particular tool in her depleted arsenal to stop him.

And in the end, even her body hadn't been enough. He'd left her anyway.

The healer's prompt return prevented further discussion and Duncan was grateful for the reprieve. Being with Jeannie again after all these years set off a multitude of conflicting feelings firing inside him. In his mind he might have relegated her to an unfortunate mistake in his past, but he wasn't as immune to her as he wanted to be.

He hadn't breathed the entire time she'd had her hands on him as she'd removed his clothes. Not just because he was steeling himself against reacting to her touch, but because at the very first whiff of her delicate scent he'd felt like he was jumping out of his damned skin.

And the feathery brush of her fingers . . . a woman's hands hadn't provoked such an intense reaction in him in years. His mouth fell in a grim line. Ten years to be precise.

He was not unused to women casting admiring glances in his direction. But when her eyes had fixed on his bare chest, widened in feminine appreciation, and then gone a little soft and hazy, it had done something to him altogether different. His body had reacted to a look as if she'd stroked his cock with her tongue. He'd gone as hard as a damned spike, blinded by a flash of lust so strong it had shocked the hell out of him. He thought he'd lost the capacity to feel like that. He'd forgotten how desire could drown everything else in its black hold.

But he was no longer a callow lad ruled by lust. Whatever power she might wield in that seductive body of hers, it was no match for his iron-clad will.

If he'd needed a reminder of her treachery it had come quickly. *Please, just leave it be.* She didn't care about right or wrong, about seeing his name cleared. She didn't want him disturbing the life she'd built on a bed of treachery. Why it disappointed him that her loyalty to her family still outweighed any justice on his behalf, he didn't know. But he'd come back for one reason only—to prove his innocence. And nothing—certainly not the woman who'd been at the heart of his downfall—would stand in his way.

The healer, a tiny old woman whose wrinkled hands possessed surprising strength and dexterity, finished her ministrations, smearing a thick pungent salve over the wound and then binding it with a clean swathe of linen. For just having been shot, he felt remarkably well.

She left him a posset to drink, which he politely declined, and bade him to rest. He thanked her, and she left. He thought Jeannie was going to join her, but she reached the doorway, hesitated, and then turned back to him.

"Why did you come here, Duncan? Why me, why now?"

"It was time." That was the simple answer. The truth was far more complicated. His sister Lizzie's note about the death of Francis Gordon and rumors of Jeannie's remarriage—possibly to Colin—had sparked an urgency he didn't want to examine.

"That's it?" she asked incredulously. "That's all the explanation I'm to receive after all this time?" Her eyes locked on his, piercing. "*You left me* without even the courtesy of a fare-thee-well. Not one word for *ten years* and now you suddenly decide it's time to return?"

The sudden outpouring of emotion surprised him as much as it seemed to her. His brow furrowed. It almost sounded as if she'd cared, as if he'd hurt her unconscionably and not the other way around. She wasn't acting guilty, she was acting wronged. *You left me.* The accusation echoed inside him. He'd heard the pain in her voice and knew its source. But his leaving was nothing like her mother—he had a reason. *She'd* betrayed *him*.

The flash of anger was as fierce as it was unexpected. "What the hell did you expect me to say? Thank you for fucking me so well—both literally and figuratively."

She flinched at the crudity as if he'd struck her. He'd never spoken to her like that. The look she gave him was filled with emotion so intense he couldn't even begin to probe its shadowed depths. But it gave him the first prickle of unease.

He took a deep breath. How did she do this to him? In the spate of a little over an hour, she'd managed to pry away years of steel layers to the raw underbelly. With all the subtlety of a nail under his fingertip.

His anger raged, but he tamped it down—an eye on his mission. He was here to prove his innocence not rehash past betrayals. "I said good-bye," he said. "What more was there to say?"

"Quite a bit, if you'd given me the chance," she said softly. "But you were so quick to judge me guilty."

"Then help me find the truth," he challenged. "Tell me what you know."

Their eyes met and held. For a moment he thought she was tempted, but in the end she shook her head. "I can't."

His face darkened. A small part of him had always wondered whether he'd been wrong. But her silence condemned her. "You mean you won't."

She shrugged at the truth, then studied him. "Ten years is a long time. You've made a life for yourself—satisfied your ambition." She motioned to his armor. "Accumulated wealth and earned infamy. I can barely walk past the barracks without hearing about some exploit of the 'Black Highlander' and his men. You have everything you've always wanted. Why come back, reopen old wounds, and take the chance that you might lose it all again?"

She'd heard of him. The knowledge pleased him more than it should. Aye, he'd satisfied his ambition. At one time he'd thought that was all he wanted. "What is wealth or reputation without freedom, and there is no freedom in exile. The Highlands are my home. And here I'll live . . . or die."

She held his gaze for a long pause—as if she understood—then turned and left him alone.

Alone. He was used to it that way—even preferred it—but being alone wasn't the same thing as loneliness. Seeing Jeannie again was a painful reminder of the difference.

Duncan had achieved everything he'd set out to do and more, but it had not come without a cost. He'd never been tempted to marry, to have a family—not since Jeannie—believing his life had no room for domesticity. And there had never been a woman who could make him think otherwise.

He breathed through the sudden ache in his chest that had nothing to do with his wound, wondering at the life he might have had had things been different. Had they not ended up on the opposite side of a war.

Chapter 11

Morning had come and gone before Duncan stirred, his limbs and head still heavy with slumber. Were it not for the pain in his belly and the urge to take a piss, he might have slept through the day.

He felt like hell.

But he'd suffered worse. It was always lying down that did it, as if only in repose did pain find its voice. There were days after long bouts of fighting where he'd woken feeling like every inch of his body had been beaten to a bloody pulp. Where his muscles had felt so stiff and spent he couldn't move. With a bullet wound, the pain was focused—at least in theory. But right now, his entire stomach throbbed with a violent burning sensation.

Gritting his teeth, he sat up. Too quickly. Pain knifed through him and he fought the sudden wave of nausea. The sickness subsided quickly, but the pain lingered, intensifying. He put his hand to the bandage, glad that it was not damp with blood or puss. But the wound hurt more than he'd expected. And it itched like hell.

If there was ever a good place to get shot, Jeannie's bullet had found it, avoiding the death zones—the places guaranteed to kill you. Still, the ball must have done more damage than he'd realized.

But not enough to keep him abed. He needed to find Leif and Conall and tell them to look around and try to ask a few questions while they were here. His men, foreigners, would not be in danger, but Duncan knew he had to be careful. There was always the chance someone would recognize him.

He was impatient to be on his way, but he knew it would be foolish to leave like this, and not before he took a look around. Another day or two and he would be well enough to travel.

He stood slowly, the loss of blood having weakened him, and tended to his more pressing needs. Even the small exertion proved taxing and he braced himself against the bedposts to catch his breath. An annoyance he was forced to repeat a couple of times as he went about washing his face and cleaning himself with the cloth and water provided.

He rubbed his chin. The two days growth of beard had begun to itch and he was thinking about calling for the maid to bring him a razor, and a shirt, when he felt an odd tingling sensation at the back of his neck.

He was being watched.

He stilled, and turned around half expecting it to be Jeannie. But there was no one there. "Who's there?"

Silence.

His gaze slid around the room, taking in the details that had escaped him yesterday. The ambry to the left of the door, the window opposite the bed, the table, chair, and small bed. A trunk for clothes, a pig's bladder ball in the corner, a crooked stick for shinty, a wooden sword, a handful of shells strung on a string, and a couple of books.

A child's room.

His heart stopped. *No.* He heard a soft shuffle from behind the door. "You might as well come out," he said. "I know you're there."

Every muscle in his body tensed, steeling himself, but nothing could have prepared him for the blow. For the sheer devastation wrought by the sight of the little girl who stepped out from her hiding place behind the door. A beautiful lass with dark red hair, pixie features, tiny red lips, and wide eyes.

She was adorable—and devastating. A miniature version of her mother except for the blue eyes and smattering of freckles across her nose.

Jeannie had a child.

The burning in his chest intensified. Why should it surprise him? She'd been married for ten years, she probably had a handful of children. What did he think, that her marriage had been a sham and she'd stayed true to him after all these years? In truth, he hadn't allowed himself to think about it. But the harsh physical reminder of her intimacy with another man was proof that hers had not been a marriage in name only.

And it stung. More than he could have ever expected.

The lass eyed him warily. He schooled his features, realizing the fierce emotion in his eyes might be scaring her. He was at a bit of a loss of what to do, having no experience with bairns. And sensing the threat, he wanted nothing to do with this one.

"What's your name?" he asked, realizing he had to say something.

She bit her lip and something hot and tight twisted inside him.

"Helen," she answered. "Helen Gordon," she added more boldly. "But everyone calls me Ella." She wrinkled her nose, her eyes moving above his head to the ceiling. "You are very tall. Taller than my father and he was the tallest man in the Highlands," she boasted with a heavy dose of Highland pride. "Do you hit your head on beams when you walk?"

"Not as much as I used to," he admitted, jarred by the sudden turn in conversation. "I've learned to duck." He gave her a hard look, realizing what she was trying to do—distract him. "And why were you spying on me, Mistress Helen?"

She straightened her back, affronted by the mere suggestion. "I was *not* spying. I was curious." Obviously there was a difference. "Did my mother really shoot you?" Her brows knitted together across her tiny nose. "You must be a very bad man."

He held his face impassive, despite the pain in his stomach, fighting the urge to laugh. "I think it depends on your perspective." She appeared puzzled by his response. "It depends on which side you're on," he simplified. "But it was an accident." I think.

She didn't look too sure either. "I wanted to see whether you were as big and terrifying as they were saying."

Duncan's mouth twitched. "And?"

She frowned. "I haven't decided." She studied him carefully. "Why aren't you wearing a shirt? You are very dark."

"It's torn and I spend a lot of time in the sun."

"You have a lot of scars. But your eyes are blue." He was having a hard time keeping track of her train of thought, but this apparently was a point in his favor. "I don't like beards," she continued. "They're too scratchy."

He rubbed his chin again. "I agree."

She nodded. "Beth said you were very handsome." She apparently was undecided. "My father was the most handsome man in the world and he never wore a beard." The mention of her father struck him cold. Duncan would have sent her away, but she lifted her gaze to his and something inside him shifted. "He died."

She said it matter-of-factly, with a challenging tilt of her chin, but Duncan could see the sadness shimmering in her eyes. "I'm sorry, lass," he said, despite the urge to keep his distance.

The little girl nodded, accepting his sympathy with a

maturity that belied her years. A thought struck him with the force of a lightning bolt. She didn't look old enough, but . . .

"How old are you, Helen?" he asked, suddenly unable to breathe.

"Almost eight. I was born on midsummer's day." His mouth quirked. *Almost.* It was still the last days of October. "My brother"—Duncan stilled, clenching his fists at his side until his fingers turned white—"says I'm short, but he's wrong. I'm petite. At least that's what my father said and he assured me there's a difference. Isn't there?" Duncan nodded, still reeling from the knowledge of a brother, but she wasn't listening. "*Petite* is a French word," she clarified. "It means 'small and dainty.' "

She expected him to be impressed and he didn't want to disappoint. "Ah," he said, nodding.

She sat down on the trunk at the foot of the bed, apparently having decided he wasn't much of a threat. "But Dougall is just jealous. I swam across the river Dee when I was only six and three quarters and he didn't do it until he was seven and a quarter."

"That's quite an accomplishment. How old is your brother?"

He was being ridiculous, but everything inside him tensed until she answered. "He just turned nine on Michaelmas." September 29. Duncan ticked the months back in his mind. She must have conceived in January. He'd left Scotland in mid-August—almost five months earlier.

The vise around his chest loosened. He didn't know whether to be relieved or disappointed. He'd never thought . . . He'd been so caught up in his own anger he'd never thought about the possibility of Jeannie being with child. But both children were too young to be his.

Ella hadn't noticed his distraction. Rather, sensing

an appreciative audience, she beamed, her adorable face growing even more animated as she chattered on about the many things girls could do that were not appreciated by older brothers. Apparently, there were a lot of them.

Having been in similar circumstances with her mother and realizing this might take a while, Duncan did what any wise man would do. He decided to get comfortable, laying back down on the bed and settling in for the long haul.

Jeannie forced herself not to check on Duncan first thing in the morning. Instead, she went about her duties, going over the accounts with the seneschal and planning the day's meals with the cook as if the man who'd walked out on her and left her heart in shreds ten years ago hadn't suddenly returned and threatened to destroy everything.

Mairghread had checked on Duncan earlier and had been pleased to find him still asleep. Rest was the best thing for him now, the healer assured her, which Jeannie in turn told the two brutes who cornered her in the hall when she was breaking her fast. The Irishman and Norseman had been none too happy about her refusal to let them see him, but Jeannie had not let those broad chests and arms the size of tree trunks intimidate her. If their leader was much improved by the afternoon, then they might be permitted to see him. She would let them know. Apparently being told "no" was new to them and she took advantage of their surprise, leaving them staring after her.

It was near noontime before Jeannie climbed the stairs from the kitchen vaults with a tray of food. She crossed the hall to the tower staircase. It was just her luck that the Marchioness happened to be descending from her chamber at the same time.

"Where are you going with that tray?" the older woman demanded.

"I was hoping the guardsman had wakened and would feel well enough to eat."

The Marchioness's eyes narrowed. "Surely there are servants capable of carrying trays. Unless there is another reason for your attentiveness?"

Jeannie's face flushed with anger, she was tired of her mother-in-law's domineering ways. She was only bringing him a tray for heaven's sake. "There are, but I shall see to this myself. It is my fault he is injured and my responsibility to see to his care."

"Do you think it is a good idea? What do you really know of this man?"

Jeannie felt a prickle of alarm. Though the Marchioness couldn't possibly have guessed who Duncan was, curiosity on her part could be dangerous. "He is a guardsman sent by my brother, what more should I know?"

"He doesn't look like a guardsman," the Marchioness said flatly.

Jeannie cursed inwardly, for once in agreement with her mother by marriage. Duncan did not look like a typical man-at-arms—not just because of his wealth, but because of his bearing. She should have made him a king, it would have been more believable. She thought quickly. "He's a mercenary."

The Marchioness's mouth pursed in distaste. "I see." She gave Jeannie a shrewd smile. "I'm only trying to think of you, daughter. A woman in your position can never be too careful to avoid talk."

Jeannie bristled at the innuendo. "What position is that exactly? I'm the lady of the keep, why should anyone talk about whether I bring an injured man a tray of food."

"You're right, of course. No doubt, I'm just being

overly cautious. I worry about you and Helen out here alone when I leave."

Jeannie hadn't seen Ella—a nickname that had stuck when Dougall couldn't say Helen—all morning. She shuddered to think about what kind of mischief her daughter had gotten in today. Jeannie was trying to be patient, but the little minx had become even more obstinate since her father's death, refusing to heed her at all. She had a mind of her own and unfortunately shared her mother and grandmother's tendency toward impulsiveness. Stubborn and impetuous was not a good combination.

Jeannie turned back to her mother-in-law. "Are you returning to Castle Gordon, then?" she asked, hoping she didn't sound too eager.

The Marchioness eyed her shrewdly as if she knew exactly what Jeannie was thinking. "I've received word from the Marquis that he has agreed to the king's demands and will sign the confessions of faith."

Again, Jeannie thought. And probably with just as much sincerity as the other few times he'd renounced his Catholicism. "Then he will be released from Stirling Castle?"

"Soon, I hope." Her mouth fell in a hard line. "Though Argyll is looking for reasons to prevent it." One more reason why Duncan's sudden reemergence could prove troublesome. "Have you given any more thought to the Earl of Erroll's son?"

Jeannie shook her head. "I'm not yet ready to think about marrying again." And when she did it would not be to a man so firmly under the Marquis's thumb. The Gordons were less than subtle in their desire to see her son's inheritance under their control; they'd already appointed Francis's cousin as Tutor.

The Marchioness nodded. She'd loved her second son

and that fondness was the only thing that tempered her desire to see Jeannie remarried immediately.

"You mustn't wait too long," her mother-in-law said. "Helen is in need of a man's influence." Jeannie heard the subtle criticism and bristled. "Just this morning I caught her hiding under the bread table, listening to the servants' gossip again."

Jeannie bit her lip, knowing she should act properly horrified, but remembering all too clearly her own hiding spots where she'd listened to the kitchen maids lusting over the latest handsome—

Oh, no! Her stomach crashed to her feet and she almost dropped the tray along with it. Ella wouldn't. But Jeannie knew she would. Muttering some pithy excuse to her mother-in-law, she walked calmly to the stairs when every instinct in her body urged her to run. To tear her daughter away from him.

She heard their voices at the bottom of the stairs. Her heart jumped to her throat. Panic welled up inside her. She told herself to calm. Ella couldn't say anything to make him suspicious and Duncan would never hurt her. Not intentionally at least. Her chest tugged. But Ella was so sensitive, so vulnerable since her father's death. And Duncan was so cold and remote—hard to the bone. Ella wouldn't understand his aloofness.

Jeannie clambered up the steps and heard Ella say, "No, this is my brother's room." *Dougall. Oh, God!* Ice filled her veins.

Then Duncan's voice. "Where is your brother—?"

Jeannie's sudden appearance in the doorway stopped him. He took in her wide, panic-filled eyes and shortness of breath.

"Ella!" she shouted.

Her daughter turned uncertainly, the abruptness of Jeannie's voice putting her on alert.

"I wasn't doing anything," Ella said automatically.

Jeannie took in the scene: her daughter sitting on the trunk with her feet tucked underneath her and Duncan relaxed, lying on the bed with his arms crossed behind his head—an indulgent look in his eye. For a moment her mind flashed to the loch. He'd lain just like that after . . .

Stop. She shook off the memory.

Feeling some of her fear subside, she forced a smile to her face as she addressed her daughter. "I know," she said, conscious of Duncan's eyes on her. Hands shaking, she carefully set the small wooden tray on the table. "But Duncan needs to get some rest. And it's almost time for your lessons."

Ella gave Duncan a glance of longing that made Jeannie's blood chill. Had her daughter fallen into the same trap as she had, becoming immediately captivated by him?

"Do I have to?" she whined, giving her mother a much put upon look.

Jeannie nodded, not swayed by those big pleading blue eyes. "Gather the others; I'll be down shortly."

Ella hopped off the trunk and bounded out of the room, auburn curls dancing behind her. Only then did Jeannie breathe a sigh of relief. She turned back to Duncan. His gaze was as frosty as the snow tops of the Cairngorms.

He stood, seemingly unhampered by his injury. "You couldn't actually think I'd hurt her?"

She straightened, not shying from his angry rebuke. But as he walked toward her, she felt the sudden urge to flee. She didn't know where to look, uncomfortably aware of his powerful naked chest. Her body heated, flushing with awareness.

How was it possible that after ten years he could still make her feel so strongly? It didn't make sense, she'd only known him for such a short time. Why after so

many years did her body respond? Why did remembering still hurt? She'd almost half convinced herself that
she'd never really loved him—that like her mother she'd
gotten carried away by the moment.

Why couldn't she be like him? Stony faced and indifferent. He looked at her with exactly the right amount
of familiarity—as someone he'd known a long time ago
who betrayed him. If he remembered their intimacy he
did not show it—even when she'd been standing naked
before him he hadn't betrayed even a flicker of desire. A
sharp contrast to the way his eyes used to smolder with
heat at every glance. Now he looked at her the same way
he did everyone else. If there had ever been anything special before, it was gone.

"I wasn't sure," she said, dropping her gaze.

It was a mistake. Her eyes fell on his shoulder at precisely the spot she'd used to love to bury her face
against. She stood transfixed for a moment, her heart
rising to her throat. Pain welled up from a forgotten
place. Her breath was forced—hard and uneven. If she
closed her eyes she could remember the warmth flooding
over her as she'd pressed her cheek to his skin and curled
into the curve of his body. The contentment. The security. The feeling that with him at her side nothing would
ever hurt her again.

God, will I ever forget?

"Look at me, Jeannie."

The hard clip of his voice snapped her out of it. Her
mouth fell in a tight line, furious at her weakness. It was
illusory. He hadn't protected her. He hadn't loved her.
He'd left her.

"You know me better than that," he said.

She met his gaze, feeling the strange urge to laugh in
his face. "Do I?" She let the question hang between
them. "Actually, I don't know you at all. Ten years ago
I thought I knew you, but it turns out two months isn't

long enough to know anyone." Though it was long enough to have your heart broken. And the pain was still there, buried in a shallow grave that his return had unearthed. She couldn't allow herself to forget it. "You weren't half the man I thought you were."

Her barb struck. His hand wrapped around her wrist and he swung her to him, the tips of her breasts skimming his chest. She gasped at the force of the connection. At the shock as her body exploded in sensation. Her pulse raced, her breath quickened, her blood rushed, and every nerve ending flared. Desire, hot and heavy, possessed her from head to toe.

"You knew me well enough," he said, the husky burr in his voice seeping under her skin. "Well enough to give me your body." His finger traced a path down the curve of her cheek to her chin. She was too stunned to move. Too overcome by sensation to turn away. Her heart tugged when his gaze met hers.

She wanted to kiss him, could almost feel the warmth of his lips on hers. The impulse came on with the force of a lightning bolt, but she fought it. She was no longer a girl to allow lust to cloud her judgment. But she couldn't completely erase the desire from her eyes.

"What's wrong, Jeannie? Remembering?" His hand slid down her throat. "Was some of it real after all?"

She heard the edge of mockery in his voice and tried to pull away. "Let go of me." But his hand gripped her wrist like a steel manacle. Their eyes met and for the first time she saw an ember flickering in his gaze. He was not completely unaffected.

Jeannie fought to catch her breath. From somewhere buried deep inside her, she felt an old spark of recklessness, an impulsive urge to provoke him right back. Heedless of the danger, she shifted her body closer, nestling her hips to his and pressing her breasts to his chest. Their bodies slid together, locking together from memory. She felt the hard column of his erection against her stomach. Heat drenched her with the force of a tidal wave. She looked up at him, letting her eyes settle on his mouth. "I think 'tis you who are remembering. Is what you came back for? Is that it, Duncan? Do you still want me?"

Every muscle in his body tensed and Jeannie wondered if she'd made a mistake. She'd wanted to prove that he was not as indifferent as he pretended, but Duncan was not a man to toy with—he was the most feared warrior on the continent for heaven's sake. The flare of heat in his eyes frightened her. *He* frightened her. She wasn't a naïve girl anymore; she knew how dangerous it was to play with fire.

He released her as if she'd suddenly scalded him. He didn't answer her question, but they both knew the answer. Instead, he returned to the original subject. "I would never harm a child, Jeannie," he said quietly. "Then or now."

A horrible thought crept into the back of her mind. She knew nothing about him. Nothing about what his life had been like the past ten years. What if she was not the only woman to fall prey to his undeniable masculine allure? "And you have plenty of experience with children?"

He gave her a hard look. "I've never married."

The twinge of relief disappeared when she recalled her own circumstances. "You better than anyone should know that is not a prerequisite."

His eyes darkened dangerously. "Just exactly what are you accusing me of?"

She shrugged. "I wonder how many black-haired, blue-eyed bairns are strewn across the continent?"

She'd pushed too far. He grabbed her by the arm and brought her toward him. She gasped, the barely restrained fury in his eyes made her heart race.

"Do you really think I'd consign a child to my burden?"

He had. She bit the words back and said instead, "Unmarried parents don't make you a bastard. Your actions do."

She saw the muscle in his neck tic and knew her barb had struck.

His mouth tightened. "I would never allow a child of mine to go unclaimed."

Her blood chilled, his words giving voice to her fears. He could never find out about Dougal. Duncan's birth had always been his Achilles tendon and he would not be rational about it. He would see her lie for what it was and his blasted nobility would never allow him to stand aside.

All she wanted was an explanation and then his swift departure. Gathering up the tattered remnants of her emotions, she pulled herself together. How did he manage to get to her like this? Couldn't they simply have a rational conversation? Must there always be this strong undercurrent crackling between them, this fierce awareness that made her feel like that foolish, impetuous girl again ready to believe in white knights and faerie tales. She was an adult now, a mother. She should know better.

She returned to the original subject. "Ella has been a trifle headstrong of late, I will make sure she doesn't bother you again."

He seemed about to object, but then appeared to reach the same conclusion as she had—better not to encourage an acquaintance.

But he wasn't quite done yet. "You have a son as well?"

She tensed, but quickly masked the visceral reaction to the danger posed by his question. She spoke carefully, feeling as if each word somehow held the potential to explode. "Yes, he is being fostered." She didn't want to tell him anything, but knew it would be better to be as honest as possible. He would sense any caginess on her part.

His reaction moments ago only solidified what she already knew. He would insist on claiming his son, even if it meant labeling him a bastard and destroying everything she'd done to protect her son from the scandal Duncan had left in his wake. She couldn't risk it—not when it was her son who would suffer. Duncan had lost any claim on Dougall when he'd left her.

She felt his eyes on her, watching intently.

"How old is he," he asked, "your son?"

She met his gaze, her expression betraying none of the raging panic inside her. She had gone to a great deal of trouble to protect her secret, she could not allow him to suspect anything.

The Battle of Glenlivet had turned out to be her salvation. The Gordons had been forced into exile. Francis hadn't gone with his father to the continent, but they'd removed to a remote castle up north with only a few trusted servants. They hadn't returned for almost two years and by then Dougall's true age was easy to hide. Moreover, there was no reason anyone should question his age. Only one person could do that.

"He just turned nine." She phrased her next words for maximum impact. "He born over a year after Francis and I were wed."

She thought something in his gaze might have flickered at the mention of her marriage.

"Where is he being fostered?"

Even though every instinct in her body urged her to say nothing more, she forced herself to appear as if she had nothing to hide. "Dougall is at Castleswene with your brother."

"With Jamie?" He didn't hide his surprise.

It was one more reason she had to be grateful to her husband. Dougall would never know that he was being fostered by his uncle, but Francis had found a way for him to be tied to his kin. "The battle of Glenlivet was a long time ago, Duncan. Old feuds have mended."

"My cousin hasn't forgotten," Duncan pointed out.

"Perhaps not, but there is no reason for Argyll to renew old hostilities."

His gaze hardened. "You mean unless I make him remember."

"Yes."

"Why does this matter so much to you? Your father and husband are both dead, not even my cousin can reach them where they are."

Jeannie's breath caught, her eyes widening in sudden understanding. *Francis.* That was why he'd come to her. "Am I to understand that it is not just my father and me you have envisioned in this conspiracy against you, but my husband as well?" The hard look on his face was all the answer she needed. "Francis had nothing to do with what happened to you."

She thought he flinched, but his even voice gave no hint to his thoughts. "How can you be so sure?"

"Because he would never do something so dishonorable as to frame another man for treason."

"And your father would?"

Her mouth tightened, anger stained her cheeks. "I didn't say that."

"Grant had to be in contact with someone in the Gordon camp and your quick marriage certainly suggests that it was your husband."

Her gaze shot to his, hearing the sharp bite in his tone. The speed of her marriage had bothered him. She felt the strange urge to laugh. If he only knew the reason why. The man who Duncan sought to drag through the mud had given his bastard not just a name, but an inheritance. Francis had known she was pregnant when he married her. Not many men would do what he'd done—claiming, raising, loving her child as his own.

Her husband had done so much for her and yet she'd never been able to give him the one thing he wanted.

Because of Duncan.

Guilt rose inside her. She might not have been able to give Francis her love, but she could damn well give him her loyalty. She wouldn't let Duncan embroil him in this mess.

"You can't deny that your father was working with your husband?"

"No." It had been Francis who'd met her father that day in the solar. "But encouraging my father to change sides in battle is an entirely different proposition from framing a man for treason. What reason could he have?"

His eyes burned into her. "The same reason as your father. You. He would not be the first man to act ignobly for a woman."

She shook her head. "You are wrong. Francis left Freuchie Castle *before* I told my father about us. My husband had nothing to do with what happened to you."

Remembering the conversation she'd overheard a few days later about the map and gold, she ignored the twinge of uncertainty.

His eyes bored into her with a strange intensity. "Prove it. Let me look through his things."

"I don't need to prove it. I knew him, and I know he wasn't involved."

Her impassioned defense of her husband seemed to enrage him. His mouth drew into a sneer. "All men can be made fools for a beautiful woman."

Including him. That's what he meant. She flushed at the scorn in his voice. "Look somewhere else to prove your innocence, Duncan. I will not allow you to besmirch my husband's good name." She owed Francis that at least for all he'd done.

But she had an even greater reason. It wasn't only the discovery of Dougall's parentage that she had to fear or even the trouble that the reminder of Glenlivet could pose for her family. By casting suspicion on Francis and labeling him a traitor, Duncan could put her son's inheritance in jeopardy and risk all she'd done to protect him.

Her eyes turned as hard as glass. Whatever sympathy she had for his plight dissolved in the face of the danger he posed to her son.

I should have turned him in when I had the chance.

Duncan could barely think from the anger pounding through his blood. How did she get to him like this?

It had been a mistake to touch her. His skin still burned from where she'd pressed up against him. For one treacherous instant his body had surged with lust, with visceral memories of pleasure almost too powerful to resist. Almost.

He hated weakness of any kind, but he had to admit she did something to him. She got to him the way no other woman ever had.

She was so damned beautiful. Standing there with her eyes flashing, cheeks flushed, her hair shining like copper in the sunlight.

All that passion, all that emotion . . . for another man.

He wanted it for himself. The primitive urge to drive away all thoughts of another man surged inside him. His fists clenched at his sides as he fought for control. His gaze met hers, hot with challenge. "How do you intend to stop me?"

Her absolute refusal to help him, to consider that her husband might have had a part in what happened to him ate through the walls of his indifference like acid.

The sanctity of her husband's name mattered more than his freedom. Mattered more than right or wrong.

What had he expected? Nothing had changed. Misplaced or not, her loyalty to her family still hung between them.

Once again the line had been drawn in the dirt and she'd chosen to stand on the opposite side. To prove his innocence he needed to investigate her family—possibly uncovering some ugly truths—and she would do everything she could to prevent it. It seemed their interests would always be at odds.

"I could call the guards," she threatened.

And she looked angry enough to do it. "But you won't," he said with more confidence than he felt. She held his gaze for a long beat and he wondered if he'd miscalculated. He used to be able to read her emotions so easily, now she was cool and controlled. Her indifference riled him. But it was her unquestioning loyalty to her damned husband that egged him to recklessness.

He took a step toward her, letting his body tower over hers, forcing her to acknowledge him, wanting to prove that it had meant something, that he wasn't the only one to remember. He could see her tense, see her pulse beating faster at her neck, see the way her senses flared. She wanted to retreat, but her pride wouldn't let her. "Because no matter what you claim, Jeannie, I think you still remember how good it was between us."

"Youthful fumblings? You forget I was married for ten years and have learned the difference."

White hot rage flashed inside him. God's wounds, she pushed too far. Just thinking about—*imagining*—her with another man drove him insane.

He pulled her into his arms, crushing her body to his. He heard her gasp, and felt the shudder ripple through her and wanted to roar with satisfaction when her nipples hardened against his chest.

God she felt good. His body exploded with hot, heavy sensation. Desire pounded through his body, so hard that he shook with it.

"I think it's you who forget," he challenged, lowering his mouth. Youthful fumblings? Inexperienced they might have been, but he remembered only too well how good it had been between them. His skills no doubt had improved over the years, but passion like they shared could not be learned. It was something in the blood, in the senses, a visceral connection that defied description.

Damn her.

He crushed her lips to his and kissed her with all the passion she'd unleashed inside him with her taunts. He groaned at the first taste of her. At the honey sweetness he'd never been able to completely forget.

Her lips were softer than he remembered; her skin and hair more fragrant. Everything was *more*.

His kiss was punishing. Hard and deep. Starving. One hand slid behind her neck, winding through her silky hair as the other moved over the round curve of her bottom to lift her against him.

He needed pressure. He needed to release the tension that had been coiled inside him from the first moment he'd seen her.

She froze as if too stunned to respond. For a moment he felt her body sag, felt her relax and open to his kiss . . .

Suddenly she made a strangled sound and jerked away, pushing against his chest and breaking free of his hold. She stared at him, cheeks flushed, breath heaving, eyes hard as emeralds, mouth swollen a deep pink. "You're wrong, I don't want you."

Her barb struck with the opposite effect than the one she intended. It didn't dissuade him, rather only made him more intent on proving her wrong. She wanted him every bit as badly as he wanted her, he knew it with every bone in his body.

He took a step toward her, lust and anger coiling inside him ready to strike. Her eyes widened.

The flash of fear stopped him cold.

It wasn't him she was afraid of, but of how easily he could prove her wrong. But it was fear all the same.

He took a step back, and forced his blood to cool. God, what the hell did she do to him? One taste of her and he turned half-crazed. His desire was too close to the surface, ready to flare at the first scent of her. He'd never had a problem controlling his base impulses, except with her.

He'd spent part of his manhood trying to ease the stain of treason and his bastard birth, gaining fame and fortune as the "Black Highlander." Honor, nobility, duty—those were what he believe in. But one day in her presence and he was acting like a damned barbarian, ready to press his point to satisfy his damned masculine pride.

He'd let her keep hers—this time. But if she pushed him again . . .

Perhaps sensing her narrow escape, Jeannie said, "One more day, Duncan. That is all. I want you gone in the morning."

And without another word she turned and left.

She was right; he needed to get the hell out of here. This place was too dangerous for him. It wasn't the threat of calling the guards that worried him, but the memories—the very sharp and visceral memories.

Chapter 12

Jeannie's body was drenched with sweat as she writhed in bed, the cool linen sheets rubbing uncomfortably against her sensitive skin. She was so hot. So heavy. So ready. Her body soft and throbbing.

She could feel his mouth on her lips, on her throat. Feel the rough calluses of his palms as his hands slid over her possessively.

His tongue was in her mouth, probing, sliding, twisting against hers. She could taste him on her lips. Feel the scratch of his beard against her skin. Feel the weight of his muscled body pressing down on hers.

Her body swelled, her breasts heavy, her skin too tight.

His hand slid between her legs. Her heart pounded. Her breath caught . . . anticipating. She wanted to cry out in pleasure at the first touch. The first stroke of his finger sliding inside her bringing exquisite relief. Her hips lifted against the heel of his hand, her thighs squeezed. She could feel the pressure building . . .

A soft rap on the door startled her awake. Jeannie opened her eyes to darkness. Her body sagged with disappointment. *It had only been a dream.* Groggy with sleep, she closed them again, rolled over, and dragged the pillow over her head. That kiss had not only shattered her peace of mind it had penetrated her dreams, rousing feelings she'd thought long since forgotten.

Her skin still tingled with heat, sensitive to the touch. Her body stirred with restlessness, craving release.

She'd forgotten what it was like to feel passion. What it was like to kiss a man and have her body explode with pleasure so intense it took her breath away. But as the memories had hit, so too did the subtle differences. There was a confidence and strength to his movements that hadn't been there before. He was no longer a youth, but a man. And he kissed like one. A very big, very strong, very possessive man.

She'd gone without passion for so long, but one day in his presence and it all came rushing back.

What if . . . ?

No, she was being ridiculous. Still dreaming. But girlish dreams had no place in her life now. She had responsibilities. Staying wasn't an option. She needed him gone by daybreak.

She heard another knock—this one more insistent.

Alarmed and suddenly wide awake, Jeannie slid from bed and tiptoed to the door, careful to avoid the pallet of the other occupant of the room who was (thankfully) still asleep.

Holding one hand flat on the wall, she cracked open the door. It was Mairghread, holding a candle to her face. Even in the shadows, Jeannie could see that something was wrong.

"I'm sorry for waking you, my lady, but you said to let you know immediately. It's the guardsman." Jeannie's heart stopped beating. "He's taken a turn for the worse."

For a moment she forgot her anger. "A fever?"

The old woman nodded.

Fear cut down her spine. Just like Francis. It had only been a small slice—an errant slip of a blade during sword practice—but it had festered. Within a week he was gone.

Jeannie felt as if the floorboards had just been yanked out from under her feet. How had this happened? Only a few hours ago he'd kissed her. She'd felt his strength, his passion, the life radiating inside him.

"I'll be right there," Jeannie said. She grabbed a plaid to cover her nightraile and slid her bare feet into a pair of soft leather slippers.

Turning back into the room, she knelt down beside the small pallet and kissed the velvety cheek, inhaling the sweet baby-soft scent. Ella wasn't a baby, not any longer, but she still smelled like one. She'd had another nightmare and Jeannie had allowed her to sleep in her room, knowing it wasn't the bad dream, but the death of her father that haunted her child. Besides, with the little termagant sleeping beside her, she was easier to keep an eye on.

Within a few minutes, Jeannie was following the healer along the narrow corridor to the stairwell and up the winding stone stairs to the garret above.

Mairghread had already woken Beth, the young nursemaid who slept in the mural chamber, to keep watch on him. Poor Beth seemed to be having a devil of a time doing so, and Mairghread rushed forward to help her.

Duncan had kicked off the bed linens and was writhing back and forth as the maid did her best to keep a damp piece of cloth pressed to his brow. But with his size and strength it was virtually impossible for the two women to keep him down and still. Jeannie should go to help them, but she was frozen.

Not from the cold. The room was hot—stiflingly so—though only a single candle burned. The heat was coming from Duncan, and her chill was from fear. Steeling herself, she forced herself to take a few steps closer.

Oh, God. She made a muffled sound in her throat and clenched her fist to her mouth. *I can't do this.*

His face flickered in the candlelight, enough for her to see the sickly telltale scarlet flush on his cheeks. His mouth was already white, soon she knew his lips would be cracked and chapped with thirst that could not be sated.

Instinctively she recoiled, taking a step back.

Mairghread read the horrified expression on her face. Their eyes met in shared understanding. The old woman knew how hard she'd fought for her husband's life and knew what the failure had cost her.

Tears sprang to her eyes. *"Be happy, Jeannie. I'm sorry."* It was the last thing Francis had ever said to her, as if he'd failed her and not the other way around.

"You don't need to be here, my lady. Beth knows what to do."

Jeannie nodded. It was what she wanted to hear. It had almost killed her to watch the man she *should* have loved die, she couldn't watch Duncan do the same. Duncan, the man she'd once loved but now hated.

At least she wanted to. But as she stood here with fear in her throat and a vise around her chest she felt the veneer crumble. It wasn't hatred that had ripped open the scar on her heart, revealing the raw and still bleeding wound underneath. It was the memories—the yearning for a past that could never be. He'd ruined her, not of her maidenly virtue but of something far more important—her heart. Seeing him again brought it all back. Kissing him . . .

She didn't want to think about this. God, why had he come back?

His body seized and he cried out as the demons of the fever possessed his body, clutching him in their fiery hold.

I could just let him die and it would all be over.

She recoiled from the thought almost as quickly as it had sprung. The malevolent impulse shocked her. Dear

God, where had that come from? It hinted of anger far deeper than she'd realized. Of wounds buried but far from healed.

I have to go. But her feet remained planted to the floor.

"My lady?" Beth asked, her eyes wide with concern.

Jeannie took a deep breath and tore her gaze from the man on the bed. "I'm fine," she answered, the terror suddenly releasing its hold. Her mind cleared. He might have left her, but she would not do the same to him. She couldn't just let him die and do nothing to save him. Not when it was her fault.

She might not be able to help him clear his name, but she could not completely turn away from him.

Squaring her shoulders, she readied for the battle ahead. With quick, determined strides she reached the bed and took Beth's place at his side. She dunked a cloth in the bowl of cool water, wrung it out, and placed it on his head, holding it to his brow and murmuring soothing words while Mairghread attended to the infected wound.

He settled at the sound of her voice. His eyes fluttered open and locked on hers for a long heartbeat before closing again. He was blinded by the haze of the fever, yet somehow she wondered whether he'd known it was her.

For two long days and nights she stayed at his side, battling the inferno that tried to consume him, not knowing whether he was going to live or die.

She wouldn't leave his side. Not Mairghread, not her mother-in-law, not even Ella's worried little face, could drag her from the room. It was no more than she would do for anyone, she told herself. It was her duty.

But it didn't feel like duty, it felt like an exorcism. The hotter he burned, the deeper her unraveling. Emotions long since buried bubbled to the surface like a volcano waiting to erupt. She spun back and forth between cursing him to the devil and praying with all she had for his life.

Then, in the wee hours of the second night, he woke. Delirious with fever, he cried out her name, before falling suddenly still. Dead still. Just like Francis.

Panic gripped her heart. "No!" she cried, shaking him. "Damn you, Duncan. You've no right to die. I'm not done with you yet." She'd never got a chance to tell him how much he'd hurt her. How it had felt to know she was pregnant and alone. How her heart had been breaking for him, how all she wanted to do was curl in a ball and cry, but she'd had to be strong. How she'd been forced to marry a man she didn't love to protect her child from her folly.

She shook him again and again, but he moved lifelessly in her hands. The healer woke at the sound of her voice, and rushed to his side. Mairghread placed her hand on his heart and lowered her cheek to his mouth. When she stood, Jeannie knew from the old woman's expression that it was bad. "I'm sorry, my lady. The fever has weakened his heart and lungs."

Jeannie shook her head stubbornly, refusing to believe that this indestructible man could be defeated. Deep in her bones, she knew he would not die. He couldn't leave her. She wouldn't let him.

She stared at the once beloved handsome face gray with sickness, a tumult of emotions pressing inside. *I hate you, damn you.* Tears streamed down her cheeks as she pressed her lips gently to his.

God, I loved you. She'd loved him with all her girlish heart. And that was what she thought of now. Laying her head on his shoulder, in that warm place she remembered, she wept, mourning the loss of the girl and of the love. She wept for the treacherous circumstances that had forced them apart, for her lost innocence, for dreams disappointed, and for her son who would never know his father. She wept until she had nothing left.

"There is nothing more you can do for him, lass," the healer said gently.

Maybe not, but she would try. Duncan was strong—stronger than any man she'd ever known. The fever that had struck with such potent destruction had weakened him, but she knew if anyone could weather such an attack it would be him.

Mairghread left her to her solitary vigil. And on the third morning Jeannie's belief was rewarded. As the first light of dawn crested over the horizon, Duncan opened his eyes—the blue cobalt every bit as clear and vibrant as she remembered.

His gaze locked on hers, weak and confused but lucid. "How could you marry him, Jeannie? How could you marry someone else?"

The emotion in his voice clamped around her heart. He didn't know what he was saying, but it didn't diminish the honesty of his feelings.

He had cared for her. Perhaps not enough to trust her, but she hadn't been the only one to suffer at their parting. Her throat tightened, moved by the unexpected revelation. "I didn't have a choice."

But he didn't hear her; he'd already slid back into sleep's healing embrace.

She stared at him for a long while, wondering what it meant.

Exhausted, Jeannie stood, legs shaky, and walked slowly across the room.

It was over. She felt as if she'd been freed from ten years of purgatory. Duncan would live, and she'd finally made some peace with her past.

Maybe now she could have a future.

*   *   *

Duncan woke the next morning feeling as if he'd just made it through hell's gauntlet. His body was battered, bruised, and weak, but he was alive.

It wasn't the first time he'd taken fever from a wound, but if the way he was feeling right now was any indication, it was the nearest he'd come to death.

"You're awake." The old healer must have been sitting in the corner and heard him stir.

He frowned, feeling a strange stab of disappointment. He'd thought . . .

Had he only dreamed of Jeannie's presence at his side?

"You'll be wanting something to drink," the woman said, passing him a cup of water.

"Aye," he said. "And a bath when one can be arranged."

The woman chortled. "Feeling a wee bit gritty, are you?"

To put it mildly.

"The lady anticipated your request and has ordered a bath to be brought to your room when you are ready. Beth will see to your needs."

"And Lady Gordon?" he found himself asking.

"Which one?" Duncan lifted his brow in question and the old woman explained. "The Marchioness has been in residence since the death of the young laird."

Huntly's wife . . . here? *Hell.* He'd met her once, years ago. Though it was unlikely she would remember the bastard son of a Campbell, he would do his best to avoid her. The old battle-ax was every bit as formidable as her husband and dealt with enemies swiftly and brutally. Not long before Glenlivet when the Chief of Mackintosh who'd been feuding with the Gordons had thrown himself upon her mercy—and with foolish bravado offered to lay his head on the executioners block in submission—the Marchioness had accepted his grandiose offer and had him beheaded. "The Mistress," he clarified.

The healer's eyes narrowed. "Getting some well-deserved sleep. She didn't leave your bedside for three days. I'll not have you disturb—"

"Nay," Duncan cut her off. "I've no wish to disturb her." He couldn't deny the swell of pleasure. He hadn't dreamed it. Jeannie *had* been here. He knew better than to put too much weight to the fact, but perhaps she wasn't as hardhearted toward him as he'd thought. For some reason that mattered.

The healer was watching him closely. Almost as if she were reading his thoughts, she said, " 'Tis no more than she would do for any man."

Duncan heard the implicit warning that echoed his own thoughts—don't put too much store in her devotion.

The old woman frowned. "Though it was difficult for her after losing the master so recently."

Duncan tensed. He didn't want to think about Francis Gordon, but he couldn't stop himself from asking, "How did he die?" Lizzie hadn't been specific in her note.

"The fever," she said bluntly. "He took a cut on his arm, during practice one day, and it festered. The sickness nearly took the lady along with it, so hard did she fight for his life."

His chest tightened. Jeannie must have loved her husband something fierce for such devotion.

This was asinine. He was jealous of a dead man. But behind the irrational spur of jealousy, Duncan realized how difficult it must have been for her to nurse him.

Was it guilt for what she'd done to him all those years ago?

He frowned. For some reason he couldn't shake the feeling that something was wrong. The old doubts he'd had before finding out she'd married were resurfacing. He'd been so certain. But was there another explanation and he'd been too blinded by anger and distrust to see it?

Unease settled like a rock in his gut. Never before had he allowed himself to ask the question: What if he'd been wrong? The ramifications were too horrible to contemplate. *"You left me."* The echo of her voice reverberated in his ears, sending a chill down his spine. If he'd been wrong, he would hand her another pistol himself.

But if Jeannie hadn't betrayed him, who had?

Jeannie heard the sound of voices as she tromped up the stairs, a leather pack containing Duncan's belongings slung over her shoulder.

She'd woken about an hour ago and after a long hot bath and quick bite to eat felt wonderfully refreshed. Realizing Duncan would likely want the same, she'd tracked his much relieved men down and asked them to bring her his things, which she hoped contained a spare shirt. Francis had been almost as tall and broad shouldered as Duncan, but not nearly as muscular. He'd been a warrior by necessity, not by nature. But even if she could find a shirt to fit Duncan, the idea of lending something of her husband's to Duncan felt strangely disloyal, and she wasn't sure Duncan would want it anyway.

But she remembered the effect his bare chest had had on her before and now that he was on the mend . . . well, she would find him something, even if she had to cover him with a sackcloth.

Given all that had happened, Jeannie was amazed by how much lighter she felt. His fever had forced her to face some hard truths. She wasn't nearly as over him as she'd wanted to believe. She'd repressed her feelings for so long, never dealing with the pain he'd caused her, forced to bury the anger and bitterness she'd felt toward Duncan for the sake of the child she was carrying. Seeing him so close to death had unleashed it with a ferocity that had surprised her.

What had happened between them was a long time ago. A lifetime ago. Too long to hold onto such anger.

She still wanted Duncan to leave—the danger to her son had not lessened—but she could wait until he recovered.

She'd almost reached the top of the stairs when the deep rumble of his laugh stopped her cold. Her chest squeezed. She'd forgotten that sound. Forgotten how it affected her. How it wrapped around her and penetrated with a bone-deep contentment. How at one time it had made her feel as if she were the most special woman in the world.

Years ago he'd been so serious that his laughter had felt like a rare gift. And now, hardened by age and battle, it was even more so.

She bit her lip, wondering what had made him . . .

She took a few more steps and the answer to her question became painfully obvious. She sucked in her breath, the lash of hurt as strong as it was unexpected.

Duncan stood in the middle of the room, knee deep in the water of his bath, naked except for the damp drying cloth slung low around his waist, with the young nursemaid Beth plastered against his chest. His muscular arms were wrapped around her. Jeannie's heart strained to beat. Both were laughing and the pretty fair-haired maid's cheeks had flushed a very becoming pink.

A sharp stab of what could only be termed jealousy landed precariously near her heart. Why should it affect her? He didn't belong to her. There must have been numerous women in his life after he'd departed Scotland. Duncan was a sinfully handsome man—strong and undeniably virile. Women would naturally flock to him. But knowing in the abstract and seeing in the flesh—very wet, naked flesh—were two entirely different things.

Both Duncan and Beth turned at the sound of her gasp and instantly (guiltily?) sobered. As always, Duncan's implacable expression betrayed none of his thoughts, but Beth had the same look on her face that Ella often did— what Jeannie called the "I-didn't-do-anything" look when caught with her hand in the biscuit jar.

Duncan released his hold on the maid and the girl stepped back quickly. The entire front of her kirtle was damp, revealing the outline of her pert young breasts.

"I slipped," Duncan said, by offer of an explanation. "And almost landed wee Beth here in the bath with me."

Was this supposed to make her feel better? "I see," Jeannie said, feeling like a humorless old goat, like her mother-in-law, actually. Why was she acting like this? There was nothing unusual about a servant helping a man to bathe—Jeannie had made the suggestion herself. She just hadn't thought it through very well.

Beth held out her arm again and this time he stepped easily from the wooden tub.

Jeannie's mouth went completely dry. Modesty had little place in a castle, and even less among warriors, and one glimpse in his direction reminded her that he had nothing to be modest about. She could see everything. Every muscle, every bulge. She sucked in her breath. Every long, thick inch of him.

Her stomach muscles clenched.

Very purposefully she kept her gaze above his neck. But even that wasn't safe. He'd shaved and her eyes were drawn to the deeply tanned skin and strong angle of his jaw. He'd always been so ridiculously gorgeous— now even more so.

Remembering the task that had brought her here, she

slid the pack from her shoulder. "I've brought you your things."

He grinned, an errant lock of wet hair sliding forward across his face roguishly. Her memory jumped to the loch, and the jabbing in her chest grew more insistent.

"Ah, thank you. I was just going to ask Beth here to fetch them."

Feeling like a fool for letting him get to her, Jeannie started to back away. She'd been down this path before. But she was no longer a girl caught up in romantic fantasies who saw something she wanted and acted without thought of the ramifications. Her life had been one big long ramification. She was wiser now and would not tempt discretion.

"I'll leave you then. I've asked one of the servants to bring you some food, and when you are ready, I believe your men are anxious to see you."

"I can imagine," he said dryly.

She turned to leave, but he stopped her. "Wait. If you have a moment, there is something I would like to speak with you about."

Very conscious of the other woman in the room, Jeannie nodded stiffly. "Of course."

Beth's gaze shifted between them. She seemed uncertain what to do. Duncan came to her rescue. "I think I can manage from here, thank you, lass. Sorry about getting you all wet."

Beth didn't look like it had bothered her at all, but she bobbed her head and quickly bustled out of the room. A room that suddenly seemed much smaller.

Jeannie hoped he didn't intend for her to help him dress. She didn't want to get any closer to him than she already was. Even five feet away, her body hummed and every nerve ending pulsed with a restless energy.

He didn't look at all like a man who'd just escaped the

clutches of death. He looked strong and powerful and more attractive than anyone she'd ever known.

His body was a thing of beauty, exuding raw masculinity that called to her on a base level she couldn't explain. It was something intangible, something involuntary, but undeniable.

It wasn't merely his physical appeal. Her husband had been a handsome man, but she'd never responded to him this way—though she'd tried and tried. The lack of passion between them had been a disappointment to them both—one that had eventually driven Francis from her bed. Despair cut through her, knowing how much her tepid responses had hurt him.

How wrong it was that one look at Duncan could provoke more desire in her than years with her husband. Her body's reaction seemed the cruelest disloyalty and one more nail in the coffin of her guilt.

He riffled through the contents of his pack, eventually removing a pair of black leather breeches and a clean linen shirt. When his hand went to the cloth at his waist, Jeannie carefully shifted her gaze. But her senses seemed unnaturally heightened and she was painstakingly aware of every movement. She knew it was impossible, but she could have sworn she heard the thin drying cloth drop on the floor. Heard the fabric stretching as he pulled the breeches over his legs. Felt the whoosh of air as he dropped his shirt over his head.

"I'm done," he said, the wry amusement in his voice made her wonder if she was totally transparent. She turned to face him and he pulled out a chair for her. She hesitated, then told herself she was being ridiculous and sat, folding her hands primly in her lap. He lowered himself to the edge of the bed opposite her—much too close for her comfort. She could smell the warm tang of soap on his skin and the dark, male essence that had always haunted her.

"I wanted to thank you for what you did."

"It was nothing," she dismissed quickly, fighting the heat that rose to her cheeks and wondering how much he remembered.

He didn't argue with her, but they both knew she lied. "I'm sorry that my return might cause you difficulty. It was not my intention to hurt you. But you had to know I'd come home sometime."

She gave him a sharp look. "Actually, I wasn't sure if you'd ever return. If half the legends are true, why would you?" She couldn't prevent the twinge of curiosity. "Did you really defeat an entire army with a dozen men?"

He looked uncomfortable. "Half of what you've heard is no doubt exaggerated."

And the other half? She noticed he didn't deny her original question. "It must have been difficult having nothing but your sword arm to make your living. You went to Ireland?"

He nodded. "I was a gallowglass mercenary for the O'Neills. When they were forced from Ireland, I went with them. First to France, then to Switzerland, Italy, Flanders, and eventually Spain. It was a hard life, but not without its rewards."

He turned the question back on her. "And what of you, Jeannie. What has your life been like? Have you been happy?"

She regretted her impulse to probe into his past—it was the last thing she wanted to discuss with him. But he'd answered her honestly and she would do as much for him. Happy? Nay, but she hadn't suffered. "I've been content. I've had my children."

"And your husband? He was good to you?"

Something in his voice caught her attention. He seemed hanging on her every reaction. "Aye, Francis was a good man." She should have loved him. Wanting to avoid further discussion of her husband, she returned to the original subject. "You've made a name for yourself on the continent, but nothing has changed here. You are still under a cloud of treason."

"Not a cloud," he said tightly. "I was convicted before I left. I would have hanged the moment they found me."

"That's why you left so suddenly?"

He shrugged. The lack of bitterness in his voice surprised her. Everyone had turned against him and he acted like it meant nothing, but it had to have been horrible.

"With my father dead and the rest of my clan convinced of my guilt, I thought there was nothing left for me here."

She could barely get the words out, her throat burned. "What about me?"

Their eyes locked and something passed between them—something deep and significant.

Jeannie swore she would not defend herself against his spurious charges again, but his silence compelled her to try one more time. It was too late to reclaim what was lost—not to mention dangerous with all she had to lose—but it seemed somehow important that he know the truth. "I did not take the map, Duncan. I would never have betrayed you like that. I loved you."

He didn't look away, but neither did he respond. What had she expected? He hadn't believed her years ago when he'd claimed to love her, why should he now when she was nothing to him.

"All those years, did you not once question my guilt?" she asked, her voice climbing higher. "Did you not once think about coming back?"

Did you think of me at all?

His eyes went flat. Cold. She wanted to pound her

fists against his granite wall of a chest, hating that he could be so unaffected when her pain felt so raw.

"You married. Rather quickly if I recall."

She sucked in her breath. The edge in his voice gave him away. Had her marriage prevented him from coming back?

What horrible irony. She'd married to give their son a name and may have prevented him from attaining his rightful one. But she couldn't look back. What was done was done. She wouldn't be foolish enough to fall for him again.

His gaze leveled on her, hard and unwavering. "If you had nothing to do with the plot against me, why did you marry so quickly?"

Her pulse jumped, knowing the danger that lurked in his question. She tried to control the frantic race of her heart, but her knuckles turned white as she clenched her hands in her lap. "My father wished it." It was the truth. As much as she would give him.

His mouth curled. "And, of course, the dutiful daughter would never think to defy him."

She heard the not-so-subtle criticism and fought to keep her temper in check. "How dare you," she seethed. "Once I would have defied my father in the worst way possible. I was ready to run off with you. I would have left everything for you. It was not me who broke the vow. *You* were the one who left. What reason did I have not to marry Francis? Should I have waited these ten years for you to return?"

"No," he said, taken aback by the emotion in her voice.

He'd never looked at what happened from her perspective. He'd taken her innocence, vowed to marry her, and then left her. He'd hurt her when he left, he couldn't deny it.

He'd thought he had reason, but what if he was wrong? She sounded so sincere. He shouldn't have asked her about her past, but he'd seen her sadness and wondered what her life had been like. But thinking about her married to another man ate through his gut like acid. The selfish part of him wanted her to have known the same emptiness he had. "You deny taking the map, but not once have you questioned my guilt. Why is that?"

She lifted her eyes back to his. "Perhaps I have more faith in you, than you have in me."

The rebuke was not without effect. Should he have trusted her when all evidence pointed against her? With Jeannie he'd let himself get carried away. He'd allowed his feelings for her to affect his judgment, something that had never happened to him before and he didn't like. When he thought she'd betrayed him, he'd been ashamed of falling trap to his emotions. He'd felt responsible for the loss of the battle and for his father's death. In his shame and anger had he rushed to judgment? It would be a horrible irony given what had happened to him.

Could he have failed her so miserably? He recoiled from the thought, reminding himself that even if she hadn't taken the map, she'd still made her choice. And no matter what she tried to claim now, it had never been him. "Faith? It wasn't in me. You never would have defied your father. Your actions are proof enough of that."

Her eyes flashed with green fire. "How can you say that?" Her tiny fist landed on his chest with surprising force. "Was my innocence not enough for you? What more proof did you want from me?"

The fact that she'd given herself to him had always bothered him. But he'd convinced himself that it had been unintentional. That like him she'd been carried away by the moment. She had cared for him, just not enough.

He grabbed her hand and held it firm against his chest, his heart pounding. "You said you loved me and agreed to marry me. Your loyalty should have been with me, but you chose your father. You knew he intended treachery and chose to say nothing. You let me ride away, knowing I might not come back." His voice shook with emotion he could no longer contain. "My father died because of that battle, Jeannie."

Tears sprang in her eyes to slide down her pale cheeks. His hand lifted but he checked the impulse. He would not comfort her, damn it.

"I'm sorry. I tried to warn you. But what would you have me do? I knew that if I told you, my father's life would have been forfeit. Would you have kept my secret and said nothing to your cousin?"

His mouth fell in a tight line. "Of course I would have told my cousin."

She dropped her gaze and tried to pull away. "Then I was right to say nothing."

But he wouldn't let her go. He held her wrist and took a step toward her, backing her against the wall, using his body to corner her. She'd started this; she would damn well finish it. "The hell you were. Where's that faith you mentioned? I would have protected you and your father, but you never gave me the opportunity."

"How could you? You were just a bastard son. What could you have done against the Earl of Argyll and his powerful cronies?"

He flushed with anger, his teeth clenched. *Just a bastard.* It didn't matter that her words had not been said with scorn, the truth still pricked. "I wouldn't have turned your father over to my cousin to be killed. I would have gone to your father first, told him that his treachery had been discovered and given him the opportunity to get away *before* any damage had been done."

Her eyes rounded with surprise, the dark velvety

lashes sweeping like a raven's wing against the pale skin of her brow. "I never thought . . ." Her voice dropped off. But when she lifted her eyes to his again, he could see she didn't believe him. " 'Tis easy for you to say now. But I remember how you were then, a young, ambitious warrior trying to erase the stain of your birth. You were the quintessential chivalrous knight—all nobility and honor with little tolerance for deception or injustice. Letting my father go would have put you at odds with your clan. You would never have done anything to blacken your name."

Fury cracked like a whip inside him, shattering whatever rein he'd had on his control. Chivalrous knight? God, it was laughable. Not with her. Never with her.

He leaned into her, her breasts brushing against his chest, his skin crackled, the flames stoking hotter. It was all he could do not to slam her up against the wall and kiss her until the raging inferno inside him quieted. How did she still do this to him? Turn him into someone he didn't even recognize?

He heard her sharp intake of breath and saw the frantic pulse in her throat that echoed the beating of her heart. He slid his fingers around her neck, placing his thumb over the tiny flutter. He lowered his face to hers, forcing her to him. "Don't you understand? I *loved* you. I would have done anything for you. *Anything.* Honor? Duty? They meant nothing compared to you."

He'd said too much, but he was past all discretion. His life had been so damned clear, he'd known everything he'd wanted until he met her. She'd changed everything.

She gazed up at him helplessly. "Duncan, I . . . I'm sorry."

He didn't want her damned pity, he wanted her help. "You're still choosing to side with your family against me. Even if you weren't responsible for taking the map and setting me up for treason, what if your father and husband were?"

"They weren't."

"Then you should have nothing to fear." He swept his thumb over the delicate point of her chin, tipping her head back to gaze deep into her eyes. The old connection surged through him. He wanted to believe that she hadn't betrayed him, but she was making it damned near impossible. "Please, tell me what you know, let me see his correspondence. Help me find the truth."

Her luminous green eyes swam with turmoil as she struggled with what to do. Her indecision chaffed against his control, already rubbed raw. God's wounds, he'd practically begged her.

His blood surged and desire fisted low in his gut. He was hot and hard, and her nearness only made it worse. Never had a woman managed to get so completely beneath his skin. She'd always been the devil's sweet temptation. His entire body ached for her. Longed for her. How could she deny this madness that burned between them?

He knew she felt it from the way her lips parted, her eyes darkened, and her breath hitched. But she was trying to fight it. "Duncan, I—"

He swore, covering her mouth with his to prevent the refusal from passing her lips. He groaned at the contact—at the taste—sinking into her, digging his fingers through her hair to bring her mouth more fully against him.

His body heated, hardened, overtaken by dark, primitive urges of a man intent on claiming the woman who belonged to him. Blood surged through his body as lust gripped him in its inextricable hold.

He wanted to punish her for denying him, for denying this, for bringing him to this barbaric state.

He wanted to sink into the warm, honey recesses of

her mouth and devour her. To force her to admit what was between them.

Not just passion. The flash of rationality pierced the black haze. It was more than passion. Something far deeper and far more meaningful. And he wanted her to acknowledge it. He forced himself to cool and eased back to coax her lips apart with gentle, deft strokes of his mouth and tongue.

But God, she was sweet. Honey on his tongue. He wanted to sink into her, to delve into the warm sugary recesses, but instead of demanding with the force of passion, he cajoled with infinite tenderness.

His forbearance was rewarded by a soft moan as she opened her mouth and returned his kiss, surrendering. To him. A bolt of pure masculine satisfaction surged through him as strong as after any battle he'd ever won.

He knew she'd felt it, knew he was not alone in the force of emotion that made his chest ache with every tentative sweep of her tongue. His tongue circled hers in a slow delicious dance, delving deeper and deeper. She sagged against him, her body melting into his. He groaned at the contact, at the incredible sensation of all those ripe curves pressed up against him.

The sound startled her out of her trance. With a cry she jerked away, the movement as emphatic as a slap. She stared at him, breathing hard. Her gaze shuttered, but she still bore the stamp of their passion in her swollen lips and flushed cheeks. "I can't. I'm sorry, I can't help you."

He flinched. "Why not?"

She shook her head, tears blurring her luminous green eyes. "I just can't. Please don't ask me again."

This time when she turned to leave, Duncan didn't stop her. His body felt coiled, ready to strike, and he didn't trust himself. His hardened heart felt the pinch. Her refusal, in the wake of his own weakness for her and the passion that still seized his body, was a double betrayal.

He clenched his jaw, biting back the flare of disappointment. He'd thought . . .

What, that he meant something to her? He was a damned fool thinking he could read emotions in a kiss.

What the hell had he been thinking? Kissing her only made him more crazed. Lust blinded him to his purpose. He was here to clear his name, not to wake the ghosts of the past.

She wanted him, but not enough to overcome whatever it was that held her back from helping him. It wasn't just loyalty to her husband, but something else. She was hiding something and he intended to find out what it was.

Chapter 13

✦

The conversation with Duncan stayed with Jeannie long after she'd left his room. She'd had her questions answered, but it hadn't made anything easier, only more complicated. The initial anger that had flared between them had been dulled both by the fever and by understanding. What had once seemed so clear was now clouded by a different perspective—his perspective.

He left me. And she would never forget it, but she was not completely without fault. Map or no map, on some level Duncan felt she'd betrayed him. By not telling him about her father she'd put her loyalty to her clan above her loyalty to him. Honor and integrity permeated every fiber of his being, she'd never thought he would put that aside to help her father. Should she have trusted him? She didn't know, but he was right—implicitly she'd made a choice.

And she'd done so again, choosing to protect her son rather than help Duncan clear his name. Guilt that she could not completely ignore gnawed at her. She'd wanted to agree to help him. The words had been right there on the edge of her tongue. But she hadn't given in to the impulse. She couldn't trust him, not with her son's future. Once she'd been willing to risk everything for Duncan, but she wouldn't make the same mistake again—not when Dougall could be the one to suffer.

But it was dangerous without having anger as a shield between them—as that kiss had demonstrated. She'd felt the undeniable tug, drawing them together. It would have been so easy to fall into his arms again. Terrifyingly easy. It was getting harder and harder for her to resist, but she steeled her heart against him, avoiding being alone with him.

She wasn't the only one to feel his magnetism. Over the next few days while Duncan recovered his strength with alarming alacrity, she'd done her best to keep Ella away from him—with little success. Every time Jeannie turned around, Ella was sneaking into his room or following him to the stables, the hall, or the barracks on some pretense or another. To his credit, Duncan did nothing to encourage her, but his indifference had the opposite effect than the one intended. Ella never could resist a challenge. And if her formidable grandmother could succumb, it was only a matter of time before Duncan did likewise.

Ella couldn't hide her fascination with their uninvited guest. Nor for that matter could most of the women under or over the age of sixty. Yesterday, when Duncan joined his men for the first time to practice his sword skills in the yard, the entire female population in the castle seemed to stand still when he removed his shirt. She'd never seen so many women gathering water from the well, which happened to be located near the practice yard, and the keep's windows had never been so clean.

Ridiculous. But Jeannie found her gaze straying more than once to the tanned chest gleaming in the sunlight. When he held his sword above his head and his muscles flexed . . . her body tingled in places she'd long forgotten. His raw masculine appeal was undeniable.

But not for me.

The truth, however, did not quiet the dull ache in her chest.

Beth's mooning grated more than the others, not because of what Jeannie had seen or because Duncan gave any indication that he noticed, but because the girl was young and pretty, and as innocent as Jeannie had been once—a long time ago.

But as trying as the past few days had been, Jeannie knew that it would soon be at an end. As his sword practice yesterday proved, Duncan's recovery had progressed to the point where he would soon be well enough to travel.

She intended to remind him of that fact. Entering the hall, she found him breaking his fast, Ella perched on the table beside him, chattering animatedly, and Beth opposite, elbows on the table, chin cupped in her hands, utterly enthralled. Both girls seemed to be suffering from the same malady—an acute case of hero worship.

He'd done nothing but shoot a few arrows and swing his enormous two-handed great sword around, but even hampered by his injury, there was something special about him. He stood out like a king upon beggars. His physical strength, confidence, and authority could not be masked, despite his best attempts not to draw undo attention to himself. She supposed his handsome face didn't hurt either. She could only imagine what would happen if it became known that he and the legendary Black Highlander were one and the same.

Gritting her teeth, Jeannie marched toward them, feeling the strange urge to smash her fist through the nearest window—or his perfect, gleaming white grin. His constant presence was like an itch she couldn't scratch and her hard-won, even-keeled temperament was starting to suffer.

"I could go with you," Ella said hopefully. "My father promised to take me hunting next spring if I practiced with my bow."

Jeannie's heart caught, hearing the eagerness in her daughter's voice. Ella missed Francis horribly and in

Duncan she'd found not a replacement, but a man to soothe an ache.

"I can hit the target from twenty paces," she added, chest puffed out and chin tilted high.

Duncan's lips quirked and Jeannie knew he was fighting a smile. "Twenty paces? A wee thing like yourself? I know laddies twice your size that can only shoot from ten."

Ella beamed. "Can I go then? Please . . . ?"

She batted her long, dark lashes at him, a clichéd feminine gesture that surely Duncan would see through. Jeannie glanced in his direction.

Oh God. He's falling for it.

Duncan looked up and saw her, no doubt reading the horror on her face. He sobered and turned back to Ella. "Perhaps another time, lass."

"No!" Jeannie exclaimed, panic causing her pulse to race frantically. Delay would only encourage her. "You can't go hunting, Ella. It's too dangerous. You could get hurt."

Ella's dainty features turned mutinous. "You always say that. Dougall went hunting when he was nine."

Jeannie bit back the response that Dougall was a boy and that hunting was part of his training, knowing it would only make it all the more tantalizing to her daughter. Besides, Jeannie had always detested that explanation when she was a girl and she'd vowed not to use it upon her daughter. Perhaps that was part of the problem. Ella wanted to do everything her brother did.

"Well, you are only seven. When you are nine we will discuss it." Seeing the argumentative expression on her daughter's face, Jeannie took a different tact. "Besides, Duncan will not be able to take you hunting as he will be leaving soon." She turned to Duncan. "Isn't that right?"

Duncan held her gaze for a moment then turned back to Ella. "Aye, it's true, lass."

"But why?" Ella asked. "Why can't you stay here? I thought my uncle sent you to protect us from the bad men—"

"Beth," Jeannie interrupted, startling the young nurse-maid out of her besotted stupor. Hearing the edge in her voice, Jeannie tempered her tone and forced a smile on her face. The girl had done nothing wrong. "Why don't you take Ella down to the kitchens? I believe the cook is going to make some biscuits." She turned to Ella. "Didn't you say you wanted to help . . ."

Her voice fell off as Ella jumped off the table and raced to the stairs, the promise of sweets proving a sufficient distraction. Rarely did one thing hold her daughter's attention for long. Jeannie hoped she would soon add Duncan to that list.

When Ella and Beth were out of earshot she turned back to Duncan. "You have to leave."

He eyed her intently, ignoring her admonition. "What 'bad men'? You mentioned some kind of trouble that first day."

"It's nothing," she dismissed. It was none of his concern.

His gaze hardened. "Humor me."

She was going to refuse, but he would hear about it soon enough—she was surprised he hadn't already. She sighed, giving him a much-put-upon glare. "Since Francis died there have been increased cattle raids." She hesitated, wondering whether to say more.

He frowned, one hand absently playing with the handle of his tankard. But Jeannie knew it was all for show—he was anything but relaxed. He was fixed on her. Tension emanated from him like the tentacles of a sea monster ready to wrap around her. "Go on," he demanded.

She pursed her lips distastefully. "About a month ago the Mackintoshes attempted to abduct me. I believe my newly widowed state and Dougall's youth has proved something of a lure for unsavory clansmen intent on bettering their fortunes."

His hand froze, then gripped the handle of the tankard until his knuckles turned white. "Why have you said nothing about this?"

His voice was deadly calm, but it sent shivers of trepidations whispering up her spine. To all outward appearances he was in complete control. But she knew better. She could read the signs of danger surging just under the surface—the slight flex of muscles, the thinning of his lips, the darkening of blue in his eyes. To her he looked like a man ready to kill.

"Because it's none of your affair," she said in her haughtiest tone. She didn't need him to protect her.

His face darkened. He looked like he was going to challenge her assessment of the matter, but instead he said, "That is why you carried a pistol with you to the loch?"

She nodded. And why she was so quick to pull the trigger.

His eyes never left her face. "It's why you've decided to marry again?"

Her eyes widened. "I've made no decisions, why would you think that?"

"My sister mentioned Colin's suit in her letter."

He said it matter-of-factly, but there was something in his voice that made her stop. She studied his face, not sure what she was looking for. His mouth tightened and the muscle below his jaw jumped. News of her proposed marriage to Colin bothered him. Her heart pounded. Had the false rumor of her betrothal to his brother finally done what months of tears and prayers could not?

"Is that why you came back, Duncan?" she asked softly.

"As I said, it was time, that is all."

He lied. Though outwardly nothing gave him away, she could feel it. He was too calm. Too indifferent. Too dismissive.

What did it mean? After all these years did he still have feelings for her?

Her chest throbbed. It didn't matter. Protecting her family was all that mattered now. They'd had their chance and failed. Girlish fantasies of "what if" had no place in her life.

She recalled her reason for seeking him out—a reason made even more pronounced after seeing him with Ella. "If you are hunting today, I assume that means you are feeling better?"

He didn't answer right away. He knew what she was getting at. Instead, he bit a piece of bread off with his teeth, chewed slowly, and washed it down with a long swig of ale, trying to harness the bloodlust pounding through him.

Someone had tried to abduct her. She'd been in danger. She could have been hurt, and very likely would have been raped before or after being dragged to the Kirk door. He couldn't stop thinking about it, couldn't quiet the rage storming inside him, waiting to unleash its violent fury. The urge to kill gripped him hard and would not let go.

By the time his gaze returned to hers, however, he was once again in control. "I am much improved."

"Good, then you'll be leaving soon?"

Duncan would have found her eagerness amusing if it wasn't at his expense. He wouldn't be surprised to find his bag packed by nightfall and Jeannie standing at the gate, ready to lift the steel yett herself to see him out.

He was on the verge of giving her what she wanted. God knows, it's what he should do. If he was caught, he was a dead man, and every day he stayed here increased the risk. He needed to find proof to clear his name before word of his return leaked out. Clearly, Jeannie had no intention of helping him. There was no cause for him to stay.

But she was in danger. And every primitive male instinct in his body recoiled at leaving her alone and vulnerable.

God's blood, what the hell was wrong with him? Why did he care? She was not his responsibility, nor did she want his protection. He should go . . .

"Aye," he said. "I'll go." His stomach twisted, his body in revolt. He couldn't do it. His mouth fell in a grim line, furious with her and with himself. "Once I can be assured that you are well protected."

Her face fell. "I'm quite well protected. Besides, my safety is none of your concern."

His eyes narrowed. "I'm making it my concern. If you think I'm leaving now, you are very much mistaken. And if you are so well protected, how did I manage to come upon you swimming naked in a loch alone?" His temper gave way. *Naked.* "What in Hades could you have been thinking, Jeannie?"

She stiffened, her green eyes sparked with defiance. "I managed well enough. Need I remind you of the hole in your stomach?"

"Your pistol was effective against one man, but what if there had been more?"

She set her tiny pointed chin stubbornly. "I had Tavish."

"Your guardsman was too busy watching the performance in the loch and was lucky to only suffer a clop on the head for his transgression."

Her cheeks flushed. "I'll not explain myself to you. You sound just like my mother-in-law."

"Then he must be a man of exceptional good sense."

The haughty voice tinged with a faint French accent could only belong to one person. Duncan tensed. *Damn.* He'd been so wrapped up in Jeannie, he'd failed to notice the Marchioness of Huntly's approach. The one person he'd been doing his best to avoid.

Jeannie had her back to her mother-in-law, but Duncan noticed her stiffen at the sound of her voice. His gaze flickered back and forth between the two women. Apparently, Jeannie's devotion to her husband did not extend to his mother.

The older woman's hawk-like gaze settled on her daughter-in-law. It wasn't with dislike, precisely, more like forbearance. As if Jeannie was a personal challenge— another cross to bear, to use a cliché for the notoriously penitent Catholic.

"From what I heard," the Marchioness continued, "I assume this man is trying to impart upon you the seriousness of your recent lapse in judgment." She made it sound as if this was a recurring situation. "You should listen to him." Thinking she'd found an ally—though Duncan hadn't decided yet—the Marchioness turned to him, bestowing what looked to be a rare smile of approval on him. "I hope you will impart to my daughter-in-law the seriousness of her situation, alone without a husband to protect her."

He remembered how Jeannie's cheeks would flush when she was angry; her emotions displayed for all to see. Now the only signs of emotion were the balled fists at her side and lips pressed so firmly together that tiny white lines appeared around her mouth. Ten years had given her a measure of control over her reactions, but still he realized the Marchioness must be bullying her into finding a husband.

He sprang to her defense. "She's not alone," he corrected, watching the Marchioness's smile wither liked a dried vine. If she was looking for an ally against Jeannie it would not be with him. He spoke boldly, without the deference a man of his station should afford her, but it wasn't in his nature to condescend—not knowing his place had always been his problem. "It's not a husband she needs, but better trained guards, which is why the lady's brother sent me." His eyes slid to Jeannie, daring her to argue. But she was watching him with a puzzled look on her face, as if surprised by his defense of her. "When I'm done, Lady Gordon will be able to swim at the loch as often as she likes."

The Marchioness's beady gaze sharpened. He could empathize with the mouse that had just crossed the hawk's line of vision. He held his expression impassive as her eyes studied his face with unmistakable intensity. "Who are you? You look familiar. Have we met?"

His pulse spiked, but he met her inquiry with a relaxed smile. "How kind of you to remember, my lady. I'm Duncan MacAllan, we met many years ago at court. I was but a lad, attending to the Laird of Freuchie." MacAllan was a well-known sept of Clan Grant.

Her mouth pursed distastefully at the mention of Jeannie's father. The Marquis of Huntly may have forgiven Grant for his former transgressions preceding his return to the Gordon fold at Glenlivet, but forgiveness was not in the Marchioness's vernacular. What would she do if she ever discovered he was a Campbell?

He resisted the urge to rub his neck.

His relaxed response did not persuade her. "Your face reminds me . . . Who is your father?"

He did not need to feign the shadows that crossed his face. "I am a bastard, my lady." That much at least was true.

"I see," she said, eyeing him down her long nose. His

bastard blood having succeeded in convincing the Marchioness, temporarily at least, that he was beneath her interest. But Duncan knew his resemblance to his father was marked. How long would it take her to connect him with her husband's enemy, the former Campbell of Auchinbreck?

She looked to Jeannie. "Come along, daughter. I've something I wish to discuss with you."

More likely she wanted to keep Jeannie away from him. But she needn't worry on that accord—Jeannie didn't need her help. The Marchioness turned on her heel and strode away as regally as a queen. Jeannie made to follow her, but glanced back over her shoulder, a worried look on her face. "You shouldn't have done that," she said in a low voice.

Duncan gave her a wry smile. "I know." In defending Jeannie he'd placed himself under the Marchioness's scrutiny. She was suspicious. But despite the danger he could not regret it. "I'll be careful."

She nodded and walked away.

Duncan knew he didn't have much time. The most prudent thing would be to leave now and continue his search for information that would clear his name. But he couldn't leave—not yet. He told himself it wasn't just because the idea of Jeannie in danger made his insides twist and curl in a confused mass. The next few days would also give him an opportunity to search the keep and solar and see what he could find of Jeannie's secrets.

But more and more, he hoped he didn't find anything.

True to his word, over the next week Duncan transformed the castle and its occupants. Jeannie couldn't believe the changes he'd accomplished in so little time. In addition to personally attending to the training of the guardsmen, he'd organized regular scouting parties, reinforced the sentries, fortified the gates, and ordered the repair of the *barmkin* wall, which had been allowed to fall into disrepair over the past few years.

After a party of cattle reivers had been met by Duncan and his men at the beginning of the week, the air around the castle had changed. Word had spread that attacks against Aboyne—against Jeannie—would be met with resistance. Lethal resistance.

Even Adam, the captain of the Gordon guardsmen, who'd been initially reluctant to cede his authority in any way to Duncan, had been won over. Mostly because Duncan gave the credit for the changes to him, though everyone knew who was responsible.

Jeannie smiled as she exited the keep into the yard, despite the bone-chilling blast of wind and the dark clouds hanging overhead. For the first time since Francis had died she felt safe. Safe. She hadn't realized how oppressive it was being locked behind the walls of the castle like a princess in a tower until the weight was gone.

And she had Duncan to thank. It was hard not to admire the man he had become, just as it was hard not to imagine what might have been.

She wrapped her plaid around her shoulders and trudged across the courtyard, misty wind pelting her face with needles of ice.

Another week or two and she might even be able to resume her morning rides. Duncan would take her now, but he'd been so busy she hadn't wanted to ask him.

After the meeting with the Marchioness he'd removed himself from the keep and joined the other guardsmen in the barracks. She knew it was the right thing to do, but . . .

But what? She missed him? *No.*

Then why did she find herself waiting for opportunities to catch a glimpse of him? Like now, timing her trip to the garden to select the vegetables for the evening meal, right around the time he was expected back from the morning hunt.

If the dark skies were any indication, this might be one of the last hunting excursions. She inhaled deeply. The promise of an early snowstorm hung in the air.

She treaded carefully along the damp path, frowning as she passed the group of women gathered round the well. Apparently she wasn't the only one with thoughtful timing. Turning the corner, she entered the small vegetable and herb garden located on the west side of the old chapel.

Not surprisingly, it was crowded with young, unmarried women, and a few married ones as well. She *was* surprised, however, to see Beth. Jeannie glanced around, but didn't see her daughter.

"Where's Ella?" she asked the nursemaid.

Beth gave her an odd look. "I thought she was with you. She left about an hour ago to join the other children for their lessons."

The hair at the back of Jeannie's neck stood on end and gooseflesh ran along her skin, but she forced herself to stay calm. "She begged off her lessons, telling me that you were taking her to see Mary's new baby."

Jeannie saw her own rising panic reflected in the young nursemaid's face. Beth's eyes widened and she shook her head.

There's no reason to panic, Jeannie told herself. Oh God. Her heart raced in her chest but she wouldn't allow herself to think until they searched the keep.

A quarter of an hour later, however, she knew there was no mistake. Ella was gone.

"Where could she have gone?" the distraught nursemaid asked, her face white and tears barely repressed.

The possibilities ran through Jeannie's mind and stopped on one.

Duncan and his men had gone hunting in the forests near the Grampian Mountains and Ella must have followed him. She thought Ella had forgotten. In the security of Duncan's taking control of the castle, Jeannie had forgotten her daughter's stubbornness—and her resourcefulness. During the day it wouldn't be difficult for her to slip away. People passed through the gates all day and the guardsmen were more concerned with who was coming in than going. She would be on foot, unless—

"One of the ponies is missing, my lady," Adam informed her on cue, his face somber. "She must have taken it when they were grazing outside the gates."

Now panic set in. Ice-cold panic that chilled her blood and penetrated her bones. Panic that made her unable to think. She felt as if she were spinning in a whirlpool trying to claw her way out.

Think . . .

"How could you let this happen?"

Jeannie turned at the sound of her mother-in-law's voice. The Marchioness had been roused from her embroidery to join Jeannie in the yard when the hue and cry had been raised to search the castle for the missing child. "I warned you that something like this could happen. Helen has been allowed to run wild—"

"Not now!" Jeannie snapped, for once heedless of offending the older woman. "You may chastise me to your heart's content when we find Ella, but right now you are only wasting precious time."

To say the Marchioness was taken aback would be an understatement. Profound shock was more apt. But she took Jeannie's set down with surprising grace. They might have their difficulties, but in their love for her children they were united.

"What can I do to help?"

Jeannie would remember to be shocked by her capitulation later. "We need to organize search parties."

Adam, the captain, stepped forward. " 'Tis done, my lady. I started the moment I heard the child was missing."

Too terrified to feel anything other than a breath of relief, Jeannie thanked him. "She'll have gone after them. Do you know where they've gone?"

"Aye. The Muir of Dinnet."

Minutes later most of the remaining guardsmen who had not accompanied Duncan on the hunt rode out through the gate.

Duncan. Where was he? She wanted—nay, needed—him desperately and was too terrified to allow pride to stop her from admitting it.

Adam was one of the last to go. "Don't worry, we'll find her, my lady. She couldn't have gone far."

But they both knew she could. Ella was an excellent rider. Jeannie nodded mutely, trying not to think about all the horrible scenarios that could harm a seven-year-old child alone in the mountains and forests. What if she took a wrong turn and got lost? The paths were fraught with danger and if she veered off she could fall down a ravine, off a mountainside, or even into the River Dee if she wasn't careful. Only the knowledge that Duncan had cleared the land prevented her from thinking about brigands.

As Adam and the last group of men galloped away, Jeannie ran up to the battlements to watch them go.

She wanted to go. To do something. Anything other than this horrible waiting.

But as a woman waiting was what was expected of her. Adam would never have allowed her to go—she would have only slowed them down.

And Duncan . . .

She shuddered. He would be furious at the mere suggestion.

This was what it meant to be a woman. Forced to sit and wait while your life played out beyond your control.

Once before she'd felt this way—this horrible helplessness. She recalled standing at the window in the tower chamber, eyes glued to the countryside, waiting for news of Glenlivet. And that's what she did now, standing at the battlements, scouring the countryside for any sign of riders. Her mother-in-law and the other women had gone inside, but she could not. Inside she would go crazy. She needed to be outside where the walls could not close in around her.

Her skirts whipped around her ankles as a great gust of wind tore across the *barmkin*. Cold from fear, Jeannie barely noticed the wintry weather, until the first snowflake landed on her cheek.

It couldn't be snowing. It was too early . . .

As if to taunt her thoughts, the flakes came down harder.

Now Ella was at the mercy not only of the harsh terrain, but the elements as well. If they didn't find her soon she would freeze to death. She closed her eyes, praying, but it did not prevent the tears from leaching out and running down her cheeks.

How long had it been? Five minutes? Ten? An hour? Jeannie lost all sense of time. She looked at the sky—dark with storm clouds, but it still looked as if there were a few hours of light left.

They should be back by now.

The Muir of Dinnet was not that far. Francis used to take Ella there to see the stone circle and standing stones. Ella loved the ancient stones that dotted the Deeside, convinced that they were imbued with faerie magic.

Could she have gone there instead?

Her heart started to beat a little faster. It felt right. If Ella had been unable to find Duncan, the stone circle would be the first place she would think of. Jeannie had to do something. Standing here doing nothing had become unbearable.

The guards tried to stop her, but Jeannie could not be swayed. Eventually, with two of the remaining guardsmen to accompany her—two more than could be spared—Jeannie put her head down low against her mare's neck and kicked her heels, racing into the storm.

Chapter 14

❖

The hunt had taken longer than Duncan planned. But then again he hadn't counted on his wee stowaway.

He had to hand it to her, Ella had done a fine job of tracking them. About an hour after Duncan and his men had left the castle, they'd tied their horses and fanned out in the woods stalking their prey: deer, the rare boar, or anything else that might add to the winter stores. And if the cold, heavy wind was any indication, winter would be here soon enough.

One of his men had caught sight of a movement. A hint of brown in between the trees and sea of green foliage. The warrior raised his bow, taking steady aim.

Duncan's neck tingled. The hair on his arms stood on end. Something was . . .

"Stop!" Duncan jerked the man's arm down so hard he almost broke it. "It's not a deer." Panic had spiked inside him so hard, his voice actually shook.

The scrap of brown started to run at the sound of his voice, but it didn't take long for Duncan to overtake her.

Aye, *her.* Because, despite the brown cap, trews, and short coat, Duncan knew exactly who had followed them. The glint of one red curl peaking our from under the cap had given her away—and saved her life.

He circled his arms around her from behind and lifted her off the ground. She kicked and tried to wrestle free, but realizing the futility, gave over to the punishment.

He hadn't meant to be so harsh, but she'd just about

taken ten years off his life and his fear had lashed out like a whip in a brutal tongue lashing.

The tears had been his undoing.

Somehow, in between the chokes and sobs, the tiny, pale face streaked with tears, the apologies, and the knowledge of how badly she missed her father, Duncan agreed to allow her to accompany them.

He suspected he'd been rather handily maneuvered, but in truth he would have done just about anything to make her stop looking at him like that. When this was over he was going to make a vow to stay away from beautiful lasses with creamy skin, big blue—or green for that matter—eyes, and red hair.

Knowing Ella would soon be missed—if she hadn't been already—and that Jeannie would be in a panic, he sent one of his men back to the castle with a message that the lass was safe and they would return soon.

But hampered by the need to ride slower—even with Ella wrapped snuggly in his plaid before him—and then the storm, it was nearly two hours later that they rode back through the gate to discover that his messenger had just arrived. The man's horse had gone lame and he'd been forced to lead the beast the whole way back. He'd run into Adam and the party of guardsmen looking for Ella and they'd called off the search.

Duncan knew something was wrong when he looked around the *barmkin* and didn't see her. The crowd that had gathered to see the lass's safe return didn't include Jeannie. His heart took a sudden jump.

The Marchioness of Huntly met him at the bottom of the forestairs. "You found her!"

Actually Ella had found them, but the lass would be in enough trouble without him making note of her skill. "Aye."

Ella had also noticed her mother's absence. She

looked around as he handed her down to her grandmother and asked before he could, "Where's mother?"

"Looking for you," the Marchioness quipped, her voice severe.

Ella bit her lip, gazing up at her with wide, guilt-filled eyes.

While the lass attempted to appease her grandmother, Duncan turned to Adam. "I thought you said all the search parties had been told to return." His voice gave no hint to the sudden disquiet that had settled over him.

"Aye, they have," Adam said. "I know nothing of this."

The Marchioness's mouth pursed with disapproval. "Jean left after the others with a couple of guardsmen when it started to snow. She mentioned a stone circle. Someplace Ella used to go with her father."

Ella brightened. "Near the loch! I was going to go there if I couldn't find you."

Duncan swore. A couple of guardsmen? Loch Kinord and the nearby stone circle were on the edge of Farquharson territory. It explained why they hadn't come across Jeannie on their ride back—she would have taken the road north of the Dee. "How long ago did she leave?"

"About an hour."

Duncan didn't need to say anything. One grim look at Conall and Leif and they were off, joined by a half dozen Gordon guardsmen.

The thunder of hooves couldn't drown out the pounding in his chest. He hated this feeling—this vulnerability he still felt when it came to her. The thought of Jeannie in danger penetrated his hard-wrought reserve like nothing else. Only his complete focus on the task at hand kept fear at bay.

But when he caught up with her . . . he didn't know

whether he was going to throttle her or kiss her until the half-crazed feeling inside him let go.

There was probably no reason to worry. With the storm it would be unlikely that anyone would be about, but he wouldn't be able to relax until Jeannie was safe and back where she belonged. With him.

Jeannie gazed around at the circle of irregularly sized boulders in the small clearing of oakwoods, feeling her heart sink with disappointment. A thin layer of fluffy, pristine snow blanketed the ground and rocks. It seemed so still. So perfectly quiet . . . except for the sound of their voices echoing through the trees.

"Ella . . ." She waited, ears honed on silence.

She'd been so convinced that Ella would be here. Now she was beginning to feel foolish.

A sharp wind blew across the clearing. Jeannie shivered and sank into the deep folds of her hooded cloak. The snow had slowed, but with the daylight fading it was getting cold—very cold. Even with wool-lined leather gloves, her hands could barely clench the reins. She'd stopped feeling her face about an hour ago.

Her heart squeezed. Ella was so small, the icy weather would be even worse for her.

William, one of the guardsmen who'd accompanied her, halted his horse beside hers. "There's no sign of the lass, my lady." He waited for her to say something, but she was too overcome by disappointment. "We have to turn around; we're too close to Farquharson lands." Both men had grown increasingly wary as they neared Dinnet.

The warning was well met. The "fighting" Farquharsons had earned their moniker. The clan was part of the Chattan confederation of clans that included—among others—the Mackintoshes. Neither of whom were friends of the Gordons.

They were treading on dangerous ground and she knew it.

Jeannie nodded, taking one last look around, seeing not the beauty of the snow-laden trees and hills, but danger and the myriad of places in which a little girl could get lost.

William gave her an encouraging smile. "I'm sure they found her by now, my lady. The wee lass is probably warming up before the fire as we speak."

"You think so?" Her voice cracked, sore and ill-used from shouting in the cold.

William's smile deepened. "I'm sure of it."

Jeannie appreciated his confidence even though she knew he could well be wrong. But at least Duncan and the other men would have returned by now. Duncan would know what to do. If anyone could find her daughter he could. Never had she needed his solid, steady strength as she did now.

Following William's lead, she turned her horse around and threaded back through the trees. They rode for about a mile before Jeannie realized that something was wrong.

They were going too fast. Instead of the steady trot they'd started out with, William had gradually increased the pace until they were almost galloping through the dense trees. Such speed was dangerous in the best of conditions, but with the blanket of slippery, concealing snow on the ground, was foolhardy.

She caught William exchanging a worried glance with the other guardsman behind her and reined in her mount to a sudden halt. The men followed suit. "What is it?" she asked.

"I think we're being followed." William motioned to the other man. "Take the lady and head out of the trees for the river, I'll hold them off for as long as I can."

They couldn't leave him. Jeannie tried to argue. "But—"

"Go," William cut her off, slapping her horse on the rear.

The mare jumped forward and shot off like an arrow through the trees. The remaining guardsman followed her, putting himself between her and their pursuers— brigands were always a fear in the countryside. They were moving at a dangerous breakneck pace, narrowly avoiding overhanging branches and brushes that lined the narrow pathway. She prayed the snow was not hiding any treacherous holes or dips.

No more than a minute later she heard shouting that sent a chill shooting down her spine. They were so close. How many were there? The number of voices was lost in the wind.

She prayed for William's safety as she catapulted through the trees, fighting for her own. Surely they must be nearing the edge of the forest by now?

Her heart was beating like a frightened hare's. Her fear wasn't just from the men chasing them, but from the terrifying speed at which she was—

A scream tore from her throat as the mare pitched forward, having landed on a piece of uneven terrain. Jerked from the saddle, Jeannie flew over the horse's neck. The hard slam of the ground was the last thing she remembered.

Duncan would never forget the sound of her scream. In that moment, he realized just how much of a fool he'd been. Indifferent? Hardly. The white-hot terror cutting through him was anything but indifferent.

He didn't know whether there was anything left to salvage between them, but he swore if Jeannie came out of this unharmed he would find out.

Closing in on them, he motioned to his men to fan out and surround them. With his men in position, Duncan ordered them to wait for his command and dismounted.

Pulling an arrow over his shoulder from the quiver at his back, he threaded it through the bowstring and trod softly through the snow and trees. With Jeannie likely captured, stealth was their best option.

She hadn't screamed again. He didn't know whether to be thankful or panicked.

He listened for her voice, praying for the sweet sound, but only heard the low voices of men.

He steeled himself for what he might see and peered around the tree. Perhaps a dozen warriors were gathered in a circle standing in a patch of snow-covered heather and bracken.

He stared harder, looking through the tangle of steel and leather clad limbs . . .

Oh, God. His heart sank and for a moment he couldn't breath as anguish laced around his chest. He could just make out the spill of bright blue velvet on the snow and the heel of one tiny slipper.

It was Jeannie they were gathered around. And she wasn't moving. Rage, fear, and helplessness combusted inside him, the flames licking like a whip.

"Get away from her," he commanded, moving out from behind the tree. Not far away from her he saw the body of one of the guardsmen who'd accompanied her lying face first in the snow, an arrow protruding from his back.

The men startled at the sound of his voice. The metallic buzz of swords pulled from their scabbards reverberated through the air as they spun around, weapons brandished. Bloodlust surged through him. If they'd hurt her, a thousand swords wouldn't be enough.

"Move away," Duncan ordered. "Now."

One man stepped forward. Tall, broad shouldered, and wearing higher quality mail than the others, with two pistols tucked into his belt, Duncan took him for their leader. His long black hair and thick beard couldn't hide the fact that he was young—no older than five and twenty.

"Who are you," he sneered. "One man to order us? We found her first. She's ours."

Duncan's nostrils flared as he fought for control. "If she is harmed I'm the last face you'll ever see."

The stone-cold promise in his voice gave the warrior a moment's pause, but he recovered quickly. "Bold words when you are outnumbered a dozen to one."

"One is enough," Duncan said meaningfully, aiming the arrow straight between his eyes. Their gazes met in silent battle. "I assure you," he added. "I won't miss."

The man's eyes narrowed. Duncan had encountered dozens of his type over the years. Young men eager to the point of recklessness to prove their mettle, young men who's every decision was based on pride. They didn't like to back down—ever. And this one with his bold arrogant swagger reeked of trouble.

He was taking too long and Duncan was of no mind to wait for him to see the light. Jeannie still hadn't moved.

His mouth fell in a cold, flat line as he drew back his hand. He did not make empty threats.

"Wait." An older ruddy-faced man stepped between them. "He means it, captain. Do as he says." He motioned to the trees. "He's not alone."

The young leader opened his mouth to argue, but a movement in the trees stopped him. He shot Duncan a venomous look, but did as the older man cautioned and stepped away from Jeannie. There was something in the way he looked at her—possessive almost—that set Duncan's teeth on edge. He thought about letting the arrow fly anyway.

But the circle of men opened, allowing Duncan to get his first full view of her.

His knees almost buckled. Jeannie lay twisted on her

side, knees bent and hand near her mouth as if sleeping. His heart lurched as he stepped forward, gesturing with his hand for his men to come out and cover him.

He felt the older man's gaze on him as he approached, but Duncan only had eyes for the woman lying on the ground.

"We did nothing to the lass," the older man offered. "She was thrown from her horse."

Duncan bet he knew why. "You were chasing her."

The older man shrugged. "They ran. We did not know it was the lady."

Duncan knelt in the snow beside her and gently slid his hand under her neck to cradle her head in his palm. Her hair had come loose and was fanned out behind her head in a red halo. His heart clenched. Her angelic face looked as pale as the snow that surrounded her.

He pressed his fingers under her jaw and stilled, waiting, his heart on a precipice.

Relief crashed over him in a heavy wave, feeling the unmistakable pulse of life beneath his hand. He wanted to pull her into his arms, but he didn't want to move her in case something was broken.

"Jeannie." He nudged her gently and repeated her name.

Her eyes fluttered open. She blinked a couple of times as if trying to clear the haze from her view and stared up at him. "What happened?"

He smiled. "You fell from your horse."

Her eyes went wide. "There were men . . ."

"Shhh," he soothed, sensing her rising panic. "There is nothing to fear."

She shot upright, her eyes flashing wildly. "Ella!"

"Safe," Duncan assured her, wrapping her in his arms and smoothing back her hair with his hand. "She's at the castle."

"Thank God." She sighed. Her entire body sagged against him, her relief visceral.

Heedless of their audience, Duncan pulled back and tilted her chin up to meet his gaze. Unable to stop himself, he dropped a soft kiss on her mouth, needing the connection.

His chest tightened at the soft, warm silkiness of her lips. He wanted to sink into her sweetness, to kiss her until the roaring in his head quieted and the tightness in his chest loosened. But he felt too raw to weather the rejection right now. He lifted his head before she could react.

Gazing into her eyes, he read her surprise and waited for the rebuff, for the curtain to drop. But it didn't.

"Thank you," she whispered.

He grinned. "Anytime."

"Not for that, you wretch." She punched him, relief spilling into a moment of lightheartedness. "For finding Ella."

He nodded, and quickly explained what had happened. Then he asked, "How are you feeling? Do you think you can stand up?"

She nodded. "I think so."

He helped her get to her feet. She wobbled once, but steadied under his firm grasp.

She was lucky. Instead of hard ground, she'd landed on bracken and heather, which wasn't to say she wouldn't be aching later. But at least there didn't appear to be any broken bones.

No sooner had she stood than she retreated against him, tucking herself into his side. An instinctive movement of protection. A movement that pleased him more than it should. He slid his arm around her and snuggled her even closer. It felt good. Too good.

What was between them had not died—not completely anyway. He felt a spark of something suspiciously like hope flare inside him. Maybe they could have another chance . . . He stopped himself. Who was he fooling? He was an outlaw. A dead man if his cousin's soldiers caught up with him before he found something to prove his innocence.

While Duncan had been attending Jeannie, his men had corralled her pursuers to one end of the path.

She gasped. He swore under his breath, realizing she'd seen the body of the dead guardsman.

Duncan's mouth fell in a grim line as he addressed the men who'd pursued Jeannie. "Who is responsible for this?"

No one answered right away. He stared at a dozen blank faces before the old man stepped forward. "We were only defending ourselves. Ours was not the first arrow shot. The lady's guardsman attacked us a short while back."

That explained the missing second guardsman— Duncan knew she'd left the castle with two men. He would have one of his men ride back to find him.

Duncan met the old man's stare, looking him full in the face, intending to demand restitution for the men's families. Instead he felt the jolt of recognition.

Hell.

He saw the shock returned on the other man's face and realized he was not alone. The older man was one of the Mackintosh warriors Duncan had rescued from certain death during the battle of Glenlivet—Malcolm was his name.

"You've come back," Malcolm said, his voice filled with awe.

"You know this man, Malcolm?" the captain asked.

Jeannie's head lifted from its place buried in his chest at the sound of the younger man's voice. Duncan felt her body go rigid. "It's him," she said, her fingers gripping the leather of Duncan's cotun. "It's the man who tried to abduct me."

Duncan went cold. Ice cold. The urge to grab the man by the throat and squeeze until his eyes bulged raged inside him.

Sensing his thoughts, Jeannie put a restraining hand on his chest. "No. It's over. I just want to get home and see my daughter."

The young captain seemed to sense how close he was to death and took a few steps back.

Duncan's fists clenched at his side, the muscles flexing up his arms and across his shoulders. A man who dared to hurt a woman—and not just any woman, but his woman—did not deserve mercy. In two strides he'd reached the man and drew him up by the neck. He tried to break free, but Duncan's arms were as rigid as steel. The Mackintoshes reached for their weapons, but Duncan's men lunged forward—the point of their claymores a sufficient deterrent.

"Give me one reason I should not kill you," Duncan seethed.

"She's mistaken," the coward gasped. "I don't know what she's talking about."

Malcolm Mackintosh tried to intervene. "We did not mean the lass any harm. We want no trouble."

Something in the man's voice pulled Duncan's gaze away from the captain's. He read the silent offer. Let the lad live and I will keep the secret of your identity. It wasn't much of an offer. If all of the witnesses were dead no one would be left to tell Duncan's secret.

"Duncan." Jeannie tugged on his arm. He gazed down into her upturned face, into the pleading green depths. "Please."

His fingers gave one last squeeze before he tossed the man away from him. The young Mackintosh landed, gasping, on his ass.

Duncan turned to Malcolm. "Go. But if he comes within a mile of the lady again, he's dead."

Malcolm nodded and said in a low voice, "Welcome back, captain. I never believed what they said of ye. No one who saw ye fight that day did."

Duncan acknowledged the man's loyalty with a nod. He heard the young captain rustle to his feet. Out of the corner of his eye he saw him bend over and . . .

Before anyone else realized what was happening Duncan reached for the *sgian dubh* in his boot and in one smooth, unerring motion threw.

There was a loud thump as the blade found its target, followed by a strangled grunt from the captain.

The young captain wobbled, the hilt of Duncan's knife firmly in his neck. The pistol he'd slid from his waist and pointed at Duncan's back wavered in the air before dropping to the ground.

A moment later his body followed.

Chapter 15

❖

It had happened so fast. Jeannie still couldn't believe how quickly Duncan had reacted. She hadn't even been able to open her mouth to shout a warning before his knife was sheathed in the other man's neck, finding the small unprotected area right below his throat and above the edge of his mail.

The flash of fear she'd felt for Duncan paled in comparison to the awe and admiration that had followed after his near effortless dispatching of the threat and cold accuracy. She'd never seen him fight before and if the dark, ruthless look that had come over him was any indication, she could see how the Black Highlander had earned his fearsome reputation.

His instincts were amazing. *He* was amazing.

She put her fingers to her mouth. She could still taste him on her lips. The kiss had been brief, but poignant. In that one kiss he'd conveyed more emotion than in the entire three weeks since he'd returned. It had not been a kiss in lust or anger, but of something far deeper—of aching tenderness and poignant reminder of feelings long sumerged.

But the truly shattering part was that she hadn't wanted him to stop. Her feelings had been right there—on the edge—ready to catapult into danger.

She was softening.

An uneven bit of road caused her to lift from her saddle and land with enough force to rattle her teeth, but her mount barely seemed to notice. The destrier (her mare had come up lame after she'd fallen) belonged to Duncan's Irishman. The beast was far too big for her, but after her fall she appreciated its solid strength.

She didn't even want to think what would have happened had Duncan not arrived when he did.

Though she would not mourn the death of the Mackintosh brigand who'd tried to abduct her, she did regret that it had been at Duncan's hand. For a moment she worried that there would be a battle, that the Mackintoshes would seek to avenge their leader's death. But after a tense moment they'd gathered up his body and left. The rash young captain had signed his own death warrant by trying to shoot Duncan in the back. He'd gotten no better than he'd deserved.

But Jeannie doubted his father would agree. The dead captain, the man who'd tried to abduct her, was the Mackintosh chief's youngest son. And there was another problem to consider. The older Mackintosh warrior had recognized Duncan. She wanted to question him about it, but there hadn't been an opportunity. As the path was too narrow to ride two abreast, conversing was impossible. In truth, she was too anxious to do so. Though Duncan had assured her that Ella was unharmed, Jeannie wouldn't truly believe it until she had her little girl in her arms.

The torches were blazing by the time they thundered through the castle gate and the ghostly mist had settled low over the gray stone walls. She didn't wait for assistance. As soon as the groomsman took her reins, she hopped down and raced up the stairs.

She burst through the door and the first thing she saw was her daughter. Ella stood in the entry, looking up at her with eyes wide, cheeks rosy from the fire, and the most abashed expression Jeannie had ever seen on her face. Her tiny mouth trembled. "I'm sorry, mother."

Tears sprang to Jeannie's eyes. Emotion engulfed her in a big, hot wave. All that she could have lost suddenly crashed down over her. She didn't say anything, just knelt to the ground and gathered her child in her arms, holding on to her as if she would never let her go.

She glanced up and through the tears saw that Duncan had come up behind her. Their eyes met. "Thank you," she whispered.

He bowed his head.

The tears flowed until Ella started to wriggle. Jeannie took her by her small shoulders and held her a few feet away from her, giving her the sternest look she could manage at the moment. "Don't you ever do anything like that again. Do you realize what could have happened?"

Ella bit her lip. "I didn't think anyone would confuse me for a deer."

Jeannie paled. "What!"

Duncan winced at her side.

Ella looked up at him uncertainly and bit her lip. "I shouldn't have said that, should I?"

He shook his head and then looked at Jeannie. "I thought I'd wait until later to fill you in on all the details."

Jeannie looked back and forth between the two of them. "One of you had better tell me exactly what happened."

Duncan sighed. "It was hard to see through the snow and trees. Ella was partially behind a bush and with her clothes"—Jeannie noticed that Ella was still wearing the clothing she'd purloined from her brother's trunk—"one of my men thought she was a deer."

Jeannie sank to the floor and looked up at him. "You stopped him." She didn't need to ask, she knew.

He nodded.

Overwhelmed, Jeannie sat in stunned silence.

Ella eyed her warily. "Mother? Are you all right?"

Jeannie shook her head. The tears and hot swell of emotion were choking her again. He'd saved her daughter's life.

Duncan held out his hand and helped her up.

"I'm in a lot of trouble, aren't I?" Ella asked Duncan. He gave her a solemn nod.

Jeannie recovered enough to find her breath. "You disobeyed me, Ella. I told you I didn't want you hunting. You can't just run off like that and do whatever you want just because it seems like a good idea."

One man had lost his life, and only by a miracle had it not been two. William had been found with an arrow in his back, but was still breathing.

Ella tilted her head, her little mind clearly at work. "Did you get in trouble for running off, too?"

Duncan made a sharp sound that he quickly covered up with a cough, but Jeannie glared at him anyway. Ella was quick witted—too quick witted for her own good. Her innocent remark rang uncomfortably true. "I'm an adult, Ella. I can make my own decisions. And I made sure people knew where I was going."

The little girl nodded, chastened.

The Marchioness had come to join them. "You're back safe." She shot a glance to Duncan. "Was there any trouble?"

Jeannie stiffened, bracing for the recriminations that were sure to follow when her mother-in-law heard about the attack.

Duncan stepped forward before she could respond. "Nothing I couldn't handle."

Though Jeannie knew it was only a temporary abeyance she appreciated the effort. "I'll leave you now," he said. Jeannie noticed how he avoided the Marchioness, having roused her suspicion he did not want to put it to the test.

"Wait." Jeannie bent down and kissed Ella on the cheek. "Go with your grandmother for a minute, there is something I need to discuss with Duncan. I'll only be a minute."

The Marchioness gave Jeannie a disapproving look, but Jeannie paid her no mind and led Duncan into the laird's solar. The Great Hall was already crowded with clansmen gathered for the evening meal, and she wanted to speak to him in private.

She closed the door behind her and turned to face him. "Thank you, Duncan." Her voice caught, but she fought back the emotion. "Thank you for saving my daughter and for finding me when you did."

Their eyes met and something passed between them. "I thought you were dead." His voice was low, rough. "I saw you lying there and thought you were dead."

The stark look in his eyes tugged at her heart. "And that mattered to you?" she whispered.

"Hell, Jeannie." He dragged his fingers through his thick, wavy black hair. "How can you ask that?"

What do you feel for me? But she couldn't ask. Not when she wasn't sure what her own feelings were. But something had changed. A barrier had shattered between them. The pretense of indifference.

"Ella was right you know. You shouldn't have left like that. You should have waited for me."

He wasn't judging her or chastising her; it was concern that spoke. Usually such references to her impetuousness would make her defensive, but she wanted him to understand. "I had to go. The wait . . ." She gazed up at him. "Every minute was agonizing. You don't know how hard it is to sit and do nothing. I was half-crazed. What if someone you loved was in danger? Could you sit aside and do nothing?"

A wry smile turned his mouth. "Nay, I don't suppose I could."

He gave her an odd look, then dropped his gaze. "You won't be too hard on her will you? The wee lass knows she did wrong."

Now that the fear had faded, anger was making an appearance. "If she doesn't now, she will in ten years when I let her take her first step outside this castle."

Duncan chuckled. "If she were mine, I'd probably do the same. I swear the chit took ten years off my life when I realized it was her."

If she were mine. Jeannie's heart stopped for a long beat and then throbbed painfully. He would be a wonderful father.

The pain sharpened and she had to turn away. After all he'd done for her, she wanted to trust him. But could she? Should she? Did he trust her?

Too much was weighing on her decision. This was not something she could decide on the spur of the moment— on a feeling. For once, she would take the time to think about it.

Taking a deep breath, hoping to hide the sudden flood of turmoil, she lifted her eyes to his again. "The man recognized you."

"Aye." He seemed disappointed by the turn of conversation. "I fought with him at Glenlivet."

"Will he say anything?"

"Before I would have said nay, but now . . ." He shrugged.

Because of the death of the Mackintosh chief's son questions would be raised. "What will you do?" she asked.

His eyes met hers. "What I set out to do. Find the truth."

He watched her expectantly, as if waiting for her to say something. To tell him she would help. But she couldn't. Not yet. "You will leave?"

"Aye, soon."

Her heart tugged. "Where will you go?"

He gave her a solemn look. "I don't know."

Duncan paused outside the door, listening for any sound that might indicate that all the occupants of the keep weren't tucked safely away in their beds. But the soft crackle of the dying fire was the only sound to disturb the empty black void of night.

Still he hesitated. He hated that it was necessary to do this, hated the need for subterfuge. Sneaking about in the middle of the night was not his way. But he'd waited as long as he could. He could delay no longer.

What had he been waiting for?

Jeannie. Part of him had hoped that she would change her mind about helping him.

He bit back the wave of disappointment. Maybe he was a fool, but after Ella's wee hunting adventure and Jeannie's near disastrous attempt to find her, he'd allowed himself to think that she'd softened toward him. That maybe, just maybe, she would confide in him what she knew.

That he wouldn't need to sneak into the laird's solar to look through her dead husband's papers because she would show him herself.

He'd thought she'd been about to offer her help, but something had stopped her. Loyalty to her family? To her husband? Or something else?

He didn't know, but he'd waited as long as he dared. Every day he lingered put him in greater danger of discovery.

And with what had happened this morning, Duncan knew his time was running out. The proverbial dogs had been unleashed and the hunt was on.

He'd sent Conall to Inverness to check for a response to the message he'd sent Lizzie at Dunoon Castle earlier this week, asking for her help and instructing her to leave word for him at an inn. Fortunately, his men were well trained and Conall had smelled the trap. From an alehouse across the way, he'd spotted soldiers beneath the battered plaids meant as a disguise.

Duncan frowned. Someone must have intercepted his note; his sister would never betray him. But who? Colin was the captain of Dunoon Castle. Had his brother sent soldiers after him? After Colin's help in seeing him safely away ten years ago, Duncan didn't want to think it possible. But in the notes he'd received from Lizzie over the years, he'd sensed her growing distance from Colin. It was Jamie she admired, Jamie she trusted, Jamie she begged him to talk to. Though Argyll was usually at Inveraray this time of year, he supposed there was always the possibility it had been his cousin.

Whoever it was, what mattered was that his return was no longer a secret. He was now the hunted. Wherever he went, he would need to be very careful. In the alehouse Conall also had heard that rumors of the Black Highlander's return were spreading across the countryside. Once word reached Aboyne, it wouldn't take the Marchioness long to figure out his identity. Though the way she watched him, he wondered if she already had. He couldn't risk staying around to find out.

They would leave tomorrow.

Originally, he'd planned to go to Freuchie Castle, but now it would be too dangerous. With rumors spreading of his return, he knew the Grant's stronghold would be one of the first places they looked. They would guess Duncan was looking for a way to clear his name. Only Lizzie knew of his connection to Jeannie, but with the Marchioness he couldn't risk staying any longer.

Over the years Lizzie had begged him to go to Jamie and it looked like he had no other choice. But he sure as hell wished he had something more to give his younger brother than his word.

He'd searched the laird's solar the night before he'd fallen ill and found nothing. But the very fact that he'd come across no personal correspondence at all had bothered him. When Jeannie had brought him in here the other day, his eye had caught on an oddity in the wood paneling of the walls near the fireplace—a gap in the carving, almost undetectable. The back of his neck had prickled, wondering if the rumors of a secret chamber were true. Before becoming part of the Gordons' holdings, Aboyne Castle had once been in the possession of the Knights Templar and rumors of a secret "monk's room" had circulated for years.

Carefully, he opened the door and slid into the solar. With no windows the inner-chamber was pitch-black except for the soft orange glowing embers of the fire. It took him a moment to find a candlestick, but with a few puffs of air he managed to light it.

Even with the candle, however, he needed time for the flame to gather strength and his eyes to adjust. When he could see well enough to get around, he headed straight for the incongruity in the wood paneling he'd noticed near the fireplace. His fingers slid over the place where the two pine planks abutted, feeling not only a distinct gap but that one side was raised slightly. He followed the gap around the top and knew it was a hidden panel—in this case a door. There had to be a way to pop it open. Perhaps the fireplace?

He tried pressing the rosettes, the vines, the shells— any part of the relief. Then he methodically started searching for any moving part . . . nothing. He was about to take out his dirk and pry the damned thing open, when he decided to reach around inside the fireplace itself and struck gold. He pulled a small wooden lever and heard the distinct pop.

A small door—about four feet high by three feet wide—opened. Holding the candle into the dark space, he could just make out the stone walls of a narrow passageway. From the dank smell and the layers of cobwebs and dust, it looked like it hadn't been used in some time. Fortunately, however, it was tall enough for him to stand in.

After ducking through the door, he allowed his eyes to adjust for a moment before he carefully stepped forward. He was glad he did, as the floor suddenly became stairs. He realized he must be in a hollow section of the outer wall of the castle. The stairs seemed to go down forever. When he reached the bottom, he realized he was below ground because he was no longer seeing stone under foot, but dirt. The ceiling was also much lower and he was forced to duck as he walked through a tunneled passageway for about ten feet. Suddenly the tunnel gave way to a small chamber—if the old alter table in the center of the room was any indication, he'd found the monk's room.

But if the layer of dust on the table and handful of chairs scattered about the room was any indication, it hadn't been used as such in a very long time. Taking advantage of the two candelabrums that still held candles, he significantly improved the lighting.

Not wasting any time, he started looking in any place that might hold documents. He noticed a drawer in the alter table, and opened it to see it stuffed with papers. His pulse sped up, certain that he was about to find something important. He removed piece after piece of parchment, reading as fast as he could, quickly discarding the more recent documents to get to those from ten years ago. There were correspondence between Francis Gordon and nearly every laird in the Highlands, but nothing to do with him or Glenlivet. A short while later Duncan found himself staring at the wood plank of the bottom of the drawer.

He couldn't believe it. He'd been so certain. Maybe

Jeannie was right. Maybe her husband had nothing to do with what happened to him.

As he replaced the papers where he'd found them and closed the drawer, he felt the distinct prickle of guilt. *Should I have trusted her?*

His instincts rarely failed him. His gaze scanned the room and landed on a trunk, tucked into a small alcove in the wall. Lifting the top, he found himself staring at a thick stack of parchment.

Every nerve ending stood on edge. This was it. He removed the papers and began to read.

Near the bottom he found the missing map, creased where it had been folded in ninths. Parts of the wax still remained where it had been sealed closed, and scribbled on the back in one of the boxes created by the folds was a note:

This came to me unexpectedly. Consider it a betrothal gift.

Grant.

His mind raced, trying to sort out what this meant. *Betrothal gift.* Had Jeannie known about this all along? He'd thought he'd been wrong, that she hadn't betrayed him. He'd wanted to trust her.

A few pages later he found a short correspondence, again from Grant to Francis Gordon, dated three days after the battle, the same day gold had been found in his belongings. It discussed the king's approach and near the end words that sent a chill down his spine: *The rumors you alluded to at our last meeting should give you no cause for concern. I have dealt with the matter and you can be assured that nothing will stand in the way of this betrothal.*

He was "the matter."

Duncan's insides twisted. Vindication was cold comfort.

He felt the subtle shift in air at the same time as a beam of flickering light spilled over his shoulder.

"What are you doing in here?"

He stiffened at the sound of her voice. He'd been so engrossed in what he'd found that he hadn't heard the approaching footsteps. Holding the map in his hand, he slowly turned to face her. Jeannie stood in at the edge of the tunnel, a candlestick in her hand.

Long red curls, blazing fiery gold in the candlelight, tumbled freely around her face and shoulders down the front of her thick velvet dressing gown. God, she was beautiful. So beautiful it hurt to look at her. He hated the doubt that consumed him.

"What are you doing?" she repeated. Her eyes shifted behind him, seeing the papers, and her face filled with horror. "My God, you're spying on me."

Jeannie gazed at him in stunned silence. To think she'd been unable to sleep because she'd been warring with herself about what to do. He'd saved her daughter's life and quite possibly her own. With all he'd done she couldn't stand aside and allow him to hang. But Dougall's future hung in the balance. She'd wanted to find a way to help him and protect her son at the same time.

Now here he was spying on her. He'd found the room. How could she be such a fool to allow herself to think that he'd changed? That he'd trusted her? Betrayal curdled in her stomach.

Her accusation hung in the cold night air. He didn't deny it. Instead he held out a couple of papers in his hand, his eyes once again cold and unyielding. "How do you explain these?"

Not knowing what to expect, her fingers shook as she took the wrinkled parchment in her hand.

Her heart thumped when she realized one of the documents was the map he'd been accused of selling to her father. She flipped it around, read the note, and then the letter.

Saying nothing, she handed it back to him. A cold chill swept across her skin. Dear God, what had her father done? She'd wanted to think he hadn't been involved, that the map had merely fallen into his hands. Had Francis been involved, too? Even posing the question felt disloyal. "This proves nothing."

His eyes flared dangerously. "It proves your husband was involved."

"What it proves is that my father sent the map to my husband. We already knew my father sent it to the Gordons. It changes nothing. Francis had nothing to do with framing you for treason." Did she say it for her benefit or for his? And if Francis had been behind it, did it really change anything? He'd still protected her and her son.

Duncan's eyes scanned her face. "What has he done to deserve such loyalty?"

She heard the raw emotion in his voice and had to turn away, lest she be tempted to tell him. Instead she turned his accusation back at him. "Why are you so quick to implicate Francis? My father even says the map came to him unexpectedly."

"And how did it come to him?"

Her chest pinched. His question shouldn't hurt so much. "I did not give it to him, if that's what you mean."

"Then who did?"

"Was there no one else with opportunity?"

"I removed my sporran twice. Once with you and once when I returned to my tent."

"And you slept alone?"

He gave her a long look. "My father, brother, and a

few of my father's closest clansmen slept in the tent as well."

"Yet you immediately assumed it was me?"

"Given your father's actions that day, you were the most logical. But I did consider other possibilities."

"And?"

He didn't say anything.

"And I am still the most logical?"

He waited for a long moment. "I don't want to think so."

Her gaze met his. He was looking at her as if he wanted to believe her. "What do you think in here?" she asked, pointing to her chest.

He flexed his jaw. "I don't."

Because he thought his heart had led him astray.

When she didn't say anything, he asked, "And what of the letter? Do you still deny your father was involved with what happened to me?"

Her gaze dropped to the floor. "He could have meant anything." It rang false even to her own ears. Her father had been involved. She knew it as well as he did.

He held her gaze for a moment longer, as if waiting for her to reconsider. To make a different choice. To choose him.

God, how she wanted to. Standing this close to him, alone, feeling his strength surround her, she ached to touch him, to take refuge in the force of the connection between them. Every instinct urged to throw herself in his arms, rest her cheek against his shoulder, breathe in the warm, spicy scent of him, and forget her troubles.

He would kiss her.

The memory of his mouth on hers was almost enough to throw caution to the wind. She knew how it would feel. How he would taste. How pleasure would crash over her like a wave, drowning out everything but sensation. Her troubles would fade away like the mist upon the dawn. For a moment. But, like the mist, when darkness came they would return.

She had to think with her head and not with her heart. The fact that he was here spying on her, accusing her, told her that she had been right not to trust him with her secret.

She would not deny that there was something between them. That in the past few weeks she'd felt twinges of her former feelings for him. That she'd found many new things to admire in the man he'd become. That when he'd kissed her she'd felt more passion, more emotion, than she'd felt in ten years. That even now, she feared he would pull her into his arms and she would be lost.

But though the old feelings were still there, so was the distrust. As much as her instincts urged her to throw caution to the wind, experience had taught her control. Duncan deserved to clear his name, she wanted him to, but she had to protect her son.

With what he'd found, Jeannie knew it was going to be harder and harder to do. She felt as if she were living in a house of cards and one by one Duncan was plucking them from under her.

He would never understand why she was doing this. To him, it would seem another betrayal. That she was siding with her father and husband against him even when she suspected their complicity in his downfall. She knew what she was sacrificing. But the thought of her son suffering for her mistakes . . .

If Duncan proved her husband complicit, at best her family would expect recrimination from Argyll. At worst, the king could refuse to grant her son sasine in his property. And if Duncan discovered the truth about Dougall's birth . . .

The scandal, the repercussions could be horrible. She remembered how it had been when her mother had left.

The stares, the whispering, the suddenly quiet rooms when she entered. Being rendered a bastard would be much worse. She couldn't do that to her son.

Her decision must have shown on her face. She could feel Duncan pull away from her. Feel the tenuous connection that they'd established snap. His face shuttered. He took a step back and placed the map and letter in his sporran. "I'll be leaving at daylight." His voice was flat, emotionless.

Jeannie flinched. *Leaving. Again.* Pain wrapped around her like a vise. It shouldn't hurt so much. She'd known it was coming. She'd made her choice, she'd have to live with the consequences. "I see." She gazed up at him, her heart squeezing like a fist. "Where will you go?"

"To my brother. Jamie is Argyll's closest advisor."

She drew back in shock. He must be mad. Argyll's enforcer was the most ruthless pursuer of outlaws in the Highlands. "He will toss you in the nearest dungeon and have a rope around your neck before you can blink."

His eyes darkened. "He is also my brother and right now my best option. My only option. It is not without risk, but it's a chance I'll have to take."

She wanted to argue. But he was right—where else could he turn? He'd come to her and she'd turned him away. But to go to Jamie Campbell . . . right into the heart of the dragon? A dark ball of fear lodged in her chest like a rock—hard and unyielding. Why did the idea of him putting himself in that kind of danger make her stomach churn? Make it feel like the bottom of her heart had just dropped out? "If it is mercy you seek, you will not find it with the enforcer."

"It's not mercy I seek, but justice," he said flatly, his eyes as hard as steel. "My brother will be as good a source as any." The rebuke stung as it was meant to. But how could she tell him that she wanted to help him, she just couldn't. "I will tell him what I've discovered and see if it will be enough to convince my cousin of my innocence."

She looked up at him, her heart in her throat, wishing there was more that she could say. "Will it be enough?"

He shrugged. "It would be better if I had a link to the gold."

"Or to the person who stole the map," she said softly.

He held her gaze. "Aye, or the person who stole the map."

He might not fully trust her, but at least he was willing to acknowledge that it could have been someone else. He'd believed her guilty for a long time—not without reason—and she could not expect him to suddenly change his mind. Even if she wished it.

It seemed neither one of them was willing to take such a leap of faith. Following her heart had almost destroyed her—she could not do that to her son.

But she hoped Jamie Campbell helped—

Dear God. Why hadn't she considered the possibility before? Panic shot through her veins. She tried to keep her voice steady though every nerve ending in her body buzzed with alarm. There was no reason to think . . . the Campbells had many castles. But still her voice squeaked when she asked, "You are going to Ascog Castle?" *Please, please, please say yes.*

He gave her an odd look. "Nay. In my sister's last missive Lizzie mentioned that Jamie and his new wife would be spending the winter at Castleswene."

No! Dread settled over her. Dougall was at Castleswene.

Her heart pounded. Surely he could hear it? The sound seemed to trumpet in her ears. Despite the cold night air, sweat gathered on her brow and hands. *Duncan would see Dougall.* Her fingers crushed the velvet of her dressing gown. Every instinct clamored against the possibility. "I'll go with you," she blurted.

His eyes narrowed, her sudden change of heart having roused his suspicion. "Why would you want to do that?"

She didn't know, but she had to *do* something. She might not be able prevent their paths from crossing, but perhaps she could distract him? All she knew was that she couldn't stay here and just wait for disaster to strike.

She held her expression impassive, panic turning her to ice. "Traveling as one of my guardsmen, you are less likely to be discovered, and," she continued offhandedly, "I should like to see my son. After what you've done for me and Ella, it's the least I can do." That much at least was true.

"And you care whether I am discovered?"

Her eyes locked on his. Her chest rose up to her throat. It hurt that he could think that of her, but what else could he think? "I've never wanted to see you hurt, Duncan," she said quietly. "I'm only trying to protect my family. The same family you seem hell-bent on destroying."

He gave her a long look, his penetrating blue gaze darkening to black. "Is that the real reason you wish to come, Jeannie? To prevent me from sullying your father's and husband's names?"

She flinched. It hadn't been what she was thinking at all, but perhaps it was better if he thought so. Anything to keep him from guessing the truth: that the thought of him within a mile of their son drove nails of terror down her spine.

I would never allow a child of mine to go unclaimed. His words echoed in her head.

She lifted her chin, not denying his accusation. "Believe what you will, but I am going to Castleswene, whether you choose to ride with me or not."

Chapter 16

In the end Duncan had ridden with her, though it had meant a day's delay in leaving in order to organize the traveling party—or funeral party, depending on whether his gamble paid off.

Jeannie's estimation of the situation was accurate. Turning to his brother for help was a risk, but it was one he had to take. He'd run out of options. Jeannie wasn't going to help him; he had to hope that his sister's assessment of their brother proved more accurate than some of the rumors he'd heard. If he was wrong, he was a dead man. He might as well be handing himself over to the executioner.

Though the true danger lay at their journey's end, the journey itself would not be without risk and Jeannie's offer to have him travel as one of her guardsmen would certainly help. But he would not have her in any danger. He picked the men who would accompany them himself, choosing the most skilled warriors, and insisted on doubling the number of guardsmen she initially wanted to take.

Ignorant of the true situation, Ella had wanted to come, but the Highlands in the winter were no place for a child—or anyone for that matter. Fortunately, the lass was still feeling guilty for what had happened to put up much of an argument.

The Marchioness had tried to persuade Jeannie to reconsider, suggesting that it was "hardly the time to go gallivanting across the Highlands on a whim to see her son," but Jeannie had proved surprisingly stubborn.

Duncan bit back a wave of bitterness, knowing the stubbornness was not for his benefit, but for her dead husband's. She wouldn't lift a hand to help him, but she would journey across the Highlands in the bowels of winter harboring the most wanted outlaw in the land to protect her husband's memory.

Something he was reminded of countless times over the next week. Each time their eyes met, jealousy and anger twisted inside him all over again. He'd thought she'd softened. He'd thought she was feeling the same emotions he was. The way she looked at him . . .

As if sensing his thoughts, she turned and met his gaze. The pang of longing in her eyes hit him square in the chest with the force of a smith's hammer. Their eyes held for an instant, before she quickly shifted her gaze, leaving him wondering whether he'd only imagined it.

Why couldn't he just accept that he wanted something that could never be his?

But he did want her—badly—and her close proximity was testing the limits of his endurance. More than once, he wished he'd insisted she stay at Aboyne—not that he was sure she would have listened to him.

Her constant presence chaffed. Together for hours on end like this . . . she was the devil's own temptation. The long days in the saddle, followed by even longer nights, knowing how close she was. Even buried beneath layers of wool, the image of her nakedness was burned on his memory.

He was at the end of his damned rope, pulled taut by jealousy and a cock that stiffened with a sharp gust of wind. He hadn't had a woman in too damned long and his hand provided only temporary satisfaction. He'd considered releasing a bit of his pent-up frustration in the willing arms of a barmaid, but somehow he sensed it would hurt Jeannie and despite his jealousy he couldn't do that—not yet. But to say he was looking forward to the journey's end was putting it mildly.

It wasn't just the close proximity to Jeannie that had him on edge. The trip had been fraught with danger and delay—plagued not only by heavy snowstorms, but also by long detours to avoid brigands and soldiers. If Duncan needed any proof that his cousin had not relented, all he had to do was count the army of soldiers scouring the countryside for him.

When they stopped at night in the drover's inns or ale-houses, the talk was either of the MacGregors or of the hunt for the elusive Black Highlander. To some he was an outlaw, to others a hero who'd taken on almost mythic proportions. It surprised him how many enemies he and his cousin had—many people were rooting for him to escape Argyll's clutches. Though given his cousin's recent debacle with the MacGregor chief's surrender and subsequent execution, perhaps he shouldn't have been.

Duncan kept his head down and did his best to avoid drawing attention to himself, but more than one person had given him a long glance. He could hide his hair beneath a knapscall and avert his eyes, but he could not hide his size.

Then, the night before they'd neared Inveraray, he'd come within a hair's breadth of capture.

They'd just finished eating—a surprisingly delicious beef and barley stew—and were relaxing before the fire with a tankard of ale before bedding down for the night when Leif rushed in. He'd been on watch and had seen the soldiers coming, but too late to make an attempt to avoid them. Leaving suddenly this late at night would have only given the soldiers cause for suspicion. Duncan knew they would have to take their chances.

But he wouldn't go without a fight. He looked at

Conall and Leif, telling them without words to be ready. Their long great swords would be of limited use with the low ceiling, but his dirk would provide all the steel he needed.

He found a seat in the corner and kept his face averted as the dozen or so of Campbell soldiers filed in. He was grateful for the smoky darkness of the old stone and thatch building, though the musky stench left something to be desired. The accommodation at the drover's inn was limited to the chamber above and the floor of the room that they were in, so the new arrivals would be bedding down in the stables. A prospect that did not appeal to the captain—a heavyset, ruddy-faced man with a crooked flat nose that had been smashed more than once, of around Duncan's age and whom he didn't recognize.

If it wasn't for Jeannie sleeping in one of the chambers above, Duncan would have welcomed the excuse to escape to the stables, but he wanted to stay close to her.

The captain took a surly attitude, and started to object loudly. The innkeeper's efforts to appease the man were falling on deaf ears.

"Who are these men?" the captain asked. "We are on the earl's business and have been riding all day. My men are tired."

The innkeeper, a thin, balding man with long wisps of white hair combed across his skull looked around anxiously. "Lady Gordon arrived with her guardsmen some time ago."

Duncan swore under his breath.

"Gordons?" The captain's surliness took on a malicious edge. The Earl of Argyll and the Marquis of Huntly might have nominally made their peace, but Jeannie was right: old hatreds died hard. Their identity had only given the Campbell captain further cause to complain. "Duncan Dubh's conspirators?" The captain's coal-black gaze scanned the room. "Perhaps they are harboring the traitor?"

The Gordon guardsmen started to protest the slur, but before Duncan or anyone could object, Jeannie—who must have heard the noise from her room—intervened.

"Is there a problem, gentlemen?" The soft, dulcet tones stopped the conversation as effectively as a gunshot.

She appeared like something out of a bard's tale. Her auburn hair was brushed to a brilliant sheen and pulled back at the crown with a tiny comb of pearls to tumble down her back. Wearing a pale ivory velvet gown, she looked wholly out of place among the rough soldiers and primitive surroundings, like Persephone descending into Hades.

The Gordon guardsmen, including Duncan, tensed, ready to do whatever it took to protect their lady. His was the first hand to reach for the handle of his dirk but not the last.

They need not have worried. The stunned expressions on the Campbells' faces were almost comical. Jeannie, however, seemed entirely unaware of the effect her ethereal beauty had on the men. She smiled at the captain and batted her long, dark lashes. "Have my men caused you any trouble, sirrah?"

The Campbell captain almost pissed himself in his eagerness to assure her otherwise. With Jeannie's arrival the surly solider suddenly became a caricature of a gallant knight. Jeannie returned his attentions with grace and charm, though Duncan could see that her smile never reached her eyes. Only the slight shake of her hands betrayed her nervousness. She knew well what was at stake.

Thanking the captain for his understanding, she offered to buy a round of ale for him and his men "to help make up for causing them a night in the stables." The captain insisted she join them. Her gaze flickered to Duncan before she agreed, but it didn't make him feel any better.

He seethed in silence as Jeannie flirted with the captain, the soft tinkle of her laugh grating like an iron mace down his spine. The knowledge that she did so only for him did not make it any easier. He gripped his tankard until his knuckles turned white. The damned lecher couldn't seem to take his eyes off her low bodice and the lush round of soft flesh that swelled above it.

When the captain's arm brushed the side of her breast, however, it wasn't only Duncan's knuckles that betrayed his anger. Instinctively, he lunged forward in his seat, stopping himself at the last moment from standing up.

The movement did not go unnoticed. The ale Jeannie had urged the Campbell captain to drink had yet to completely dull his warrior's instincts and he'd sensed the threat.

Duncan felt the other man's piercing scrutiny as he leveled his gaze on him. "You there," he said. "Come forward where I can see you."

Duncan's relaxed position on the bench gave no hint of his sudden alertness. All it would take was one swift movement and his dirk would be buried in the captain's gullet. The lecherous fool deserved as much for daring to touch Jeannie and for the lewd thoughts that were surely running through his mind.

Despite the temptation, Duncan would not act precipitously. Although he was confident he and his men could escape, there was Jeannie to consider. She could be hurt easily in the melee that ensued.

Duncan brought his tankard to his mouth and drew a long gulp. Lazily he put it down on the table, but made no move to do the other man's bidding. The Campbell captain held no authority over him.

The captain's face flushed an angry scarlet as the silent

standoff continued. Eventually he rose from the table and crossed the room to stand before him, only then did Duncan stand. To his credit, the Campbell captain didn't flinch when Duncan rose above him, looming over him by at least half a head.

"I'll have your name."

Duncan was tempted to give it to him. He sensed Leif and Conall's readiness at his side, but he also knew brandishing weapons in a small place like this was dangerous. It wasn't in his nature to back down, but he wouldn't take a chance with Jeannie's safety.

Even if it meant his capture.

The realization shocked the hell out of him. In spite of all that had happened, in spite of her unwillingness to help him, he would give his life for hers without hesitation. He was still grappling with the implications when Jeannie suddenly appeared at the captain's side.

"You'll have to forgive my guardsman, captain. They are a fiercely loyal and protective lot and will follow no one's orders but my own. I'm sure this man meant no disrespect to your authority."

The Campbell captain appeared mollified, not by her words as much as the dazzling smile she bestowed upon him. He puffed up like a bloody peacock. " 'Tis the king's business we are on, searching for the traitor Duncan Dubh. Your man has the look of him."

Duncan tensed, knowing that right now Jeannie was all that stood between him and death.

How far would she go to help him? Would she help him? If she wanted him gone, this was her chance.

"You can't think my guardsman could be *the* infamous Black Highlander?" Jeannie asked incredulously.

Abashed, the captain's flush grew even redder. "He's said to be a man of unusually large height and build with black hair and blue eyes."

It wasn't just the Campbells' eyes that fixed on him.

He could feel the weight of the Gordon guardsmen's gazes as well. Duncan was a common enough name in the Highlands, but the captain had perhaps raised a connection in more than one mind. Even if they suspected, however, Duncan knew they would not defy their mistress.

Jeannie put her hand on the Campbell captain's arm, threw her head back slightly to reveal the long ivory column of her throat, and laughed. Duncan's gut clenched. The entrancing musical sound lulled like a siren's song. And with his stunned, wide eyes, the captain had the look of a man who'd been mired in darkness and then had a blazing torch thrust before him.

"Oh, Captain. If you are going to arrest every tall, black-haired, blue-eyed man in the Highlands you are going to have a very crowded dungeon." She smiled, green eyes twinkling. "Why you are a tall, well-built man yourself." She blushed coyly as if just realizing what she'd said. "Were your eyes blue instead of brilliant green, you might qualify."

Duncan seethed as she took the captain's arm and gently steered him back to the table, leaning forward to give him a healthy view of the deep cleft between her breasts.

Brilliant green? The ridiculous compliments worked. Although Duncan could feel the man's gaze on him a number of times throughout the long evening, the Campbell captain did not trouble him again. How could he, when Jeannie kept him utterly entranced. Duncan had never seen her play the coquette before and watching her do so now set his teeth on edge. That she did so only for his benefit did not ease the storm of dangerous emotions surging inside him.

The gratitude he felt was no match for the jealousy and desire gnashing around inside him like an angry lion. He had to hold himself back from marching over there, tossing her over his shoulder and taking her up-

stairs where they would settle this thing between them
once and for all. Savage and barbarian, perhaps, but
bloody well effective.

He raked his fingers through his hair and poured over
his tankard. How the hell did she manage to do this to
him? He reverted to every primitive instinct when it
came to her.

There was one tense moment when Jeannie excused
herself for bed, but the captain went off willingly to the
stables when she suggested that he join her to break his
fast in the morning. Duncan was saved, however, from en-
during another long meal when the Campbells were called
away early in the morning by rumors of a sighting of the
Black Highlander near Inverness only the night before.

Despite the false rumor, Duncan knew the noose was
tightening.

Thus, it was with some relief when late in the afternoon two days later the formidable towers of
Castleswene appeared in the distance. The thick gray
limestone walls seemed an oasis of stone against the brilliant sapphire seas sparkling beyond. Still, the edginess
did not completely leave him, knowing he could be
riding to his death. Jamie's reception could be far from
cordial and his brother—unlike the Campbell captain—
would not mistake his identity.

The wind intensified as darkness fell as they neared
the coast. Castleswene was one of the oldest stone castles in Scotland, having been built over four hundred
years before to guard the mouth of Loch Sween. What it
lacked in modern conveniences, however, it made up for
in durability and fortitude with ten foot thick walls. The
original four buttressed wall structure had been added
to over the years, including the addition of a squarish
corner hall tower on the east and a round tower with ad-
jacent barrack's on the west. The castle had been given
over to the Campbells for their service and loyalty by

Robert the Bruce after the castle was taken from the MacSweens during the Wars of Independence.

Duncan rode beside Leif and Conall, but kept his eye on Jeannie, half afraid that she might blow away. He knew how weary she must be after the long journey, but she kept her head down against the biting wind and did not break her pace until they rode through the gate and into the courtyard.

They'd said little to each other since the night he'd come so close to capture. He knew he should thank her—she had stood up for him after all and lied about his identity at great risk to herself—but every time he thought about the way she'd flirted with the captain . . . He wasn't ready to be reasonable.

She'd sent a rider ahead, alerting Jamie of their arrival and there was a crowd of men gathered at the bottom of the forestairs to greet them. By now, the sun was a distant memory and only the orange flicker of torchlight broke the black shroud of night. Mist rolled off the water like dragon's breath, filling the night air with black haze.

The man that stepped forward with an unmistakable air of authority was every bit as tall and heavily muscled as Duncan. His features were strong and blunt, his jaw square. Even in the darkness, Duncan could see the hard unyielding glint in his eye. It was a look of absolute command that did not brook defiance.

He shifted his head, giving Duncan a different angle of his profile, and the shadow of a memory hit him. Only then did he realize that the imposing fortress of a man before him was his "little" brother Jamie.

"Lady Gordon," Jamie said, helping her down from her horse. "I was surprised to receive your message."

"I hope we are not intruding," Jeannie said.

Jamie shook his head. "You are always welcome. Your son is anxious to see you and my wife is looking forward to meeting you." A wry smile turned his mouth, the first hint of emotion in the otherwise stony façade. "It was the timing that surprised me. We have only just arrived from Dunoon ourselves—my sister was recently married—and the winter storms have made the roads treacherous."

Lizzie married? Duncan felt a pang in his chest, the knowledge bittersweet. He was happy for his sister, but how he would have liked to see Lizzie wed. But it did explain why she hadn't responded to his missive.

"I'm afraid this visit could not wait," Jeannie said.

Jamie cocked a brow, intrigued. "Oh?"

Though he'd been glued to the conversation taking place before him, Duncan had stayed back in the crowd of guardsmen who'd dismounted behind their lady as she greeted the man known throughout the Highlands as Argyll's Enforcer—the position that would have belonged to him had treachery not driven him from home. Surprisingly, it wasn't resentment Duncan felt but pride.

The time had come. He stepped forward out of the shadows into the circle of light.

He felt his men tense at his side, knowing the moment of truth was upon them. He'd made Conall and Leif promise that if he was taken they would return to the rest of his men in Spain. When Leif reached for the handle of his dirk, Duncan shot him a look of reminder.

Catching the movement, Jamie glanced over Jeannie's shoulder and stilled. He did not need an introduction, recognition flickered in his eyes. The slight tightening around his mouth was the only visible reaction in his otherwise implacable façade. Their eyes met for a long pause. "I see the rumors were true," Jamie said flatly. "I've been looking for you."

Duncan tensed at the ominous greeting, half wondering whether his brother was going to call for the guards. "Happy to see him" would be a stretch.

He was saved from finding out by the sudden appearance of one of the most beautiful creatures he'd ever seen. She rushed down the stairs, cheeks flushed, a wide smile of greeting turning her sensuously curved mouth, and long ebony hair tumbling loose around her shoulders. Unless he was mistaken, this lovely creature was the infamous Caitrina Lamont, now Campbell.

She started to apologize for being late, when she caught one glance at her husband's face and stopped midsentence. She hurried to his side. "What is it? What's wrong?"

As Jamie's face was about as expressive as stone, Duncan wondered at her keen ability to discern her husband's moods. Had his brother made a love match? It seemed out of character for what he remembered of his practical, duty-bound brother. Though he better than anyone should know that love struck blindly—neither beggar nor king immune to its blow.

Jamie didn't answer, but turned his gaze to Duncan. Caitrina followed the direction of his stare and startled with such immediacy that Duncan knew the resemblance between the brothers was more pronounced than he'd realized. She wasn't as proficient as her husband at hiding her emotions and Duncan could see shock register across her exquisite features. He half expected her to cross herself—if Scotland were still Catholic she probably would have.

"Jesu!" she muttered instead. She immediately put her hand on Jamie's arm as if to calm him. Remarkably it seemed to work and some of the tension dissipated.

Caitrina recovered from her shock, recalled her duties as hostess, and turned to Jeannie to offer her a greeting. After exchanging pleasantries, she said, "You must be exhausted after such a long journey. I will have baths set up for your men in the kitchens and one will be sent up for you in the tower. The evening meal will be in about an hour—if you need anything before then you only have to ask. I hope you will be staying with us through Hogmanay?"

Jeannie shook her head. "I must return to Aboyne Castle well before the New Year. If I am not back before Christmas my daughter will never let me hear the end of it. I'm afraid I can only stay a week or so."

Duncan stiffened. He could hear it in her voice: Her duty was done. Getting him here safely had repaid any obligation she might have felt.

Caitrina continued, "May I suggest we reconvene in the Great Hall?" Her gaze slid meaningfully to Duncan. "Your men will join us, of course."

Jeannie nodded. "Thank you for your hospitality."

"It's a sacred obligation in the Highlands, but in this case also a pleasure," Caitrina said with a charming smile. Her smile turned to a warning when she looked at Jamie. "Isn't that so, husband?"

The less than subtle reminder was not missed by his brother. "Aye," he drawled, "even a traitor is safe tonight."

And with that ominous warning, Jeannie was led into the keep by the laird and lady, leaving Duncan behind.

He supposed the initial reunion had gone better than he expected—at least he hadn't been tossed in the nearest dungeon. Whether Jamie's forbearance continued, however, remained to be seen.

He waited, hoping . . .

But Jeannie never looked back. She'd done as she vowed and brought him to his brother's, now it was up to him alone to make his case and keep the rope from his neck. He wished he knew how to keep the ache from his chest.

*　　*　　*

The two men stared at one another across the table, alone, after what seemed an infinitely long meal.

In the bright candlelight of the laird's solar, Duncan could better see why Caitrina Lamont had reacted as she did. Except for hair color and the difference of a handful of years between them, he and Jamie could have been twins. If his identity had been secret before, to anyone who saw them together it wouldn't be any longer. He'd done his best to sit far away from Jamie during the evening meal and keep his face down on his meal, but undoubtedly some of the clansmen had realized who he was, which gave him even less time in which to convince his brother.

Duncan presented his case matter-of-factly, leaving out nothing except for what had happened between him and Jeannie at the inn, though he suspected Jamie guessed the rest. When he was done, he handed him the map and correspondence between Grant and Francis Gordon. Jamie frowned when he read the last.

He didn't say anything right away, taking time to consider all that Duncan had said. Eventually, he gave Duncan a long look and said, "So you believe that someone took the map, gave it to Grant, and then planted the gold later."

"Aye. Grant was anxious to be rid of me and when suspicion turned to me, he found a way to ensure that I was eliminated. It worked. But he had someone to help him. Someone with access to my belongings."

"And what is Lady Gordon's place in all of this? I take it by her presence here that you no longer believe she took the map?"

His gut reaction was to say he trusted her, but he could not rely on his gut. He hedged. "I need to consider all possibilities, including others who had an opportunity."

"You think one of our men might have betrayed you?"

"Aye, though it would help if I knew why someone would want to do so."

"Can you think of anyone who might have a grudge against you?"

A wry smile curved his mouth. "Perhaps one or two."

Jamie nodded, understanding. Their father had given him authority and position. It was easy to see how others might resent that a bastard had been given so much. He'd earned his way, but people saw what they wanted to see.

Jamie rubbed his chin thoughtfully. "Who had something to gain?"

Duncan had been thinking the same thing himself with little success. Once he'd begun to consider that Jeannie had not been involved, it had opened up possibilities Duncan had not fully considered before.

They went through the list of men who Duncan could remember had slept in the tent that night. Of the handful of men besides his father and Colin, one of them had died in a battle a few years back, but there were a few others that Jamie would look into, including a man who Duncan had ordered punished for dallying with a lass when he was supposed to be watching the gate and Padraig—one of his father's most trusted guardsmen—who thought he should have been named captain instead of Duncan.

The one name neither of them wanted to consider was Colin, but it lay between them like a beached whale rotting in the sun.

Duncan sensed that Jamie wasn't telling him something. "Tell me about Colin. Where is he?"

Jamie's mouth fell in a grim line. "Keeping himself out of sight if he's smart." At Duncan's quirked brow, Jamie explained. He told him of the recent troubles with the MacGregors and of the circumstances of his own marriage—how Colin had led a battle against Caitrina's father for harboring the MacGregors, during which her father and brother had been killed and her home destroyed. How Jamie had convinced her to marry him, Duncan couldn't imagine.

"It wasn't easy," Jamie said, guessing his thoughts.

Then Jamie told him what had happened afterward—how the MacGregors had risen in revolt following the execution of their chief, Alasdair MacGregor, and how Colin had exacted revenge for the rape of a Campbell lass by ordering the rape of a MacGregor lass.

Duncan grimaced—not just because he found the act abhorrent, but at the thought of the brother he remembered doing something so dishonorable.

But it was worse: The MacGregor lass was not only Lizzie's sister by marriage, but also the beloved of Niall Lamont—Caitrina's brother. And Niall Lamont was scouring the Highlands for Colin right now with justice on the mind.

The question of how Lizzie had ended up married to a MacGregor would have to wait. "You're sure?" Duncan asked. The rash attack on Caitrina's family sounded like the hot-headed brother he remembered, but to order the rape of an innocent lass . . . 'twas a dark side of Colin that he found difficult to reconcile. "That doesn't sound like Colin."

Jamie nodded. "There's no mistake. You've been gone a long time. We've all changed, including Colin."

"You can't think it was Colin who did this to me?"

Jamie shrugged. "I don't know. I'd like to think not, but I no longer know what he is capable of."

"But it doesn't make sense. Colin is the heir; he had nothing to fear from me."

"He was jealous of you, or rather of father's favoritism toward you."

"Perhaps," Duncan conceded. But could Colin really hate him that much? Would he have put their clan in that kind of danger because of a grudge? It seemed a stretch, despite the dark side of Colin's temperament, of which he'd just learned.

"What about the lass? Wasn't Colin betrothed to Lady Gordon? Yet you had a . . ." Jamie hesitated. "Relationship with her?"

Duncan shook his head. "Colin didn't know about my involvement with Jeannie."

As the hours passed, Duncan grew steadily more hopeful of Jamie's support. Argyll's Enforcer was reputed to be a man of uncompromising adherence to the law. By all rights, Duncan was a convicted traitor and should be arrested on sight. That Jamie was willing to hear him out at all was more than he expected. And Jamie did not appear to be immune to Duncan's claim of innocence. If anything he seemed to believe him.

"But why didn't you stay and defend yourself?" Jamie asked. "When you ran it made you look guilty."

"I'd been tried and convicted. No one would listen to reason. Everyone seemed ready to believe the worst of me—Archie, Colin—and father was dead."

"I would have listened," Jamie said quietly.

Duncan nodded. But they both knew the word of a lad of seven and ten would not have held much weight.

Duncan finally asked the question that had brought him here. "Will it be enough?"

Jamie shook his head, a grim look on his face. "I doubt it. Archie still flies into a rage at the mere mention of your name or of Glenlivet. It will take more than a map and vaguely worded letter to convince him of your innocence."

The surge of hope that had filled his chest deflated. Duncan had his answer. He didn't need any more disappointment, but he couldn't prevent himself from asking, "And what of you, little brother, do you believe me?"

A corner of Jamie's mouth lifted in a half-smile. "It

won't matter if our cousin gets his hands on you, but aye, I do."

But Jamie was wrong. It mattered. Quite a lot in fact. With Jamie and Lizzie's belief in him, maybe Duncan wasn't quite as alone as he'd thought.

But one question haunted him. He'd dreamed of clearing his name and proving his innocence for ten long years, thinking it would be enough. But would it?

On the continent he'd achieved everything he'd ever wanted—satisfied his ambition twice-over. But no win on the battlefield could fill the emptiness inside him. He feared only one person could do that.

Jeannie sat on a boulder in a secluded corner of the courtyard along the south wall, her chin in her hands, content to sit and watch her son for hours. She was so proud of him. Dougall had taken to his training with enthusiasm, blossoming under Jamie Campbell's tutelage. With his shock of dark auburn hair, big blue eyes, and handsome boyish features, he still resembled the child she'd held in her arms more than the man he would become. It had always bothered her son that he was smaller than the other boys of his age—more so if taking into account his real age—but she was happy to see he'd gained confidence in the short time he'd been here.

This was the first opportunity they'd had since she arrived three days ago for her son to demonstrate his progress. Winter had relented long enough for her to sit outside. It was still cold, but the snow that had stormed down upon them for the last week had abated, revealing the sun that had seemed forgotten behind the thick curtain of gray.

Dougall drew back the bow, aimed at the butt about fifty paces away and let the arrow fly.

He let out a whoop and turned to face his mother. "Did you see that?"

Jeannie laughed and clapped her hands. "Of course I saw it. It was a magnificent shot, right in the middle. You've obviously been practicing."

He seemed to grow five inches, his narrow shoulders stretched as wide as they could go. "Every day." He made a face. "It's the only *real* weapon we're allowed to use."

Thank God! The thought of her nine-year-old son with a steel blade in his hands made her stomach queasy. But try explaining that to a boy who'd been waiting to hold a sword in his arms since the age of two when he'd toddled over to Francis and managed to pull his dirk from its scabbard.

Dougall was much like his father: Warfare was in his blood.

Her chest pinched at the thought of Duncan. He'd seemed so distant and angry on their journey, and it had only gotten worse after the incident with the Campbell soldiers at the inn. That had been close. Too close. Her skin still crawled when she thought of that soldier's eyes on her. But the distraction had worked. She pursed her lips. Not that she'd get any thanks from Duncan. Instead of gratitude, he acted as if she were the whore of Babylon. Well, next time, she thought angrily, he could save himself.

Duncan's mood hadn't improved any since their arrival at Castleswene. Despite her efforts to avoid him, he watched her with a hot, predatory intensity that augured a reckoning. From across the hall she would feel his eyes on her, and her body would prickle with awareness. Suddenly self-conscious, her hands would start to flutter, her laugh would turn high-pitched, and her mind would start to wander from her conversations.

He had her completely on edge and unnerved. The way she always was around him. You think she'd be used to it.

She realized Dougall was waiting for her to respond. Ah yes, swords. "I'm sure you will be allowed to practice with steel as soon as the captain determines you are ready."

Hopefully Jamie Campbell would find that day a *very* long time in coming.

"Wooden swords are for bairns. All the other boys use steel." Never one to complain for long, Dougall added, "But the captain says as soon as I can hit the target nine out of ten times from fifty paces with my bow, I can learn to use a gun."

Mother Mary. Jeannie repressed a shiver, while her son's eyes lit up with excitement. She knew there was no fighting it. Guns had steadily made their way into the Highlands over the last generation and anyone who could afford one needed to learn to use it. Even she had learned to use a pistol—with nearly deadly results.

Dougall frowned. "I don't see why I can't start practicing now. In a few more years, no one will be using swords and bows anymore anyway."

"I wouldn't be so sure of that."

Jeannie's heart stopped at the sound of his voice, and then suddenly rushed with panic. She looked over her shoulder to see that Duncan had come up behind her. He was staring at Dougall, an enigmatic expression on his face.

She wanted to jump up and throw her arms around her son, to cover him up, to protect him. But she forced herself to calm. But how could she when everything she'd struggled for hung in the balance?

She'd known this meeting was inevitable—they were bound to cross paths at some point—but the moment she'd been dreading since she first realized it was Duncan who she'd shot was upon her.

Chapter 17

Duncan didn't look at her, but took a few strides toward Dougall. "A warrior must learn to use any weapon at his disposal. But the first weapon of choice to a Highlander will always be his sword." He took a pistol out of his belt and handed it to Dougall. "Take it." Jeannie opened her mouth to object, but he cut her off. "Don't worry, it's not loaded."

Dougall practically tore it from his hands. Duncan stepped back a few paces. "Try to shoot me."

The boy looked at him uncertainly before lifting the pistol and pointing it right at his chest. Duncan moved with the speed of lightning. Before Dougall could cock the gun, he'd reached over his shoulder, pulled the two-handed great sword from its scabbard, and landed a blow on Dougall's arm hard enough to make him drop the gun.

Dougall made a sound of pain and held his upper arm where the blow had landed. Jeannie leaped to her feet, but her son's expression of horror checked her and kept her from running to him. He wasn't hurt and didn't need his mother treating him like a bairn, especially in front of another warrior.

Dougall reached down, picked up the pistol, and handed it back to Duncan. "How'd you do that? I've never seen anyone move so fast."

"Practice," Duncan said, returning the weapon to the belt at his waist. "Hours and hours of practice. Even if you had managed to get the shot off with a gun you have only one chance. My sword will be faster than your ability to reload every time. The Highland sword is a noble weapon, a part of our history. A symbol of our past, passed on through each generation."

Dougall was listening to him with ill-concealed awe, no doubt having heard the speculation of Duncan's true identity. Jeannie just wanted to bury her head in her hands and cry at the look of rapt adulation on his face.

The thought of what might have been tore her apart. The bitterness she'd held for so long resurfaced for a moment before she tamped it down. Blaming Duncan would not help, and one look at the two of them together told her that his lack of trust in her had cost him far more than her broken heart. Being part of Dougall's childhood could never be replaced.

For one moment she wanted to tell him. But she knew she could not take the chance. He would insist on claiming his son and Dougall would be the one to suffer for both their mistakes.

Duncan placed the blade flat in his hands and held it out for Dougall to examine. The enormous sword had to be at least a few inches taller than her son. "This belonged to my father and before that his father—passed down from father to son all the way back to my ancestor who fought alongside King Robert the Bruce at the great Battle of Bannockburn. It's stained with the blood of freedom." There was a deep, reverent tone in his voice that Jeannie had never heard before.

Dougall stared up at him, eyes wide with awe, hesitating.

"Go ahead," Duncan said with a smile. "You can touch it."

Dougall traced his finger over the bone carving. "What are these designs? It looks like a spider web."

"It is," Duncan said, but didn't elaborate. "Maybe

one day, I'll tell you about it. Would you care to hold it?"

Would a wolf like a juicy leg of lamb?

Dougall didn't need to be asked twice. He reached out and grasped the horn handle in his small hands. When Duncan released it, the tip of the blade dropped almost to the ground before Dougall managed to get it under control. He tried to swing it around, but it was clear that the sword was too big for him. His cheeks mottled with color. "I hope my ancestors weren't quite so tall."

He meant it as a joke, but Duncan must have discerned the embarrassment behind the comment. "How old are you?"

Jeannie sucked in her breath so sharply, she was glad Duncan was focused on her son. "I was nine last Michaelmas."

Only when Duncan nodded did she exhale. "I was smaller than the other boys at that age, too," he said.

Her moment of relief vanished in the immediate jump of her pulse. There was no reason for him to make the connection. Her son had her features and the dark auburn hair of—

His uncle. Dear God, why had she never noticed before? Dougall had the same color hair as Jamie Campbell. She felt the panic closing around her and forced herself to breathe evenly. There was no reason for him to suspect, she kept telling herself.

Then why was her heart racing as if she'd just run a marathon?

"You were?" Dougall asked, his eyes narrowing skeptically.

Jeannie didn't blame him. She found it hard to picture Duncan as anything less than the rocky mountain of a man he was now herself.

"Aye. It made me work harder to prove myself. Find your strength here first," he pointed to his head, "and you will know how to use the other when it comes. There are other advantages to being small."

"Like what?"

"I can show you if you'd like."

No! Jeannie thought with barely concealed horror.

"When?" Dougall asked, unable to hide his eagerness. He broke into a wide smile, the dimple in his cheek an exact mirror of the man standing before him. They looked nothing alike, but the signs were there if you looked closed enough. She prayed no one did.

Duncan chuckled. "You'd best check with Jam"—he stopped to correct himself—"the captain first."

"I'll do it right now," Dougall said and ran off toward the keep. Jeannie opened her mouth to stop him, but snapped it shut again, deciding to let her son go. The way Duncan was looking at him made her uneasy. *He couldn't guess.* But saying it over and over did not stop the panic from eating at her.

In Dougall's eagerness, he'd neglected to return the bow and arrows he'd been practicing with to the armory. Jeannie walked toward them, but Duncan cut her off. "You don't want me around your son, why?"

The suspicion in his voice chilled her blood. He was too damned observant. She forced her gaze to his, holding it steady and unflinching. *No reaction.* No emotion. "What good can come of it?" she said brusquely. "In a few days you will go your way and I will go mine. It is better that way."

"A clean break, is that it?"

There was a dark edge to his voice that made the hair on her arms stand up straight. Jeannie didn't think of herself as a coward, but her first instinct was to turn and run. That dangerous energy she'd sensed in him on their journey was right there, just under the surface, threatening to break free.

His fingers wrapped around her wrist and brought

her toward him. "Do you really think that is possible, Jeannie?"

She wrenched her arm away. "Yes." It had to be. But her heart called her a liar. And he knew it.

Just leave me alone! She picked up the bow and quiver and marched toward the armory. The small wooden building was cold and dark and smelled of damp. After replacing the weapons, she turned to leave, but Duncan blocked the door, his tall, well-muscled physique an imposing silhouette.

"I'm not finished."

It had been a mistake to turn her back on him, to let him corner her. She didn't trust herself. His being close like this always made her unable to think straight.

He closed the door behind him, making the room feel even smaller. The musty air of the armory darkened with his masculine scent and the cool air heated with the fire crackling between them. Thin rays of light streamed through the spaces between the wooden planks, providing barely enough light to see. But she could feel him; her senses honed on everything about him. Every inch of his tall, muscled frame. Every strand of silky black hair. Every thin line etched around his mouth.

He was using his size—his masculinity—against her, as if challenging her to ignore the desire taut between them. She wouldn't let him intimidate her. But she felt a flash of sympathy for the men he'd faced on the battlefield.

"Well, I am," Jeannie said, trying to push past him. But he wouldn't let her go, catching her to him, their bodies brushing against one another, yet to her it felt as if she'd just caught fire. "There is nothing more to say." Her voice shook, her nerves fluttering wildly.

"I think there is much more to say." The deep brogue of his voice seeped into her bones. His jaw was pulled taut and his piercing blue eyes seemed to tear away her secrets as he stared down into her face.

Her heart thudded with premonition. She sensed his curiosity about Dougall and knew she had to distract him.

Or maybe that was just her excuse for what she did next.

She did the only thing she could think of when he surrounded her like this. When her body hummed with sensation. When she looked up at his mouth and her body flooded with desire.

She kissed him. Not a chaste touch of the lips, but a full meeting of mouth and body. The rope holding them apart snapped and all the passion building between them over the past weeks exploded into fierce, drowning need.

They tore at one another, trying to get closer, trying to douse the flames that threatened to incinerate them both.

His heat enveloped her. His maleness. The seductive power of his rock-hard body. There was something primitively satisfying about a big, strong man taking you in his arms.

It felt too good. Too right. She wanted to cry out with the perfection of it. This was what she'd been missing, this was what had haunted her for all those years.

His mouth moved over hers, hungrily, passionately. Every touch a brand.

He groaned, opening her lips with his, devouring her with his mouth, with bold thrusts of his tongue, with his hand as he cupped her bottom and brought her against him. His erection rose hard between them, the thick steel column nudged erotically between her legs.

She felt his size. His power.

She quivered—softened—and felt the hot pulse between her legs. Her hips circled, rubbing against him as she tried to ease the restlessness, the anxiousness, the urgency.

All she could think about was him inside her. Filling her. Making her his. Again.

Duncan was out of control. The hunger raged inside him, wild and ravenous. The taste of her passion was like ambrosia to a starving man.

He couldn't get enough. He kissed her harder. Deeper. Drinking her in with his mouth and tongue. With every breath.

He'd forgotten how good she felt in his arms. How soft and feminine. How she smelled like some kind of exotic flower. The silky soft waves of her hair tumbled down her back over his hands. He remembered how it had felt spilled out over his chest and he groaned, sliding his tongue in her mouth with long, insistent strokes.

Her kiss had taken him by surprise, but the flare of passion that burst between them did not. For ten long years this primitive part of him had been repressed, but one taste of her and the chains of civility snapped like a silken thread.

His body raged as hot as a blacksmith's fire. Control a distant memory. The feel of her lush curves pressed against him was too much to take. The sweet feminine surrender an aphrodisiac too powerful to deny.

Every barbarian instinct in him urged to take her. To lift her skirts, thrust inside her, and make her his. Again. But this time he would never let her go.

It had been too damned long. He cupped her bottom and lifted her against him. Blood rushed to his already rock-hard erection, pushing him to near bursting. When she rocked against him, he pulsed and nearly came. Her body told him what she wanted.

Knowing it was going too fast, that he was being too rough, that he could hurt her, he gathered every last ounce of his control and tried to slow down. To tame the wildness.

But she wouldn't let him, moaning her protest. She circled her hips against him insistently, rubbing, and kissing him with all the frenzy he'd tried to temper.

He growled, the last remnants of nobility ripped to shreds. His need for her drove him over the edge.

Breaking the kiss, he trailed his mouth down the long column of her throat. Tasting the warmth of her skin, inhaling her fresh scent. He loosened the ties of her cloak with one hand, and then opened the top buttons of her velvet doublet to kiss her chest. To slide his tongue below her sark along the edge of her stays.

She moaned when his tongue flicked the taut bead of her puckered flesh and gripped his shoulders as if her knees had just given out.

From the edge of consciousness he realized how dangerous this was—they could be discovered at any moment—but that only heightened the excitement, the urgency. Later, there would be time to strip her naked, to lick and suck every juicy inch of her, but right now they were both too ravenous.

His tongue circled the hard peak of her nipple, teasing, as his hand lifted her skirts and bunched them around her hips.

She sucked in her breath at the blast of cold air, but he didn't give her time to protest. His hand found her heat.

His cock jerked at the erotic touch, at the soft silkiness sliding under his fingertips. He stroked her, a long gentle swipe along the slit of her womanhood.

"God, you are so wet," he groaned.

She didn't say anything, but made a soft sound in her throat and her body quivered.

He felt the dampness spread between her legs and couldn't wait for her to come. For her body to contract

and shudder around him, for her to cry out with pleasure as she shattered.

He slid his finger inside her. A slow thrust first and
then more insistently. Circling, teasing. Rubbing that
sensitive little spot until her breath hitched in short, demanding gasps.

He loosed the ties of his breeches. His erection sprang
free, the cold air a relief to his red-hot skin. A drop of
anticipation glistened on the tip. Hooking one shapely
leg over his arm, he bent his knees a little to find the
angle . . .

His stomach muscles clenched as the heavy head of
his cock nudged damp swollen flesh. The muscles in his
neck and shoulders tightened, straining against the urge
to drive up high inside her.

He held her there just like that—flesh to flesh—and
forced her to look at him. To see him. To know that it
was he who was pleasuring her. That it was he who
could make her feel like this. That she belonged to him.

The mindless surrender of her body was not enough.

Her gaze met his, half-lidded, soft and hazy. Her
beautiful features slack with desire. "Duncan," she said,
her voice pleading.

A pure shot of masculine satisfaction surged through
him, but he needed more. He wanted all of her—body,
heart, and soul. The need to hear her say it outweighed
even the lust raging inside him. "Tell me you want this,
Jeannie. Tell me you want me." *Only me.*

Her eyes widened, she appeared startled as if out of a
dream. "I—"

She hesitated.

His body chilled, sensing the words before she spoke.
The bite of disappointment snapped down on his chest
like a spiked steel trap.

*   *   *

Jeannie fought to hold on to the passionate haze that dulled her senses—the shimmery effervescent wave, the tingling, the frantic quickening of her pulse—but it slipped through her fingers like water through a sieve. The moment was gone and unwanted lucidity forged a path of cool rationality in her mind.

Her body throbbed with complaint at the sharp curtailment of pleasure. It felt as if she'd been brought to the very edge of paradise only to be shoved forcefully back to earth.

An irrational burst of anger hit her. Why did he have to do this? Why did he have to force her to acknowledge what was happening? Why couldn't they just forget about everything else and let desire take over?

She stilled. For the same reasons she couldn't just say, "Yes, I want this. Yes, I want you," and give over to the pleasure he wrought within her.

They'd both changed. They were no longer careless youths to be swept away by passion. She better than anyone knew the consequences of that.

She pushed herself away from him, horrified by the madness that had come over her. By what she'd nearly done. "I'm sorry. I . . . I can't do this."

His face was a mask of pained restraint, every muscle tight. His eyes pinned her, biting into her with a searing intensity. "Why?"

The dull hollowness of his voice made her chest pang. She'd hurt him.

Tears burned behind her eyes. She looked up at him, trying to find the words to explain. "I don't know."

"You want me."

She didn't bother trying to deny it. How could she when her body still wept and trembled from his touch. She'd always wanted him—only him.

"But something is holding you back," he said. He caught her arm and held her to him, his face dangerously close. "What are you hiding from me, Jeannie? Does it have something to do with your husband?" She didn't say anything, fear clamping around her throat. "With your son?"

He was holding her so close, looking into her eyes, and he saw it. The flare of panic in her gaze she could not hide.

"It's your son you are protecting." His eyes searched her face. "Why?"

Jeannie's heart raced as she wrestled with something to say, with some kind of explanation to steer him from the truth. Everything she'd fought so hard to protect seemed poised on the very precipice of disaster. She was scared to open her mouth, fearing the truth would somehow slip out.

"How could I possibly hurt your son?"

Anger welled up inside her. Though she'd gone to every effort to prevent him from doing so, part of her wanted him to guess. His genuine perplexity, his blindness, grated, shattering her already frayed emotions. Tears broke free as the pressure of all she'd been keeping inside finally burst.

"Don't you see that your very presence here is a threat to him? If you implicate my husband in this plot against you who do you think will take the blame? You can destroy my son's future, everything I've fought so hard to protect," she lashed out, coming dangerously close to the truth, but for the moment not caring.

Her accusation took him aback. "He's a child."

She scoffed. "Do you think that will matter to your cousin or the king?"

His silence said it all. Giving voice to her fears was a relief, she realized. It hadn't been the entire truth, but enough of it to feel as if a weight had been lifted.

After a moment, he dragged his hands through his hair and said, "Why didn't you tell me this before?"

"Would it have mattered? Should I have trusted you?" She challenged. "Did you trust me?"

Their eyes met, each knowing the answer.

"And this is why you've refused to help me? To protect your son?"

She sensed the urgency in his voice, as if her answer was somehow very important to him. "What should I have done? Help you destroy him?"

"I would never allow that to happen, Jeannie," he said, tilting her chin and forcing her gaze to his. For a moment his expression was devoid of the anger that had hardened it only moments ago—almost tender. "The boy carries no blame for what happened. I swear to you he will not be harmed."

"How can you make such a promise?"

"I can do nothing about your father, but I will ensure that your husband's name is kept out of this."

She sucked in her breath. Her eyes scanned his face, seeing only cold resolve. "You would do this for me?"

He nodded. "Aye. You have my word."

She wanted to believe him. Looking at him it was hard not to. In his fine black leather and metal-studded garb, he looked every inch the fierce, indestructible warrior—the black knight of legend ready to defeat all who challenged him. His head nearly touched the ceiling, his shoulders were as wide as the door, his chest as hard as a shield—every inch of him honed to a steely weapon of war. But it was more than his size and clothing. The stamp of authority was plain not just on his proud, noble features, but engrained in every movement, even in the way he spoke. He seemed more a chief than an outlaw.

But he *was* an outlaw—a dead man if his cousin's soldiers caught up with him. How could he protect her son?

Yet, all her instincts cried out to throw herself into his

arms, close her eyes, and give over to the powerful force that drew them together. It seemed so easy, but she'd learned to be wary of easy.

It wasn't just him she didn't know if she could trust, she realized; it was herself. When it came to him, her judgment had never been sound.

Her uncertainty must have shown on her face. His hand fell from her face and he took a step back away from her. "I can't undo the past, Jeannie. Nor can I force you to move beyond it. I wronged you. I should have listened to you and given you a chance to explain. But I'm not the same man now as I was then." He gave her a long penetrating look. "God knows I tried, but it seems I couldn't forget you. You are in my blood—in my bones. I want to see if there is anything left to salvage between us, but I cannot do it alone. I can't force you to trust me, but neither will I have half of you."

The cold resolve in his voice left her no doubt he meant what he said. Duncan had thrown down the gauntlet at her feet: all or nothing. Wasn't that always how it had been between them?

Never far from her mind was the knowledge that he could be taken at any time. The close call at the inn came back to her in full force. What if she decided and it was too late?

Before she could respond he turned and left, never once looking back. She stared at the door, the panic that she'd felt moments ago welling up to claim her heart. Her heart that shouldn't care. But the armor of the past had rusted away, leaving her unprotected and vulnerable to him.

Don't go. The voice of the girl she'd been escaped before the resolve of the woman she'd become could quiet it.

Would it ever be completely quiet?

She feared she knew the answer.

* * *

Duncan left the armory, cursing stubborn women. Jeannie was his, damn it. Couldn't she feel it?

He refrained from slamming the door and venting some of his considerable frustration, and clenched his fists at his side instead.

The disappointment that had knifed through his chest at her refusal to acknowledge what was between them had done nothing to take the edge off the unspent lust that still coiled through his veins. He felt like an angry tiger in a cage and heaven help anyone who got in his way right now.

She sure as hell better make up her mind soon, because time was the one thing he did not have.

There were a few people milling about the courtyard, but they took one look at his face and turned the other way. He glanced in the direction of the practice area, near the place where he'd first seen Jeannie. He'd hoped a good sword fight would help ease his tension, but had been disappointed to discover that the guardsmen had yet to return from their morning ride. Jamie had thought it better that Duncan stay within the walls of the castle until they determined how to proceed. Having already come across more than one party of soldiers looking for him on his way south, Duncan was inclined to agree and not press his luck.

He crossed the yard, heading toward the keep, half expecting the lad to come bounding down the stairs and intercept him.

It was the boy she was protecting—not her husband. Why hadn't he realized it before? It put an entirely new perspective on her refusal to help him—one not burdened by jealousy. But it infuriated him to think that she didn't trust him to protect her son.

Duncan almost regretted his offer to show the lad some of the hand-to-hand combat moves he'd learned as a lad . . . almost. But he'd heard the shame in the boy's voice and it had struck a chord. He remembered only too well what it was like to be picked on. His bastardy had made him a target, and when he was Dougall's age, his size had made him an easy one. Fortunately for him, he'd grown quickly and significantly in adolescence.

But even if the lad stayed on the small side, it didn't mean he couldn't distinguish himself as a warrior. Duncan felt a strange urge to help him, but knew it wasn't his place. Jamie would see to his training.

Still, like Ella, something about the lad unsettled him—even more so. He'd felt that same heart-squeezing pain upon seeing him, and a fleeting moment of wistfulness, knowing that had circumstances been different they could have been his. With a certain amount of wishful thinking, he'd studied the boy's face, searching for a connection and seeing only the stamp of Jeannie's features. From what he remembered of John Grant, Jeannie's brother, the boy looked quite a bit like him.

Duncan frowned. Except for the hair color. Like Francis Gordon, John Grant had blond hair. But then she'd kissed him and he'd forgotten everything but the passionate woman in his arms. Had that been her intention? Had she been trying to distract him?

He was halfway up the stairs when a woman cried out his name, "Duncan!"

His heart stopped. For a moment he thought it was Jeannie. But even before he turned and set eyes on the tiny, wisp of a woman who'd just come storming through the gate he knew it wasn't her. Disappointment cut through him.

The woman didn't bother waiting for anyone to help her down, much to the outrage of the man beside her— if the black expression on his face was any indication— but jumped off her horse and started running toward him.

The hood covering her hair flew back, revealing a crown of white-blond hair.

"Duncan," she cried again, tears streaming down her cheeks.

Blue eyes met blue and recognition hit. A hot wave of emotion rose up to grab him by the throat. There was only one person who could be this happy to see him. "Lizzie," he choked out and opened his arms.

Chapter 18

❖

Jeannie knew she should leave. She should take Dougall and return to Aboyne Castle for the Christmas and Hogmany celebration while Duncan was occupied clearing his name, before his curiosity could take hold about her son.

If she were smart, she would do just that. But she'd never been smart when it came to Duncan Campbell. Torn between wanting to run after him and wanting to run away, Jeannie had just turned the corner around the practice yard on her way back to the keep when she heard the woman's cry.

She froze midstep, seeing a tiny woman catapult herself into Duncan's arms.

Her heart tumbled to her feet. The spur of jealousy was as strong as it was unreasonable. For a moment she couldn't breathe, transfixed by the sight of another woman in his arms. In her stupor, it took Jeannie longer to realize who it was. It wasn't until the woman released her hands from around Duncan's neck and pulled back to hold his face that Jeannie recognized Elizabeth Campbell—his sister.

The sigh of relief that poured through her was telling. Slowly, the tension eased from her neck and shoulders. After taking a moment to compose herself, Jeannie walked toward the keep, staying back so as to not interrupt the poignant reunion taking place between the siblings.

Rarely did Duncan display emotions, but his love for his sister was plain on his face.

Once he looked at me like that.

Guilt pricked at her. This is the welcome he'd deserved, she realized. The difference between Jeannie's greeting (with a pistol!) and that of his sister's couldn't be more glaring. In spite of his betrayal of her, it did not change the fact that Duncan had been forced from his family, his home, his country, for a crime he didn't commit. Likely because of her father and possibly her husband. And the only person who'd been glad to see him—who'd welcomed him back—was his sister. By contrast, Jeannie had tried to stop him every step of the way.

At first it had been warranted. But what of now? Could she trust him?

"You're back," Elizabeth said, just loud enough for Jeannie to make out her words. "I almost gave up hope. Oh, Duncan, it's been so long, I thought I would never see you again."

She buried her head in his shoulder and started sobbing even harder. Duncan stroked her head and soothed her with words Jeannie could not make out.

Quite a crowd had gathered at the commotion caused by the new arrivals. Jamie and Caitrina had appeared at the top of the stairs, and a tall, powerfully built man with a black look on his face had quickly dismounted from his horse and followed Elizabeth to hover protectively a few stairs below.

With his dark hair, brilliant green eyes, and finely chiseled features, he was a strikingly handsome man, though it had taken Jeannie a moment to realize it, probably because of the fearsome expression on his face.

"Lizzie, you're overwrought," the man said. "It's not good for you or the—"

"I'm fine!" Lizzie said, giving him an exasperated

look over her shoulder. "As I've told you a hundred times in the last hour, I'm fine. I'm pregnant, not made of glass."

The man's eyes narrowed dangerously. "Lizzie . . ."

"You're having a babe?" Duncan asked, holding her back to look in her face.

Elizabeth nodded, a shy smile playing upon her mouth.

"I'm happy for you, lass," Duncan said. "Congratulations."

The other man moved up behind Lizzie, sliding his hand around her waist. "She *insisted* on coming when she received the hench"—he stopped at the sharp glance from his wife and cleared his throat—"Campbell's note that you'd arrived." It was clear from his disapproving tone that he'd tried to convince her otherwise. "Despite the less than ideal travel conditions."

Elizabeth rolled her eyes and turned back to her brother. "This overbearing, aggravating man is my husband, Patrick MacGreg—"

"Murray," he cut her off with a nod to remind her of their audience.

Jeannie had moved closer to hear the conversation and gasped when she realized what Elizabeth had been about to say. Elizabeth *Campbell* had married a *MacGregor*?

Jeannie eyed Jamie Campbell, Argyll's Enforcer, waiting for the call to arrest the outlaw. Though he didn't appear happy to see the man, he didn't seem inclined to toss him in the dungeon either. But she didn't miss Caitrina's restraining hold on his arm.

Elizabeth had heard the sound Jeannie made and her gaze shot to her. They stared at one another in silence. Though they'd crossed paths a number of times at court since that day when Jeannie had arrived at Castleswene looking for Duncan, until now they'd avoided speaking to one another.

Except for the initial surprise, Elizabeth's expression gave no hint of her thoughts at finding Jeannie here with her brother. She gave a short nod of her head. "Lady Gordon."

Jeannie returned the curt gesture. "Lady Murray."

Elizabeth's husband had had enough. He took his wife's arms and tucked it firmly in his. "Why don't we finish this inside, where you can rest?" The suggestion came out as more of a growled order.

When Elizabeth started to protest, her husband bent and whispered something in her ear. Her eyes widened in outrage, but MacGregor appeared unmoved. He gave her a look as if to say "try me." MacGregors were a wild, fearsome lot and Patrick gave proof to the reputation.

But Jeannie fought back a smile. Unless she'd missed her mark, Patrick MacGregor/Murray had just threatened to carry his wife in whether she wanted to go or not.

With her solemn expression, Jeannie would have said Elizabeth followed her husband meekly up the stairs, but she'd caught the glint in Elizabeth's eye that promised retribution.

Jeannie hung back as the crowd dispersed and Duncan followed his sister and her husband up the stairs. Her chest squeezed with longing that she couldn't deny. She wanted to go, but it wasn't her place. He had his family; he didn't need her.

When he reached the top of the stairs, he turned. Embarrassed to be caught staring, she quickly looked away, but he called down to her. "Will you join us?"

Her heart pounded. "I wasn't sure . . ."

His gaze held hers. "You're a part of this," he paused,

"if you want to be." Not waiting for her response, he turned on his heel and disappeared into the keep.

Jeannie watched him go, knowing he was forcing her to make a choice, which meant she had to make a decision.

Duncan kept his eye on the door to the laird's solar. The adjoining great hall had already started to fill with clansmen awaiting the midday meal and the solar would enable them a small measure of privacy.

The minutes ticked by. He sat stiffly on the bench, his neck and shoulder muscles tight with tension. He didn't expect her to come.

It doesn't matter.

But when the door opened a moment later, he knew that it did.

Her gaze went immediately to his. Seeing the uncertainty on her face, he gave her a reassuring nod. There was still much to be said, but she was here, and for now it was enough.

Lizzie lifted her brow at him in question, but he ignored it and offered Jeannie a seat on the bench beside him.

Her very presence at his side gave him an unexpected charge. He felt stronger. Lighter. And for the first time since he'd arrived back in Scotland bolstered by hope. Hope that not even Lizzie's next words could dampen.

"Archie has men looking for you everywhere since he heard the rumors of your return." Her gaze flickered to Jeannie. "Please tell me you've found something to prove your innocence."

Duncan shook his head. "Not yet."

He repeated what he'd told Jamie, leaving out the part about meeting Jeannie at the alehouse. When the time came, Jamie removed the map and letter from his sporran and handed it to Lizzie who read it and passed it around to the others. Jeannie shook her head when it came to her—she knew what it said.

He could feel the weight of the question that was surely on everyone's mind: With her father and husband implicated, what was Jeannie's role in the plot against him? Instinctively, he moved closer to her, angling his shoulders like a shield, as if by blocking her from view he could protect her.

Not knowing the history between them, Lizzie's husband Patrick asked, "But how did Grant get the map? You said you had it in your sporran."

Jeannie stiffened at his side, her fingers gripped the edge of the bench. He covered her hand with his, and for once, she didn't jerk it away. "Not the whole time. I removed my sporran when I returned to my tent the night before the battle."

He was facing his sister and brother, but he could feel the weight of Jeannie's gaze on his profile.

Lizzie and Jamie were watching him with equal scrutiny. It was his brother who spoke first. "No one else could have taken it?"

Jeannie froze, her hand like ice under his. They both knew what his brother was asking: Did he still believe Jeannie had betrayed him?

Nothing had changed. He had no proof with which to disprove his original assessment. No proof but the certainty in his heart.

Jeannie hadn't betrayed him. He'd stake his life on it, which, in a way, he supposed he was.

Ten years ago he hadn't been able to give her the blind faith and loyalty that she deserved. He'd been too young, too unsure of himself, too caught up in ambition and the need to erase the stain of his birth. But he was no longer that unsure lad. He'd achieved everything he'd ever dreamed of—wealth, reputation, infamy—but had lost the one person that had made any of it matter.

It wasn't rational, but what was between he and Jeannie had never been so. It had been passionate and undeniable. A connection so strong he'd never felt anything close to it since.

He loved her and always would. The realization didn't surprise him as much as it should. She'd always been a part of him, even for the years they'd been apart. If there was a small chance for them, it was worth the risk.

He didn't hesitate, meeting Jamie's gaze full force. "Nay. No one else could have taken it."

He heard Jeannie's sharp intake of breath as shock rippled through her, but he didn't trust himself to look at her. Not with a room full of people. Not when admitting that he'd been wrong meant he'd taken her innocence, promised to marry her, and deserted her. The girl who'd lost her mother and who'd looked to him as a rock to hold on to. God, what had he done?

Lizzie turned to Jamie. "Surely you can do something? Archie will listen to you."

"I'll try," Jamie said. "But I doubt it will do any good. You know how stubborn our cousin can be. He's believed Duncan guilty for ten years. It will take more than a map and a vaguely worded letter to convince him otherwise."

Duncan sensed his sister's rising agitation. "But we have to do something." Her voice held a frantic edge. Lizzie turned to Duncan. "If you don't find something to prove your innocence before Archie's men catch up with you . . ."

"Don't worry, Lizzie. I don't intend to make it easy on them," he said.

Her husband put a hand on her arm to try to calm her down. "From what I hear your brother can take care of himself. He can take refuge in the hills with Niall Lamont if need be. Getting yourself upset won't help him."

Lizzie nodded and took a deep breath. "I'm sorry. You're right. We should focus on finding proof that will convince our cousin. What of the men in the tent that night," Lizzie said. "Who would have a reason to see you or the Campbells harmed?"

"And who would my father know to approach?"

Duncan turned to meet Jeannie's gaze, surprised by the observation. He wasn't the only one. Her cheeks heated as Jeannie suddenly found herself the center of attention.

She was right. Grant must have been fairly certain that the person he convinced to steal the map would do so.

"Who was in the tent that night?" Patrick asked.

Duncan repeated the names he'd told Jamie, but when he got to Colin, Patrick and Caitrina reacted instantly. Both stiffened, but where Caitrina's gaze flashed with pain, MacGregor's turned ice cold and deadly. Having learned of Colin's role in both of their tragedies, Duncan could understand why.

Lizzie paled, putting her hand on her husband's arm in a silent offer of comfort. MacGregor cooled a bit, but his eyes still burned with hatred. "If Auchinbreck was there," he said. "You can be damn sure he had something to do with it."

Caitrina looked as if she wanted to add to his assessment, but seemed to be biting her tongue.

"Jamie told me what happened," Duncan said to them both.

"Colin? What has he done?" Jeannie asked, surprised.

Duncan shook his head and murmured that he would explain later. To Patrick he said, "I know you've reason to distrust my brother, but there are others with better motives."

"Auchinbreck doesn't need a motive, only an opportunity," Patrick said through clenched teeth.

Duncan looked at Jamie and Elizabeth, both of whom looked as uncomfortable as he felt. None of them wanted to think that Colin could be responsible.

"I was no threat to him," Duncan said. "Colin had everything he could possibly want. If anyone should have been envious it was me. I was the first born, but he was the heir." Duncan glanced at Jeannie, his throat suddenly hoarse as the memories flooded him. "He was the one betrothed to the woman I wanted to marry." He turned back to the others, one corner of his mouth lifted in a wry smile. "Not that I can blame him for that. No one knew." Catching Lizzie's frown, he corrected himself. "Except Lizzie and my father when I returned from court."

Lizzie's frown turned to a grimace. "Colin *did* know."

"After I left," Duncan said.

Lizzie shook her head. "No, he must have known before. When Jean—Lady Gordon—had come to Castleswene looking for you, Colin was furious. He said you should have gotten over your attachment to her after his betrothal. That you'd been a fool to think you could ever marry her."

Duncan didn't know what to make of Lizzie's pronouncement. Had his brother purposefully engineered a betrothal with Jeannie to hurt him or had he, like Duncan, simply fallen for the same woman? Colin's recent efforts to secure another betrothal seemed to suggest the latter.

Jamie seemed to have reached a similar conclusion. "Colin's actions have been reprehensible, but he's always been loyal to the clan and to our cousin. It's hard to believe he would turn traitor over jealousy. Our father died at that battle."

"But what if he didn't know what my father intended?" Jeannie posited.

"She's right," Lizzie said. "We've all been assuming that whoever took the map was conspiring with Grant to betray the Campbells, but what if it was simply to discredit you? What if Grant's defection to the other side was just as much a surprise to him as it was to everyone else?"

Jeannie tried to slip her hand away, but Duncan held firm. Her father's actions hadn't been a surprise to everyone—not to her at least—but he found he no longer blamed her for not telling him. He'd been too angry to realize the difficulty of the position she'd been in—choosing between him and her father. It was a choice no one should have to make. She'd done what she could, he realized. At great risk to herself.

Something about Lizzie's words rang true. "And then the gold was planted afterward to cover it up." Aye, it was possible. And rash enough to sound like something Colin would do.

But still he wasn't convinced.

Something was missing—a piece of the puzzle that would make it all fit into place.

In any event, right now all they had was conjecture, which wasn't enough to keep him from the hangman's noose.

"Where is Colin?" Duncan asked Lizzie.

It was her husband who answered. "If he's smart not within a hundred miles of Niall Lamont."

Lizzie shot him a look and then glanced back at Duncan. "Last I heard, he had returned to Dunoon."

Damn.

"What is it?" Lizzie asked, seeing his expression.

"That's where I sent your letter—the letter intercepted by the person who sent troops to wait for my man in Inverness."

*   *   *

Jeannie lay in bed on her side, watching the candle flicker and melt into a soft blob of gooey wax. Her ears pricked at any sound in the darkness, but the silence of the night surrounded her like a tomb. Shadows flickered across the plastered walls, cast from the bedposts and ambry—not from a man.

She'd retired hours ago. After the troubling conversation in the solar, the midday meal had been a somber affair. Duncan had disappeared with his brother afterward, and when she'd seen him again at the evening meal he'd barely spoken to her.

Had she been wrong? When he'd asked her to come to the laird's solar with his family, and made his unexpected declaration as to her innocence in taking the map, she'd thought—

She startled. Though all her senses had been honed to the door, the sound of it opening and then quickly closing shut still made her heart jump and nerve endings flare.

She sat up, instinctively tugging the bedsheets up to her neck, her breath stuck high in her throat.

All but his form was hidden in the darkness, but she didn't need light to know it was Duncan.

He'd come.

He stood dangerously still, looming in the shadows like a lion ready to pounce. Tension radiated from his powerful body, his muscles flared. He'd changed from his battle garb to the simple shirt and belted plaid of the Highlander, but if anything it only served to make him appear more overwhelming. More daunting.

"Tell me to leave, Jeannie." The husky lilt of his voice wrapped around her in a dark sensual vise. She could hear the tightness underneath—the strain of a man held by a very taut string.

He'd come to her like this before. All those years ago.

But the danger that emanated from him now was not from anger and betrayal; it was fueled by desire.

She shivered. Not from fear, but from anticipation. Her body flushed with awareness: her skin prickled, her nipples beaded, and the tiny little hairs on her arms stood on edge. But mostly, the soft juncture between her thighs quivered. The heavy warmth of desire spread through her body. It was a woman's desire. Desire forged in the fires of heartbreak and disappointment and made stronger by experience.

She could no more tell him to leave than she could deny her heart a beat. She'd wanted him from the first moment she'd ever seen him, and that wanting had never stopped but only grown more intense with the passing of years.

This moment had been inevitable since the first moment he'd set foot on Scottish soil. And she no longer wanted to deny it.

"Tell me," he repeated, his voice angrier . . . tighter . . . harder.

She shook her head, her heart beating wildly. "No. I don't want you to leave."

He swore and crossed the distance between them in a few long strides. He stood at the edge of the bed and stared down at her. In the candlelight, she could see the fierceness of his need for her drawn harshly in the lines of his handsome face. A sharp feminine thrill shot through her. He was magnificent . . . and all hers.

For a moment she thought he'd reach out, pluck her from the bed and ravish her senseless. She could tell he wanted to, but he held his arms tightly at his side, fists clenched, his control strained to the breaking point.

Piercing blue eyes bored into her. "You know what you are saying, Jeannie?"

She nodded, wide eyed. She did. It terrified her, but

she knew exactly what she was doing. He trusted her, and she would have to try to do the same.

The sheet had slipped to below her breasts. His gaze heated, lingering on her puckered nipples visible through the thin cotton of her sark. A hot flush spread across her skin as she recalled the feel of his mouth enveloping her, sucking her.

"God knows I want your body, but it's not enough. I need all of you. Can you give me your trust and forgive me for not giving you the same?" He paused, the stark pain of regret burning in his eyes. "God, Jeannie, can you ever forgive me for leaving you?"

The thick emotion in his voice snapped the last thread of doubt—he cared, then and now. They'd both made mistakes and had paid for them in different ways. But what he was offering her was something she never thought they'd have: a chance to try again.

She remembered the loneliness, emptiness, and anguish she'd felt when he'd left her all those years ago. He'd broken her heart and nearly destroyed her. The stakes had grown even higher now: his life . . . their son. But losing him again would be much worse.

It had been so long since she'd taken a chance, since she'd listened to that little voice at the back of her head, but he was worth the risk. He always had been. For so long she'd thought of what had happened with Duncan as a mistake; it was a shock to realize she wouldn't change it, not if it meant never having loved him.

Heart pounding with the significance of what she was about to do, she slid her legs under her bottom, lifted up on her knees to face him, and wrapped her arms around his neck.

He made a harsh sound at the contact—halfway between a groan of pain and one of pleasure. His body was as hard as granite, his muscles coiled under her fingertips like thick steel ropes. She pressed her body against his, savoring the strength and solidness of his broad chest. Their hearts drummed in unison. He was so warm, heat radiated through the fine linen of his shirt and plaid. She could smell the peat from the fires in the wool and the faint, intoxicating scent of whisky on his breath.

She moved her mouth to his ear, inhaling the dark spicy scent. She wanted to devour every inch of him with her mouth and tongue. "Make me forget, Duncan," she whispered.

The primitive challenge of her words broke the last link in the steel chain of his control. With a fierce growl he pulled her into his arms and covered her mouth with his in a deep, primal kiss. It was a kiss of possession. Of hunger. Of need.

A kiss to make her forget.

It was as if all the years had disappeared and once again everything was right. More than right . . . it was perfect. For when he was holding her like this, kissing her like this, the world disappeared and there was only them. Unburdened by duty and clan loyalties, by treason and by secrets.

His mouth moved over hers—tasting, devouring. She felt the raw urgency as her own and returned it full force, melting against him and opening her mouth to his tongue.

Youthful fumblings? It hadn't been true then, and such a claim was laughable now. He knew exactly what to do to bring her pleasure. Every caress of his lips, every deft stroke of his tongue was calculated with deliberate precision to arouse.

He cupped her bottom tight against him with one big hand as the other plunged through her hair to cradle the back of her head. She melted against him, drowning in heat and passion. She could feel the warm press of his fingers on her scalp, bringing her even closer. The rough stubble of his beard scratched the sensitive skin around her mouth, as he kissed her deeper and deeper, leaving no part of her unclaimed.

Her body shuddered at every long, carnal thrust of his tongue, as he mimicked the rhythm of the pleasure he would give her. Molded against him, with only a few thin layers of clothing between them, she could feel the source of that pleasure hard against her stomach.

It had been too long. Desire came over her in a big, crushing wave. The strength of it, the force of it, surprised her. That part of her life had been quiet for so long, she'd forgotten how it felt when desire—passion— took hold and swept away everything else in its path. But her body remembered the sensations. The rasp of his beard on her skin, the pressure of his hands on her breast, the heat of his mouth on her nipple, the dark, spicy taste of his kiss, the weight of his body on top of her. The fullness of him inside her.

Her body flooded with those memories.

She didn't want to think, she only wanted to feel— him, inside her, filling her. Her hips circled against him, rubbing the thick column of his manhood. He felt so good. Too good. She couldn't wait . . .

He broke the kiss with a groan, his breath coming hard and fast; his eyes burning hot with desire. "Not so fast, my sweet. Not this time."

Jeannie wanted to cry out in protest, but she could see the resolve tight on his face and knew he would not be dissuaded.

She knew what he was doing, forcing her to acknowledge what was between them every step of the way. No longer would she be able to hide behind blind passion. He wanted to strip her bare—not just her clothes, but her soul. The thought of what he could reveal terrified her, but she was beyond caution.

Without another word, he started to remove his clothes, holding her gaze to his the entire time.

Jeannie couldn't move, couldn't breathe, utterly transfixed by the incredible man before her. He unfastened the thick leather belt at his waist and tossed it to the ground. The intricately wrapped plaid came next, the thick, heavy folds falling into a pool at his feet. He still wore his brogues and sat on the edge of the bed to remove the soft leather boots. He stood again to remove the linen shirt, but she stopped him.

"No, let me," she said, her voice husky.

His eyes locked on hers. If he was surprised by her bold request, he did not show it. Instead his gaze seemed to burn even hotter.

She was not an innocent girl any longer, but a woman who knew what she wanted. And right now she wanted to touch him more than anything in the world. To spread her hands across the wide spans of muscled chest and feel his heat, feel the raw energy pulsing from him.

To know that this was real and not a dream.

His eyes followed her every movement as she reached forward and slid her hands under the front edge of his shirt. She gasped at the contact, at the erotic sensation of hot, smooth skin. Just touching him made her dissolve into a puddle of hot, liquid need.

Duncan made a sharp sound and jerked, his jaw clenched and the muscles under her fingers suddenly rigid. He didn't seem to be breathing, but she had no doubt what she did to him.

His reaction only encouraged her—she felt emboldened by the sensual power she wielded over this fierce warrior. She splayed her fingers over the steel bands of his stomach, marveling at their precision, yet wickedly aware of the thick, swollen head of his erection jutting just below her wrists.

He wore nothing under his plaid which meant . . .

She looked down, a bold, naughty streak she didn't know she possessed taking hold.

Her mouth went dry. Her memory hadn't exaggerated. Thick and long, the round head swollen and heavy with blood, his manhood rose prominently a few inches above his waist between heavily muscled thighs giving proof to his virility. She blushed, realizing she'd been staring. But the wanton attention only seemed to make him grow even larger.

She reached out, but he grabbed her wrist to stop her from touching him. His jaw was clenched tight and the muscles in his neck bulged. He shook his head. "Nay," he said, his voice harsh and pained. "Not yet."

Blushing harder, but strangely pleased, she returned to removing his shirt.

Slowly, she skimmed her hands up his chest, lifting the shirt. When she reached his shoulders, he raised his arms and she had to stand on the bed to take it all the way off.

Tossing the shirt beside the plaid, she ran her hands over his shoulders, his arms, his back, as if memorizing every ridge, every bulge of muscle with her palms. He was completely naked, and utterly magnificent. His muscles sculpted to perfection, every ounce of his flesh hard-wrought steel. His virile strength was daunting.

He stood completely still, but she could tell from the harshness of his breathing that her exploration was torturing him.

She tore her gaze from his chest and looked into his eyes. "You've changed so much," she said softly, unable to keep the wistfulness from creeping into her voice. The boy had become a man. He'd left her a promising warrior, and returned an indestructible legend. Her fingers absently traced scars, the remnants of battles she knew nothing about.

"I hope for the better," he said lightly, cupping her

chin and forcing her gaze to his. His tone turned serious. "There's still time, Jeannie. It's not too late."

Her heart squeezed. She hoped so. Uncertainty clouded her consciousness, until he dropped a soft kiss on her lips. A kiss that quickly turned insistent. Demanding. Wiping out all thoughts of the troubles facing them and returning her to the moment at hand.

She circled her arms around his neck and pressed her body against his, a body that she'd primed with her touch. She could feel the fire blazing under the surface, ready to engulf her in flames. All too aware of his nakedness and that only the thin linen of her nightraile separated them, she sank against him, sliding her body down to position him between her legs.

He drew back, his eyes dark with passion and shook his head. A predatory glint sparked in his gaze. "Now it's my turn."

The sensual promise in his voice quickened her pulse. She eyed him warily. Though she was far from a maid, she could hardly be called experienced in the art of lovemaking. She fought back the needle of guilt for the failure to her husband. Francis had deserved more than duty and quiet acceptance.

But she could no more force her body to passion than she could her heart to love. She knew that now. With Duncan she never had to try, it was always there. Bone deep. On an elemental level that could not be feigned. With Duncan she'd never felt self-conscious. Never been uncomfortable. Making love to him seemed the most natural thing in the world.

She was still standing on the bed before him, and she was suddenly aware that her breasts were right at his eye-level. Slowly, he worked the ties of her nightraile, the heel of his hands brushing the hard tips. She couldn't see his eyes, but she could feel them on her, caressing her with their heat.

Her knees wobbled when his hands cupped her breasts and lifted them to his face. He circled her nipples with his thumbs, creating a gentle friction with the fabric, until she throbbed. She wriggled, her body restless.

But his exquisite torture had just begun.

Chapter 19

Duncan called on every last ounce of his restraint. Her bold desire for him was like a powerful aphrodisiac, her open admiration for his body a siren's call almost impossible to resist. And then when her gaze had fallen on his cock . . .

He groaned, the memory sent a fresh surge of blood to the already throbbing head.

His body urged him to give her what she wanted. To rip off the flimsy piece of linen that covered her, toss her down on the bed and swiv her until the demon of desire that had possessed him let go. Until he could think straight.

She did something to him—she always had. She touched something inside him that unleashed a primitive side that he'd never known existed. Good intentions. Control. Honor. All fell by the wayside in the face of his desire for her.

It was everything he had not to give into it. Not this time. Explosive passion wasn't enough. He wanted everything. Her trust. Her heart. Her soul.

If only her breasts weren't so spectacular. He weighed them in his hands, lifted them to his face to bury his nose in the deep cleft between them and inhaled the soft fragrance of her skin.

No one smelled like she did. Clean and sweet, with the faint scent of honeysuckle. It filled his nose, his lungs, his body. He wanted to drown in it, in her.

Her nipples beaded under his fingertips. Gently, he

rolled them between his thumb and forefinger to a stiff pink point. Too sweet a temptation. He'd wanted to undress her slowly, but he couldn't wait another minute to have her naked. Images of her gorgeous body had haunted him since that day at the loch. Taking the hem of the nightrail, he slowly drew it up the length of her body and over her head.

When it was off, she blushed and instinctively tried to cover herself. But he would have none of it. "No. Don't. You're so damn beautiful." He smiled, seeing her pink cheeks. "Especially when you're blushing."

Slowly she removed her hands, revealing her creamy nakedness to his view.

God's blood, he thought, taking in the heavy round curves of her breasts, the slim contours of her waist and hips, and the long shapely legs. *I'm a lucky man.*

His silence had given her the wrong idea. "I've changed as well. I've had two children."

He slid his hands around her waist. "You've only become more beautiful." How could she not see it? He traced the heavy contour of her breast with the back of his finger and looked into her eyes. "Beautiful."

Needing to taste her, he scooped the soft, round flesh in his hands and lifted her breasts to his mouth, placing a gentle kiss on each tip.

She made a sharp sound that told him she'd forgotten her embarrassment.

He caressed her with his hands, with his mouth, with his tongue. Sucking her nipples one at a time deep in his mouth. Her skin was so soft and smooth. Velvet under his tongue.

She moaned, her back arching. His cock jerked hard against his stomach. She was so damned responsive, he could make her come by just sucking her breasts.

But he had other plans.

He wrapped his hands around her ankles and looked

into her eyes. Through the soft, haze of passion he saw her anticipation.

Slowly he moved his hands up, sculpting the long, slim legs that were every bit as shapely as he remembered. He stopped just above her knees.

He heard her breath catch, and felt her legs wobble.

His fingers brushed the soft skin of her inner thighs. Now she was shaking, trembling with desire. And deliciously wet. He bent down and replaced his fingers with his mouth, nuzzling her, inhaling the soft scent of her womanhood.

Her hands clasped his shoulders, as if her legs had suddenly given out. He slid his hands around to cup her bottom, to bring her more fully under his dominion.

"Duncan," she said, in weak protest. "You can't—"

She stopped when he licked her, her tight, round bottom clenching in his hand. A devilish chuckle rumbled through his chest. "Oh, yes, I can. And I will—very thoroughly." He licked her again, tasting her deeper.

She gasped, moaned, shuddered. He lifted his gaze to hers. "Look at me, Jeannie. I want to see your eyes as I pleasure you."

Her green eyes met his, wild and full of passion. Her lips were parted, her breath panting.

His chest tightened. God, she was beautiful. And shaking with desire.

Holding her gaze, he kissed her again, drawing his tongue along the damp opening, then easing slowly inside. He sighed into her, his tongue thrusting and circling in long delicious strokes. All the while holding her gaze, watching as green turned black. As lids fluttered. As cheeks turned pink with the flush of pleasure. He sensed her restlessness, sensed her fighting release, and pushed her harder, deeper, closer to the edge. He kissed her until she cried out. Then he held her there, sucking until she shattered. He felt the spasms take hold as her body clenched and pulsed with her release.

When the last pulse had ebbed, she collapsed against him, her body limp. Satisfied, but by no means finished, he showed a little mercy and lowered her to the bed.

But it would be the last she saw this night.

He gazed at her soft and languid on the bed, overcome for a moment by his love for this woman.

The tightness in his chest would not let go. He knew just how fragile was the truce they'd established.

His own future was anything but certain, but when he was done with her tonight, he would leave her no doubt that she belonged to him for as long as that future held.

Duncan was staring at her with the strangest expression on his face.

Jeannie reached up to put a hand on his cheek, rubbing her palm against the stubble of the dark beard that shadowed his jaw. He looked so serious. "What is it? Did I do something wrong?"

A slow smile curved his mouth. It landed like a blow across the chest. For a moment he looked like the boy she'd lost her heart to.

"Nothing is wrong, though I hope you don't intend to take a nap."

He was sitting on the edge of the bed leaning over her, and she let her gaze travel over the broad muscled chest and down to the prominent evidence of his arousal. She cocked an eyebrow at him. "You mean we aren't done?"

"Do I look done?"

She bit her lip playfully. "Hmm. I can't tell." She lifted her gaze to his, seeing his blue eyes turn dark. "Perhaps I should touch and see?"

All signs of playfulness fled. "God, yes," he groaned.

She reached down between their bodies and circled him. Her hand looked so small holding him, her fingers weren't even able to close around him. His skin was hot, but velvety soft and rock hard at the same time.

He showed her how to stroke him, how to bring him pleasure. She loved to watch the way his stomach muscles clenched as her rhythm quickened. To watch the emotions play upon his handsome features. She scooted closer, pressing tiny kisses along his clenched jaw, on his neck, on his chest. She loved the taste of his skin. The warmth. The crisp, clean saltiness.

She heard his breath hitch as her mouth dipped lower. As her tongue slid over the steely defined bands lining his stomach.

Her hand paused. What would the rest of him taste like?

She lifted her gaze to his, his expression more fierce than she'd ever seen it. Every muscle in his body seemed clenched tight. He read her silent question and nodded. Barely. He seemed unable to move.

He pulsed, a pearly drop seeping from his tip and she licked it off with her tongue, tasting him. He swore, and nearly jumped off the bed, his body shaking with pleasure. She lowered her head and pressed her lips around him, taking the heavy head of his erection in her mouth. He groaned, clenched hard, then lifted his hips to slide deeper into her mouth. Her senses filled with the tangy male essence of him. Everything was deeper . . . darker . . . more intense.

She closed her eyes and gave over to the powerful sensations, exploring him with her mouth, with her tongue, sucking him deeper and deeper down her throat. His responses—the groans, the stiffening of his body—were her guide. With each stroke she grew more confident. The knowledge that she was driving him mad with pleasure only increased her own.

"No more," he said, lifting her head from him, his voice rough. "I need to be inside you."

Gently, he laid her back down on the bed and slid beside her, skin to skin. She snuggled against his warmth, savoring the incredible sensation of his long, powerful body stretched against hers.

He lowered his head and kissed her, coaxing with deep sensual strokes of his tongue. His hands possessed her body, the hard calluses of his palms marking her. There was no part of her he left untouched. Her breasts, her legs, her arms, her feet. He left her warm and whimpering for more.

His hand slid between her legs, as his mouth held her in a deep kiss, his tongue and finger acting in perfect unison.

She pressed against his hand, against his body, dissolving into a pool of fire. Sensation pushed to the edge of every nerve ending, waiting to be set free. She couldn't think, lost in the throes of passion so thick and heavy it was like trying to see through a dense mist.

He moved over her, positioning his hands on either side of her shoulders, the plump head of his erection poised at her entry. Holding her gaze, he slid inside her slowly, inch by inch, possessing her with his body, with his soul.

It was too intense. Too powerful. The tightness in her chest too much.

She gasped when he'd reached the end, then gave one final nudge and held her there. Letting her feel him. His weight. The incredible sensation of him inside her . . . filling her. Making her complete. With his eyes, he forced her to acknowledge the connection that bound them together. Not just their bodies, but something far deeper. Something elemental. Something that could not be put into words, but that she could see reflected in his piercing gaze.

Her heart welled up, overcome by an emotion she'd never thought to feel again. An emotion so intense it frightened her as all that she had to lose became clear.

Then he started to move, thrusting with long deep strokes. Strokes that reverberated through her body from head to toe, each staking a further claim. It was the most erotic, intimate moment of her life.

No other man could make her feel like this because no other man existed for her.

Duncan didn't think anything could feel more incredible than Jeannie's soft, pink mouth stretched around the head of his cock, her tongue stroking him, her mouth sucking him deeper and deeper into her throat.

But he was wrong.

Raw lust was nothing to the emotion that gripped his heart as he sank into her inch by incredible inch. Her eyes pulled him in. Deeper and deeper. To touch her soul.

She was so warm. So wet. So sweetly tight. He'd forgotten how it felt to be inside her. How her body felt under his. She was so tiny and soft he worried that he would crush her, but she pulled him down, seeking the connection of skin on skin. Her breasts were crushed to his chest as he thrust high inside her, her nipples raking him.

He closed his eyes, sensation showering over him in a warm, tingling wave.

He thrust again, groaning. It felt too good. The pleasure too intense to contain. Her body clenched around him like a fist, pumping, milking.

She moaned and lifted her hips, meeting him, circling in a slow, delicious dance.

Blood pounded through him, concentrating at the sensitive head. Sensation coiled at the base of his spine in a hot pulsing fist. He was going to explode.

Sweat poured off his forehead as he fought to hold on. He thrust high and hard, forcing her . . .

She cried out, calling his name as her body racked

with the spasm of her release. The sheer ecstasy on her face pushed him over the edge. He drove into her one more time and stiffened, then jerked with the force of his own release as pleasure crashed over him in a hard, earth-shattering wave.

He stayed inside her until the spasms ebbed and the last drop of pleasure had been wrung from him. But even then he was reluctant to break the connection. Only the knowledge that he was probably crushing her forced him to slide from the warm embrace of her body. Rolling to the side, he gathered her up in his arms, cradling her against his shoulder. The night air cooled his heated skin.

They were silent for a while. After what had just happened it seemed fitting. Words would be lacking.

Her finger weaved absently through the thin triangle of hair below his neck, following the thin trail down to his stomach. He could tell she was thinking.

"Did you mean it?" she asked, gazing up at him.

He didn't need to ask what she meant. "Aye."

"What made you realize that it wasn't me who took the map?"

He twirled a lock of silky red hair in his finger, letting it fall in a soft puddle on his chest. "It wasn't any one thing. I suppose I started to see beyond the 'proof' and listened to my gut. Your reaction had a lot to do with it. I realized how much my leaving had hurt you. You acted wronged, not guilty." He felt a hard burning in his chest as the ramifications of what he'd done hit him. "God, Jeannie, I'm sorry." He heard her voice in his head begging him not to leave and tried to shut it out. By all rights she should hate him. "I should have trusted you. I should have given you a chance to explain. Can you ever forgive me?"

"Why were you so quick to find me guilty?"

She wasn't asking about the specific evidence against

her, but the more difficult question of why he believed it. He thought back, remembering. He'd been so young, barely a man, still making his way in the world and couldn't quite believe he could be that fortunate to find someone like her. "I'd seen you with your father, and knew how much you loved him, knew the loyalty you felt to your family. You were young, beautiful, and could have had your pick of any man in the Highlands. Part of me couldn't believe you'd give that all up for a bastard with nothing to his name." He made a harsh sound. "Who didn't even have a name."

She lay perfectly still. "I saw the man you were. I believed in you, Duncan, not in your birth. Did I ever give you reason to think it mattered to me? Did I ever make you feel like you were anything less than the most wonderful, amazing man I'd ever known?"

The anger in her voice took him aback. "Nay," he admitted.

She relaxed, her body easing into his once again.

"Why believe me now?" she asked. "What's changed?"

"Me. You. We aren't the same people we were then. I guess I didn't give either of us enough credit. I didn't see what you did, that we make our own destiny not by our birth, but by our actions."

Jeannie peered up at him, a strange look in her eyes. "Do you really believe that?"

He sensed there was something behind her question—something important. "Aye, I do."

She held his gaze for a moment, then nodded. She was quiet for a few minutes, lost in thought. Finally, she said, "What can we do?"

He cocked an eyebrow, a wry smile on his lips. "We?"

"I want to help."

He'd been waiting a long time to hear those words. "Could you persuade your brother to allow you to go through your father's papers?"

She shook her head. "It wouldn't help. Little was left after the fire."

His stomach sank. "Fire?"

She nodded. "After Glenlivet when the king marched north, seeking vengeance against those who'd fought against him, he razed many castles, including Freuchie. The great hall and my father's solar were destroyed. When he died, I went through what remained. There was nothing from around the time of the battle."

Duncan swore. The chance of finding any documentary proof had been slim, but now it appeared to be nonexistent. His only option appeared to be tracking down the men who might have been involved. But the idea of questioning his brother didn't sit well.

"You're thinking of Colin?" Jeannie said.

He gave her a look out of the corner of his eye. "Remind me to be careful what I think around you." She grinned. "Aye, it's difficult to conceive that Colin could have anything to do with this."

"It's hard staring at the sun all the time."

He gave her a wry look. "I'm not perfect, Jeannie."

"To a younger brother you might have seemed as such." She bit her lip. "Colin said something of the like once. I didn't think much of it then, but jealousy can drive people to do horrible things. I wonder though if there could be more to it." Resting her hand on his ribs, she propped her chin on the back of her hand. "What do you know of your mother? You never talk about her."

He stiffened. "There's nothing to talk about," he said flatly. He tried to ignore the wounded look in her eyes. But it felt as if he'd just failed some test. She'd wanted him to confide in her—to share feelings that didn't exist for a woman he'd never known. Hell, he'd rather have his teeth pulled.

But he knew he was treading a treacherous path, this connection they'd established was tenuous. So he took a deep breath, forced the tension from his body, and splayed himself open for her digging. "She was a Mac-Donald. Nursemaid to the chief's children. She left me with my father when I was but a few months old. I assume my birth caused her great shame and she was eager to be rid of me. I'm afraid it wasn't much better for my father. The Campbells and MacDonalds were engaged in a bloody feud at the time. My grandfather hated me on sight."

She pressed a kiss to his chest. Strangely, it helped. Perhaps because he knew she could understand. "Your father must have cared for her greatly to risk his clan's wrath."

He shrugged. "I never thought about it, but I suppose you're right."

"Did you ever try to find her?"

He kept a tight rein on his anger and managed to say calmly, "No." He might have come to terms with his birth, but that didn't mean he'd wanted anything to do with the woman who'd abandoned him. He gave her a measured look. Did his parentage matter more to her than she'd let on? "Why are you asking me about this?"

She shrugged her naked shoulders. "Just curious." Her nose scrunched. "I wondered if there was more to the story, that's all. Your father never said anything more about her?"

"Nay—" He stopped and frowned.

"What is it?"

"Nothing." She got that look again and he sighed, resigned. "Something my father said right before he died." He recalled his words: *Mother . . . Find . . . MacDonald.* "He seemed to want me to find my mother, but he was delirious with fever."

He saw the excitement leap in her eyes. "What if he *did* know what he was saying? What if he wanted you—"

"Nay," he said, cutting her off before she could get

carried away. For a moment he caught a glimpse of the spontaneous, exuberant girl who'd snuck out of the castle and joined him in a midnight swim. "I have no interest in a reunion with my mother. If my father wanted me to make peace, I'm sorry to disappoint him."

"But what if your father wanted you to find something?"

"Like what?"

"What if your mother didn't really leave you? Or what if there is something about your birth—"

"There is nothing," he said in a voice that boded no argument. "Don't look for a faerie tale, you'll only be disappointed. I'm a bastard, Jeannie, and nothing is going to change that. I thought you accepted it."

She pursed her sensuous mouth into a thin line. "I do. This is not about me, it's about you. I'm trying to help you clear your name, and what if finding your mother can help?"

His jaw flexed. "It can't."

She mumbled something about stubborn oafs.

"What's that?" he asked.

She threw him an annoyed look. "The isle of Islay is close. We could be there and back in a day or two." She gazed up at him beseechingly. "What harm can it do?"

Plenty—to his peace of mind for one. Not to mention that half his cousin's soldiers seemed to be looking for him. But she practically bubbled with excitement and he hated the idea of crushing her enthusiasm. And he was running out of options.

He gritted his teeth, every instinct resisting yet at the same time desperately wanting to please her. She didn't know his father. He wouldn't have lied to him. "I'll think about it."

She looked like she was about to argue, but then a slow smile curved her lips, a naughty gleam in her eye. She slid her hand down the length of his chest, drawing little circles with her soft fingertips low on his stomach. He hissed, his spent muscles jumping back to life.

"Perhaps I shall find a way to convince you?"

He grabbed her hand and wrapped it around him. He was already hard as she began to stroke him. Heat spread across his limbs. Each pull of her hand sent him deeper and deeper into the black vortex of pleasure.

He knew he would eventually grant her request, no matter how much he didn't want to. He feared there was very little he would not do for her. But it didn't mean he couldn't have a little fun in the meantime.

"You can try," he groaned, then closed his eyes and let her.

Chapter 20

❖

For the next two nights Jeannie did her utmost to persuade him, but Duncan was proving to be an exceedingly stubborn man. Though she was beginning to suspect it was simply that he enjoyed her efforts too much to ever give in. He wasn't the only one. As she lay in bed, contemplating getting up, her body was still limp and sore from their lovemaking.

She couldn't seem to get enough of him. Passion had been absent in her life for so long, it was as if she was trying to make up for lost time.

And always at the back of her mind was the knowledge that *time* was the one thing they did not have.

If he was captured before they found proof . . .

Her stomach turned as she fought back the suffocating crush of fear. He'd only just come back to her; she couldn't bear the thought of losing him again.

Jeannie knew that they probably wouldn't find anything on Islay, but right now his father's deathbed deliria were all they had. She couldn't explain it, but all her instincts told her that finding his mother was important. And she was far too desperate not to heed them.

They were safe at Castleswene, but Jeannie knew Duncan would not stay here long, when to do so would further jeopardize his brother's place with their cousin. Coming here had already placed Jamie in an awkward position—he wasn't just harboring a fugitive, but his cousin's most wanted outlaw. Duncan and Jamie had argued about it last night. Duncan was adamant that he would not foist his troubles on his family, and Jamie was just as determined to not turn his back on his brother again.

Apparently the brothers had reached some sort of impasse. By the time Duncan had slipped in beside her, he said that it had all been sorted out.

After dragging herself from bed, Jeannie called for a bath. She did not linger. The gentle heat from the peat fire was no match for the chilly morning air. Dressing quickly with the help of one of the young maidservants, she went in search of Elizabeth Campbell. If she could not persuade Duncan herself, she would have to call on reinforcements.

She found his sister in one of the mural chambers, a small room carved out in the thick castle walls, looking out the window with a book in her lap. She had a strange pensive look on her face.

"I hope I'm not disturbing you."

Elizabeth jumped at the sound of her voice and looked at Jeannie as if she were an apparition. She shook her head, a wistful smile on her face. "Nay. I wasn't feeling well this morning and Patrick insisted I rest if I want to go to Inveraray. Normally I would not succumb to blackmail, but in truth I was tired."

"It's been an emotional few days."

A wry smile curved Elizabeth's mouth. "That it has."

"You are going to Inveraray to speak with Argyll on Duncan's behalf?"

Elizabeth nodded. "With Jamie and my husband. I hope it will help."

But Jeannie could hear in her voice that she didn't think it likely. Elizabeth looked back out the window and Jeannie drew closer to see what captured her attention. Through the frosty pane of glass she caught sight of the warriors in the courtyard. A few of the men were practicing their swords, others their archery, and a few lads were standing in a circle around—

Her stomach sank. *Oh, God.* She schooled her features, trying to hide her reaction, but she knew what had so captured Lizzie's attention.

Duncan had kept his promise to show Dougall his maneuvers. He and her son were locked in a playful demonstration of hand-to-hand combat. Dougall tried to dart by him, but Duncan captured him, enfolded him in a big bear hug, and lifted the squirming boy off the ground. Dougall must have said something funny because Duncan tossed his head back and laughed.

She felt a sharp pang in her chest. Watching them together was torture, but she could not turn away. Her conscience tugged. More than once over the past two days she'd fought the urge to tell him, but she still couldn't be completely sure how he would react. Would he see it the same way she did or would he insist on claiming his son? She would trust him with *her* future, but could she trust him with her son's?

She wanted to, but something was stopping her. It wasn't just the fact that he was an outlaw—a man fighting for his life—though that certainly played a part. They'd just started to rebuild what had been almost destroyed. This connection between them, growing stronger with each passion-filled night, was as yet too fragile. There had been no talk of the future—how could there be with Duncan's being so uncertain.

She could feel the weight of Lizzie's gaze on her. "I believe that is your son," she said.

Jeannie stepped back from the window, her heart pounding. "Yes." She met Lizzie's gaze. "His name is Dougall."

"He looks to be about ten years old."

Jeannie's heart stuttered to a terror-struck halt. "He was just nine last Michaelmas."

Lizzie didn't say anything for a moment, just stared at her with those crystal clear blue eyes. Jeannie met her gaze unflinchingly though every nerve ending in her body stood on edge.

"I was thinking about the day you came to Castleswene."

Jeannie tensed.

Elizabeth continued. "I thought it bold of you to come looking for Duncan after what you'd done to him—or what he'd accused you of," she amended. "You seemed so upset to discover he'd left. I was surprised to hear you'd wed so quickly afterward. It seemed to confirm Duncan's accusation, but I wonder if there was perhaps another reason."

Jeannie's fists curled into tight balls at her side. "If you have something to say, just say it," she said through clenched teeth.

"One day he will see what I see. Once he does, the difference of four or five months will not deter him. Somewhere there is a person who will remember something and be able to tell him the truth. That person should be you."

Elizabeth Campbell had no right to tell her what to do. "What you are suggesting is wrong. You know nothing of what you speak."

Lizzie put her hand over her stomach, an instinctive gesture of protection. "Actually I think I do. This babe is not yet born and already I know there is very little I would not do to protect my child. I'm sure you felt the same." Her voice grew quiet. "But Duncan has a right to know."

He'd given up that right when he left her.

Or had he?

Deep in her heart Jeannie knew that if they were to have a chance, eventually she must tell him.

Elizabeth shifted her gaze, seeming to realize she'd said enough. "Did you wish to see me for something?"

It took Jeannie a moment for her emotions to subside before she could compose herself to respond. She forced Dougall from her mind and said, "I was hoping I might get your help in persuading Duncan to make a quick journey to Islay. He'd remembered something your father said—"

"But he's going tomorrow. It was decided last night. I'd assumed he'd told you." Lizzie looked embarrassed. "Though it was late, perhaps you haven't seen him."

Apparently Elizabeth had correctly assumed their sleeping arrangements and was now wondering if she'd made a mistake.

She hadn't.

Jeannie's mouth drew in a tight line. The wretch.

"I'm sure he was intending to tell you," Lizzie offered.

Aye, probably after another night of her trying to "persuade" him when it was too late for her to accompany him. Her eyes narrowed on the imposing man below in the courtyard. "I'll just bet he was," she said. She excused herself and marched purposefully down the stairs. If he thought he could exclude her, he was quite mistaken.

The practice had just broken up for the morning when she exited the keep and made her way down the forestairs. Duncan was speaking with Leif and Conall with his back toward her and didn't see her approach. His men took one look at her and made their quick excuses right before she tapped Duncan on the shoulder.

He turned, his face instinctively breaking into a smile when he saw her.

For a moment she forgot her anger under the powerful onslaught of the devastatingly handsome man standing before her. His black hair glistened in the sun, his blue eyes sparkled like the sea, his teeth flashed white behind a wide grin that made him appear younger than his years. She could smell the heat of his practice on his skin. The crisp, harshly masculine scent called to her on a dark primal level. There was just something irresistible about a heavily muscled, well-worked warrior.

Furious that she could be so easily distracted, she gritted her teeth and glared up at him. At times like this she really wished he wasn't so tall. It was difficult to be intimidating with your neck cranked back. "I hear you've decided to take a wee journey."

He had the good grace to wince. "Ach, you heard about that did you?"

"Didn't you think to tell me?"

His grin grew wider, wickedly wider. His eyes slid down the length of her, lingering in all the warm spots, then returned to her mouth. She could almost see what he was thinking, what he was remembering, and her cheeks flushed. "Now why would I want to do that? I was having too much fun with your methods of persuasion."

Her eyes narrowed on the grinning lout. "You are a wicked man."

"I'll show you just how wicked later tonight."

Her skin tingled with anticipation—in spite of her intention to not allow him to affect her. It was a foolish intention, he always affected her. She drew up her spine. "I'm afraid I will be busy this evening."

His smile fell. "Busy?"

"Yes." She smiled sweetly. "Packing for our journey."

His jaw hardened. "You're not going."

Determined green met equally determined blue. "And how do you intend to stop me? You've no authority over me, Duncan Campbell."

His gaze narrowed, the tic beneath his jaw jumped to life. "Do not challenge me on this, Jeannie. It's too dangerous."

"Unless they are searching the waterways, I don't see why. No one would think to look for you on Islay."

His lips fell into a thin line, not pleased by her argument—because it was true. They could embark directly from Castleswene and land right at Dunyvaig, the MacDonald's stronghold on the eastern seaboard of Islay. They never need even sit upon a horse.

"I don't want you involved," he said.

"I am involved. If my father had anything to do with what happened to you, it was partially because of me. With a good wind we could be there in a few hours. Besides, you can't deny I helped you before."

"The same trick will not work twice. No doubt your friend the captain has discovered his mistake."

Jeannie placed her hand on his arm. "Please, Duncan. This was my idea. I want to go to see it through. I want to be there with you." Tears burned behind her eyes. "I can't sit and wait and worry about what is happening." Her eyes met his. "You wanted my help, now you have it. Don't turn me away."

She held her breath, watching his face. His jaw flexed. "If there is trouble you will say I abducted you. What is one more crime when I've already been convicted of treason?"

She bit back a smile. She would do no such thing. She would defend him with her last breath.

Duncan breathed easier once they left the coast of Knapdale behind them and entered the open sound, safe on one of his brother's *birlinns*. It was a small party—better to avoid too much attention—just Duncan, his men, and a handful of the loyal Gordon guardsmen. And Jeannie.

He'd been fooling himself to think he could leave without her. It wasn't the danger—she was right, the sea was probably the safest place for him—but if anything went wrong, he didn't want her to see him captured. But would hearing of it later be any better? Probably not.

Like it or not, she was involved. He couldn't turn her away now. Not when he wasn't sure how much time they had left. For purely selfish reasons, he liked having her with him. If he had his way they would never be apart again.

More than once he'd thought of asking her to run away with him. To leave Scotland and the noose poised over his head. He had wealth enough to last for a dozen lifetimes. Perhaps if it had been just the two of them, he would. But she had her children and he could not ask her to deprive them of their future.

He was done hiding. He wasn't alone anymore. It was time to face the charges against him and hope that justice would be done.

Duncan kept a close eye on the coast falling away behind them while the Norseman Leif, holding true to his seafaring heritage, sailed them across the sea. Their departure would hold the most danger—if anyone was watching Castleswene, they would attempt to follow. So far, however, they appeared to be alone except for the occasional fishing boat.

The sky wasn't exactly blue, but the soft gray was about as much as they could hope for on a cold December morn. Away from the buffer of land, however, the wind held quite a nasty bite.

Keeping one eye on the water behind them, he took the seat behind Jeannie who had bundled herself up to her nose in plaids. It was a stark contrast to the way he'd left her this morning, her naked limbs tangled in the bedsheets and red-gold hair spilled across the pillow.

He'd suffered well for his wee trick—very well. She'd tortured him for hours. First with her words, whispering all the wicked things she was going to do to him, then with her hands, and finally with her mouth and tongue.

He hardened at the visceral memory of her teasing. How she'd refused to allow him to touch her as she brushed her tight nipples across his chest, across his mouth, across his turgid cock. As her smooth, silky skin slid against his. How her tongue had circled the heavy head of his erection, traveled the long length licking, flicking, and circling until he'd been forced to grab the mattress to keep from surging into her mouth. How when she'd finally taken him between her warm, moist lips he'd almost come. And then how she'd milked him in her mouth, caressed his bollocks in her soft hands, and forced him over the edge.

He would submit to her punishment any time. But as demanding as she'd been in bed, she'd been unusually quiet afterward—quiet that had extended into the morning. He attributed it to concern over their journey and the precarious state of his freedom, but he wondered if it was something else entirely.

She'd seemed so excited about the trip before. "Is something bothering you, Jeannie?"

The question startled her from her reverie and her eyes quickly shaded. She shook her head a little too vehemently. The wool slipped from around her mouth, revealing a bright smile. "Nay. 'Tis cold, that's all. How much longer?"

Duncan was not fooled. *She's hiding something from me.* He hoped she would confide in him, but he would not force her. "Another two hours or so, if the wind stays the same. We should be docked at Leodamas before noon. I'll send word requesting an audience with my . . ." he couldn't quite get the word out, "the nurse as soon as we arrive. With any luck we can see her this afternoon and only be forced to stay one night on the island." He took another glance behind them, scanning the waves and seeing nothing, before turning back to her. "I don't know how long Jamie and Lizzie will be at

Inveraray, but I'd just as soon be at Castleswene waiting for them when they return."

Jeannie tilted her head a little to look at him. "We are docking at Leod's Harbor? I assumed we'd stay at the castle for the night."

He shook his head. "I'd rather not avail myself of MacDonald's hospitality any longer than necessary. In fact, I hope to avoid the chief entirely."

"You think he will recognize you?"

Duncan nodded grimly. "Aye. My brother Jamie is well known to MacDonald—the chief also knew my father." Though not engaged in a blood feud at the moment, relations between the Campbells and MacDonalds were always uneasy.

Her eyes widened. "I didn't realize . . ."

"There's nothing to worry about. Even if we do run into him, he'll not break the bond of hospitality by holding me. If he sends word, we'll be gone before anyone can arrive." He grinned. "I'm afraid it means you'll spend the night in a rustic alehouse or inn and not in the luxury of Dunyvaig."

Jeannie returned his smile. "I've done so before."

"I remember."

Their eyes held for a moment. Surprisingly, the memory no longer held pain for him. Further conversation was forestalled however, by the glimpse of a sail behind them. It turned out to be nothing, but by the time they'd made sure, the wind had changed, requiring Duncan to take his turn at the oars.

As promised, two hours later they sailed into the small harbor. Once they'd secured the boat, Duncan set two of Jeanie's guardsmen to the castle with the note from Jeannie requesting an audience with the old nursemaid—he didn't even know his mother's name. The rest of them located the nearest inn. Fortunately, the innkeeper was also a decent cook and they'd just finished a hearty bowl of beef stew with a hunk of the local cheese and barley bread when the guardsmen returned with their reply.

The lady would see them.

Duncan arranged for horses and not long afterward, he, Jeannie, and the two Gordon guardsmen were riding up the hill through the landward gate of Dunyvaig Castle, or Dun Naomhaig as it was known in the Highlands.

The castle, once a stronghold of the Lords of the Isles, was situated high on a rocky promontory along the eastern edge of the Bay of Lagavulin, overlooking the sound and, on a clear day, the coast of Kintyre.

It was an impressive fortress with a seven-sided walled enclosure, encompassing the entire hill. The castle was two levels—the sea gate and outer courtyard below, the tower keep and inner courtyard above—joined by stairs. A large bastion overlooked the bay, giving the guardsmen clear warning to all who approached.

Duncan had ordered Leif, Conall, and the other guardsmen to stay outside the gates to keep watch of any messengers coming or going from the castle. If something went wrong, he'd rather have his men safe on the outside where they could help.

While Jeannie's guardsmen waited outside, they were led into the great hall, located on the second floor of the tower keep. Jeannie sat in a chair before the fireplace. Duncan stood behind her.

He was too restless to do otherwise. For years he'd refused to think about the woman who'd abandoned him, but now that the moment when he would meet her was upon him, he couldn't deny the increased pounding in his chest or the anxiety building in his stomach.

Sensing his tension, Jeannie put her hand on his and gave it an encouraging squeeze.

At that moment the door opened. Jeannie stood, and

Duncan went completely still as the woman walked into the room.

She was small and thin to the point of frailty, with snow-white hair partially visible beneath the black velvet French hood popular with the prior generation when Mary had been queen of the Scots. Her skin was as wrinkled as a dried apple.

She had to be at least seventy years—far too old to be his mother. Some of the tension dissipated. But why had the nurse—his mother—not come?

The old woman had focused on Jeannie, but eventually her eyes lifted to him. Her skin grew sickly pale and her eyes widened in shock, as if she'd seen a ghost. She wobbled a little and both he and Jeannie reached out to steady her.

She didn't faint, but they carefully lowered her to the chair. Jeannie retrieved a fan she carried in the purse at her waist, the heat from the fire making the room warm and stuffy. The woman appeared too overcome by emotion to speak.

"I apologize," Jeannie said. "We didn't mean to cause you any distress."

The old woman shook her head and seemed to collect her senses. She stared at Duncan. "You've the look of him—and her. She had the blackest hair, like a raven's wing they said. With eyes as blue as the Irish Sea."

Duncan's stomach sank. He hadn't missed her usage of the past tense.

"There appears to be some misunderstanding, my lady. We were here to see the chief's old nursemaid."

"Forgive me, Lady Gordon," the woman said. "I am Mary MacDonald. Sister to the old chief, aunt to the present. It was I who received your note. I'm afraid you can't see, Kathrine." She gave Duncan an apologetic look. "She died, ten years passed now."

It was what Duncan expected, but it didn't stop him

from feeling as if he'd just taken a blow to the chest. He'd never wanted to know his mother, but to know that he couldn't was surprisingly difficult to hear. *Kathrine*. It was the first time he'd ever heard her name.

Jeannie put her hand on his arm. The old woman noted the gesture and looked back and forth between them.

"What happened?" Duncan asked, his voice emotionless.

"She slipped and fell off a cliff onto the rocks below. It was a terrible tragedy."

Ten years ago. "About the same time as my father died," he noted.

The old woman nodded. "Aye, we'd just heard that he'd fallen in battle. News of your troubles had not reached us." He heard the implied "Thank God." "When did you return?" she asked.

"A couple months ago."

"You've been exonerated?"

He and Jeannie exchanged a look. "Not exactly," he explained. "That is why we are here."

"Is there anything you can tell us about her?" Jeannie asked.

A slight wariness appeared in Mary MacDonald's eyes. "Why don't you tell me what you know."

Duncan answered. "That she was a nursemaid to the present laird's children, that she had an affair with my father, and that she left me with my father not long after I was born," he couldn't quite keep the edge from his voice.

"Do not judge your mother too harshly, lad. 'Twas not easy for her to do what she did. My brother would have killed you had he discovered what she'd done. The MacDonalds and Campbells were locked in a vicious blood feud."

The vehemence in her voice took him aback. But from

what he'd heard of the old laird he did not doubt her. The old MacDonald chief had a well-earned reputation as a harsh and merciless leader. "She must have been a favored nursemaid."

A strange look crossed her face. "Aye. Your mother was a special lass. Everyone loved her."

Yet she'd given away her child and never looked back.

Jeannie seemed to sense his thoughts and moved to get them back on course. "Can you think of any reason why Duncan's father would send him to find her? It was his dying wish."

The old woman held Duncan's gaze for a long moment before turning back to Jeannie, a sad look on her wrinkled face. "I can't think of anything." She paused. "I'm sorry, I wish I could be more help."

It was no more than Duncan expected, but it did not lessen the disappointment. One more road had led him nowhere. Sooner or later (and he suspected the former), he was going to have to deal with the very real possibility that there was simply no proof to be found.

Chapter 21

They'd stayed only a short while longer, declining Lady MacDonald's offer of a glass of claret and cakes, in favor of returning to the inn. Duncan was anxious to leave the MacDonald stronghold—not wanting to chance running into the laird—and Jeannie couldn't blame him. Any hope of learning something important had died ten years ago.

It seemed strange and sadly ironic that both his parents had died within months of one another. She'd wanted to question Lady MacDonald further, but it was clear the subject was a painful one for the old woman, as it was for Duncan.

Not that you would know it by looking at him. She glanced over at him, so big and strong riding atop the powerful black horse, utterly in command, his handsome face devoid of emotion as he spoke in low tones with Conall. But the stoic façade did not fool her. She'd seen the flash of pain in his eyes when Lady MacDonald had spoken of his mother's death.

Jeannie's heart went out to him. She, too, had lost her mother without being able to say good-bye. Worse, she knew, was the lost opportunity to confront the person who'd caused so much pain.

It was only a few hours past midday, but already the light had begun to wane as they navigated the narrow path back to the village, which consisted of a handful of buildings that had sprung up around the port. Duncan seemed preoccupied and for once Jeannie was not inclined to disturb him. Did he blame her for delving into a painful past unnecessarily?

She didn't blame him if he did. By the time they reached the inn, her stomach was tied in knots. She'd been so certain they would find something. Now she just felt foolish—impulsive—having dragged them across the sea on a silly madcap adventure. It felt distinctly like something her mother would have done. Shame crawled up her cheeks.

Duncan had a quick conversation with the men—she assumed giving them instructions for the evening—before joining her and leading her to the small private chamber he'd secured for her, for them, she hoped.

The inn was more of a large cottage—a two-story stone building with a thatched roof that hadn't been built with men of Duncan's build in mind. With his broad, muscular shoulders, he could barely negotiate the narrow wooden staircase up to the second floor. They reached a small landing where it appeared that three very small partitioned chambers had been created from one space. Fortunately, the room he'd selected for her was in the back, overlooking the port. It was also the most private. He had to duck his head through the doorway as he showed her inside, putting down the small bag of belongings she'd brought with her on a side table.

The room was barely functional—only a small bed, side table with basin and chair—but appeared clean.

"If you'd like, I can send for a bath," he offered.

She nodded, biting her lip. Did he mean to leave?

"Would you care to eat your meal up here or downstairs with the men?" he asked.

She twisted her hands, looking at him anxiously. "Are you very angry with me?"

His head jerked back with surprise. "Angry? Why would I be angry with you?"

She gazed up at him, tears in her eyes. "You didn't want to come, but I wouldn't let it go. I'm sorry for dragging you all the way—"

"Stop." He cupped her chin and tilted her face to look deep into her eyes. "You've nothing to apologize for. You didn't drag me anywhere. I should have come years ago—when my father asked me to. It was I who was foolish with pride. I didn't want her to think I needed her."

He was only trying to make her feel better, which only succeeded in making her feel worse. "You think I'd learn my lesson by now. Whenever I feel something strongly it always seems to get me in trouble."

"We aren't in trouble." She shot him a glare and he grinned. "Well, no more trouble than I was already in." He smoothed his thumb over her cheek. "I love your passion—your joie de vivre. In truth, it was what first drew me to you."

Passion and joie de vivre? She supposed that was one way of looking at it. "I think my father used to call it flightiness."

Duncan's expression hardened. "You aren't your mother, Jeannie. You follow your heart, but not without thought. Stop punishing yourself for her mistakes."

She nodded and pulled away. "I didn't mean to keep you. I know there are things you need to do—"

"They can wait." He closed the door behind her and reached for her, pulling her into his arms. His eyes bored into hers intently. "Leave with me. We can sail to France right now. Within the week we can be in Spain. You shall want for nothing and we will be safe."

Jeannie gasped, her eyes searching his face. He seemed to be in complete earnest. "But I can't."

"Don't you want to be with me?" He challenged, bringing her closer so that she nested into the hard crevices of his body. "I love you, Jeannie. I've never stopped loving you. I'd hoped that you loved me."

"I do," she said without hesitation. It took a minute to realize what he'd said—he loved her—and then what she'd said. She loved him. She couldn't help it. She'd tried to bury it, to push it away, but it didn't work. Her heart had belonged to him from almost the first moment she'd seen him. But her girlish love had only grown stronger as she'd come to know the man he'd become. "I love you, Duncan, but I could never leave my children—"

She stopped, realizing what she'd said.

He smiled and dropped a soft kiss on her mouth. "See? You are nothing like your mother."

The realization took her aback. He was right. She might be impulsive, but unlike her mother it wasn't without bounds. Her mother had run off without care to those she left behind. She'd been fun and carefree, but also, Jeannie had to admit, selfish and irresponsible. Jeannie loved Duncan with all her heart, but not even for him would she ever abandon her children.

She had another realization. Her mother had fallen in love at the drop of a pin, but Jeannie had only loved once. She might have some of the impetuousness of her mother, but she also had duty and loyalty that her mother did not.

She eyed him warily. Perhaps he'd only been trying to teach her a lesson. "Did you mean what you said?"

He gave her a jaunty grin, the dimple in his left cheek making her heart squeeze. "About leaving or about loving you?"

"Both," she whispered, her heart pounding. He was horrible to tease her like this.

"Not about leaving, I intend to stay and fight the charges against me. But about loving you . . . ?" He ran the pad of his thumb over her bottom lip, his voice turning husky. "Aye, Jeannie, I love you. From the moment I first saw you, there has never been another woman for me."

The hot wave of emotion rose up in her throat. She'd forgotten what it felt like to be truly happy. "It's the same for me. I've never stopped loving you. I thought my heart had broken when you left, but my love for you never died."

The fierce look in his eye sent shivers of anticipation shooting through her body. "You don't need to say that. I have you now, that's all that matters."

He thought she'd loved Francis. She opened her mouth to correct him, but he covered it with his in a kiss that left no room for argument so thoroughly did it consume her.

His tongue wrapped around hers in an insistent dance. She knew what he needed because she needed it, too. To give proof to their words in the most basic of ways.

Within minutes he'd divested them both of their clothes and their bodies came together in seamless abandon. His hands stroked her skin, smoothing over her back and cupping her bottom to lift her against him. His erection rose hot and hard between them.

Gently he lowered her to the bed, his hard warrior's body looming over her. She reached up to touch him, to run her hands over the thick slabs of muscle and pull him down on her. She loved his solidness, his strength.

She throbbed between her legs, growing damp with her need for him. His eyes burned into her intently, holding her gaze the entire time. Spreading her legs, he looped his hands under her knees and positioned himself at her entry, nudging forward.

Duncan had never felt like this, his heart seemed too big for his chest. *I love you.* Hearing those words was far more powerful the second time around, for now he knew how precious they were. He knew disappointment, heartbreak, and the emptiness of what it was like to live without.

But the mistakes—the distrust—of the past were behind them. He felt as if he'd been given a second chance at life. Not even the threat hanging over him would interfere with this night. Tonight, nothing would come between them.

He wanted her aware of every moment of their joining. He didn't touch her, didn't kiss her, didn't make her half-crazed with passion. Instead, he held her gaze, looking deep into her eyes and entered her. Inch by inch. Slow and purposeful. All their senses honed on one place.

She gasped as he filled her, her soft pink lips parting with the erotic hitch of breath. Her round ivory breasts with the tiny pink nipples lifted as her back arched to accommodate him. To take him deeper.

It felt incredible. Her warm, wet body closed around him like a tight velvet glove. He stopped about halfway in, forcing himself to savor every second of sensation. But it was the tightness in his chest that truly moved him—the sheer intensity of emotion. How every time he looked at her, his heart seemed to expand. He never thought this would be his again. Fortune, it seemed, had smiled on him at last. A fierce wave of emotion rose up and took hold. This time he would never let her go.

He continued his slow possession, sinking into her until at last they were one. She was his: his heart, his soul.

"I love you, Jeannie. More than I ever thought possible."

She smiled and reached up to cradle his cheek in her tiny palm. "And I love you."

He held her there—at the deepest part—and then looking into her eyes took her a little farther. Her eyes widened and the little moan of pleasure nearly undid him.

He moved in and out with long, delicious strokes. Loving how her body milked him, how it fought to hold on to him.

She wrapped her legs around his buttocks, drawing him even closer. He lowered his chest to hers, his skin searing at the contact, and thrust. Harder now. Faster. Demanding.

Her moans drove him on. He couldn't wait for her to come.

He watched as the sensations clouded her expression. As her gorgeous features grew soft, as her eyes grew dreamy with the pleasure he was giving her.

He felt the first spasm as she arched underneath him, her taut nipples pressing deeper into his chest.

She cried out his name. She cried for God. And then she cried out for her release.

The hot spasms quivering around his cock were too much.

His ass clenched. Pleasure intensified at the base of his spine with all the subtlety of a lightning bolt. His bollocks tightened and he began to pulse. The force of his climax possessed him body and soul. Surging one more time, he drove into her, threw back his head, and let go. Crying out as it shattered over him in a torrential wave of hot pleasure. Pleasure that seemed wrought from the deepest part of him. Pleasure that so consumed him it seemed to stop his heart from beating. For a minute he thought he'd died and glimpsed Valhalla.

When it was over and his mind could once again form a coherent thought, he rolled her under his arm, tucking her against the length of his body.

Everything that had needed to be said was said.

They were meant to be together. Whatever future he had would be with her.

*   *   *

Jeannie must have dozed because when she opened her eyes it was dark outside. Duncan had lit the candle and sat at the edge of the bed, pulling on his clothes.

He turned at the sound of her stirring, and swept his gaze down the length of her naked body. A lascivious grin turned his mouth. "Sorry to wake you, but I need to go check on my men and make sure everything is in readiness for our journey tomorrow."

A chill of foreboding swept over her as his words brought her back to the reality of their situation. It wasn't fair. Duncan wasn't an outlaw. Argyll should know the type of man he was, should know that he would never betray him. It infuriated her that he must go through this.

"How do you do it, Duncan? How are you not bitter with all that has happened to you?"

"What good would it do? Raging against the injustice will not set me free. I prefer to think that justice will eventually win."

She studied the strong, noble features of his face and smiled. "Don't tell me that the most feared warrior in the land is an optimist?"

He laughed. "Nay, a realist. Eventually the truth will come out. It always does."

The truth. The cold, hard truth. After what they'd just shared, how could she keep it from him? How could she tell him she loved him one moment and then the next keep the truth of their son from him? But she was scared. Scared what he would think and scared what tomorrow might bring. Tears gathered in her eyes and she spoke her thoughts aloud. "What are we going to do?"

He bent down and kissed her eyelids. "Don't give up on me just yet, love. I intend to live for quite some time. Long enough to marry you and see a babe or two suckling on those beautiful breasts."

The surge of guilt took her breath away. *He has a son. Tell him.*

"I'm done running," he said. "If I can't find Colin, I've decided to go to Inveraray and take my chances with my cousin."

Her eyes widened with the sudden icy blast of panic. "You can't do that!" She grabbed his arm. "What if he doesn't believe you? You'll be executed on the spot."

"I hope it won't come to that." He dropped a soft kiss on her mouth. "Have faith in me, love."

"I do," she said. "It's Argyll I don't trust." He was doing this for her. She couldn't let him go through with it. She had to do something. "What if all of us were to come with you—me and the children. We'll go wherever you want to go until the truth comes out." Even if it meant sacrificing everything she'd worked to achieve for her son.

He gave her a long look and shook his head. "I'd not ask you to do that. I'll not strip your children of the future that rightly belongs to them. I'll not see your son deprived of his—"

"He's not Francis's son," she blurted. The words were out before she could take them back.

The room went completely still. He didn't move a muscle. The eyes were black as coal, boring into her with a cold intensity she'd never seen before. "What did you say?"

The change in him was instantaneous. His voice was so hard and flat it was nearly unrecognizable. Panic fluttered wildly in her chest. Knowing this moment was inevitable didn't make it any easier now that it was here. But she trusted him. He would understand. He would do the right thing.

He grabbed her arm and pulled her naked from the bed, holding her more harshly than he ever had before.

His hand felt like a steel clamp around her upper arm. "Tell me what you said," he repeated.

She lifted her chin, bracing herself for the maelstrom. "Dougall is your son."

He looked at her as if she'd just shot him again. His fingers bit into her arm. He swore—a vile curse she'd never heard him use. "You lied to me. How could you keep this from me?"

The cold accusation in his eyes cut her to the core. He was looking at her as if he didn't know her. He was looking at her the way he'd looked at her that night ten years ago when he'd snuck into her room and accused her of betraying him.

The look shattered the rein she had on her control. How dare he act as if she'd wronged him! She'd done the best that she could under the circumstances. All she'd done had been for her child—for *their* child.

She jerked her arm out of his hold and shoved him away from her. "It was you who left us, Duncan. *You* left me pregnant and alone." His head jerked as if she'd slapped him, but she didn't care. He wanted the truth, he would hear it. "I swallowed my pride after you'd so cruelly accused me of betraying you and went to Castleswene to tell you that I was carrying your child only to discover that you'd left. How do you think I felt? What was I supposed to do?" Her voice shook with emotion. "I was terrified of what would happen if anyone found out. I couldn't bear to think of the scandal my mistake would bring down on my innocent child. I knew what it would be like for him—as I'm sure you do." He flinched, but she didn't care. "So when Francis Gordon asked me to marry him I did what I had to do. Don't you dare judge me."

His eyes narrowed. "You deceived him, too."

She balled her fists, for the first time in her life close to striking someone. "I told him everything. Every ugly bit of it. The man you sought to blame for your predicament, who you wanted to destroy, knew the child I carried was yours, but vowed to love and raise him as his own. A vow he kept." That stopped him for a moment, but it did not stop her. Anger erupted inside her. Anger that had been contained for a very long time. "And what did he get in return? A pitiful excuse for a wife. A woman who could not love him, because her heart still foolishly longed for the man who'd broken it."

"You never loved him," he said flatly.

She turned away, removing the plaid from the bed to wrap it around her. Suddenly she felt naked and cold. "Nay, I couldn't even give him that. To both our great disappointment."

Duncan didn't want to hear about the saintly Francis Gordon—the man who'd raised his son. He didn't want to hear her bloody excuses.

The betrayal cut deep and raw. *My son, damn her.* How could she keep something like that from him? He'd convinced himself to believe in her, and she'd been lying to him the entire time.

He'd known. Part of him had known the boy was his, but he'd chosen to believe her. Fool. "How did you do it?" he asked stonily. "How did you hide his birth?"

She sat on the edge of the bed, weary, as if her impassioned defense had taken everything out of her. "After the battle, Huntly and most of the high-ranking clansmen involved were forced into exile. Francis didn't go with his father to the continent, but we removed to one of the Gordon's remote castles up north. We took only a few trusted servants with us and didn't return for two years. There was no reason for anyone to question our story." She paused. "I think my father suspected, but he never voiced his suspicions."

"How convenient for all involved. Gordon stole my son and no one ever questioned it."

Her cheeks flamed. "He gave your son everything you denied him when you left."

Knowing that there was an element of truth to what she said didn't make it any easier to hear. Duncan was so angry he didn't trust himself to stay another minute—he might say something he would regret. That they both would regret.

"That will change."

Her face paled. "What do you mean?"

He met the panic in her gaze with determination. "What do you think? I intend to claim my son."

"I can't let you do that."

He laughed, throwing the words she'd once said to him back at her. "How are you going to stop me?"

She grabbed him, holding the blanket tight around her neck with one hand and his arm with the other. "You can't do this. Don't you see? You'll destroy everything I've done for him."

Duncan stilled as the impact of what she'd said hit him. His stomach turned, the truth tasting as bitter as bile. If he claimed his son, he'd make him the very thing that had haunted him his entire life: a bastard. Not just any bastard, but the bastard of an outlaw. And, if he didn't, he would allow his son to bear another man's name and to inherit land and property that did not belong to him.

What kind of hellish choices were those? It was like choosing to die by a gun or a knife—either way, he was dead.

His eyes burned as he stared at the woman he'd held in his arms not an hour ago and made love to. Who he'd thought loved him. If she'd wanted to hurt him, she could not have chosen a more painful way to inflict her pain.

He's my son. I want him.

Never had he blamed anyone for the brutal card that had been dealt him, but he did now. Cursing God, cursing his father, cursing Jeannie, cursing himself for the injustice. Had he reached too high again? Reached for happiness only to be shoved roughly back down to the ground.

He didn't bother to finish dressing, just grabbed his boots and weapons and went for the door.

"Wait! Where are you going?"

He heard the fear in her voice but it didn't penetrate. He sensed her move up behind him but kept his back to her—looking at her hurt too much. "Anywhere but here," he said tonelessly. And before she could say anything else he left, the door slammed hard behind him.

Chapter 22

❖

Jeannie stared at the door for hours certain that he would return. He needed time to think, then he would realize that there was nothing else she could have done.

But he'd been so angry. He'd looked at her as if she'd hurt him unbearably, as if she'd destroyed him. She wondered if he'd even heard her explanation.

The sick feeling in her stomach rose and rose. As the hours passed, she was forced to accept what she'd known the moment the words blurted from her mouth: Once again her impulsivity had led her to make a huge mistake.

But was it a mistake?

She was so confused, she no longer knew what was right. But she did know that Duncan wasn't ever going to see it her way, not when it meant perpetuating a lie. And that's exactly what she'd been doing—good intentions or not. She would have gone right on doing so, too, for the sake of her son, if Duncan hadn't returned.

For so long she'd fought to protect Dougall, thinking only to save him from living under the shadow of scandal and the difficulties inherent to being labeled a bastard. But in protecting him, it also meant she was denying him a chance to have a father again. Did she have that right? Francis was dead, but Duncan was not.

Hadn't she once told Duncan that it wasn't his birth that made him a bastard, it was his actions? Had she truly believed that or were they just words? If she believed in Duncan, didn't she have to believe in her son?

She hated the thought of the pain it would cause him, but Dougall was strong and with their help he would weather the storm. Jeannie would never forget what Francis had done for her, but couldn't deny Dougall a chance to know his father.

And she would tell Duncan as much if only he would come back. In another hour it would be dawn, surely he would return by then?

He wouldn't just leave her . . . would he?

The sound of a knock startled her. Her heart leaped. She jumped from the chair, raced to the door and tore it open. "Dunc . . ."

The word died in her mouth. It wasn't him. It was only the innkeeper's daughter with a tray of food. The flare of hope that had soared crashed to the ground in a fizzled, gnarled heap. The girl was about seven and ten with dark hair and a pleasant round face consistent with her figure. In addition to serving food and ale in the public room below, she was also apparently the inn's maidservant.

"Is it too early, my lady?" Jeannie could see the concern on her face. "I can come back? I heard you moving around and thought you might wish for something to break your fast."

"Thank you," Jeannie said, opening the door and letting her in. The steaming bowl of beef broth and fresh bread smelled delicious, but she wasn't hungry. "I thought you were one of my guardsmen."

The maid shook her head. "They're still sleeping off my mother's ale before the fire. Except for the leader—the tall black-haired man." She gave Jeannie an uneasy look. "He left a short while ago."

Left? Jeannie swallowed the lump in her throat. "Do you know where he went?"

"To the docks, I think. He was heading off in that direction."

Jeannie nodded and tried to stay calm. He was probably just readying the boat to leave. He wouldn't leave without her. The girl set the food down on the side table and offered to bring some fresh water for the basin, which Jeannie declined.

"I can help you with your gown," the girl suggested, seeing that Jeannie was wearing only her linen sark.

Though Jeannie was in no mood for company, she knew she could not get dressed on her own and accepted the girl's help rather than wait for Duncan. It might be some time before he decided to come for her.

"You had business at the castle, my lady?" the girl asked conversationally, lacing Jeannie's stays.

Jeannie nodded. "I'd hoped to see the old nurse, Kathrine."

The young maid looked at her in surprise. "Katy?"

"Yes, I was sorry to hear of her passing."

She nodded. "Aye, it was a horrible tragedy." She lowered her voice. "Poor Katy must have slipped on the cliffs while walking home. She washed ashore a week after she went missing. The only way they could identify her was by her hair. Like spun gold it was, twisted with the kelp."

Jeannie grimaced, not needing the gory details. But wait—she frowned—gold? "I understood her to have black hair." Like her son.

Maid shook her head. "Nay, mistress. Katy's hair was as bright as the sun. 'Twas her pride and joy, those curls."

Jeannie felt a prickle of excitement and tried to tamp it down. Hair "like a raven's wing," Lady MacDonald had said. Perhaps Jeannie had misunderstood. But she hadn't. Maybe the old woman had been confused. That must be it.

But she hadn't seemed confused.

The niggle at the back of her neck that something was wrong wouldn't leave her. Had Lady MacDonald lied to them?

All her instincts—

She stopped. *Instincts.* That alone should prevent her from going any further. She already felt foolish for insisting on dragging Duncan on this journey in the first place.

It was probably nothing, an innocent mistake.

But what if it wasn't?

She couldn't let it go. If there was a chance that Lady MacDonald knew something she had to take it. But Duncan was eager to leave. And the way he felt about her right now, she wasn't sure he'd be willing to listen to anything she said. She turned to the maid who was watching her with an expectant look on her face. "Could you arrange for someone to take me to the castle?"

"Aye, my brother Davy could take you, but don't you want to wait until your guardsman returns?"

"Actually, I'd rather he not know that I've gone." At least before he could order her not to go. This way, if she was wrong, he need not ever know. "If he comes to look for me . . ." She thought quickly for an explanation. Seeing the small fan she'd used to help revive Lady Mac-Donald peeking out of her purse, she shoved it down and tied the bag around her waist. "Tell him that I forgot my fan yesterday at the castle and have gone to retrieve it. I will return as soon as I can."

The maid bobbed. "Aye, my lady. I'll go find Davy right now."

"Before you do, if I could trouble you for one more thing?"

The girl nodded.

"Might I borrow a plaid?"

The maid hardly blinked—Jeannie suspected she was not the first person to sneak out of this inn. "Of course."

A short while later, Jeannie tiptoed down the stairs, avoiding the main room where she knew the men were and passing into the kitchen instead. The maid led her out the back door, past a well and small garden to the stables.

Her brother—Davy—was a few years older than his sister and as thin as the girl was round. He stood waiting for her with a sturdy Highland pony. Knowing that Duncan would have a guardsman stationed outside, Jeannie adjusted the borrowed plaid over her head like a hood and kept her face down. Though her "disguise" wouldn't hold up under scrutiny, she hoped the guard would take a quick glance and think her a woman from the village.

It must have worked because no one stopped them. They made quick work of the three mile or so journey, arriving at the castle just as the cock had begun to crow.

Once inside the courtyard, they tethered the ponies near the stables and Jeannie went to beg her second audience with Lady MacDonald, praying that this time it proved more fruitful.

Colin Campbell had waited until dark before landing in a small inlet just north of Leodamas, using the night to shroud his arrival on Islay. If reports of his brother's battle skills held true, which he did not doubt—Duncan had always been annoyingly accomplished at everything—he would need the benefit of surprise to capture him. Just to be sure, however, another *birlinn* waited outside the bay to cut off any attempt at escape.

Colin knew Duncan was here. As soon as his men had seen the boat leave Castleswene and head down the sound, Colin guessed where his brother was heading.

The spy he had in Dunyvaig amongst the MacDonalds' guardsmen confirmed it. They were on Islay—at an inn at the village. They'd left the castle yesterday after a short meeting with Mary MacDonald.

The fact that Duncan was here meant he was too close. Though Colin was certain he'd taken care of everything, there was always a possibility he'd missed something. He'd hoped this wouldn't be necessary, but he couldn't take the chance.

But Colin wasn't without filial sentiment, the thought of what he had to do held no enjoyment for him. He'd always looked up to Duncan—had wanted to be just like him—which he supposed had always been the problem. He was destined to fall short.

It's either him or me, he reminded himself. On some level he'd always known that.

That damn map. He'd just wanted to make Duncan look foolish, instead it was he who'd been fooled. Grant had used him. Used his jealousy against his brother. And Colin had trusted him, thinking himself engaged to Grant's daughter. The devil's spawn Grant had betrayed them both, and Colin had been forced to hide the gold to cover up his part in the debacle.

The note had been the last straw. Colin had recognized the feminine lettering and known that it was from her. *My* betrothed. Duncan knew they were engaged, but he'd gone to meet her anyway. He'd fucked his bride, damn him. Like he was probably fucking her now. Anger dulled any sympathy he might have felt for his brother. Duncan deserved exactly what he got.

Unlike their father. He'd never wanted his father to be hurt, but with what he'd threatened after Colin admitted to knowing about Duncan's feelings for Jean Grant before proposing the betrothal, perhaps it was better that he did. *I should have made Duncan my heir.* Colin had been outraged. Humiliated. But he hadn't believed he would actually do it—not until his deathbed ramblings sent any icy chill down his spine.

Colin buckled the scabbard at his waist and tucked the two brass-handled pistols into his belt as his men finished clearing the camp on the small forested hill above the village where they'd slept. It was about an hour before dawn—the perfect time to catch them unaware. He knew Duncan had only a handful of men with him, but he did not underestimate his brother. Duncan did, however, have a weakness. Colin just had to get his hands on her.

Why couldn't Duncan have stayed away? The moment Colin had heard his brother was back on Scottish soil he'd known what he would be forced to do. He hoped Duncan gave him a reason. He didn't want to have to shoot his brother in the back.

Duncan walked the short distance to the inn from the beach, trying to shake the water from his hair. But the frozen clumps snapped against his cheeks, releasing little—if any—of the icy sea water. Overnight the mist had settled low around the island in a damp, bone-chilling fog that the dawn had yet to thaw. But cold had never bothered him. He'd been raised in the Highlands near the sea; he was used to it. Though admittedly, not all Highlanders swam in the sea in the middle of winter. Perhaps he had more Norse blood in him than he realized.

The village was quiet, but showing the first signs of life as he approached. Gentle swirls of smoke billowed out of the rooftops as the servants lit the morning fires.

It had been a long night. When he'd left Jeannie he'd joined his men in the public room below. He'd been wound tight, looking for a way to unleash the dangerous emotions swirling inside him. It was either fight or drink, and as he did not trust himself not to kill someone, he chose the latter.

Gauging his dark mood, Conall and Leif gave him a wide berth. A handful of tankards of the innkeeper's best *cuirm,* however, had barely taken the edge off his anger or the gnawing burning in his chest.

He'd spent a few restless hours before the fire, before giving up on sleep and deciding to try to clear his thoughts in the sea. But the clarity he'd hoped to find in the icy waters had eluded him.

I have a son. It was still difficult to comprehend. But what the hell was he going to do about it? Make him a bastard? He better than anyone knew what that was like. He'd come to terms with his birth, but it hadn't been easy. Could he foist that kind of black mark on his son?

Why hadn't she told him earlier? *Because she didn't trust you.* Why should she? *You left her.*

He shook off the annoying voice. He didn't want to see her side, his anger was still too damn raw.

He turned the corner around the empty market stalls and the inn came into view. As always, he scanned his surroundings. Something was wrong: The Gordon guardsman he'd left was not in position.

Senses honed, he realized it was too quiet. Too still.

He looked down at the muddy ground and saw the unmistakable signs of footprints coming from all directions around the building. A score of men—at least. He suspected there were others positioned in and around the building, hidden in the backdrop of trees. Too many for the handful of men he had with him, particularly since Leif had left early this morning to scout the castle. He took a few steps back out of view, but they'd already seen him. His skin prickled with the sensation of being watched.

It was a trap. One in which he would not be caught.

Then he remembered. He swore, dread settling low in his belly. Jeannie. He'd left her alone, and in doing so had given them the perfect weapon. His muscles flared and fists clenched. If they hurt her, touched her in any way, they would not see another sunrise. He didn't care if there was an entire army in there.

His eyes darted to the second floor window, not seeing any movement. He tried not to let it alarm him, but she had to have heard the noise below when the men rushed in. If she wasn't in her room, it meant she was—

A muffled woman's scream tore through the morning air, turning his blood to ice.

Without hesitation he ran.

About twenty feet from the door, the loud shot of musket fire pierced the quiet morning air.

Colin couldn't believe it. It had been almost too easy—well, except for the big Irishman. His men had taken the inn with nary a shot fired, a dirk had taken care of the sole guardsman outside, and the other men had been virtually helpless while they slept, only to discover that neither his brother nor Lady Jean Gordon were here. His fury was nearly uncontrollable, buoyed by fear that they'd found something.

The wounded Irishman and the four Gordon guardsmen had been bound and gathered in a group on the floor. The innkeeper, his wife, and his young daughter had also been brought to him. "Where are they?" he demanded of the big man.

Blood was gushing from the Irishman's nose and cheek where his face had been smashed by the butt of a musket, but he smiled and asked, "Who?"

Colin barely contained his irritation. Only his desire to catch his brother prevented him from ordering the man killed instantly. "The outlaw Duncan Dubh."

The burly red-haired man shrugged. "I don't know any outlaws."

Colin put the barrel of his pistol right under the man's chin. "Are you sure about that?"

The big man didn't flinch. "Aye."

He could see it in his ruddy face—this man would never betray his leader. Colin was about to pull the trigger when out of the corner of his eye he noticed the young maid open her mouth.

His gaze narrowed on her. "Do you have something to say? Do you know where the outlaw and the woman are?"

The girl looked scared enough to crap herself. "I . . ."

"Bring her to me."

She screamed when his men grabbed her. "They're n-not h-here," she said, her words barely intelligible behind the frightened sobs. "We didn't know he was an outlaw. We don't want no trouble. I saw the black-haired man leave a while ago, heading toward the harbor. I heard them arguing last night and I was concerned about the lady so I went to check on her. She left not long after he did—"

Her words were cut off by the sound of a gunshot.

Colin supposed it was too much to hope that someone else might have done his job for him.

Jeannie's heart raced to near bursting as she urged the pony faster. The wind ripped through her hair and pounded against her cheeks. Tears streamed from her eyes, but she hardly noticed. All she could think of was getting back to the village. She couldn't wait to find Duncan and tell him what she'd discovered.

Refusing to back down, she'd confronted the old woman with what she'd learned. A few pointed questions was all it had taken and like a dam that had been waiting to break, the whole sordid story had come pouring out.

Davy shouted something that sounded like "be careful" just before she caught sight of a man plunging out from the trees on the right side of the path, cutting her off. She was forced to rein in her mount to avoid colliding with him or veering off the path into the trees and bracken.

It all happened so fast it took her a moment to realize it was Duncan's man Leif. In the best of circumstances the Norseman made her uneasy, but with the glacial look on his face right now he made her blood run as cold as his ice-blue eyes. He was an incredibly attractive man, if you could get past the fearsome expression, which she'd yet to do. Hard, emotionless, scary: that about summed him up.

"What are you doing at the castle?" he demanded, his voice as biting as the wind.

She didn't like the way he was looking at her or the suspicion in his voice. She would wager he was well aware of the argument she and Duncan had last night.

Davy cowered behind her, eyes wide and shoulders shaking.

She resisted the urge to tell the giant Norseman that it was none of his blasted business. He had no right to question her. It was only that she knew he was motivated by concern and loyalty to Duncan that prevented her from telling him to go to the devil. More importantly, she didn't want to waste time arguing with him. "I found it. I found the proof we were looking for." Reaching in her purse, she pulled out a wrinkled piece of parchment and handed it to him, hoping he could read Latin.

Skeptical of her pronouncement, the Norseman kept one eye on her as he carefully unfolded the parchment and read its contents. It didn't take long.

Some of the hostility on his face slackened on the first pass. He read it again and then stared at her, unable to conceal his shock. She could commiserate.

"Where did you get this?"

She bristled at the arrogance in his tone and said, "Lady MacDonald."

He swore and shook his head in disbelief, then handed her back the parchment, which she carefully replaced in the jewel-encrusted purse at her waist. "Now, if you don't mind I'd like to find Duncan," she said.

"I'll take you myself."

If that was an apology, his manner left much to be desired. They rode hard the remainder of the short journey back to the inn, Davy struggling to keep up with their lightning pace. They'd just crested the hill above the village—only a few hundred yards away—when the shot rang out.

No! Her heart plummeted, an icy chill of premonition running down her spine. She covered her mouth to stifle the scream that rose to her throat.

Leif swore and reined in his horse, motioning for them to stop.

She looked at him helplessly, not daring to think what was happening down there—they could see the barn and garden, but not the front yard of the inn.

A bit of Leif's icy hard demeanor cracked and he gave her an encouraging grin—at least she thought it was a grin as one side of his mouth lifted. "Don't worry, lass, the captain can take care of himself."

But his confident words could not spell the frantic pounding of her heart. This couldn't be happening. Not when they were so close! She had the proof. She only needed to get it to him.

If he'd been caught, he could be executed on the spot. Had that been the shot? Tears swam in her eyes. Her chest tightened painfully. It was too horrible to contemplate.

As their horses would only be a hindrance now, Leif instructed them to tie them up, leaving Davy to watch over them until it was safe—a task the frightened young man was most willing to accept.

Cautiously, they crept down the hill, Leif scanning their surroundings the entire time. After what seemed an hour, though was probably only a minute or two, they approached the stable of the inn. Two soldiers stood guarding the kitchen door, presumably to prevent any escape. They could hear voices and shouting coming from the yard.

Leif pressed his fingers to his lips and motioned for her to follow him. Using the barn as a shield, they skirted around to the front of the inn.

It was what they feared—soldiers. At least a score of them. One man stood with his back to her. There was something eerily familiar . . .

He turned, giving her his profile.

Jeannie stopped dead in her tracks. The blood slipped from her face.

Dear God. It was Colin Campbell.

And then she saw Duncan.

Anticipating her reaction, Leif pulled her into his arms and put a hand over her mouth to prevent her cry.

Duncan barely noticed the burning as the musket ball grazed his shoulder, but blood poured down his arm. He was fortunate the soldiers' guns didn't have better accuracy. From their distance in the trees—perhaps fifty yards away—they would have been much better off using their bows. He pulled out his dirk, knowing the pistol at his waist would be useless as he'd yet to prime it for the day.

The noise from the shot had alerted the men inside to

his approach and the door opened. A few men funneled out before he saw the one who was familiar to him.

Their eyes locked.

"Colin," he said. His brother had changed over the years. Not as dramatically as Jamie, perhaps, but still significantly. He was a few inches shorter than Jamie and Duncan, but more thickly built. But he looked unwell. On edge. As if he hadn't slept in weeks.

Colin nodded his head in greeting. "Duncan. It's been a long time."

Duncan thought he detected a glint of regret in his eyes, but it was quickly smothered by cold resolve. In that one glance he knew: If he was looking for an ally, he would not find it with his brother.

His gaze darted behind Colin's shoulder through the door, but there was no sign of her. "I heard a woman scream," he said. "Where is she?"

Colin's eyes narrowed, he thought with a gleam of calculation. "You mean you don't know?" He held his gaze and laughed.

A chill swept across the back of his neck. Had something happened to her? "Let them go," Duncan said. "I'll go willingly, if you let them go."

Colin's eyes turned black. "Willingly or not you'll go. You are hardly in a position to bargain."

Duncan fought to stay calm. A score of soldiers wouldn't stop him if he wanted to escape. "They have done nothing wrong. You've no cause to take them."

"Harboring an outlaw is crime enough," Colin said. He stared at the dirk Duncan had in his hand. "Drop your weapons and I can promise that no one will get hurt."

Duncan didn't hesitate. He dropped his dirk, removed his pistol and tossed it down as well, then unbuckled his sword and handed it over to his brother.

Colin took one look at it and his face nearly exploded

with rage. "Father's sword! You stole it after he fell. You've had it this whole time."

Duncan didn't defend himself. The sword had never rightfully belonged to him. But he'd wanted it. Taking it had been a spurious decision in the shock of his father falling in battle.

He allowed himself to be bound, flexing his wrists to ensure a little slack in the rope.

"Make sure it's tight," Colin said, guessing his intentions. "And check him for hidden weapons." When they were done retrieving the two other knives, including his *sgain dubh,* Colin shouted to his men inside, "Bring them out."

Duncan waited anxiously, needing to see that she was all right, but he was to be disappointed. He saw Conall, beaten badly but alive, and three of the Gordon guardsmen who'd accompanied them—he knew it didn't bode well for the fourth. Leif, he hoped, was safely away.

He kept his face impassive, hiding the cold fear cutting through him. Jeannie wasn't there.

If Leif hadn't been holding her, Jeannie would have rushed forward. Duncan thought she was inside with Colin's soldiers and that's why he was giving himself up. She had to stop him. At best he would be imprisoned in some ghastly pit prison, and at worst . . .

She couldn't think about at worst.

"His brother?" Leif whispered in her ear.

She nodded, and he relaxed his hand around her mouth.

"You can't help him. Not now," he said.

As much as she didn't want to hear it, Leif was right. She was more certain than ever that is was Colin who was responsible for what had happened to Duncan. Her proof would hold no weight with him; if anything it would give him even more reason to kill Duncan on the spot. She wondered why he hadn't already done so.

"Where is she?" she heard Duncan say. For a man tied up, his voice held the unmistakable promise of danger.

"Not here," Colin answered. "Don't tell me she ran out on you again?" To one of his men he said, "Bring out the girl."

Jeannie saw the poor maidservant dragged out and she had to fight the urge not to rush out and do something to help her.

"Wait," Leif whispered. "We don't want to interfere unless we need to."

She relaxed just a little. Duncan trusted this man, she would have to as well.

"Where did the lady go?" She heard Colin ask.

The girl could barely speak she was so scared. "T-to the castle. She d-didn't want him," she gestured to Duncan, "to know."

"Why would she do that?" Colin asked. Jeannie heard the suspicion in his voice.

The maid shook her head. "I don't k-know," the girl stuttered. "She was upset, she looked like she'd been crying all night. I heard them arguing."

Jeannie's cheeks heated. The walls at the inn were thinner than she'd realized.

"She betrayed me," Duncan said flatly. "I wouldn't be surprised if she went to alert the MacDonald to my presence on the island. Leave her to them."

Jeannie gasped. How could he think that?

"He doesn't mean it, lass," Leif whispered, but he didn't sound quite as confident as he had before. He'd seen Duncan last night—no doubt he'd also seen how furious he was.

"Yet you were willing to surrender your life for hers," Colin pointed out shrewdly.

Duncan nodded. " 'Twas my fault she was here. 'Tis

no more than I would have done for any woman in my care." *Even one who did not deserve it.* Jeannie filled in the words he'd left unsaid.

Colin recognized the truth in that, as did Jeannie. Duncan was unfailingly chivalrous.

Colin gave him a hard look. "Why were you here?"

"I hoped to find my mother."

"And were you successful?" Colin asked nonchalantly, though Jeannie knew he was anything but.

"Nay," Duncan said. "She died ten years ago."

Colin nodded, satisfied. "After what Jean Grant did to you last time, I'm surprised that you sought her out at all."

"I hoped she might have come to regret what she'd done, but I was wrong. She's as false of heart as she is fair of face."

Colin studied his face, not sure whether to believe him. "I'm interested in hearing what Lady Gordon has to say all the same. I'll send some of my men to the castle to see if we can't retrieve her." Colin's smile sent a chill down her spine. "Our cousin has ordered me to bring you both to Inveraray. He wishes to see you before you face the charges against you."

Jeannie breathed a bit easier. She had her explanation for why Colin had not executed him on the spot. She felt the inconceivable urge to thank the Earl of Argyll.

Duncan shrugged. "Do what you wish. She can swim home for all I care."

A tear ran down her cheek. Her heart squeezed. *He doesn't mean it*—no matter how convincing he sounded. But the look on his face last night when she'd told him about Dougall was still too fresh in her mind.

Colin started to order his men to take the prisoners to the *birlinn*. Slowly, Leif backed them away to the safety of the inn's stables. "He's trying to keep you safe, lass."

Jeannie sniffled and nodded. "I know." *I hope*. She

wiped her eyes with the back of her hands. She couldn't think of this now. Later her heart could break, right now she needed to help him. "We have to get to Inveraray before they do. Argyll will kill him. What are we going to do?"

The fearsome Norseman smiled—really smiled this time. It might have been more blood-chilling than his frown. "Beat them," he said. Her surprise must have shown. "We aren't just infamous for murdering and pillaging, you know. No one can best a Norseman on the water."

Jeannie didn't know whether to be relieved or terrified. *Murdering and pillaging, good God!*

Chapter 23

❖

Duncan breathed easier when Colin's men returned from Dunyvaig Castle empty-handed. Lady MacDonald claimed that Jeannie had left the island first thing this morning. Whether it was true, Duncan didn't know, but he wanted her as far away from his brother as possible.

He allowed himself to be loaded onto the *birlinn,* trying to put aside his fear for Jeannie. He knew it was far safer for them both if he left the island without her. He didn't think Colin had completely believed his avowal of indifference and he didn't want to put it to the test. If she wasn't with them, Colin couldn't try to use her against him. Moreover, it might not be necessary to escape, but if it was, Jeannie's presence would make it a much more difficult proposition.

Still, the thought of leaving her went against every protective bone in his body.

She'll be fine, he told himself. If she'd gone to the castle, Leif would have seen her. And the Norseman would protect her with his life.

But why *had* she gone to the castle?

The thought that she might have left him as Colin had suggested, or turned him in as he'd asserted, had entered his mind for a fraction of an instant, but he'd never truly considered it. Whatever reason she'd had to return to Dunyvaig, he knew it wasn't that. She loved him. She would never have told him about Dougall if she didn't trust him completely.

And he trusted her. He knew it with a certainty that defied explanation. He could be looking at a mountain of evidence against her and still he wouldn't believe it. He didn't know what had changed, what had caused his trust not to waver, but it didn't. Not a hair.

He supposed he had Colin to thank for giving him the clarity he'd sought. When he'd heard the woman's scream everything had crystallized. He'd been angry at Jeannie for not telling him about Dougall, but the real source of his fury had been directed at himself. He was to blame for leaving her alone and with child. His lack of trust had cost him not just the woman he'd loved, but his son. It was a mistake that he would never be able to rectify, but he swore he would do everything he could to try.

He thought back to last night, regretting more than ever what had happened. He should have been falling to his knees, begging her forgiveness, and instead he'd walked out on her and threatened to destroy all she'd done to protect their son.

He supposed he wouldn't blame her if she had left.

But he swore he would make it up to her—if he had the chance.

Wisely, Colin had separated him from his men. But Duncan wasn't interested in escaping—not yet. Not until he had a chance to question his brother. Colin, however, did not seem eager to renew their bonds of brotherhood and had situated himself well away from Duncan on the boat. He'd have to wait until they landed at Tarbert. From there they would carry the *birlinns* (Colin's second boat had joined them as soon as they'd left the harbor) across the narrow one mile long slice of land that joined Kintyre and Knapdale to Loch Fyne which would take them north to Inveraray.

On the boat, Duncan took the opportunity to watch his brother's interactions with his men, and what he saw

Duncan stood slowly. Out of the corner of his eye, he saw his brother's hand move toward his belt, reaching for his pistol.

The knowledge that his brother hated him enough to try to murder him ate like acid, but he was ready. Hands still bound, he spun and kicked as hard as he could. His booted foot connected with Colin's arm just as he'd raised it, knocking the gun to the ground. Before Colin could recover, Duncan kicked him again, this time in the head as he instinctively bent over his injured arm. It stunned him long enough for Duncan to ram into him with a fierce battle cry, taking them both to the ground.

Conall responded to his signal with a cry of his own and the battle was on. Though with two against nearly two score, it remained to be seen how much of a battle it would be—despite rumors to the contrary, there were limits to his abilities. Their odds would improve some if Conall managed to free the Gordon guardsmen.

Colin grunted with pain as Duncan jabbed his elbow low in his stomach, reaching for the hilt of his brother's dirk. He grabbed it and managed to slice his hands free just as Colin recovered enough to land a blow to his temple. Though Duncan wore a studded leather cotun and chest plate, his steel knapscall had been left at the inn and his brother connected hard enough to make his head ring. Whatever his brother's shortcomings, he did not lack in strength.

Duncan returned the blow to Colin's jaw, hearing the satisfying crunch.

Holding the knife in one hand, Duncan sprang to his feet—he could hear the sounds of fighting closing in and wanted to make sure he was in position to fend off any attackers.

It was dark and foggy, but he could just make out the shadows of approaching men.

Colin struggled to his feet, facing him. "Damn you," he said, massaging his jaw.

"I wasn't the one trying to murder my own brother," Duncan bit back through clenched teeth.

But the ugly truth only seemed to infuriate him more, sending Colin reaching for his second pistol. He swung it around to fire and Duncan got his arm up just enough to send the shot careening over his shoulder and not through his heart. Colin swore and reached for the sword—their father's sword. But before he could pull it from the scabbard, Duncan surged forward, pinning him to a tree with one arm across his shoulders, the other holding the long, sharp dirk to his throat.

Colin struggled to break free, but Duncan was immoveable—every muscle flexed. Blood pounded through his body as he fought to control the urge to strike back at the man who'd just tried to kill him— twice. His own brother.

"Why?" he asked, the edge of the dagger biting into Colin's neck.

If he hoped for a confession, he was to be disappointed. Duncan knew his brother would go to the grave with his secrets. "You won't do it," Colin sneered.

Duncan glanced in the direction of the fighting and hesitated. He realized why no one had come to Colin's aid. The men that he'd sensed approaching moved out of the shadows. The leader looked enough like his sister for Duncan to recognize him.

He turned to his brother, feeling an overwhelming sense of sadness. "You're right," he said. "I won't."

"But I will," the other man said.

Colin's head jerked around to the sound of the voice. He paled.

Duncan stepped back, releasing Colin from his hold. "Lamont?" he asked.

The man who'd become an outlaw to seek vengeance

for the rape of the woman he loved bowed his head in acknowledgment, but his predatory gaze never once left Colin. Though it was dark, the force of the rage and hatred that radiated off the Lamont warrior was palpable.

The two men drew their swords and squared off to face each other. Lamont raised his two-handed great sword over his head and attacked with a ferocity that seemed superhuman. The shatter of steel upon steel reverberated like a thunderclap. Lamont came at Colin again and again. Unrelenting. Landing blow after herculean blow that his brother couldn't even begin to fend off. He fought with a force behind him that was undeniable.

This battle had only one possible outcome. Duncan knew it, and from the look in Colin's eyes, he knew it as well.

Not wanting to watch the inevitable, Duncan turned and walked away. He wished he could feel sorry for him, but Colin had forged his own destiny, and now was the time for his reckoning.

Colin was dead.

Lamont and his band of MacGregor outlaws disappeared into the darkness as quickly as they'd come—their battle, it seemed, had been with one man.

Before they could be rounded up again, Duncan sent Conall and the Gordon guardsmen back to Islay to find Jeannie. The big Irishman wasn't happy about it, but understood what Duncan had to do. Like Colin, the time for Duncan's reckoning was here. He hoped his had a better outcome.

He did not grieve for the brother who'd tried to kill him, but for the boy who'd trailed after him when they were young, who'd laughed with him, wrestled with him, and trained beside him.

Duncan might have had difficulty convincing the re-

maining clansmen not to kill him on the spot were it
not for Gillis. The young warrior had happened to
look back just as Colin had tried to shoot him. The lack
of honor in their chief did not sit well with any of the
Highlanders and given Duncan's willingness to submit
to their authority the danger of immediate execution
passed.

After tending to the wounded and gathering the dead,
it was near dawn by the time the somber procession
passed through the *barmkin* gate of Inveraray Castle,
the Earl of Argyll's formidable Highland stronghold.

Half expecting to be tossed into the pit prison, Duncan was surprised instead to be lead into the laird's solar.

It had been a long time since he'd been at Inveraray
and he'd forgotten his cousin's penchant for extravagance and luxury. The castle was fit for a king—one
with rather garish taste, to his mind. Heavy velvets,
thick brocades, ornate furnishing and fixtures, silver
plate and candelabrum, and just about any surface that
could be gilded had been.

His pulse fired as he considered what he would say to
the man who held his life in his hands. Coming here had
been a risk—no doubt a rash one—but one he had to
take. He had to trust that the truth—justice—would
win. Though, he had to admit, he did wish he had more
to go on than his word and a loosely worded note.

He stiffened when the door opened and turned. His
heart caught, stunned. "Jeannie?"

She bit her lip and took a few cautious steps into the
room. She seemed to be waiting for him to make a
move. He did, closing the gap between them in two long
strides and pulling her into his arms.

She sagged against him, her relief palpable. He
pressed a kiss atop her head and inhaled the soft floral
fragrance in her hair, savoring the feel of her in his arms.

Holding her back, he looked at her, needing to make sure that she was real. "How did you get here—"

He stopped himself. Leif. His face darkened. The Norseman's damned never-ending pride could have killed her. Leif thought he could sail through anything—a storm, a gale, no matter how treacherous the seas.

Reading his mind, she said, "Don't blame Leif. We had to come." She gave him a pained look. "If it wasn't for him, I might still be swimming."

He winced, remembering his cruel words. "You heard that, did you?"

She nodded.

"I didn't mean it," he said. "I was trying to steer Colin away from you."

"I know." She smiled tentatively. "Or at least I hoped. But after what I told you, I wasn't sure you wanted to see me at all."

The wounded look in her eyes struck him to the core. His chest tightened and he drew her into his arms again, holding her, cherishing her, knowing that if it were up to him he would never let her go. "I'm sorry. God, I'm sorry. I should never have walked out on you like that. I was angrier at myself than at you." He cupped her chin and stared deep into her eyes. "I know what you did to protect our son and I'll never do anything to change that."

Her eyes scanned his face. "What are you saying?"

He took a deep breath. The words were not easy to say. "I lost the right to claim my son when I left you ten years ago."

Her eyes widened. "You would do that for me . . . for us?"

"Aye."

The radiant smile that lit her face was one of pure happiness. She threw herself into his arms. Unable to resist a moment longer, he covered her mouth with his.

Kissing her tenderly. Lovingly. Knowing that the memory of his kiss might have to last him a very long time.

Her lips were so soft and sweet under his.

His chest tugged. God, he loved her.

He wanted nothing more than to sink into her and loose himself in her sweetness. But now was not the time. Reluctantly, he broke the kiss and met her gaze. "I love you, Jeannie."

"And I love you," she replied. "But you don't need to sacrifice your son. Hiding the truth will only lead to more pain. Dougall deserves to know his father."

It was his turn to be surprised. "Are you sure?" Then he sobered. "We need not decide anything right now. You may think differently if my cousin is not persuaded of my innocence."

An even bigger smile broke out on her face. "But he is—"

She didn't finish because as if on queue the door opened and his cousin, Archibald "the grim," the seventh Earl of Argyll strode into the room.

Instinctively, Duncan spun Jeannie around behind him, blocking her with his body from his cousin's view.

As happy as he'd been to see her, he hadn't realized what her presence could mean. If Archie thought he'd take his anger out on her, he better damn well think again.

He met his cousin's cold stare, noting how his dark, angular features had sharpened with age. Though they were close in years, Archie looked far older. His face was lined, his hair thinned and receding at the temples, and patches of gray dotted his dark pointy beard. The stress of the intervening years had taken their toll. Duncan took in the elaborate court costume, observing that his cousin's penchant for extravagance extended to his clothing as well. At least the silk was black, he supposed, and not peacock blue.

Argyll shifted his gaze to Jeannie. "I though I gave you enough time," he said.

Jeannie blushed. "I was just starting to explain."

"She has nothing to do with this," Duncan said.

Argyll's eyes narrowed. "It's thanks to Lady Gordon that you are not sitting in a dungeon right now." All of a sudden, his expression changed. Duncan could see the weariness come over him. "Is it true about Colin?"

Duncan nodded. "Aye."

Jeannie hadn't heard. "What happened?"

Duncan quickly recounted the details of his journey from Islay, including Colin's attempt to kill him and Niall Lamont's timely arrival.

Archie scowled at the mention of the outlaw. "The king won't be happy to hear about another case of 'Highland justice.' "

Aye, an eye for an eye, a tooth for a tooth. That was the Highland way.

Argyll smiled deviously. "Though perhaps having your case settled will make up for his disappointment."

Archie's tone gave no hint to his thoughts, but Duncan remembered his cousin well enough to know he was up to something. "Did Jamie bring you the documents I found?"

"Aye, your brother and sister descended on me en masse a few days ago with Grant's missive and the missing map." Argyll dismissed them with a wave. "The note could be interpreted many ways."

Duncan flexed his jaw. "Then you are determined to see me hang for a crime I did not commit."

"Duncan." Jeannie tried to interrupt, but he brushed her off.

He took a few steps toward his cousin, towering over him by a good half foot. To his credit, Archie didn't give an inch. "Hell, Archie, how could you even think I would betray you like that?"

Argyll's mouth twisted. "I don't."

"You don't?" Duncan repeated, confused.

Jeannie stomped up behind him. "If you'd let me finish, I would have told you that you've been pardoned."

"What?"

Shocked would be putting it mildly, Jeannie thought. Incredulous better captured the expression on his face.

The door opened and this time it was Lizzie who came bursting into the room, followed by her husband, Jamie, and Caitrina. Lizzie threw herself into Duncan's arms. "Isn't it wonderful?" she gushed.

Jeannie laughed. "I'm afraid he hasn't heard the whole story yet."

When she'd asked for five minutes in private first, she hadn't planned on that kiss. Next time it might be safer to ask for an hour.

She looked at Duncan. "You never asked why I went to the castle."

He shrugged. "I figured you had a good reason. To be honest, I was just grateful you weren't at the inn when Colin and his men arrived."

So was she. She shuddered to think of how differently it could have all happened. She supposed her instincts weren't always wrong. She explained about the maid's mentioning of Kathrine MacDonald's hair.

He frowned. "The old lady was confused?"

"That's what I thought, but it didn't make sense. It seemed an odd mistake to make, but it turns out your mother *did* have black hair." She pulled out the piece of parchment and handed it to him. It was a page from a church registry. "Your mother's name was Anna. Anna MacDonald."

Duncan's eyes narrowed. He took the page uncertainly and scanned it. What he saw there drew the color from his face. His eyes gazed into hers. "I don't understand."

"Your father and mother were married. Your mother was Catholic and they wed secretly in a church on the other side of the island."

She could see the confusion, the conflicting emotions traverse across his face and hurried to explain. "Your mother was Mary MacDonald's baby sister, though with nearly twenty years between them she could have been her daughter. She was the youngest daughter of the old chief. She and your father met at court, but the vicious blood feud between the clans prevented them from seeking permission to wed so they did so secretly, with only the nurse and Mary as witnesses.

"Eventually, they hoped to be able to tell their families, but until then they were forced to meet in secret. Your father wanted to run away, but Anna refused. She didn't want to be forever cut off from her family. But the stress of the situation finally caught up with them and they had a horrible fight. By the time your father returned, intent on claiming his bride, it was too late—your mother had died in childbirth and the family had gotten "rid" of her bastard, sending you off to be raised by the nurse. Your mother had refused to name the father. But your father tracked the nurse down and brought you to live at Castleswene."

Duncan was remarkably calm given what Jeannie had just told him, but his emotion revealed itself in his voice. "But how could my father do this? How could he lie about something like that?"

It was Jamie who answered. "Because of our grandfather." Duncan turned to him. "He hated the MacDonalds. Think how he was when he thought you were simply the bastard son of a maidservant. He would never have let a MacDonald be in line to inherit the chieftainship."

"Your father must have been trying to protect you," Jeannie said. She could well understand the lengths a parent would go to protect their child. Duncan's father's lie had deprived his son of an inheritance while hers had given one.

She could see the anger burning in Duncan's eyes and her heart went out to him. No matter his father's reasons, it was a horrible betrayal.

"That might explain why he lied initially," he said. "But not why he let it continue."

"To claim you, he would have had to disinherit another son. And there was my mother to consider," Jamie said.

"He must have changed his mind," Argyll broke in. "I only realized the significance when Lady Gordon brought me the document, but Auchinbreck had told me the night before the battle that he'd decided to make you his *tanaiste*."

Jeannie could feel the muscles in Duncan's arm bunch under her fingertips as he waited for Argyll to continue.

"It wasn't unheard of to make a bastard an heir, but I told Auchinbreck there would be trouble. He said not to worry about it, that he would explain everything when the time was right." Argyll shrugged. "After he died and you were accused of treason, I was glad he hadn't made his intentions known."

"Do you think he'd told Colin?" Lizzie asked.

Duncan thought for a minute. "He might have—after I went to him about marrying Jeannie. I sensed that he and Colin had argued about something."

"Colin had to have found out something," Jeannie said. "He went to Dunyvaig not long after Glenlivet and started asking questions."

Duncan looked at her, suspicion in his gaze. "Kathrine?"

"I don't know, but Mary MacDonald thought so. The

church where your parents were married burned down a week before Kathrine disappeared—only days after Colin supposedly left the island. Were it not for the page Mary had ripped out of the registry to prevent your MacDonald grandfather from finding the truth years before, we might never have known."

"Why didn't Lady MacDonald tell us that first day?"

"She was scared. Colin didn't know that anyone other than the nurse knew. Given what had happened, I can't blame her."

Duncan looked to his cousin. "And even without Colin's confession, you are satisfied that I did not take the map and sell it to Grant?"

Argyll winced a little. "I'm satisfied that you were not the only one with motive."

Duncan cocked his brow, holding his cousin's gaze. It was Argyll who eventually conceded. "Very well. I wasn't exactly in the most generous frame of mind at the time, but I shouldn't have been so quick to find you guilty."

"Careful, Archie," Jamie teased. "That almost sounded like an apology."

Argyll shot him a black frown, murmuring something about insolent henchmen.

"What will happen to Colin?" Lizzie asked.

Jeannie winced. Duncan and Argyll exchanged a look.

Argyll looked at his cousin, and Jeannie was surprised to see how much fondness was in his gaze. "Come, Lizzie, I've something to tell you, but I think your brother would like some time alone with Lady Gordon." He glanced at Duncan. "If I were him, I'd be thinking of ways to thank her."

Lizzie nodded solemnly, perhaps sensing what her cousin was going to say, and followed him out of the room with the others.

"It's not like Archie to be so perceptive," Duncan said wryly. "He's gone soft in his old age."

Jeannie snorted. There was nothing soft about Duncan's powerful cousin. It was Lizzie who had the soft heart. She bit her lip. "Do you think she'll be all right?"

"Aye. Lizzie's strong. But it won't be easy. It's hard to believe the brother we knew as a child could have changed so much."

"I'm sorry," she said, realizing how difficult it must be for him as well.

"It's a lot to take in." He shook his head. "Married. God, I can't believe it." He gave her a wry smile. "I guess you were right to believe in faerie tales."

Jeannie smiled. "I'd like to take credit, but I could never have imagined such a story." She paused. "I feel sorry for them."

His face hardened for an instant. She knew his feelings for his father must be horribly conflicted. But then some of the tension seemed to dissipate. "Aye. They must have loved each other greatly to risk so much."

"He loved you, too, Duncan. What he did was wrong, but he was trying to make it right."

He nodded, then sat down on the chair and pulled her onto his lap, cuddling her in his arms. She laid her cheek on his chest, savoring the warm strength of him.

She couldn't quite believe it was all over.

"It's strange how my father's life mirrored mine." His eyes met hers. "Except for one thing."

"What's that?" Jeannie asked softly.

"I have the chance to make amends that my father did not." He took her hand and brought it to his mouth, pressing a soft kiss on her fingers. "Ten years ago I asked you to marry me. I don't deserve a second chance, but say you'll marry me again and I'll spend the rest of my life trying to make it up to you."

Jeannie tried to swallow, but the lump in her throat

made it impossible. Her heart swelled with love for him, with long overdue happiness, and with disbelief that all her dreams were finally coming true.

She nodded, tears streaming down her cheeks. "Yes, I'll marry you."

He grinned, and brought her mouth to his. This time when he kissed her, he didn't stop.

Epilogue

Beltane, 1609, Dunoon Castle

Jeannie paused at the entrance to the great hall, surveying the festive scene of celebration before her, momentarily overcome by emotion. It was almost too perfect. Maybe she should pinch herself to make sure it was real.

She'd waited over ten years for this wedding. It seemed fitting that it be on Beltane, the ancient festival of fertility and spring—a day for new beginnings—and the true day of Dougall's birth.

The back of her neck prickled and her senses seemed to come alive. Her heart skipped a beat, then shot forward with anticipation. She felt the warm, hard strength of his body behind her as he slid his hands around her waist, clasping them over her stomach and nuzzling his face in her neck and hair.

The soft warmth of his breath near her ear sent a shiver of desire rippling down her spine. "Is it everything you hoped for, wife?"

Wife. She didn't think she would ever get tired of hearing it. Unwilling to wait while everything was worked out, they'd been married secretly over four months ago, but today they'd done so publicly with all their family gathered together to witness their celebration.

She tilted her head slightly to peer up at him, her heart

catching at his boyish grin. Looking at him now, it was easy to remember the handsome young warrior she'd seen across the hall at Stirling Castle who'd captured her young girl's heart. Her love for him had never changed; it had always been there. She'd only had to become strong enough to trust it.

"It's perfect," she said softly, adding, "Chief." Her eyes sparkled with mischievousness, unable to resist teasing him. She was rewarded by the faint tinge of color on his face. He had every right to be proud. He'd stepped into the role with ease, already earning the respect and admiration of his clansmen. She knew the position felt strange to him and that he still was getting used to the fact that he was Chief of Auchinbreck, but he'd been a leader for years—all that had changed was his title.

It was hard to believe all that had happened. They were truly blessed.

She gazed around the room, seeing her brother and his wife, her two younger sisters and their husbands—even Huntly and the Countess had put aside his differences with Argyll for the day to be here. Telling them about Dougall had been one of the most difficult things she'd ever had to do. Lady Gordon had just one question. "Did my son know?" Jeannie's assurances that he did had been enough. The Countess's fierce love of family might not ever include Jeannie, but it did her children. Both of them.

They'd yet to tell Dougall the truth of his birth, but would when the time was right. But he was so perceptive—much like his father—that she wondered whether he'd already guessed the truth. She frowned. "Where are Dougall and Ella?"

Duncan cocked a dark eyebrow, his blue eyes twinkling. "Take one guess."

She groaned. Ever since Duncan had told the children of how his sword had been used by his ancestor to save the life of King Robert the Bruce, they'd acted like it was something akin to Excalibur. "Fighting over the sword again?"

He nodded. "I'm going to have the cleanest sword in the kingdom." He grinned. "Don't worry, they promised to come down and eat when they were finished."

"Which means we shall have about an hour of quiet before Ella gets hold of you."

He chuckled and drew her a little closer. "I don't know, I think I've been replaced in her affection."

Jeannie caught the direction of his glance. "I think you're right. I'm glad Jamie and Caitrina could be here after all."

"Aye, it was thoughtful of my wee niece to make her appearance a few weeks early so they could make the journey."

The tiny cherub was the most beautiful child Jeannie had ever seen—not surprising given her parents. Ella was almost as fascinated with the child as she was with the sword—high praise indeed. "Perhaps she'll leave with a name?"

He laughed. "I doubt it. The last I heard Caitrina wanted to call her 'Peace' because it was the last Jamie would ever know or 'Penance' for what he would pay later when the lass is old enough to catch a male eye or two."

Jeannie giggled. "Or hundred." Her gaze caught on Jamie's sister who was holding the as-yet-unnamed youngest Campbell. "I was surprised Patrick agreed to let Lizzie come this close to the babe's birth."

"With all those silk pillows he makes her sit on, I'm more surprised he didn't carry her in on a litter."

Jeannie raised an eyebrow. "Don't give him any

ideas." Her gaze fell on another guest. This one had been a surprise. "It was good of you to invite her."

Duncan held her gaze, not needing to ask who she referred to. "Without her, I might never have known the truth. Lady Mary protected me and my parents' secret for a long time."

"I always knew the truth," she said.

He gave her an amused look. "How's that?"

She turned around to face him, reaching up to cup his cheek in her hand. Though he'd just shaved, his skin was warm and rough with the dark shadow of his beard. "I knew from the first moment I saw you that you were destined for greatness." She smiled. "It was always there, Duncan. Your parent's marriage doesn't change who you are."

The love reflected in his gaze took her breath away. He bent down and placed a tender kiss on her mouth.

"If we didn't have a room full of guests waiting for us, I might suggest we sneak off for a swim in the loch." He gave her a wry grin. "Though this time I hope you'll leave your pistol at home."

Jeannie laughed. "I don't know. A girl can get into a lot of trouble swimming in a loch. You never know what kind of scoundrels might be lurking about."

He chuckled. "Don't worry, I'll protect you."

"Oh, I'm sure you will." She laughed, not missing the wicked gleam in his eye. "Like a wolf protects the sheep."

"A hungry wolf." He gave a long sly look. "Perhaps I can convince you to meet me another time? Have you ever gone swimming by the moonlight?"

"Once or twice."

His eyes narrowed. "Twice?"

"Or once, who can remember?"

He spun her into his arms with a growl, their guests temporarily forgotten. "Perhaps I shall have to refresh your memory?"

"Perhaps you shall," she said breathlessly. And later that night he did, very very thoroughly indeed.

Author's Note

❖

Though Jeannie and Duncan are fictional characters, the Grants of Freuchie and Campbells of Auchinbreck are real clans who played a part in the battle of Glenlivet.

The battle was fought in 1594 (not 1599). It is often viewed as a religious war between the Catholic Earls of Huntly and Erroll against the Protestant King James and Earl of Argyll, but it is perhaps most significant as a victory of artillery and horse over infantry.

The loss was a humiliating defeat for Argyll who at the time was only eighteen. As I describe in the story, he is said to have fled from the battle crying. King James was furious about the defeat, but apparently not about Argyll's humiliation. The king (who Argyll was fighting for) is reputed to have famously said, "Fair fa' ye, Georgie Gordon, for sending him [Argyll] back looking sae like a subject!"[1] As my mom used to say, Argyll must have been getting a little too big for his britches and the king was happy to see him brought down to size.

I changed a few details, but much of the battle occurred as I described. A council of war was held the night before at Drumin Castle, and Argyll ignored the order to wait for reinforcements and decided to attack. Though Argyll certainly acted precipitously, it seems clear that treachery was also afoot.

[1]Alastair Campbell of Airds, *A History of Clan Campbell*, v. 2, pg. 115, Edinburgh University Press Ltd., Edinburgh, 2002.

Colin's perfidy is based on that of Campbell of Lochnell, who allegedly gave Argyll's position to Huntly. In a fitting case of poetic justice, however, Lochnell had his head blown off by the first fire.

The Chief of Grant was also suspected of treachery. He and his men fled the field after the first fire, crippling Argyll's vanguard. The chief at the time, however, was not my fictional Jeannie's father (who was already dead), but her brother John. An interesting aside to readers of my first series, Isabel's (*Highlander Untamed*) father, the MacDonald of Glengarry, was handfasted to Helen Grant (John's aunt), and their son "Angus" was Glengarry's heir and Isabel's half brother.

Campbell of Auchinbreck (Duncan's father) did die by taking a shot meant for Argyll. Also, the Chief of MacLean, who readers might remember as the villain in *Highlander Unchained,* did distinguish himself fighting. Argyll's boast that his standard (some sources say his harp and pipes) would fly on Gordon's castle of Strathbogie did come back to haunt him when it did just that—not in victory, but in defeat.

Huntly and Erroll's victory was short-lived. King James was furious at the earls and about a week after Glenlivet, destroyed both their castles (Strathbogie and Slains respectively). The earls were forced into exile for a couple of years. Still, despite Huntly's part in Glenlivet and his continued religious defiance, King James seemed to show him an odd favoritism. In 1599, five years after Glenlivet, the king made him a marquis. Argyll, however, was to remain an earl (his son would be the first marquis). Ten years later, the Marquis of Huntly was again in trouble with the Kirk and imprisoned in Stirling Castle. He was eventually released in 1610.

The Marchioness/Countess of Huntly was reputed to have been just as ruthless as her husband. The story of her chopping off the chief of Mackintosh's head after his foolish offer is one of the few stories that appears in the clan history about the woman.

Had Duncan arrived on Islay in the winter of 1608 to search for his fictitious mother, he would have been a few months too late. Angus MacDonald of Dunyvaig, chief of Clan Donald at the time, had been forced to surrender Dunyvaig Castle to Lord Ochiltree and Andrew Knox, Bishop of the Isles, in August 1608, leading to the forced signing of the infamous Statutes of Iona by the island chiefs the following year.

A note about the castles mentioned in the book. Freuchie Castle is also known as Balloch Castle and later as Castle Grant. The story of the old chief who locked his daughter Barbara in the tower when she refused to marry is part of the castle lore. The tower where she died is indeed known as Barbie's Tower. Comyn's skull was kept at the castle for years, although its location now is unclear as the castle was abandoned for years and then sold a few years ago.

Today Strathbogie Castle is known as Huntly Castle.

Aboyne Castle, also known as Bonty or Bunty Castle, was really once a possession of the Knights Templar—replete with a rumored secret passageway and monk's room. For more information and pictures of some of the sites mentioned in the novel, visit my website at www.monicamccarty.com.